HER COVERT PROTECTOR

VICTORIA PAIGE

Edited by: edit LLC
Content Editor: Edit Sober
Proofreader: A Book Nerd Edits
Photography by: Wander Aguiar
Model: Jose Luis Barreiro

PROLOGUE

JOHN GARRISON WAS a beast between the sheets.

Though, technically they were not between the sheets.

Currently, he was wrecking Nadia against the couch. He had her back against the armrest, thighs spread, her right foot on the floor while he used his body to keep her left leg pinned against the back of the couch.

He thrust.

He grunted.

He rode her hard.

"Don't lock me out," he ordered.

"But it's so good like this," Nadia moaned, her legs squirming at the pleasure pulsing below her pelvis, her body arching to meet his hammering hips. His cock slid in and out of her pussy, its girth stretching her inner walls to pleasurable extremes. The throb was so exquisite, it made her a slave to the relentless pounding of the man between her legs.

"I'm not ready to end this," he groaned. His words triggered a distant alarm in her head, but the heat that flared between them since they crossed that line minutes ago had incinerated all sense of logical thought. John wasn't a man to let your guard down around. But when he opened the door, and when she saw he was alive, nothing else mattered. Not even her pride. He scoffed at her tears of relief, then turned his back on her, leaving her standing in the foyer. She probably shouldn't have followed him. It should have been enough to see him alive. But she needed more assurance that he was okay, never thinking it would have gone this far.

That she would surrender herself to his animalistic way of fucking and loving it.

"Gonna come, babe," he grunted above her, his cock growing impossibly hard as he drove her harder into the couch. "Fuck."

Babe.

That was the first time he called her that. She was usually Powell to him. Like just moments ago, when he made her see red so soon after feeling relief that he made it out of Mexico in one piece.

"Part of the job, Powell. Don't get sentimental."

John climaxed and collapsed on top of her, his weight heavy on her chest, much like the remorse that started pushing itself forward from the back of her mind. He must have felt her stiffen because he raised his head, still breathing hard, a sheen of sweat on his brow.

"You're still an asshole," she whispered.

An arrogant brow arched. "An asshole who's given you an orgasm."

She pushed against his chest and he exhaled a heavy sigh, pulled out of her and rolled away. He stood and disappeared to the bathroom, presumably to get rid of the condom.

Nadia sat up, glanced around for her panties and spotted them under the coffee table. She picked up the evidence of her momentary lapse in judgment and tucked them into her backpack. She straightened her tight skirt, thankful that John didn't rip it apart when he shoved it to her waist. Her cheeks burned at how shamelessly she'd submitted to him. It was the guilt, she told herself. The guilt that it was her failure that stranded him and his team in Mexico, running for their lives.

When John returned to the living room, he was wearing a Hawaiian shirt, board shorts, and flip flops. He was fastening a giant watch on his wrist, a duffel slung on his shoulder.

She rose to her feet on unsteady legs. "Going on vacation?"

The levity of his outfit belied the expression on his face. A stoic mask. "I need to leave. Take all the time you need. Just lock up behind you."

"You trust me to lock up?"

He shrugged. "I don't keep anything of importance here. This is just a place to crash."

Somehow Nadia doubted that, and yet somehow she knew he was also right. If there was something the CIA officer kept here, it would be useless to someone who planned to steal it, because it would be protected by several layers of security.

"So, that's it?"

His jaw hardened. "This can't happen again."

A bitter taste saturated her tongue, before she managed a humorless laugh. "You need to be clearer about that, John. *This* as in dragging me into your clandestine ops any time you please or *this*"— she motioned to the couch—"which was a normal reaction to us blowing off steam because of Mexico."

He regarded her steadily. "So you're clear, then, that this is just us blowing off steam? A one and done?"

A corkscrew twisted at the center of her chest, making breathing difficult. Obviously, this was just another casual encounter for him. Hell, sex might be his way of coping whenever he'd escaped life-or-death situations. He was still charged with testosterone, and Nadia appeared conveniently for him to unload. She winced at the term. No need to make things awkward, but now knowing how John felt inside her, she wasn't sure if she could look at him any other way without remembering.

"Yes." Her chin jutted out.

His gaze narrowed. "Powell, what happened in Mexico could have happened to any comms officer. You need to get over it."

She gritted her teeth. "See, John, I can't just get over it because it wasn't my job. You put me in a situation I wasn't ready for. You blackmailed me into agreeing."

He strode past her. "Don't have time for this. Suck it up."

"I don't want to suck it up!" she yelled. "Can you even imagine how I would feel if all of you got captured, or even worse, killed?"

He stopped right at the door. His back to her. He didn't even turn around, just cocked his head to his side. "Lock up."

With those two words he left her behind. Nadia didn't know how long she stared at the door that shut behind him. But when she came back into herself, she made a decision. She slipped out the agency-vetted phone that Garrison had given her. Extracting the chip and without thinking twice, she dropped it to the floor and crushed it with the heel of her boot.

Then she gathered all that was left of her dignity and left the house.

1

THE SUN WAS JUST HITTING the horizon when Nadia pulled into the resident's entrance of the SkyeLark apartments. Before entering her code into the security panel, she glanced at her side mirror, watching a black Explorer roll to a stop at the curb behind her. She was used to Levi James shadowing her at work and looking in on her and her dad. She waved him off, letting him know she was secure.

Nadia knew he would wait until she was safely behind the apartment gates.

North Spaulding Street was quiet at this ungodly hour of the morning. She wished her favorite grocery store was open so she could save a trip, but such was the life of an LAPD crime analyst.

Crime didn't have a schedule, and neither did she or the people she worked with. She pulled her Subaru SUV through the entrance and rounded the complex, coasting into her parking spot. Cutting the engine, she dragged her weary form from the vehicle and made her way up to the third floor where the promise of sleep awaited. When her boots hit the second level, she remembered to tiptoe past the door of the apartment in front of the staircase. But when she ascended a few more steps, the sound of a knob being turned reached her ear.

She suppressed a groan. So much for making it past her nosy neighbor.

"Good morning to you, Missy," Clyde's cigarette-roughened voice greeted her.

Nadia ducked back so she could see her neighbor. Clyde was pushing eighty and the oldest resident in this cozy apartment complex. But the man had an alert mind and kept up his daily walks and poker nights with his buddies who also lived in the building.

"Hey, Clyde."

"Overnight call out?" he asked.

"What else is new?"

"Which mobster is it this time?"

Nadia bit back a smile. "Not every DB is a mobster." DB meant dead body, but Clyde in his inherent nosiness, must have memorized a cop lingo book at one point in his life and understood every LEO term she threw at him.

He stared at her dubiously. "That's not what I'm reading on the internet."

"Not if you keep reading the *Hollywood Tattler*."

"Touché," Clyde gave a disgusted snort. "You're right. The End of Days cult in the Valley has been warning of a Los Angeles Armageddon if people don't repent for their sins. They said the Ebola scare two months ago was just a warning."

Nadia yawned. It was a real yawn and not an effort to get rid of Clyde. "Well, you can sleep better at night. All perpetrators involved in the plot have been arrested."

"Looks like you're ready to crash," Clyde observed. "Catch some z's and catch you later." Without waiting for her reply, he shut the door.

Clyde could be chatty. At times he could be abrupt like he was just now, but she was used to his quirks.

Nadia continued to trudge up the stairs. There were four apartments on the highest floor. She rented one and her dad had leased another. The remaining two units were occupied by Clyde's buddies.

Grumpy old men surrounded her—no, not really. They usually made her laugh and were only sometimes grumpy. A smile touched her lips.

The sun cleared the horizon, and its rays reflected on her apartment's windows. She glanced at her watch before she fished out the keys to open her door.

Six.

She didn't have to be back in her lab until noon that day. Entering her digs, she booted the door close and headed straight for the kitchen. She lowered her patch-laden backpack on the counter before opening the fridge. An unfamiliar foil-covered plate sat in the middle shelves. Unfamiliar because Nadia hadn't put it there, yet familiar in a way she *knew who put it there*.

A beep on the phone alerted her to a text message.

Even without looking, she knew it was from her dad.

"Goulash in the fridge."

Going on a hunch, she headed to the pantry and opened it. A smile formed on her lips. Her father also stocked up her cupboard. They kept separate apartments and agreed to do their own groceries to maintain a semblance of independence as well as sanity. And yet, a dad would always be a dad. Always worrying if Nadia was taking care of herself given her long hours with the LAPD.

She exited the backdoor of her kitchen to go see her father.

The apartments on the third floor shared a rooftop garden. The majority of the plants were vegetable crops, and the rest were flowers. She made her way to Stephen's unit and let herself in. He was sipping coffee and browsing the news on his mini tablet.

"Morning." She walked over to him and kissed him on the brow before heading to his fridge to grab the carton of milk, which she knew he kept for her as well. Maybe this semblance of independence from each other was a myth in her mind. "Thanks for the groceries. You didn't have to do that."

He merely smiled.

"Didn't expect you to be up already," she continued. "You've been bingeing on *Hodgetown* until the early hours of the morning." Stephen had a habit of sending her random texts of his activities for the day, which was how she found out he was cheating on her by streaming their favorite series and watching it without her. Nadia didn't always respond, especially when she was on the job, but it had always been that way with her dad. It had been the two of them for the longest time until Clyde and his buddies butted into their lives.

"Have you started season four?" he asked.

"One episode." Nadia poured herself a glass of milk and settled in front of him.

"Well, you have to catch up," her dad said. "There's—"

"Don't tell me," she cut him off with a warning glare. He also had a habit of spoiling a show. Like he couldn't wait to tell someone about his theories. Nadia longed for their lazy weekends of all-day television. With the explosion of streaming, it was a wonder they did anything else when they spent time together. They loved the same science-fiction and horror shows. *Hodgetown* was the perfect combination of the two genres, and they had bonded over the series.

"I wasn't," he defended. "But please tell Gabby to tell Theo his acting chops are getting better and better with each season." Gabby Woodward was a detective on the LAPD task force that Nadia was attached to and, technically, her boss. Theo Cole was her son and the star of the hit series.

"Okay."

"Maybe drop a hint that she should guest star on her son's show." Gabby also used to be a popular teen actress of a zombie apocalypse series that still had a cult following to this day.

Nadia laughed and sipped her milk. "You know, we give her a hard time about it at work, especially since everyone who's above thirty remembers Gabby in *Dead Futures*."

"Not only that." Stephen lowered his tablet and rested his elbows on the table. He took off his spectacles, letting them hang from his fingers, and leaned forward as though he was about to tell her a great idea. "The studio would be crazy not to capitalize on the sensational headline from a year ago."

"Daaaad," Nadia gaped. "I can't believe you're all for exploiting that."

He shrugged. "There's a three-part mini-series on that baby swap scandal, right?" That story, so mind-boggling, it could only come out of Hollywood.

"That's not a done deal yet. Gabby and Declan are not too keen on the invasion to their private life, but Theo is all over it."

A yawn escaped her.

Her dad frowned. "That's the second day this week you hit the late shift."

"They needed someone to break into the deceased's laptop."

"Foul play?"

"It appears to be suicide, but Gabby isn't calling it yet. The guy was on the news recently…" Nadia rubbed her eyes. Thomas Brandt was an executive with SillianNet, a software company that had been embroiled in a hacking scandal the year before.

"Go to bed, *sonyashnyk*, before you get called again. You can tell me what a whiz you are this weekend. We're still on this Saturday, right?"

She loved his pet name for her. The Ukrainian word for sunflower. Looking at her father, no one could tell he was a former CIA asset who'd been a Ukrainian scientist forced to work in a Soviet-era bioweapons lab. Because of his defection, Russian death squads targeted them, and the assassins had been successful in killing Nadia's mother. Stephen and Nadia escaped execution when the agency had given them new lives and identities in the United States. She'd been six-years-old at that time, and her memories were blurry. She didn't find out about their circumstances until years later.

Recently, a faction of the Ukrainian Brotherhood targeted her father, intent to exploit his work. Technically, the threat was over, but just as a precaution, Levi had been assigned as her security escort. The LAPD also assigned regular patrols around the apartment complex.

"Yep," she said. "You're going to regret watching *Hodgetown* all by yourself."

"I'll watch it again with you."

"If you promise to hold your silence for the duration of each episode—"

"The Locke Demon appears to have—"

Nadia shot him a quelling look. The Locke Demon was her favorite character—as well as that of half of the *Hodgetown* fandom—from last season. A creature who used to be a man and cursed to be the guardian of the Ethervale, the thin curtain that separated *Hodgetown* from the dimension of monsters. In the finale of last season, the demon hesitated in killing Billy Mayhem, Theo's character, when he was trapped in the Ethervale.

In the opening episode of season four, the demon let Theo escape back into *Hodgetown*, so she was hopeful for the creature's character arc. She chugged down the rest of her milk and stood. "Well, I'm gone."

"Have the goulash for lunch."

"You didn't have to put it in my fridge, I would have come over."

Her dad looked at her dubiously. "Chances are you'd be running late, and I wouldn't see you for the next few days."

He knew her so well.

POTOMAC RESERVOIR, Maryland

JOHN GARRISON PULLED his SUV into the parking lot of the Potomac Reservoir. Fishing was not his preferred hobby. In fact, he didn't know if he had one. John was always on the move with no free time to indulge in leisure activities, although he'd taken up a few for the purpose of supporting a cover identity. The person he was meeting definitely loved fishing, and John couldn't fault this ideal spot for a clandestine meet. Two men standing side by side, shooting the shit for hours on end, waiting for a bite on the hook, certainly wasn't out of the ordinary for a place like this.

He was getting his fishing gear from the back of the silver Toyota Highlander when his phone rang.

"Garrison."

"Victim is Thomas Brandt," Levi's voice came over the line.

"Fuck. Nadia has his laptop?"

The SillianNet executive had been on the NSA watchlist ever since hackers breached their network monitoring tool via a software fix they provided to their clients. A routine task much like how one would apply a software update to a computer, it had infiltrated countless companies' networks, paralyzed their operations, and caused billions of dollars in lost revenue and productivity.

"Yup. Gabby made sure she was the one who processed all the computers and disks that were in his office."

"Good. We need to dig into his files."

"I'm sure Nadia can get something out of it now that she's in possession of the computer."

"Keep me posted."

Before Garrison could hang up, Levi asked, "Are you not going to ask me about Nadia?"

"You've been giving me reports," he said. "Is there something else you're leaving out?"

"Those were official business. Are you not interested in her personal life, like where she's hanging out after work, what time she got home this morning—"

"No—"

"Who she's dating?"

The line crackled with silence, and that question hung between them for a stretch of seconds.

"None of my business." John's grip on his phone was so tight, he was surprised it didn't shatter. "I need to know two things about Nadia Powell. That she and her father are safe, and what she can get out of Thomas Brandt's computers."

He ended the call without waiting for a response from Levi.

His phone buzzed with a text. "Sure, boss." Sarcasm jumped at him from those two words.

John tucked the phone back into his windbreaker and slammed the back of the SUV closed while cursing Levi James. The man was pussy-whipped trying to win his wife back, he didn't need to spread his misery around.

It had been eight weeks since he'd slept with Nadia, and three weeks since he'd seen her when he asked for Stephen's help with the bioweapon antiviral. John was perfectly fine with the status quo, and that included keeping his ass away from the west coast.

Balancing his fish and tackle box in one hand and his fishing rod in the other, he headed to the rendezvous point, keeping his head on a swivel. One could never become complacent, especially when the person he was meeting was the acting Director of National Intelligence.

He spotted the DNI's bodyguards, and they nodded to

him in their own fishing spots equidistant from an older man standing rigid at the edge of the water. John would recognize that military stance anywhere, even if the DNI was wearing a mariner's cap and a suede jacket. The Indian summer left Maryland weeks ago. Fall moved in quickly, bringing with it a chill to the air, and the cloudy sky blanketed the Potomac river in desolation.

John strode to his side and dropped his tackle box. "Admiral."

Benjamin Porter turned slightly his way. "John. Been a while."

"Three months isn't that long between us."

"True." The admiral stared off into the lake. "I was hoping we wouldn't meet under these circumstances again. Coming out of retirement after having only been in it for two years to clean up after my predecessor isn't really fun."

"Things went south when you retired."

Porter sighed. "I'm not planning to stay un-retired. I'm just glad my wife is more understanding."

Garrison finished setting up his line and whipped it into the water before glancing at Porter. John was aware of the admiral's predicament. His wife Pru didn't want to get married to a man who kept secrets from her after her first husband turned out to be the leader of an Asian crime syndicate. John had known Porter a long time. In fact, the admiral was the very person who told John to stop being idealistic and get a reality check. It was the admiral who told him that to be a successful spy, you needed to live and breathe the job. Porter didn't straight out say that having a family made you weak, but John could read between the lines.

The people you loved could be used against you.

The people you loved would hate the secrets you kept from them.

Ultimately, it was a losing situation, and it would only be a matter of time before resentment and bitterness eroded a relationship. That is, if the enemy didn't destroy it first.

"Is that why you haven't fully committed to the Director position?"

Porter shrugged. "I told the president that my agreement was temporary. He was desperate when my predecessor mucked things up by replacing you and your team."

"Yeah, the agency is not a big fan of publicity." John had to bite back a smile at how casual Porter mentioned the President of the United States.

"But it appears our problems didn't end with the Z-9 bioweapon threat." He glanced his way again. "Am I right?"

"Yeah. Thomas Brandt committed suicide."

Porter regarded him for a beat, and then, "Can't say we didn't see that coming."

"I'm assuming you mean that our Ukrainian friends got to him and made it look like suicide, because his profile points to an egomaniac who thought he could get away in compromising the nation's infrastructure. Taking his own life is unlikely."

Although with the bad press and the lawsuits, who knew what the man's mental state was. One malware could cause companies millions of dollars of downtime and headaches to repair their infrastructure—the U.S. government included. The breach was blamed on the Russian mafia-backed Argonayts—a segment of the Ukrainian underworld that specialized in cybercrime, extortion, and murder. Word on the street was this led all the way up to the Kremlin. John wouldn't be surprised. Brandt knew too much of their operations and with the feds breathing down his neck, the Argonayts considered him a loose end.

"Is that why we're meeting here?" Garrison asked. "You don't want the FBI to know the CIA is doing its own digging?"

Porter turned to him and smiled. "This is not even going to touch the agency. You're doing this personally for me."

"Fuck," Garrison said. "Don't fancy being banished to Antarctica."

"With your penchant for going rogue, I'm surprised you haven't been already."

John blew out a breath. "You want me back in LA?"

"Why do I sense hesitation?"

A tug on John's fishing line allowed him time to form his answer. He reeled in a catfish. It was a tiny one, so he unhooked it and threw it back in. "I don't like circulating in one place for long."

"Is it because of the place or the people?"

"Place. I've worked with the same operators for a long time. You know that. Roarke, Bristow …"

Garrison met Porter's steady gaze. The admiral studied him. Garrison returned his regard with an unflinching stare. He could play this game all day, and Porter knew it.

"LA is huge, but people start to recognize you," John added. "Especially since I use Roarke a lot. Damned Ranger had to marry into Hollywood royalty."

"Yes, that's a shame," Porter stated baldly. "But Gabby Woodward and their son could be gold mine assets."

"No," John clipped. "I'm not using the kid."

Porter returned his attention to his fishing line and was quiet for a while. "You've changed, John."

"Surely you're not insinuating that I'm turning soft."

"Aren't you?"

"Fuck no."

"Good. Then I'll need you to secure another asset before the Ukrainians get to him. Feds haven't had any luck with him." The admiral made a tsk sound. "The problem with these cyber-tech millionaires is they're suspicious of the government."

Garrison chuckled. "Could it be they've already hacked into our secret databases and know how twisted our institutions can be?"

"As acting DNI, the thought of that gives me nightmares," Porter said.

"Who's the asset?"

"Kenneth Huxley."

"Shit. That man's got an ego the size of Texas."

"Not many people can boast of hacking into Homeland Security's database and not end up in jail," Porter said dryly.

Garrison snorted. "Smith should be the one in jail. You never dare a legendary pen test genius to break into your security." In business, penetration testing was done to test the security of a company's IT infrastructure.

Smith was the United States Secretary of Homeland Security. At one of the cyber security conferences, the Secretary dared Kenneth Huxley to break into the department's database. Scotch at a bar may have been involved.

Needless to say, the hacker was successful, and DHS ended up with a huge embarrassment. In Huxley's defense, he claimed what he did fell under ethical hacking.

"You need to convince him to put his Crown-Key technology under DHS protection. I cannot stress how dangerous this would be if it ends up in the wrong hands."

"You've heard chatter about it?"

"I've been in this game for a long time," Porter said. "Cyber-warfare has taken center stage in the last decade. Companies developing technology for our military and intelligence community are also vulnerable."

The NSA's cryptologic centers around the country had been defending against cyberattacks from rogue states like Russia, Iran, North Korea, and China. It had been a constant battle.

"With Brandt's supposed suicide and the SillianNet hack last year, getting a bead on where Huxley is going with his Crown-Key technology with its ability to infiltrate secure networks is a matter of national security."

John was annoyed at the anticipation he was feeling at the

thought of returning to LA and struggled to keep an expression that gave away nothing. Like him, Porter knew how to exploit personal weaknesses in the name of the greater good. "I actually know just the person who has access to him."

The admiral angled his eyes at him and smiled.

2

"WHAT THE HELL DOES HE WANT?" Nadia checked her phone as she got out of her Subaru in front of the apartment complex.

An unknown number flashed on her phone. It was a text message, ordering her to pick up, and she had no doubt that it was Garrison who'd been blowing up her phone for the past few hours. She shook her head and slipped the phone into her backpack and walked to the staircase. Well, he could wait until hell froze over. She was done jumping to do his bidding. And couldn't the man leave a voice message?

Wednesday night was poker night for her dad and his buddies. And, if Nadia remembered correctly, it was Clyde's turn to host. As she passed her neighbor's apartment on the way to the third floor, she could hear their arguments and grumblings. She smiled. Maybe she'd join them later. The night was still young. Kelso would have invited her out for a beer if he wasn't on his "shredding phase" as he called it. She shook her head. If there was a health nut on their squad, that would be him. Gabby seemed to get sucked into his healthy regimens, much to the horror of her husband, because that would mean kale shake was on the menu. They were a fun bunch. She loved her team.

Reaching the third floor, she froze upon seeing the lights on in her apartment. Levi had stopped walking her to her door two weeks ago. It was unnecessary, but Nadia wondered if Murphy's Law was at work.

Or maybe it was a case of Garrison breaking in again.

It wasn't the first time.

Was he in LA? Was that why he tried to reach her?

Her heart pounded.

She wasn't sure if it was from anticipation.

Perhaps her blood pressure just spiked at his audacity.

She stopped and unslung her backpack from her shoulder to get her stun gun.

A figure detached from the shadows behind the stair wall.

She jumped, yelping.

"I sure hope you're not thinking of using that on me," a voice said.

"Asshole!" Nadia whisper-yelled, her hand on the weapon which was still in her bag. How did he know she wasn't just reaching for her keys? "Would you stop sneaking up on people?"

John revealed his face under the hallway lights. "I thought I gave you enough warning." He jerked his head toward the lit apartment.

"And stop breaking into my place."

"Maybe if you'd install the necessary security I've been telling you to—"

If smoke could come out of her ears. "Is this your way of proving a point?"

"Take it however you please." His eyes glittered and he nudged her forward. "Can we take this inside?"

"What's the matter?" she retorted, stalking away from him. "Hallway conversations too uncomfortable for your spooky ass?"

"Not at all," he returned mildly. "Especially since your nosy neighbors are playing poker."

Nadia clamped her mouth shut. Of course he knew what was going on in this apartment complex before he graced it with his presence. He probably knew what time each resident walked their dog and took out their trash. When they came upon her door, she didn't even bother with keys and twisted the handle knowing it was unlocked. Entering the apartment, she flung her backpack on the armchair before spinning on the heels of her scuffed boots to glare at her unwanted visitor.

"Why are you here?" she gritted.

He closed the door behind him and leaned against it, casually crossing his arms. "You'd know if you'd answered your phone."

God grant her the patience not to throw the vase on the console table at his head. That would be a waste of vase and flowers. "I don't answer calls from numbers I don't know. You should have left a message."

"I don't leave voice messages on phones I haven't vetted."

Nadia raised a brow. "Unfortunately, I don't answer to terse texts like 'answer your fuckin' phone'."

A telltale muscle ticked beneath his right eye.

"I need your help," he replied without inflection.

How could he so blatantly stand there and ask for her help? "So cut to the chase. Tell me what you need, and I might consider helping you."

Or not.

"Kenneth Huxley."

Her eyes narrowed. "Ken? Don't tell me he's on the government watch list. If that asshole from Homeland Security hadn't goaded him to break into their database, he wouldn't have tried."

Garrison straightened from his lean against the door. "Ego has a way of making the smartest men do the stupidest things."

Nadia couldn't argue with that. She'd known Ken before he'd gained notoriety in the DHS hack. They'd moved in the same IT circles since she'd been a gamer. As her work in the LAPD took her into the branch of forensics science, she'd lost touch with him. Until two years ago when she'd been called as a character witness by the feds in their investigation into Ken. She stood up for him even if she thought he was an idiot for hacking into Homeland Security.

"If you're asking me to spy on him …"

"Have you heard of his Crown-Key technology?"

"Yes. It's an improvement from what he used when he targeted DHS."

"We want to offer him protection."

"He's not going to go for it, especially after the government tried to crucify him."

Garrison left his position at the door and prowled toward her.

Nadia stood her ground. She wasn't tiny, but even at five-seven, John towered above her. She put his height at six-three, give or take. His dark hair was thick and needed a cut, but those gray wisps that winged his temples and threaded a trim beard made him a walking, talking, sexy male specimen of rakish charm and mature confidence.

It was a wonder women didn't throw their panties at him whenever he ambled by. Maybe it was a blessing he stayed in the shadows. Nadia doubted she was the only female who felt the mating call whenever John was around. Sensuality oozed from this man's pores.

Bad. Bad. Powell.

A cocky gleam entered his indigo eyes as he studied her face. *Shit*, did he know where her mind just went?

"It's a matter of national security," he said, the smirk teasing the corners of his mouth.

"Ken wouldn't do anything to hurt the country."

"Rogue states would love to get a hold of his technology."

She stilled. "Where did you hear this?"

Garrison turned away and walked to the couch where Nadia noticed his duffel sitting beside it on the floor. "I haven't heard anything yet."

"Bullshit." She stepped toward him. "You wouldn't be here if that were the case."

He spun toward her and pinned her with a stare. "My job is not to react, Powell. My job is to anticipate possible threats to this country. I don't have to tell you that wars among nations are not staged with guns and troop movements. It's gone cyber. The clusterfuck of the SillianNet malware is only the beginning, and now Thomas Brandt is dead, and we know it's not suicide."

Nadia remained silent. Kelso hadn't mentioned that the Counter Terrorism Task Force (CTTF) was working with Garrison again, so she wasn't commenting on the investigation or her findings.

His eyes squinted at her. "You're not talking."

"I don't comment on ongoing investigations."

The tic under his eye returned. She'd gotten used to his tells. Currently, he was trying not to say something that would piss her off and derail his chances of gaining her cooperation.

He backed up a step as though to give her space.

Another sign he was trying to make her feel more relaxed.

However, that had the opposite effect and made her more wary. "I told you. I'm done helping you. You're the CIA. You have resources at your disposal, especially since you report directly to the DNI."

"Right now, you're my best resource."

"Get out," Nadia fumed. "Take your things with you." She turned away from him and grabbed her backpack off the armchair. "See yourself out and lock the fucking door."

"I have an upgrade to your Wasp 10k."

She paused and then slowly turned around. "What?" she

asked weakly. Her geeky heart pounded with the rhythm of a thousand drums.

John approached her stealthily much like a jungle cat would prowl toward its prey.

As for Nadia, she was feeling like a fly being lured into a pot full of honey.

His mouth twitched. "Weren't you complaining about the camera?"

"Yes."

"You've got higher resolution and faster frame refresh rate. The new Wasp is installed with a visual intelligence app."

"You're kidding."

"Nope."

"Tell me more."

John grinned. Damn him. He knew he had her hook, line, and sinker.

After enumerating the Wasp's new features, he asked, "Do you want to see it?"

"Yes, but what do you want in return?"

"It's all yours if you go with me to this event tonight."

"Event?" she frowned. "Tonight?"

"I've secured us an invitation to Huxley's shindig at his penthouse."

She pulled back her shoulders. "It's sneaky of you to take advantage of my gadget-loving heart." Or gadget-whore heart, but she didn't say that aloud. "But you need to give me more than a future cyber threat if you want my help. I'm not following you blindly, John. I need to know it's worth it before I piss off the best pen tester on the planet and have his wrath rain down on me."

"Didn't figure you for a chicken."

Nadia's eyes narrowed. "Chicken. No? But pissing off Ken Huxley is suicidal and that I'm not. And you know that to be true, otherwise the DHS would've used more convincing methods to get him onboard."

John's mouth tightened as they squared off. "We're concerned with the Ukrainian hacking group."

"Argonayts?"

"Yes. Since you're not keen on sharing, I'll tell you this. I believe Brandt's death is not suicide, but an effort by the Argonayts to silence anyone who can expose them."

"You have proof of that?"

"I have an asset in Ukraine who has the evidence, and I believe there are more targets."

"Huxley's Crown-Key."

"Yes. If Huxley comes under Homeland Security protection, he will have the backing of the U.S. government to go after any rogue state or cyber actor that tries to exploit his technology. He will not end up dead like Brandt with our hands tied to go after his murderer."

Damn, he made a strong point, and if the Argonayts were in any way connected to Brandt's murder then …

She rubbed her brow before peering at John. "You're going to do the talking. All I have to do is get him to a place where you can make your case."

"Fair enough."

"And you're going to hand-over that Wasp right now."

John headed to the black duffel laying on the floor and lifted a black case from its depths and held it out to her. "Done."

She suppressed the urge to snatch it from his hands, calmly taking the black container from him and flipping the lid open. There, nestled in foam that had been laser cut to accommodate the shape, sat three shiny Wasp drones looking more badass than her last ones.

Her geeky heart did a happy jig.

NADIA STARED at herself in the mirror, feeling a tiny bit of guilt in agreeing to Garrison's plan to draw Ken into the protection of the spy agency. Of course, it wouldn't be the CIA on record. They would still be Homeland Security. Ken had always had a crush on her. Before he hit his first million and aside from the gaming community, they were both into cosplay. One year she dyed her hair black and dressed in full-goth after getting the dragon tattoo on her right arm.

Right then and there, she became Ken's dream girl, and he called her Lisbeth—as in Lisbeth Salander, the hacker genius in the book "The Girl with the Dragon Tattoo."

She wasn't about to dye her hair black again. Honestly, she'd been thinking of going back to her strawberry blond roots. However, Nadia had been digging the platinum blonde hair lately and more than debated in bleaching it almost to white until her trusty hairstylist advised against it, saying it would make her look ghostly.

Decisions. Decisions.

Good thing shoes were an easier choice.

Just buy more of them. Nadia was a lover of funky shoes. She peered at the pair currently hugging her legs. Suede over-the-knee boots paired with a black, slinky cami-dress that hit above mid-thigh. The style certainly displayed the dragon tattoo on her arm. Dark kohl lined her eyes, and her lipstick was darkish red, almost maroon.

Garrison said to dress sexy. He intended to use her for a distraction in their plan to lure Ken to an area where he could talk to the tech millionaire. Flirting with Ken with John's encouragement somehow soured her stomach.

Her eyes flared as she saw herself in the mirror.

Dress sexy.

She would show him sexy.

She exited the bedroom just as Garrison was buttoning up a black dress shirt that he left open at the collar. Gold chains hung around his neck, and he had a gaudy gold ring on his finger. He had sleeked back his hair and she was suspicious that he'd done something to his nose. It looked a bit wider at the base and he appeared to have slathered on an orange tanner. He had the seventies Italian mobster vibe down pat.

Nadia smiled inwardly when John's eyes darkened, and his jaw clenched into a hard line.

"I said to dress sexy, not give Ken Huxley a heart attack."

She shrugged her shoulders while she strutted further into the living room. The three-inch heels on her boots certainly gave her more elevation so she could stare more closely at John's face.

Eyes narrowing at his nose, she asked, "Is that a prosthetic appliance?"

He frowned and touched it briefly. "Is it obvious?"

"Only because I know what your real nose looks like."

"I can see the outline of your nipples. Maybe you should change into something else."

"Why? I'm proud of my boobs," she retorted. "Do you know how many chest exercises I had to do so these girls stay up without support? Besides, I don't get to dress like this often."

She backed away and made a full turn, knowing that John had probably spied her bare ass cheeks because she was wearing a thong. Nadia thought she heard him give a strangled groan, but when she turned back to face him, his face was impassive.

"Are you ready?" he asked brusquely.

"I'll just grab my wrap."

"Good idea," he muttered when she disappeared into her bedroom.

When she returned to the living room, Nadia was surprised to see her father scowling at John. Surprising, because her dad used to like Garrison. But this time, displeasure emanated from her father's body language.

"Are you dragging my daughter into another one of your secret missions?" Stephen asked.

John said nothing.

"Dad, stop it." She inserted herself between them. "Garrison needs a little help, that's all."

Her father's scowl deepened. "Then why are you dressed that way?" His gaze lifted past her shoulders. "You disappear for weeks and, when you return, you're taking my daughter to a club. What's this, a date?"

Nadia's face flamed. "No! John needs help—"

"With one of her contacts," Garrison inserted smoothly. "I swear, Stephen, this has nothing to do with you or the Ukrainians who were after you. Everyone involved has been arrested. This is something else entirely."

"Can you leave us for a minute, John?" Her father looked at her. "I'd like to speak to my daughter."

"We were getting ready to leave, anyway. I'll wait for you outside." Without saying another word, John left her alone with her dad.

He didn't say anything for a while, just stared at her. Not able to hold his gaze, she looked away. "Why are you here? It's too early for poker night to be over."

"We ran out of whiskey. I was heading to my apartment but I saw your lights on and thought to say hi. I was not expecting to see John here." Stephen sighed. "I don't think it's a good idea for him to keep dragging you into things. You have enough on your plate with the LAPD."

Nadia would agree if Garrison's case wasn't so related to hers.

"And I don't like that you're disappearing into yourself."

Not sure where her father was going with this, she caught his gaze. "What do you mean?"

"I can't keep track of who you are," he said. He gestured to her outfit. "This is not you."

"Dad, this is sort of a disguise."

"A disguise? Or is it because you don't know who you want to be?"

"You never said this when I cosplayed."

"You were in your teens." He stared at his feet. "And it was my fault."

"Dad, we've talked about this."

He raised his eyes, and her heart cried at the torment in them.

"I should have been honest with you about our situation here in America from the start."

She gave a sad smile. "You were trying to protect me."

"You went from being a precocious and confident child to a teenager trying to hide from the world."

Stephen was talking about that day they were suddenly uprooted from their suburban home in Virginia after an agency leak exposed them to Russian assassins once more. She was twelve when she discovered the truth of their immigration to the United States. Her father had been a defector and not simply a pharmacist. Eight months of safe houses ensued, and, with it, the need for disguise. In Nadia's young mind, that was coloring her hair, or changing her hair cut, wearing different styles of clothes, or noticing how wearing glasses changed her look drastically. It wasn't until Halloween during their sixth month of hiding that she discovered the power of costumes, and how she could transform into someone else.

She reached out and gave her dad's arm a squeeze. "I turned out okay, didn't I? And I enjoyed cosplay. Being a geek is my calling."

"I was happy when you found a job with the LAPD."

"See?"

"But somehow I feel like you've reverted into not knowing who you are again," he sighed. "I think John is a bad influence."

"I'm not arguing there," Nadia laughed. "But not in the way you mean."

"Do you really think that man knows who he is?"

Stephen stared at her for a few seconds longer, and then he gave one shake of his head and disappeared out her back door.

NADIA HADN'T SEEN Ken Huxley since the DHS investigation. She'd known he was making the ultimate ethical hacking device. Of course, *ethical* was just a way to market his invention to make it sound legal. Garrison was right. In the wrong hands, it could cause a lot of damage the likes of which would be hard to comprehend. Stealing classified information or taking down the power grid. Even water treatment plants were computerized nowadays. Nadia wasn't up to date yet on the newest version of the Crown-Key. Ken had made millions around the world by selling his services and using the device to do it.

Case in point. He now lived in the penthouse of one of the swankiest buildings in LA. According to Garrison, he paid roughly thirty million dollars for this property. Nadia had seen pictures of him on society pages and with a new personal style suited to his success, giving up those garish glasses and opting for frameless spectacles. The Ken she used to know wore thick-lensed square glasses, had hair that had not seen a barber in months, and a fashion sense belonging in the nineties.

"You still okay doing this?" John whispered beside her.

They were standing in front of a wall of glass mounted under stainless steel. The elevator doors glittered like stamped diamonds.

They hadn't talked much on the ride here. Nadia sensed disapproval in the CIA officer's body language, and she was sure it had everything to do with the way she was dressed.

"I was never okay with this deception," Nadia replied out of the corner of her mouth. With his closeness, she could smell his cologne.

And it was nauseating.

"But as you're always fond of saying, it's for the greater good. And I'd feel better if I'm there when you make your case." Her nose twitched. "And please don't get too close to me. Did you pour the whole bottle on you?"

He grinned, leaning even closer. "It's part of my disguise."

"What? Making sure people give you a wide berth?"

"Just you watch."

And she did.

As a crowd gathered around them, she noticed more than one woman ignoring their dates while edging closer to John.

"This elevator is taking too long," one person in the lobby crowd said.

"That's the problem with being fashionably late to Huxley's parties that people live for," another replied.

The elevator finally arrived, and everyone surged forward. Nadia was surprised when John put his arms loosely around her and guided her in. Somehow, he ended up at the back of the elevator with Nadia's butt pressed against a part of his anatomy. As the elevator car started moving, she became aware of a hardness growing behind her.

She didn't mean to squirm.

John's fingers tightened around her arms.

"Stop moving that ass," he hissed by her ear.

Goosebumps lifted on her nape and she shivered. Heat pulsed between her thighs causing her to squeeze them. But she had to move her legs because she was standing at an awkward angle … and she had to move her hips.

"Nadia," he rasped. "If you don't want me walking around with a hard on …"

His chest heaved in and out behind her. Sweat beaded on her upper lip. She stared at the numbers on the elevator.

Six more floors. The elevator made several stops, but as people got off, more would get in.

"Did he invite the whole fucking building?" Garrison derided.

By the time they arrived at the penthouse, Nadia felt feverish. It was a blessing when the elevator doors opened, and the throng of people dispersed.

John's palm slipped into hers, and they walked out together hand-in-hand. "Are you okay?" she asked.

"I'll live," he grunted. "There's a reason I memorize baseball stats."

Speakers were blaring with the party already in full swing. A DJ was set up at the center of the penthouse in front of a stone column. Nadia spied Ken holding court in the living room. The whole penthouse had twenty-foot ceilings and wall-to-wall glass, treating everyone to a sweeping view of Los Angeles. Nadia identified with geeks like Ken who could talk endlessly about a topic they were passionate about. And the technology nerds? They were in one corner wishing they were somewhere else, but when you were invited by a tech messiah you aspired to emulate one day, making an appearance was a must. In a way, Ken Huxley was representative of the bullied demographic in high school. The ones who weren't popular enough, the ones who were socially challenged when most of the focus was on the jocks and sports that would bring prestige to the school.

Good thing Stephen instilled in her the importance of an education. Nadia wasn't one of the popular girls in high school, and it reminded her of the conversation with her dad earlier that evening. She was twelve when she found out the real circumstances surrounding their life in the U.S. The inciting incident triggered the importance of not calling attention to herself. Yet, after the danger had passed, Nadia couldn't seem to shed the need to constantly reinvent herself with different looks. Cosplaying was a way to feed that need without seeming paranoid. As for her finding kinship with the nerds and geeks? Science and technology were her best way to assume control. Math and equations gave her finite solutions. She hated uncertainty, which was why she hated what happened in Mexico.

There were men walking around in khakis and black shirts, wires hanging around their necks or comms appliances stuffed in their ears. There were over half a dozen of them scattered all over the penthouse from what Nadia could see. A thread of anxiety tightened in her gut. She glanced up at John.

"Security," he mouthed, then he nodded in Ken's direction.

Nadia's gaze followed his signal when her old friend spotted her, a smile splitting his face. Ken waved her over.

"Guess it's showtime," John said on their approach. Ken broke away from the people he was entertaining, and his eyes immediately flicked to Garrison before returning to her.

"Nadia, long time, no see." Ken glanced at Garrison again. She shook her hand loose from John's hold and stepped up to Ken to give him a hug.

"How's my Lisbeth?" he asked.

"You're still stuck on that nickname?" Nadia laughed.

"You'll always be Lisbeth to me." This time he gave John his full attention. "I don't believe we've met."

Garrison extended his arm. "Gian Ferraro."

Slick. That way if Nadia accidentally called him John, with the noise levels here, it wouldn't be an obvious mistake.

"Boyfriend, Lisbeth?"

"Just friends," Nadia said. "I wasn't sure if you'd have time to chat with me. I didn't want to show up alone, you know?"

Sympathy flashed across Ken's face, and he lightly put his hand on the small of her back and led her to the group of people he was talking to earlier. "This is my design team. Any of them would hang on your every word. Just talk to them about the drones you use at the LAPD. Ladies and Gentlemen," Ken said with flourish. "Let me introduce the lovely Nadia Powell." A fond smile broke through his face. "My gaming pal and my Lisbeth ... and oh." He turned back to her. "Are you going to StreamCon this year?"

"You betcha," Nadia replied. StreamCon was similar to ComicCon but for streaming networks. It was a big event for cosplaying.

"Oh, I'm going, too!" A young woman with bangs and squarish glasses bounced up to her. "Are you going in costume?"

"Of course." Nadia grinned.

"I heard the *Hodgetown* cast has a panel." Another of Ken's computer engineers joined their conversation eagerly. "I'm going as a—"

"Now, Rupert," Ken cut his employee off. "Let's not monopolize Nadia's time with StreamCon."

"But you brought it up, boss," Rupert argued.

"Because I know she likes to cosplay. I want to hear who she's going to go as, not you," Ken retorted and spun Nadia away from his tech horde. "Sorry about that."

"Those are our people, Ken." Nadia kept the smile on her face but couldn't keep the ice from her voice.

"Always standing up for our kind, but ..." he paused. "I want to catch up with you. I don't want to hear about them because I spend my time with them day in and day out."

Nadia barely understood his words because the music drowned out the chatter and that only made people speak louder. She was all too aware of the weight of Garrison's stare burning a hole in her back. She also noticed that Ken's security moved closer, but her friend waved them off.

"So, how has the infamous Homeland Security hacker been faring so far?" she asked.

"Doing well. I just came back from Hong Kong where I audited the infrastructure of a major bank." Ken was almost yelling, and she could see his spittle flying.

Ew.

She surreptitiously inched away. "Must be exciting being so in demand."

Her geeky friend laughed … well geekily. A sound she'd associated as a Woody Woodpecker laugh punctuated with snorts. On the old Ken, it was adorable, but somehow for a successful businessman, it was jarring.

"I have everyone who stood up for me during the investigation to thank for that," he said with a smile.

She shot him an enraptured gaze. "So, tell me what your genius is up to now?"

Ken's smile transformed from warm to sly. He stopped a server with a tray of drinks and grabbed a red, fruity cocktail. Nadia declined. Her liver didn't agree well with alcohol and she frequently only drank at home where she could roll directly into bed.

"Gian?" Ken said politely.

"I'm good right now," Garrison grunted.

Her friend took a sip of his drink. "Have you heard about my Crown-Key?"

"Vaguely. It came up last year during the SillianNet hack." It was a wonder she said that with a straight face.

A genuine sadness came over Ken's face. "That's terrible. I've offered my services to them before. Is that why Thomas Brandt committed suicide? I heard your task force was on the case."

"I can't comment. You know that." They'd ventured

through an arched hallway and the sound of the music faded into a pounding bass.

"Wow." Nadia glanced around.

"Special acoustics." Ken stopped, casting a wary glance at Garrison. "I didn't mean to ignore you."

"I'm here for her," John responded.

"You can leave her with me now," Ken said. "Why don't you enjoy the open bar?" He waggled his brows. "And there are plenty of chicks that dig the seventies gangster look. Tony Montana, right?"

"I'm not channeling Tony Montana," John bit out. "And I'm fine tagging wherever."

Nadia turned away to stifle a smile. John shouldn't be offended. He was in disguise anyway.

Ken exhaled a long-suffering sigh. "Well then, Nadia and I can't go to my office where I want to show her my latest upgrade to the Crown-Key." He grinned indulgently at her. "Geeks only allowed. And you, Mr. Ferraro, are not one."

Two of his security guys appeared at the mouth of the hallway. That explained Ken's renewed bravado. He hadn't changed his taste in clothes, but they were higher quality—even designer—from the looks of them. He still wore flannel over a t-shirt and his beloved checkerboard slip-on sneakers. He'd traded his jeans for dark slacks. His unruly hair was tamed by pomade or gel. But underneath all those designer threads and new hairstyle lived the geek who still hated the jock. And, right now, Ken had the power, and he was relishing it.

Her gaze locked with Garrison's. At this moment, if he approached Ken with his offer to put his company under Homeland Security, they'd be thrown out by his security detail.

Ken's face lost its affability and turned cold. "Do we have a problem?" He glanced at Nadia. "Are you sure he's just a friend?"

"Gian, I'll be fine." She slipped her arm into the crook of the tech millionaire's arm. "Ken and I are old friends. I told you that."

Nadia swore John's right eye twitched. Dammit. This wasn't exactly their playbook, so she was improvising. Without waiting for the CIA officer's reply, she said, "Go grab a drink at the bar." She glanced over her shoulder and winked. "Or like Ken said, a hot chick."

Ken broke into his trademark laugh again, and it grated over her nerves but at least their whole operation hadn't crashed and burned.

Yet.

"WHISKEY. NEAT."

John needed a drink, and he needed one now. Otherwise, he'd rip Nadia away from that two-faced pen-test wonder boy. The second John met him, he didn't buy his "aw, shucks" act one bit. Ken Huxley personally oversaw his company's deal negotiations, including one with a Chinese conglomerate that was a financial powerhouse. He wouldn't be intimidated by John with his security surrounding them, nor would Huxley's ego pass up this opportunity to impress the girl.

The whiskey appeared and he tossed it back and asked for another.

He damned near swallowed his tongue when Nadia strutted out of her bedroom wearing a scrap of fabric she called a dress and fuck-me-boots that made his cock thicken. Her platinum hair cascaded over her creamy skin, reminding him how smooth it felt underneath his palms. Heavy liner accentuated her hazel eyes to almost tawny. She might be wearing contacts, but the effect was the same. He was sucked into their depths. The dark red shade she painted on her mouth invited him to devour her with a kiss. And what the hell was that twirl back in the apartment? Letting her skirt do a peekaboo, taunting him with the sight of her bare ass?

She was playing with fire, but maybe he was doing the same because John seriously questioned his plan to use her as a distraction. At that moment, his concentration was shot. He'd been hoping to exorcise his attraction to her once and for all, but once he set eyes on Nadia again, he recognized the futility of that attempt. It was a good thing Stephen Powell showed up when he did because John's erection promptly deflated. But once Nadia met him outside her apartment, he had to try very hard not to wonder if she was wearing panties.

She clearly wasn't wearing a bra.

The ride to Huxley's penthouse was pure torture.

The ride up the elevator was heaven in hell.

John kept a grip on her shoulders when what his fingers itched to do was slide under her skirt, rub her clit, and finger fuck her until she'd come against him in an elevator full of people.

It would be so easy with how short her skirt was, so easy to slide down that strap and cup her naked tit.

He sat up when visions of Huxley pawing Nadia assailed his thoughts, of that son of a bitch chasing her around the office with his zipper down, and his dick in hand, wanting to thrust it into her pussy.

Fuck this.

Nadia going in there alone wasn't even close to the game plan. If it were, he would have suggested she wear a wire. He was not down with that at all. He was crashing into that room and yanking her out of there. To hell with the consequences.

Another drink appeared in front of him. He tossed that back too and sprinted back to the hallway that led to the millionaire's office.

Two of Huxley's security guys ran past him and headed the same way.

Fuck.

He quickened his steps but was blocked by security before he cleared the hallway.

"You're leaving with me, Mr. Ferraro."

"Not without—"

"Don't touch me!" Nadia's yell echoed from inside the room framed by open double-doors.

Before the security man in front of him could react, John punched him across the face and cracked his head against his knee.

Nadia appeared at the open door, two more of Huxley's security clutching her on either arm. "Let me go! I'll walk out on my own."

"Throw her out of here," Ken said from behind her and then spying John, he scowled. "I should have known better. You're a Fed, aren't you?"

John stalked toward them. "Get your hands off her …"

"Or what?" Ken challenged as he nodded to one of the men holding Nadia. That man pulled a gun and aimed it at John. "You're on my property. Invited, but now I'm uninviting both of you."

Nadia turned to Ken. "You don't know what danger you're in. Look what happened to Brandt."

"Please," Ken scoffed. "You know the chatter on the dark web is that Thomas Brandt was responsible for the SillianNet mess last year. Someone probably took him out." He glanced at John. "I wouldn't be surprised if it was the government since it affected several institutions including the Justice Department, and the Office of Personnel Management. Now there's a big leak. Every single background check of every person who worked for the government is stored in there. That's what the government should be worrying about, not me—a man who makes an honest living by helping companies improve their security."

The man had a point, but it didn't lessen the urge to wipe

his smug expression on the floor, especially with Nadia looking so agitated.

"I'm not going to repeat myself," John said evenly. "Get your fucking hands off her."

"Or what?" The security challenged with a laugh.

John probably didn't look intimidating with his gold chains and his dark unbuttoned shirt, looking like a disco-era has-been. But he knew the background of every man in Huxley's security detail, and the one who would have given him the most trouble was unconscious.

Now this man with the gun, who he'd nicknamed Dumb and the guy on Nadia's right he'd called Dumber, both barely passed Basic and had hardly seen any action when they were deployed. Besides, John could easily read them.

He advanced a step.

"John," Nadia admonished.

Go ahead and struggle, sweetheart. *Now is when I need the distraction.*

"Stay back, Mr. Ferraro." Dumb's hand holding the gun wavered.

Another step. He hated that alias. It was pretentious.

It did serve his purpose. On his third step, and when he was within reaching distance of Dumb's gun, Dumber went for his weapon too.

"Stop it!" Nadia squirmed.

Without taking his eyes off Dumb's alarmed ones, John deftly slapped the barrel to the left with his right hand, and with his other, yanked it forward while disarming and unloading the magazine. Before Dumb could react, he elbowed him square on his face, and blood splattered, making him release his hold on Nadia. John grabbed her arm and yanked her forward while Dumber still fumbled with his weapon, giving him an opening to kick him above the knee.

Dumber collapsed to the ground.

By this time, John had Nadia behind him and backed away with her.

Ken stared at him open-mouthed and then at his crew who were groaning on the ground.

Another three security men rushed in with weapons drawn. The one John knocked out in the hallway staggered after them.

"We're leaving," John said. This would have ended more civilly if they hadn't put their hands on Nadia. "I gave you all fair warning to let her go."

"I wasn't going to let them harm her," Ken protested. "I just don't like being deceived." He glared at Nadia. "I knew working for the LAPD would corrupt you. Now you're like everyone in the government."

"Think this through, Ken," she implored. John had moved them around the perimeter, never taking his eyes off Huxley's men.

"Get out of here," the tech millionaire demanded.

He wrapped his arms around Nadia, and moved her along, keeping her shielded as they left Huxley's penthouse.

4

"OH MY GOD," Nadia pressed an arm across her belly. "That was wild."

As much as she hated admitting it, Garrison had been incredibly hot, swooping in so calmly and disarming Ken's security. Her lady bits definitely noticed and ... Was it hot in here? Taking a peek at the brooding man beside her, he hadn't said more than two words at a time since they left Ken's soiree. In fact, he only said two sentences.

When the elevator arrived.

"Get in."

When they got to the Escalade.

"Get in."

Terse. Angry.

She exhaled a heavy sigh. "You're mad at me."

He cut her a brief glance. "I wonder why that is."

"There was no other way. He wouldn't have let you in there. So I said your piece for you."

Electricity zinged between them. It was as if she were tethered to him and felt his every emotion. He was displeased with her.

No. Displeased was putting it mildly. He was angry.

Furious.

"You said my piece for me." All his statements were controlled and monotone. She was used to this from John. He rarely lost his composure. Except that one night a couple of weeks ago.

She blocked that memory before it took form. No way was that happening again.

"You were in there for ten minutes—"

"It felt longer than that," she said. Maybe because she wasn't that comfortable without John at her back.

"What," he gritted. "Happened back there? Did he show you any of the Crown-Key at all?"

"Yes. It's an upgrade all right." And what it could do gave her the chills.

"And?"

"Without the visual he showed me, it's hard to explain, but I understood right away what it could do. I'm not a fan of government involvement myself, but this is akin to a cyber-weapon in the wrong hands."

John let out a string of expletives. "We'll talk at the house. Right now, we're making a detour."

"What?"

"We have a tail."

"Oh."

"He probably knows where you live," he said.

"I don't think Ken is capable of murder, but, dammit, I hope he doesn't hack into the LAPD."

"Not in his profile to do anything malicious that could land him under fed scrutiny again. He's got too much to lose. Not that he won't try and make you sweat a bit."

That didn't give Nadia the warm fuzzies, and she worried for a moment about the security of her team's computer network.

Garrison glowered at the rearview mirror. "Taking you back to Assassin's Hill."

"I need to get my laptop and log into work to make sure everything is secure."

"You can do it at my place. Your task force gave me log in credentials a while back, remember? I'm sure you can configure one if I don't have it."

"Yup." She had her phone on her person. Her authenticator app was installed on it. So why were her lungs suddenly tight? What exactly was going to happen when they arrived at Garrison's house? The last time they were alone, they didn't do much talking.

"Text your dad not to look for you tonight."

"I'll call—"

"No. Text. He'll ask too many questions."

"Are you afraid of my dad, John?"

A derisive chuckle rumbled in his chest, but he didn't answer. Guess he was busy trying to lose the tail.

As he made turns at breakneck speed, Nadia's fingernails bit into the dashboard and the side of the door. Big SUVs weren't made to turn on a dime, but John seemed to wield this one expertly without flipping them over. They pulled into a neighborhood she didn't recognize. It looked shady as hell, and when they approached an alley, John shot past it before bumping the gear in reverse and backed between two buildings. Vehicles sped by them, and when a black, or maybe midnight blue, sedan flashed past them, Garrison muttered, "Gotcha."

"That the one?"

"Yes."

"Maybe you can take me home now," she said when their SUV pulled back onto the road.

The tether between them grew taut.

"No."

"But—"

"We have things to talk about—you and I."

"I'm sure this can wait for tomorrow."

"I won't be here tomorrow."

"Oh, another clandestine op?" she huffed. What else is new? "What exactly do you want to know? I can't explain it to you without graphics. I need to write down what I remember so I can let our graphics guy model one for you."

"No need. We already know it's capable of breaking into most networks and taking control of the system."

"Then what?"

"Why did you wear that dress, Nadia?" John was looking straight ahead. "Was your plan to drive me crazy?"

"You told me——"

"Don't bullshit me."

"Excuse me? You told me to dress sexy."

"I was expecting you to be wearing your skin-tight jeans and that low-neck top," he gritted. "Not strut around in a barely-there dress, no bra … are you even wearing panties?"

"Yes."

"All I saw was your bare ass which I really wanted to see in a shade of red."

Nadia's mouth turned dry, and she clenched her legs tighter.

"You like that don't you, babe? I came close to finger-fucking you in the elevator." His filthy words kept rolling off his wicked tongue, and she was pretty sure her thong was drenched. "I was feral, and you had the audacity to wiggle that ass against my dick."

"It was crowded."

"You were begging for a fuck, weren't you?"

"No," Nadia replied icily. "You were pretty clear what we did when you got back from Mexico was a one and done."

John laughed and cast her a mocking glance. "You and I both know what's between us isn't a one and done."

Nadia glanced out the window. They were close to Assassin's Hill now. "Then you snuck out like a coward."

"The schedule was tight."

"Sure," she retorted. "Whatever you say won't negate the fact that you said it's not going to happen again."

The familiar rust-colored gate of John's house trundled open. He parked under the carport, cut off the engine, and turned in his seat to face her. "I lied."

JOHN HAD KNOWN many women in his life. He'd slept with some and in his early years as a CIA operative, a few of his lovers even tried to kill him. He learned fairly quickly that the life of a spy didn't fit with indiscriminate sex, especially when that one-night stand was sent to seduce you and slit your throat.

A thorough background check was a must. Sometimes he lost interest, but with Nadia Powell, every little thing he uncovered about her made him hunger for more.

"What?" Her eyes widened.

No. Once with her wasn't enough. John had been delusional then because he would give anything to feel her tight pussy clench around his cock like a slippery fist once more. And his dick was already thickening beneath his jeans.

He leaned across the console and brought his face close to hers. She didn't shrink away. Good. She was learning how to deal with him. "Are you saying your panties are not soaked right now?"

Her chin tilted up. "Why don't you find out?"

He smirked at the challenge and gripped her knee, slowly tracing the tender skin inside her leg. Nadia parted her thighs at the same time her breathing hitched. He stroked her through her panties and could feel her dampness against his fingers.

He dropped his forehead to hers, and groaned, "You'll be the death of me."

Wrenching his hand away, he shoved out of the SUV and

slammed the door shut. "Out." He rounded to the front, irritated that she hadn't budged.

"Now, Nadia. Unless you want to be fucked on the side of the vehicle."

John vibrated with need. He tore off his prosthetic appliance and marched to the mudroom to rinse off the atrocious orange foundation and remaining glue on his nose. He also ran the water over his neck, including his hair to get rid of the cheap cologne smell.

He removed the gaudy gold chains from around his neck, took off the dress shirt, dried himself with the expensive silk, before balling and tossing it into a hamper. When he exited the mudroom, Nadia was standing at the threshold, uncertain.

He stared at her. She peered at him.

Without breaking his lock on her gaze, he stalked toward her, his hands hit her hips as he backed her toward the door. He reached past her shoulder and shoved it closed, then he slammed her against its surface and sank to his knees.

"John …I…"

He glanced up with determination. "My mouth has been dying to taste you here." He wedged his hand between her legs and massaged the top of her pubic bone. "All fuckin' night, babe." He stripped away her panties, snagging it on her ridiculously high heel, and then slung her fuck-me-boot encased leg over his shoulder. He ducked under her skirt and went straight for her pussy. His tongue licked in broad strokes, savoring all her wetness before fastening on her clit.

"John! Jesus," she cried out. Fingers dug into his hair. "Ah … ah… ah shit."

He growled against her pussy, pressing his palm over her pelvis to keep her still. Her taste was sweet like honeysuckle, and combined with her own unique musk, it was the closest taste to heaven. And damn did she gush over his tongue while he greedily lapped every single drop. A taste that would haunt his dreams. Well, no more. He wasn't denying himself any longer. He continued to feast and flick his tongue. His finger joined the festivities and sunk into her channel to prepare her for him. He found her sensitive spot and made her shudder. She cried out again and her legs began to shake.

Letting go of her leg, he rose to his feet and pressed his hips against her, making her feel every hard inch of him.

"See how crazy you make me," he snarled against her mouth. She was breathing as hard as he was, her chest rising and falling in a fractured rhythm. Without waiting for her answer, he captured her lips, letting her taste what he had plundered. He palmed her tits. John loved delayed gratification, and though he couldn't wait to sink inside her, he wanted to explore every inch of her that teased him to the breaking point.

He abandoned her mouth to travel down the side of her jaw, his tongue darting out to lick the shell of her ear. Her whole body shuddered, her breathing serrated.

"You like that, don't you, babe?" he whispered by her ear. Garrison was intent on Nadia's pleasure. His balls were begging to explode, but somehow, he got off on making her shudder. Making her want him because he wanted her with an intensity that should scare him. He continued his slow exploration, sometimes nipping, sometimes kissing, giving her small little bites. He found the pulse on her neck and teased it, then with his teeth, he removed one strap of her dress and deftly freed her arm from it. He pressed a kiss to her shoulder and stood back.

Her liner had run, and her lips were swollen from his kisses. Her dress was lopsided with a breast exposed; a nipple ready for his taking. He wet his index finger and circled her nipple ever so lightly, his eyes watching her face carefully.

"John," Nadia gulped. "Stop teasing."

"You think I'm teasing?" He gave a pained chuckle. "I'm about to explode."

"Then why don't you just fuck me?"

"Because … I want to do this." He bent his head and captured the taut bud between his teeth, grazing it lightly, flicking it with his tongue. Nadia arched against him and he wrapped one arm around her back while his other hand dug into the flesh of her ass cheek, fingers working into her pussy from behind as he continued to worship her tits. First the naked one, and then the other through the thin fabric of her dress. She pushed her hips against his and hooked her leg around him to bring him closer. "John … I'm coming again. Harder …"

He wasn't sure whether she meant finger-fucking her or sucking her tits, so he did both. Hard. She was slick and ready for him. Somehow they landed on the couch and John levered up and stood. With her dress hiked up and still wearing those boots, Nadia was a wet dream all splayed on the couch

"Don't move an inch. You're fucking perfect." He proceeded to unbuckle his belt and lowered his zipper. The tip of his cock already beading with precum. Fuck. Condom. Reaching behind him, he extracted one from his wallet.

He braced himself over her with his elbows. Nadia spread her thighs and cradled him. "Perfect."

He lined his cock and plunged inside her, not quite to the hilt. Nadia's body bowed but she arched again and tilted her pelvis forward, and this time every inch of him slid into her. Her muscles clenched around him, and he gritted his teeth.

"Jesus, if you do that again, I'll come before I even thrust." He dropped his forehead to hers. She squeezed again.

"Nadia," he groaned. John withdrew and punched in. This time he didn't give her a chance to torture his cock again. He pounded her hard into the couch and she rounded her limbs around him. But he needed more, because he wasn't getting as deep as he wanted to with the softness of the couch. He surged up, balls deep, and shuffled to the door, throwing them against it and continued pumping.

"See what you do to me," he snarled and drove harder into her. "You want my beast to come out and play?"

"Is that all you got?" Her hair was plastered all over her face in sweaty pieces.

She was glorious.

"You asked for it." He pounded her relentlessly against the door. Nadia screamed and her nails scratched down his shoulders. John wasn't a gentle lover. He fucked hard and he was elated that she met him thrust for thrust. There'd be bruising for her and scratches for him. Nadia sank her teeth into his shoulder to muffle another cry. So he'd bear bite marks too.

No. Fucking. Problem.

He was close, and with her pussy tightening around him again, John increased his pace. She felt so fucking good. The thought about taking her bare ...

"Jesus." He never went without a condom and always used his own. But just the thought of doing it skin to skin with Nadia sent his mind blind to anything else and he started coming. He continued pumping while every last drop of his cum filled the rubber.

"John ...John..." Nadia called. "Condom."

"Shit." He pulled out before he compromised the rubber and let go of her legs, helping her stand. She was about to sink to the floor, so he swept her up in his arms and thought to lay her on the couch. Changing his mind, he headed for the staircase.

Taking the steps two at a time, he got to the second floor and went straight for his bedroom. It was the first time he'd had a woman in there. Not even Nadia during the first time they fucked.

"Are you sure you want me in here?" she cocked her head.

Apparently she remembered as well.

She added, "Coz' I don't want to hear any commitment-phobic regrets later."

John wasn't ready to analyze his actions. "Don't overthink this. Besides, you did me a solid tonight."

He was being an ass.

But she had his number. "Wow, is that the best insult you can come up with?"

John turned his back to her and strode to the bathroom to get rid of the condom. "Just stating facts. Don't want this to get complicated."

"So, what's the rule? After this, we're done again?"

No, he didn't want them to be done. A foreign emotion rattled in his chest when he saw Huxley put his hand on Nadia's back as if he was the one with the right to be by her side.

One word roared in John's head.

Mine.

He tied up the condom and tossed it into the trash can.

He stopped short of entering the bedroom, crossed his arms and leaned against the doorframe, surveying the woman on his bed. "No. I don't want to give you a definitive answer. See, babe, I'm confused myself."

"Confused?"

"It's a damning feeling. I'm sure you're familiar with it." He deadpanned.

She gave a shake of her head. "You don't get confused."

"Exactly," he said. "Which is why this is confusing."

"How confusing can it get?"

John grinned. "I think a shower will clear our heads."

Her eyes narrowed, but he saw the gleam of anticipation. "Our heads? Do you mean yours? I'm not the one having this existential dilemma of continuing this arrangement, but we need boundaries or rules."

John straightened from his nonchalant lean and held out his hand. "We can talk about it in the shower."

·   ·   ·

THEY HAD WILD SHOWER SEX, another round on the floor of the bedroom, until finally, they made it to the bed. Not a word was said. Nadia did a lot of moaning and crying out, while John grunted and cursed a couple of times. He was nowhere near making a decision about whether to continue this affair with Nadia. It wasn't fair to her. He'd be going on an op again the next day and wasn't sure when he'd be back.

Except his regret wasn't that he'd slept with her, it was that he'd accepted this assignment in Ukraine. He wanted to see where this weird emotion he had for her was heading, but he also knew if his brain did the talking, he was better off following the lead on the Ukrainian Brotherhood. He received a text from the Admiral that was time sensitive. But he had a few hours.

Right then, he was enjoying the view of the sexy analyst wearing his shirt while she checked the security of the LAPD networks.

"How much longer are you going to be?"

She cast him an irritated glance. "You should sleep. Didn't you say you have a plane to catch at seven?"

"That's another three hours. I can sleep on the plane. I don't want to waste the time we have."

Nadia didn't say anything. Her fingers flew over the keyboard. Minutes ticked by, and John swore he could hear the second hand on his watch. Finally, her screen blanked, and she turned to face him. "What are we doing here, John? Am I your booty call whenever you're in LA?"

He tamped down a surge of impatience. This was the problem, wasn't it? The women he slept with always wanted more. And the confusing part? He wanted more with Nadia, too, but he didn't want to define what they were at the moment. He'd stashed her neatly in one of his compartments. She needed to stay there.

"You know the nature of my job," he said in an even tone.

"You can't promise anything."

He nodded once. "I can't even promise to return."

She frowned. "Is this mission dangerous?"

And that was another mark against defining what this was. He didn't want people to worry about him because that was just something else to feel guilty about. "Always a degree of danger, babe. But this is strictly intel gathering."

"Is this about your asset in Ukraine? About the Argonayts' activities?"

John's mouth flattened into a straight line. In the purple light of dawn, he realized he'd probably told her too much already.

Nadia must have sensed his unease. She stood and walked to the window where the bright lights of Los Angeles still flickered despite being four in the morning. "I think you should stop asking me for help."

Something constricted in his chest, but he didn't say anything.

She turned and gestured between them. "We've crossed the line twice now. You're already admitting to being confused." Nadia smiled sadly. "You know what I think it is, John? You're forming attachments to this place. And I'm not talking about me. Declan, Levi, and Migs. Their lives are here. Bristow, I guess, can work anywhere." She blew out a breath. "And I deserve more. The first time we crossed that line, I was worried about you and what happened in Mexico. We can chalk that up to the intensity of what happened. But you didn't like that, did you? Someone caring about you."

Fuck. How had she just read his mind?

Her lips trembled, but she sucked in another breath. "That's why you upped and left. I'm surprised you trusted me enough to lock up." She waved her hand to indicate his house.

Nadia didn't need to know that he had Roarke check up on this residence since his friend lived close by.

"I'm sorry for that," John said, and he was. "That was a shitty thing to do. This time I'm personally taking you home."

He glanced at the clock. "I have plenty of time to make my flight."

"No need."

A corner of his mouth lifted. "You're going to walk over to Gabby and Roarke's and hitch a ride?"

"No. Kelso is coming to pick me up."

"I can take you home," he bit out.

"I'm not going home. I'm hitting the gym with Kelso." At his hiked brow, she added, "I have a change of clothes at the station. We're heading there first."

"Nadia …" Frustration rose inside him.

Her phone buzzed.

Her smile was small. She walked over to him and gave him a kiss on the cheek.

It felt very much like a final goodbye.

John clenched his fists to stop himself from grabbing her. He jumped out of bed. "I'll walk you…" At her protesting look, he snapped, "And, fuck, if you say 'no need' again, I'm going to throw you on that bed, and Kelso can wait until I fuck this pride out of you."

"Pride? Try self-respect," she shot back. "How many times have you asked me to work for you? The first time, I would have done it anyway because it was for Gabby. But this whole Carillo thing? That wasn't an LAPD op. Did you know how scared I was when you guys were left running for your lives in a hostile place crawling with the Mexican Army?"

John groaned, "Not this again."

"I could have gotten you all killed!" She jabbed a finger at his chest. "You put that on me, John. I wasn't ready for a military assault of that caliber. You blackmailed me. Holding my father's cover identity over my head, and I had no choice—"

"I gave you a chance to prove yourself—"

"Can't you get it through your thick skull that I fucked up?"

"You did the best job under those circumstances. Ask any

of the guys. They were reaming my ass for losing you as our analyst."

Nadia brushed past him to get to her clothes. She yanked his shirt over her head, folded it neatly while he admired the arch of her back and the swell of her ass. After putting on her dress from last night, and slipping on those sexy boots, she faced him again, expression stoic. "I have to go."

5

JOHN CAUGHT up with her before she reached the door. Nadia was glad he put on some clothes at least. As if her walk of shame to Kelso's car wasn't embarrassing enough. And Nadia had to ask herself. Why did she keep doing this to herself?

He grabbed her arm. She looked to the spot where he held her before flicking her glare to his face. The tick below his eye appeared, and he dropped his hold on her. "We'll talk when I get back."

She shrugged and walked up his driveway toward the gate.

"Don't give me that attitude," he snapped behind her.

Nadia started counting to ten. Scratch that. With John, it was probably one hundred, but she was fed up with him not giving in an inch. She realized he would only give so much of himself to gain her cooperation. Nothing more, nothing less. And he would go with less if he could.

"Nadia." He strode past her and put his hand on the pedestrian door of the gate, stopping her from leaving.

"Let me out, John."

"Not until you listen."

"What more can you say? You said yourself you don't know when you're coming back."

He stared at her for a beat. "Monday."

"Five days from now?" This was the first time he gave her a definite day when he'd show up.

"Yes."

"Why did you say you weren't sure you're coming back?"

"Because what I gather from this op might lead me to another, but I'm passing the baton."

"What does that even mean?"

"It means I'm passing on what I find to another case officer."

"You'd do that?"

"I owe it to you."

The back of her eyes burned. "I don't need scraps of your attention." The sudden urge to cry hit her. Nadia fought it back with everything she had. She mastered the art of keeping her tears at bay in high school, not wanting to let the bullies win. She summoned that same strength now, and when she speared John with a glare, he flinched. "Let me out."

His jaw clenched hard.

"Now!"

He finally opened the smaller gate to let her through.

Kelso had the lights on inside his car and she could see him nodding his head to music as well as tapping on the steering wheel with his palm. She opened the door, and he shot her a shit-eating grin that slowly faded, morphing into a thunderous expression before glowering over her shoulder. She got in and shut the door, staring ahead, not looking at John who was still standing by the gate.

Kelso lowered the volume on Tim McGraw. "Do I need to kick the shit out of someone?"

Her lower lip trembled. "No, but I do need you to take me to the gym to kick some heavy bags."

And imagine they were John Garrison.

"Are you sure? Because it's looking like that fucker did something shitty."

"Let's just go, okay?"

He revved up the engine of the Explorer. "You got it, nerd girl."

THE CLANGING of the gates reached his ears. That was Hank Bristow picking him up for their flight to Ukraine, and John was running late. He'd bet the former SEAL was wondering why he wasn't already waiting with his bags packed at the front door.

A task as mundane as doing his own laundry kept him from being punctual. Most of his colleagues would just buy new clothes and dispose of their old ones, but John had a few he was attached to. His good luck charms, so to speak. Speaking of disposal, his trash needed to be collected and burned. The agency had a service for this. Spies didn't leave their garbage to be collected on the curbside for any reason.

He tossed his two duffels into the foyer just as Bristow walked in.

"Those are ready to load," he said brusquely.

"Good morning to you, too, G," Bristow said a bit too cheerfully.

"I'm running late," John went to the kitchen to yank out a trash bag and doubled back to take the steps two at a time to the second floor. His mind backtracked to verify that Nadia did collect her panties from the floor. On her mad dash to leave the house, she swiped them from the couch and stuffed them into her purse, making John all too aware that she wasn't wearing underwear when she got into the SUV with Kelso. There was no evidence of their tryst in the house, except the scent of her left in his bedroom.

"Are you okay?" the ginger-haired SEAL asked. "It's so unlike you not to be waiting by the door. You're always raring to go."

"I'm fine." His mind was still cursing Nadia for taking up too much space in it. He entered his bedroom and headed to the bathroom and picked up the trash can.

Then his quickly wolfed-down breakfast churned in his stomach.

He dropped the waste bin as though it was a scorpion about to sting him with poison before peering at the object that seemed to be playing tricks on him.

He blinked.

Nope. Nothing changed.

A torn condom.

Motherfucker.

How could he be so careless.

He dumped the trash can with its contents into the black vinyl bag, then he fished out his phone and dialed Nadia. No answer.

Fuming, he waited for the voice recording to come on.

He nearly blurted out, "Call me." But knew that terse message would get him nowhere and he wasn't risking it. Anything longer than that would defeat his spy craft protocol. Voice analysis software was so advanced now, John was careful not to have any sample of his own on an unvetted agency phone. Even then, he was always brief. In that way, he was still old school. He didn't want his voice to be manipulated to make false recordings. He typed in a text instead.

He erased, typed back, and erased it again before he settled on: "Answer your phone next time I call."

Then he let out an extended breath and added, "Please."

"Garrison, chop-chop, man, I was cutting it close, picking you up because you're always ready. Our pilot is already texting asking where the hell we are."

They were flying in a transport plane with crates of wine from Northern California.

"Fuck this." John stuffed his phone back in his pocket and

hurried out of the room. He'd try her again when he got to the airfield and had a chance to be alone.

He walked past Bristow, who still hadn't loaded up the SUV, and headed into the mudroom to deposit the trash. Then he made a call to the cleaner to come in to do a sweep and incinerate.

"Let's go." He grabbed his bags and stalked out the still-open door. Bristow locked up behind him, not saying anything, but he could feel the SEAL's eyes boring into his back.

When they got into the vehicle, the ginger-haired operator said, "Are you sure you're up for this trip?"

"We're not running an op. We're just gathering intel. Maybe negotiating a deal."

Bristow revved up the Escalade and backed up the driveway. "You're unfocused."

"Got a lot on my mind."

"Hmm ... try again," Bristow said.

"It's personal and it's none of your business."

"It may be personal, but it's my business when your head is not in the game."

"Those are my words." Garrison glared at Bristow.

The SEAL was focused on traffic. "Exactly. So practice what you preach."

Scathing words backed up his throat. He was taking out his irritation at Nadia on his crew. It was not his style to let personal shit affect the way he handled his team. Nadia was occupying more compartments in his mind faster than he could create them. That broken condom only accelerated this dilemma.

His phone rang. John almost felt relief, but when he saw who was calling, he wasn't sure whether to pick up. He probably wouldn't be able to talk to her for another week and ... shit ... he forgot.

Swiping the screen, he said, "Ma, Happy Birthday. And I haven't forgotten."

A sigh came over the phone as Bristow cast a brief glance at him. The SEAL knew about Fiona Mason. John's mother was a happily retired schoolteacher who spent her days going through every single series on Primeflix or attending cardio classes at the local gym.

"I'm sixty-seven, Jacob. I'm too old to hold a grudge against my son if he forgot my birthday, especially with your job as embassy liaison. Travel can mess up your time clock."

"It does."

"So what adventures have you been on lately?"

He thought back to Mexico but decided not to revisit that mission at the moment.

"Rio." John gave his mother a brief made-up story about having to negotiate with the Brazilian ambassador regarding the preservation of the Amazon.

"They have pretty beaches and even prettier women."

He sighed, knowing where his mother was going with this.

"I haven't given up yet, you know?" she continued. "You're forty-two. The instructor in my Zumba class—"

"Christ, Ma—"

"Just saying, son, you're not getting any younger. The last time I saw you was two years ago, and you were starting to turn gray."

That was the time he returned from Yemen when he had a slight existential crisis because he nearly lost his head to a terrorist's machete.

"I want some grandbabies to dote on," she said. This line of their conversation was nothing new but served as a reminder of the broken condom. John got lightheaded if not a bit nauseous. His mother's voice faded and in and out of his hearing like a bad reception.

"I don't know where your dad—God bless his soul—and I turned you off on marriage—"

"You and Dad did nothing wrong," he managed to bite out.

It wasn't his parents. John had a solid middle-class, Midwest upbringing. Star quarterback in high school, on a scholarship to college before he dropped out in his second year and joined the Army. When September eleventh happened, he'd been invited to try out for the Delta Force. He got in, but his idealism slowly drained out of him. Being Delta puts you in contact with the dregs of society. You see all that shit you can't talk to anyone about or question. The classified shit that gets shoveled internally until it poisoned everything you'd once seen through rose-colored lenses. War and its horrors, the deals made with genocidal maniacs to preserve the greater good, had a way of stripping away the once-noble reasons for becoming a soldier.

"Well, we must have. I'd hate to see you waste good Irish stock. Your uncle's daughters married all these weak-jawed Wall Street types who probably don't know how to ride a bull or run their ranch."

John had to chuckle at this. "I don't think cousin Nessa would like to live on the ranch and neither did I for that matter."

"But you became a soldier. You did me and your dad proud."

But he wasn't that young man anymore. In fact, John wasn't sure who he was except a weapon for the agency. "Listen, I got to go."

"Where are you off to this time?"

"Romania."

"Lots of pretty girls there too."

"Goodbye, Ma."

"Take care, Jacob."

He ended the call.

"Man, you almost sound human talking to your mother," Bristow deadpanned.

"Yeah, almost."

The SEAL gave a brief chuckle. "So, is Mrs. Mason still trying to marry you off?"

"To her Zumba instructor this time, apparently."

"I don't know how you managed to keep her in the dark with what you do all these years."

"She's learned not to expect me on holidays."

"How long since you've seen her?"

"Two years."

"Christ, G, don't you ever get tired of the job?" They arrived at the bottom of Hollywood Hills and made the turn onto Sunset Boulevard.

"What's the matter? You want it?"

Bristow shot him a flash of teeth before shaking his head. "Nah, I like this freelance shit too much. If I get tired of your spooky ass, I'll find another boss."

That spooky ass comment reminded him of Nadia, whom he suspected picked up the term from Bristow. The familiar connections started an unease roiling through his stomach again.

When he started this gig in LA on the trail of the bioweapon, his friend Kade Spear who owned a security company, floated the idea of possibly reuniting Gabby and Declan. Spear's intentions were honorable, while John's wasn't entirely benevolent. He figured if he rolled the dice and had a connection inside the LAPD, that would smooth the way for running counterterrorism operations in the city. Nadia was a surprise. He didn't know who she was until he'd gone through the files of everyone in Gabriel Woodward's orbit.

It also didn't escape him that in the less than two years since the operation began, his operatives and assets kept falling like flies.

Falling into the marriage trap.

Declan and Gabby.

Migs and Ariana.

Antonio wasn't technically an asset. The man had a heart of ice, and yet it melted for Charly. He knew they were getting married in a few weeks.

John started to sweat. He needed time to think.

It was time to get the fuck away from Los Angeles.

HOURS LATER, he and Bristow landed in the private hangar of Kiev businessman Ilya Kravets who was an importer of American goods. There was a limo waiting for them, the usual front, a luxury welcome wagon for business associates. As John and Bristow alighted from the aircraft, the door to the vehicle opened, and Ilya alighted.

His suit was disheveled, and his face was covered in bruises.

"Fuck." Bristow dropped his backpack, drawing his gun, head on a swivel.

John did the same.

"What the hell are you doing here?" John growled at the businessman.

Ilya gave a resigned smile. "The Order found out."

Three black SUVs converged around them and armed men stepped out.

A gun clicked behind them. Their pilot had turned on Ilya.

Fuck.

It was a trap.

6

THE MERRY old men of SkyeLark apartments (MoMoS) were at it again. She groaned and dragged a pillow over her head to muffle the noise. It was Sunday and probably close to noon, but she'd stayed up into the early hours of the morning with Stephen, binge-watching *Hodgetown*'s fourth season. The Locke Demon featured widely again in the season finale and its fate, as well as that of Billy Mayhem, was unknown. They both fell through the veil into the monster dimension with the biggest baddie of all awaiting them. Nadia was tempted to have Gabby badger Theo regarding spoilers for next season.

Thinking of Gabby reminded her of the Thomas Brandt case. The medical examiner ruled out suicide. No surprise there. The chat room that could've been their lead into Brandt's shady dealings and that might have eventually led them to his killers was shut down.

The Feds had taken an interest in the case and had been around their CTTF office. It was the last time she was letting them into her crime lab. The Fed team wouldn't stop touching her drones and her other toys, questioning how she got them. She did relish telling them that they didn't have the clearance because she was a beta tester for a company that did business for the DoD.

It was partially true. They didn't have to know most of them were bribes from John.

Each time he asked her to do an op, he brought her a new CIA gadget. These devices were designed by Defense Advanced Research Projects Agency (DARPA) and were never commercialized.

Son of a bitch. She always thought it was a bribe, but what if he was wooing her the only way he knew would get to her. That was how she'd fallen for the bastard. He didn't do it with roses, or dinners, or movie dates. It didn't fit into his agenda or his lifestyle. So he gave her things that would make her happy.

But Nadia was finding out it wasn't enough.

John Garrison was too dangerous for her heart. He represented risk, excitement, and authority. And Nadia found nothing sexier than a bossy man. Unfortunately, what made him attractive also made him an unappealing prospect as the man in her life.

He didn't represent stability.

Every interaction she'd had with him ended in chaos.

Ugh. Why is he in her thoughts again?

Thankfully, the *Hodgetown* series and her job kept her occupied, but thoughts of the man had a way of sneaking back in like a bad habit. They'd had sex twice—well multiple times on each occasion. Nadia kept telling herself the first time was due to her relief that he was alive but would cop to the second time being solely about lust.

She had no excuse for it to happen a third time.

"Don't touch my fucking grill." A voice boomed from the outside. That would be Dugal Cameron. Nadia's apartment was between his and her dad's. One of Dugal's sons owned the complex—a stuntman who was in demand in action films.

"I was checking if it's ready. I'm starving," Clyde said.

"We'll wait for Nadia to get up ..." The rest of his sentence was muffled as if he remembered he was loud and was going to wake her up. Her dad mumbled an intelligible response.

Nadia sighed. Looked like she needed to make an appearance with the MoMoS as she fondly called them. She didn't turn up at their Wednesday night poker because of John's idea to crash Ken's party—

Ugh. Again, with John intruding into her thoughts.

Tossing the pillow aside, she jumped out of bed and headed to the bathroom to freshen up, putting on matching velour sweats and her platform step-in sneakers before she heard a light knock on her bedroom door.

She opened it to her smiling father.

"You heard Dugal, I presume."

A pained smile formed on her lips. "Yes."

"Sorry, *sonyashnyk*, but they missed you. Besides, Dugal's son is visiting."

"Please tell me this is not another matchmaking attempt."

They walked through her kitchen and Nadia pushed open the back door. Briefly blinded by the sun, she paused to slide on her shades.

"There's our sunflower," Clyde beamed, while rocking his stocky form in one of those outdoor deck recliners. Dugal strode to the grill to fire it up. "It's about time, lass. The natives are hungry."

"You all didn't have to wait for me. I wanted to sleep in."

"You can go back to sleep after I put some food in ye." Dugal was the biggest and most fit among the MoMoS. At sixty-two, he was over six feet, his head was shaved, and he sported a salt-and-pepper beard. He owned a butcher shop—Cameron and Sons Butcher—and had forearms that were twice as thick as hers. Maybe more. Besides the stuntman, he had two other sons who worked on and off in the Hollywood circuit when tough-looking Scotsmen who rocked a kilt were needed. Most of the time, they helped their dad out in the shop. "Did you eat that goulash I sent over?"

"Yes. Dad made sure I ate it."

"You've become skin and bones," Dugal clucked as he shut the cover of the grill to let it heat up. "Are you still hanging around that meathead detective and working out too much in the gym?"

"Stop bullying our girl," the fourth man of their group, Arthur, stepped forward. At sixty-eight he was the most soft-spoken of the bunch. He lived in the fourth apartment, the one beside her dad. He had a slender frame like Stephen and was frequently Clyde's walking partner in the mornings. Arthur also tended the rooftop gardens. Sometimes he and her dad would mess around with chemical compounds from the plants.

"I'm not bullying, just reminding her she doesn't need to hang around that detective when I have two perfectly able-bodied sons whose muscles don't come from that powdered crap who could take care of her and feed her."

"Marriage is more than about the care and feeding," Clyde put in, turning his shrewd eyes on Nadia. "It has to be about chemistry."

Nadia froze. Had Clyde seen John? She glanced at her dad who shrugged and dropped his attention to the appetizer spread of cold cuts. He didn't seem to understand the question in her eyes.

Ever since Stephen retired from the pharmacy, Nadia was worried he would become bored. He still liked to tinker in his makeshift lab in the second bedroom of his apartment. As long as he didn't blow up shit, and it wasn't illegal, Nadia was onboard with what kept her dad busy. Being around these guys also helped, dispelling her worry about her dad getting lonely.

"Chemistry, bah," Dugal scoffed. "Worry about that later. Make sure he can support ye, take care of ye. Teresa came to love me very much after we were married." He grinned slyly. "She gave me strong sons. I can tell ye that came from chemistry—"

Nadia covered her ears with her hands. "Lalala. Don't want to hear it, but I get both your points." Dugal was about to brag again about the very active sex life he'd had with his wife who died six years before from cancer. It was after that tragedy that he moved into his son's apartment from their house that was also in West Hollywood. Too many sad memories, he said.

"Colin is on his way," Dugal said, momentarily distracted with his phone. "He's just taking care of one last customer before he heads over. Better get these bangers on the grill. Colin made them last night." He waggled his brows at Nadia.

"He's laying it on thick," Clyde grumbled, still rocking back on his chair and drinking his beer. "If any of my sons were unmarried, I'd fix you up with one of mine too."

"Guys," Nadia said, feeling like she needed a drink. "Do I look desperate for a man?"

"No, but I'd hate for an unworthy one to snatch you," Dugal grumbled at his grill before glancing at Stephen. "We'd make good in-laws."

"Stop badgering my daughter before you burn the sausages," Stephen said dryly.

"They're called bangers," Dugal insisted. "How many times do I have to tell ye that."

"When in Rome …" her father started but let it hang.

"Here," Arthur came up to her, holding a pink drink with a stem of rosemary.

"Mimosa?" Nadia asked.

"A grapefruit one mixed with my own rosemary extract." Arthur adjusted his spectacles. His wild, unkempt, long hair framed a narrow face. His lips were thin but distinctly contoured and sharp; intelligent eyes peered from behind rectangular frameless glasses. He had the look of a mad professor. Arthur and her dad were always mistaken for brothers with their similar builds.

The MoMoS continued to bicker amongst themselves. Well, usually it was Dugal who grumbled, Clyde who riled him up more, and then her father would step in as referee, with Arthur standing back and making the drinks.

Colin arrived. He was Dugal's middle son. Unlike his two brothers and his father who had dark hair, he had coppery strands that matched his trim beard and eyes that were almost amber. Besides playing a brutish Scotsman on a Hollywood set, he modeled as well.

And he was thirty-five. Right now, he was staring right at Nadia, so she willed herself to give him a flirty smile. She needed to get past her infatuation with he-who-shall-not-be-named.

"Colin."

He leaned in to kiss her cheek. "I'm here to rescue the rose among the thorns." He glanced at Dugal. "Did I hear you arguing with Clyde about who makes better tatties?"

"It's mashed potato," Clyde said. "Where I grew up in the South, there's only one way to make mashed potatoes."

"Well, I'm making bangers and mash and that's that," Dugal returned.

They went into another round of bickering until the older Scot glared in the direction of the stairs. "For fuck's sake."

Dugal grumbled, "Can't the lass have a relaxing day without you cops pulling her into shit?"

Nadia turned around to see Kelso entering the rooftop courtyard from the opening between apartments. His face was serious, so this wasn't a social call.

"What's up, Kelso?"

"Tried to call you. Figured you were out here."

"I slept late. I left my phone inside."

"It's cool," the detective replied, glancing around the rooftop. "I'm sorry to pull Nadia away, but we need her."

"Brief me while I throw some clothes on and get my gear." The menfolk were used to this from her. Her father sighed and walked back to his apartment where she figured he was going to pack some food for her to take.

Sprinting back to her own apartment with Kelso keeping pace with her, he said, "You know our victim."

Nadia braked right before the door to her bedroom and spun around. "Who?"

"Kenneth Huxley."

"THERE HAS to be a connection between Thomas Brandt's murder and this one."

Gabby and Kelso walked into Ken's office where Nadia was busy marking evidence for the crime scene techs. She was the most flexible in the group and sort of a Jill-of-all-trades for the forensic department. She had her own lab, which Kelso had christened "The Nerd Lab" that was equipped with the latest technology. Another one of Nadia's specialties was comms, and hence, her arsenal of drones. She was the eyes and ears on the ground for the team. At the moment, she had on her digital forensic hat.

"Why were you and Garrison here last Wednesday?" Kelso asked.

"He wanted to use my friendship with Huxley to coax him to put his Crown-Key technology under Homeland Security protection."

"Which really means CIA," Gabby said. "It looked like his concerns were valid. What exactly does it do?" She paused. "Give it to me in layman's terms quick-like, so we know what to look for."

"It's a two-part system," Nadia said. It took her almost an hour to get through her contact with the Feds to allow the manufacturer of Ken's computer to give her the backdoor into his machine. Nadia put in her own clearance code which was still valid from when she worked on Thomas Brandt's computer, and she was in. But that was the easy part. Like Brandt's computer, she needed to unlock several partitions. The app was installed, but that only performed surface-level hacking. "To be fully functional, we need the hardware as well." She glanced up from the screen to look at the detectives. "Ken showed me a simulation last Wednesday. If it truly does what I've seen, we're in deep shit."

"Explain," Gabby said.

She nodded for her colleagues to get behind her. "It's a device that can analyze networks for vulnerabilities. It uses an AI program to project feedback and maps out several paths to what Ken calls the Crown—the top of the food chain. Not only that, but it can also figure out a path from a less secure computer, and move laterally, if it has to, and then up."

"What does that even mean?" Kelso asked.

"Let's say our hacker has targeted a company. Lower-level computer users are more lax with authentication credentials because they have less access to critical data. If the hacker has the credentials of, say, a personal assistant to a low-level manager. He's already in the network, he can move laterally to another computer with higher security clearance on the same network, and continue hopping across and then up the chain until he gets what he wants."

"And the Crown-Key simplifies this?" Gabby asked.

"It's one of its features," Nadia said.

Both detectives were quiet for a while, contemplating the impact of her words. Finally, Kelso said, "Tell us what to look for."

"We're looking for a device eleven by nine by two inches," Nadia said. "Ruggedly built like military laptops, Ken said its case is made of titanium. I doubt he keeps it here. I would have the techs search for something like it."

"Got it." Both detectives made a turn to leave the room, but she recalled their attention. "Oh, and guys…"

Both turned to look at her.

"I don't see one of his security guys among our DBs." It was the guy Garrison knocked out first.

"We'll have you identify him when we get back to the station. I'm sure a couple of them are off-duty," Gabby said, and then smacked her head when Nadia grinned. "Oh, right, you're the one who'll be giving us that information."

"This should be interesting," Kelso said. "When your crime analyst becomes the witness." He addressed Gabby. "You think Nadia is too close to this? Maybe we should have someone else take over."

Gabby shook her head and strode out the door. Nadia might have heard her muttering about John Garrison dragging her team into his shit.

Back at the CTTF HQ, the team was assembled in the war room where a link chart was already started. One white board held everything they knew about Thomas Brandt, while another link chart on Huxley was taking shape on a second.

"Huxley was found dead in his bedroom," Kelso said. "Two shots to the chest. The rest of his security was systematically eliminated. One by the elevators, two in the kitchen, one by his office and the last was just before his bedroom."

"Nothing on the surveillance footage?" Joe Henderson asked. He was a veteran detective who used to work the Robbery and Homicide Division.

"No," Nadia said, fingers flying over the keyboard. "The video had been tampered with and we're missing a whole eight hours of surveillance that included the timeframe when the murders happened.

"Though not a suspect yet, Nadia identified a person of interest." Kelso flashed a picture of a blond-haired man, with rough features on the screen. "Cain Morris is a former Navy SEAL who worked for a private military company that did a lot of business in Ukraine. He's not the head of Huxley's security, but he did most of the hiring."

"If he, indeed, is the mastermind, that would explain the poor security," Nadia said.

"Gabby and I went to his residence," Kelso said. "No one is answering. We've filed for a search warrant."

"He's got to know that he'd be an immediate suspect given his background," Gabby added. "If he's guilty, we're sure he's already planned an escape route."

"What's this Crown-Key you all have marked there with an asterisk?" another officer on their team asked.

Nadia repeated what she told the detectives when they were at Ken's condo.

"Motherfucker. Why would Huxley create such a device?" Henderson asked.

Ego. Nadia didn't say, but there it was. Ego was the root of most evils. However, maybe Ken had an altruistic purpose. "Ken has long criticized the government and other major corporations for easily exploitable weaknesses in their infrastructure."

"So he created this to prove a point?" another officer on their team scoffed.

"Or, maybe, so he could help strengthen it against attacks."

"We don't think Morris has the device at this point," Gabby said. "Nadia indicated Huxley wouldn't be keeping it in the same location. We also believe that Huxley was killed elsewhere and dumped in his bed. Forensics and the medical examiner are confirming this."

"So why kill Huxley?" Another detective asked. "And why didn't they take his laptop?"

"Maybe they're afraid it has a tracker the LAPD would have access to and don't want to risk it. Ken also has it locked up tight. There's only the app on the machine. The source code is somewhere else, but I think I can run a program through his files to find his code repository," Nadia said. "As for killing Huxley, I have a feeling he was starting to consider Homeland Security protection, and maybe Morris knew he was out of time."

"You think he cut and run?" Kelso asked.

"He must have gotten something out of Huxley," Gabby said. "What do you think, Nadia?"

"We'll need to review every single piece of evidence from the penthouse," she replied.

"Agreed, but I want you to concentrate on digital forensics. Find that source code," Gabby told her. "I'll tell the other techs to work on latents and other evidence."

"Sounds good."

7

THE CHAIN STRINGING him up was released, and John dropped to the floor with a grunt. The day's interrogation was over, and he wondered if his ribs were broken this time.

"He didn't give up anything useful." His interrogator, a man who was a hulk at six-seven with a physique that matched, spoke in Russian to a skinny man half his size. "Are you sure I can't break his legs?"

"Unfortunately, no." The smaller man with a scar across his eyes said. "Boss said no visible injuries."

John wasn't surprised with that directive. The mob liked to intimidate American operatives, but history had shown that the U.S. had a taste for swift retribution when one of their own was harmed. Unlike terrorists, who would love nothing more than to get their hands on the enemy, organized crime preferred to fly under the radar of the law. Not that John was the law.

Steel toe boots appeared in his line of vision before he was kicked from his kneeling position, sending him flat on his back. Three hundred pounds leaned on the sole of a boot to express the air from his lungs.

"Just a jab to the face, boss," the Hulk said. "I want to see him bleed."

Normally, John would treat his captors with smartass comebacks, but self-preservation drove his silence for the past three days. Visions of leaving Nadia alone and pregnant had been giving him cold sweats and nightmares.

"Enough. Things are happening as we speak, and we don't want a damaged or dead CIA officer to add to the complication," Scar-Eye said.

"Are we sure this is the guy named Stryker?" Hulk asked.

"Ilya said he is."

Son of a bitch. Not that he could blame Ilya for giving him up. The man wasn't trained to withstand torture, but, for his transgression, the Ukrainian Brotherhood would be keeping the businessman on a tight leash. John would worry about that later.

"Take him back to his cell. We're scheduled for a call with the boss."

The weight on his chest eased, and John was yanked to his feet. His wrists were bound. Even so, he could probably take on Hulk and Scar-Eye, but there were other men with guns outside the torture room, and he had Bristow to consider.

He was led down the stairs back to the basement. From what he could tell, they were being kept in a house that had a staircase that led straight into a dungeon that used to be part of the Odessa catacombs. It was rumored to be used by smugglers. Real estate developers had filled up majority of the tunnels, but no one really knew how many remained. He wouldn't be surprised if the Odessa Order found use for it as well.

Stacked stones served as retaining walls and formed their asymmetrical cell. The ceiling revealed excavated earth and rock, and John hoped there were enough foundation and support beams to hold up the ancient structure. A bulb strung in the middle of the room provided lighting and, depending on how fond their captors were of them at any given day, it would be switched on and off. He and Bristow memorized the path to the buckets at the corner of the room that served as their toilet. It would suck if they made a mess. Food and water were provided once a day. If one could call stale bread food.

Hulk found it necessary to march him down the steps. He was followed by two guards—one to make sure Bristow didn't try anything funny, and the other was in charge of swapping the buckets.

When they were left alone, John leaned against the wall and slid slowly to the ground. Bristow didn't budge. He was flat on his back with an arm over his eyes. He was recovering from his own interrogation earlier. At least they were lying on earth instead of a cold slab of granite.

"How did it go?" Bristow murmured without turning his head.

"Same." He suppressed a groan when his ribs bitched as he tried to get more comfortable. They never discussed anything about their business with Ilya, given that their dungeon may be bugged.

There was no question they were in an Argonayts' base of operations. Despite the dilapidated state of the house, both he and Bristow spied a room full of computers with operators at the helm. Their laptops were the first to be confiscated. But since they were on the trail of hackers, they didn't bring their agency laptops, but ones that provided their cover as wine merchants. However, John doubted they bought their cover since the interrogations continued.

"But something big is happening, and it may be connected to why they detained us."

"Think they'll let us go after?" Bristow asked. "'Coz it seems they were detaining us because they think we're going to expose whatever shit they're planning."

"Don't know."

"The guy with the scar threatened to ship us off to

Siberia."

"Shut the fuck up."

He could feel the burn of Bristow's gaze on the side of his cheek.

"You've been acting strange."

"In case you missed the memo, we're in a fucking dungeon." John looked around. They'd done a quick assessment when they were first thrown in this hole. The only way out was up the stairs. Four guards roamed the halls. But John had seen as many as twenty soldiers congregate in the living room, especially during their first round of interrogations. He had a feeling he and Bristow were being paraded as prized catches.

Catch and release. For all the times this had to happen, it had to happen when he promised Nadia he was returning Monday. Tomorrow.

Fucking Ilya. Did the businessman lure them here on purpose? Did he really have information at all regarding the brains behind the Argonayts? Their endgame. Ilya said the information was too delicate to communicate even through secure channels. They had to do it face to face.

Fucker.

"I can hear you fuming over there," Bristow said.

John sighed. He was so fucking tired. And the SEAL's stomach rumbling reminded him that the two big rolls of bread this morning were not enough sustenance.

"That's called thinking," he answered.

The SEAL levered up and sat against the wall. "While you're at it, can you find a way to get us out of here? Or sweet talk and rustle us some more food? Man, what I wouldn't give for a cheeseburger right now …"

His own hunger pangs gnawed at his gut, so he tuned out Bristow's irritating yammering and fell asleep.

The clanging of the door jerked John awake, and he glanced over at his cellmate. He must have passed out while

Bristow was droning on about food. Footsteps shuffled down the steps. When he saw who it was, his heart jumped to his throat.

"Nadia?"

He blinked. She was standing in front of him in a loose dress, but it couldn't hide the bulge at her stomach. "You said you were coming home Monday," she accused.

"What the fuck are you doing here?" he roared.

He started choking. He couldn't breathe.

"Wake up, fucker!"

John's eyes flew open and gripped a wrist while trying to get his mouth free from the hand, ready to flip his attacker over, when he registered it was Bristow.

And the man stunk.

For that matter, John figured he did too.

He jerked his head to acknowledge he was awake and in control. Bristow removed his palm, and sat back, eyeing him warily. John scooted against the wall, his heart still pounding, his heaving lungs making his ribs ache.

"The fuck's wrong with you?" Bristow whispered harshly. "You've been off since we left the U.S."

He leaned closer and whispered in Bristow's ear. "Broken condom."

When John pulled back, the SEAL was staring at him, mouth gaping open in a comical way. "Fuuuuuck. Is it her?"

"Don't know who you mean."

"Stop your denial."

"Let's say it is … theoretically."

"Holy cow … I still can't …" Bristow gave a low whistle and couldn't hide the mirth in his eyes. "Way to liven up our stay here."

"Would you stop it?" he snapped. "They might think you've gone crazy."

"Well, that's certainly an excuse to let me go."

"Or ship you off to Siberia."

Bristow started laughing, then suddenly stopped and cleared his throat. "Do you need to talk to someone?"

John eyed him suspiciously. The corners of the SEAL's mouth were twitching. "Glad I can be a source of amusement for your boring stay."

"Seriously, man." The other man shrugged. "I mean, there's nothing else to do over here. I can pretend to be Dr. Phil."

John might never live this down but the urge to unload was overpowering. He needed to figure this shit out that was completely foreign territory.

"I already broke a promise to her," he said quietly.

Bristow moved his head closer. "Sorry for my foul breath, but spit it out, G."

"I told her I was returning Monday."

"Damn. That's tomorrow. Is it serious?"

A defensiveness rose inside him. "That's what I'm trying to figure out because I sure as hell don't know how to do real shit like this."

"You mean relationship shit?"

"Yeah."

His fellow prisoner sat back. "Enjoy the feeling."

"Oh, and you're an expert on feelings?"

"Oh...ho...ho..." Bristow's brows rose. "Someone is being testy. And I'm no expert. Far from it."

The dungeon door slammed open and footsteps hurried down the steps. Hulk appeared and glowered at them. "No whispering."

John and Bristow stared at each other. No question. They were being monitored.

Sixth day of captivity

. . .

"I'M SAYING, man, you can't have it both ways," Bristow said. "Something's got to give. I know marketing California wine has its appeal, but the constant travel'll get old." Even if their captors probably knew they were not wine merchants, they decided to continue playing their roles.

"You just want my job."

"Told you I don't. Like this freelance shit. And you?"

"I've got responsibilities."

"Well, looks like you'll have more depending on how the wind blows."

Anxiety pinched his gut. The idea of becoming a father was front and center in his thoughts. Maybe the lack of food was making him paranoid. He cycled between thinking he was overreacting and reacting just right. He knew Nadia was on birth control, but the pill was only as reliable as the person who took it.

"But that still can't be the reason why you stay together. Just saying … It isn't fair."

To the kid. John felt the same way.

He sighed. "I think we're jumping too far ahead."

"Best to be prepared for all possibilities."

TENTH DAY *of captivity*

JOHN WAS close to losing his damned mind, and he couldn't blame the lack of food or water. Earlier that morning they were each treated to a big bowl of oatmeal and a bag of jerky. He and Bristow scarfed those down, hoping they were finally going to be cut loose.

But, five hours later. Nothing.

"Hmm … I wonder if that was our last supper?" Bristow asked.

He glared at the SEAL. "I can make it yours."

Instead of a smartass comeback, Bristow looked apologetic. "Sorry, man."

In the past few days, he was riding a razor edge of anxiety. Though they hadn't been interrogated again, John felt a pall that had fallen on the mobsters. Yesterday, he and Bristow were hosed down. Scar-Eye probably didn't want them dying of a flesh-wasting disease, so even when his balls shriveled up in the stream of ice-cold water, he welcomed getting the layer of grime off his skin. From what he'd gleaned from the men talking, their boss's op didn't go exactly as planned, and there was going to be an attempt to salvage their objective.

There appeared to be a reduction in guards at the house, and there were fewer people in the computer room unlike the first few days that John and Bristow were here. Were they getting ready to move? What about him and Bristow? Were they fattening them up to be shipped off to Siberia?

The nightmares around Nadia were constant. Every time he closed his eyes, he could see her in his mind. Her belly round with his baby, and even one time, she was holding hands with a little girl.

Fuck. He had to get back to her. He wasn't giving up. John was getting out of this hellhole. The longer she believed he brushed her off, the harder it would be to set his plan into play. She was the only woman in his long life as a CIA officer who made him hunger for a home.

"We need to get out of here."

Bristow's face brightened. "Finally. Have you snapped out of your melancholy?"

He glanced at the SEAL. "Don't be dramatic."

"Just saying. So, what's the plan?"

FOURTEENTH DAY of captivity

. . .

JOHN DROPPED to the ground after getting pistol-whipped on the back of the head.

Their great escape failed.

He and Bristow would have been successful, too, if Scar-Eye had not returned with more men after three days of absence. Hulk was left in charge and thought John and Bristow were his docile pets. The man found out that attack dogs should never be pets.

Scar-Eye loomed over John, pointing the barrel of his Kalashnikov between his eyes. "This just proves you're a spy. Only a man with your training could take my biggest man down."

John and Bristow executed their escape plan after one of their hose-downs. The aftermath of their botched exit left Hulk with two holes, bleeding and yelling like a stuck pig. Two guards lay dead on the ground.

"Maybe I like watching action movies," John responded, and then, "You okay, B?"

"I'm good," Bristow grunted. His partner in crime was also flat on his back with a gun pointed to his head.

Scar-Eye's gaze trailed down the length of Garrison's drenched t-shirt, athletic shorts that had seen better days, and to his bare feet. "Maybe I should let you walk on broken glass." His mouth curled cruelly. "Let me see you act all die hard, huh?"

John hid his frustration with their attempted escape with a crooked smile. "Yippee-ki-yay, motherfucker."

"Can we just kill them?!" Hulk roared from his position against the wall and being tended to by his comrades.

The smaller man's fingers tightened on the trigger. "At this point, it would give us less trouble."

"Just tell Maxim they tried to grab the guard's guns," Hulk shouted. "That they shot themselves."

Despite his dire situation, Garrison's ears perked at Hulk's slip, naming the mastermind behind their abduction.

"Now I take issue with that," Bristow grumbled from his dicey position on the floor. "That's a false narrative."

John chuckled darkly. Defiant until the end.

And as he stared down the barrel of a gun, his chest contracted painfully at the loss of a life he could have found with Nadia.

And if he had a kid?

His lungs compressed into a heavy weight.

Fuck. He wasn't okay with this.

"Any last words?"

He wasn't going down without a fight. No matter how futile this seemed.

A blast rocked the house, throwing Scar-Eye off his feet. Flash-bang grenades erupted and filled the room with smoke.

Simultaneous gunshots exploded and an exchange of artillery fire followed but was short-lived.

John kept his position on the ground as he tried to see through the fumes, alert to react.

Two figures materialized from the haze.

Roarke and Spear.

A whoosh of relief escaped his lungs.

Off to the side, Levi and another guy John didn't recognize tended to Bristow.

John was grinning so wide, his jaw hurt. "It was about time you motherfuckers got here."

Kade loomed above him. "Do I need to carry you?"

"Hell no."

The other man extended an arm to give him a hand up. "Then we got here at just the right time."

8

MOTHERFUCKERS.

Take that!

Breaking into Huxley's computer was easy. Finding the Crown-Key itself was trickier. But almost two weeks later, Nadia was finally able to break the encryption on a sector of Huxley's code repository in the cloud and secured the Crown-Key source code on their own CTTF server. She harnessed part of her own decryption program and her familiarity with Huxley's character to break into it. Part of hacking involved guesswork.

She passed it into their own encryption program when Kelso walked in. "Hey, nerd girl, you ready?"

"Yes, just locking up." She blew the hair from her face.

"You worked hard on this, Nadia." Kelso came up behind her. "Any more info on that malware you found lurking around the sector you decrypted earlier?"

"No, but I was able to set up a shield so they couldn't access the code."

Kelso peered over her shoulder and at multiple split screens. "How do you read that shit? All I see are brackets, parentheses, and gibberish words."

"It's another language to me."

Kelso chuckled. "That's why guys over here are intimidated to ask you out. You're smarter than they are."

She angled her gaze at him. "And I have no patience for men who are intimidated by a woman with a brain."

Her friend gave a snort. "Gotcha. I'll clue them in." After a few seconds, his face turned serious, although mirth still gleamed in his eyes. "Have you informed Homeland Security?"

"Yup. Sent them a secure transmission."

"Good," Kelso said again. "No lead on the device yet?"

She sighed. "None."

The detective checked his watch. "Your dad must hate me and Gabby by now. You haven't had a break in two weeks."

"I've had worse. And the rest of the team worked just as hard. Any insight from the Hux Technologies employees you interviewed?"

"Nothing solid. Kenneth Huxley is the classic introvert."

"Except when he's entertaining." But Nadia knew it was a mask. The real Ken liked solitude and to tinker on his programs. "I feel bad for them. I don't think anyone is in a position to take over."

"Yeah." Kelso pinched the bridge of his nose. "Okay. Enough work talk and let's get out of here. Let me feed you at least."

After packing up and locking her lab, they passed a group of the night-shift detectives who gave them a knowing look.

"Ugh, you've been seeing me home for a week now. Where's Levi?"

"What? You sick of my company already?"

They made it out to the parking lot. "No. Just wondering where he is."

"He had an emergency."

"Are Kelly and the girls all right?"

"It's work related."

Nadia tried to keep from asking another question. John didn't show up that Monday as he promised. More than two weeks later, there was still no communication from him. He tried calling her the morning he left, but, as usual, his paranoid ass refused to leave a message. She hadn't heard from him since. Good thing her determination to solve Ken's murder left her no time for anything else. He was murdered in one of his Santa Monica properties and then his death was staged back at the penthouse. But why? Was that where he kept the Crown-Key device? A wave of dizziness hit her, and she stumbled while walking.

Kelso gripped her arm. "Hey, you okay?"

"Haven't eaten since lunch."

"You've been working too hard. Have you been drinking water?"

"No," she smiled sheepishly. Kelso was such a drill sergeant about water intake even when he plied her with sixteen-ounce caramel macchiatos as incentive to prioritize his requests.

In the past three days, the detective had been picking her up for work after his workouts at the gym and taking her home in the evenings. He and Gabby had been working overtime like she was. With Homeland Security already involved, it could become stickier and more complicated if a rogue nation was involved.

When they got into the SUV, he immediately handed her a bottle of water.

"Fancy eating gyros?" Kelso asked.

"At the Athena Loft Deli?" It was a Greek and Mediterranean grill with an attached grocery. "At this point, I'll eat anything. And Dad mentioned picking up pomegranate paste if I get to a store that had it before he did." Nadia uncapped the bottle and drank a healthy dose of water. She was parched despite guzzling too much caffeine not two hours ago. Kelso threw her a look and gave a shake of his head.

"What?"

"Nothing."

"No, really."

"You finished that bottled water."

"I thought you wanted me to hydrate."

"Carefully," Kelso shot her a look again. "Anything over four ounces every half hour is wasted."

"Where the hell did you read that?"

"Somewhere," was his flippant reply. "Besides, we're going to hit traffic."

As they merged onto the 101, heading for the Middle Eastern neighborhood near her place, Nadia wanted to pound her head on the dashboard. "Shit."

"Yup," Kelso said wryly. "If your bladder is as tiny as Woodward's, it's going to be either a tolerable ten minutes or a tense forty-five."

Up ahead, the braking red lights of vehicles taunted her.

"No," she groaned. She was already feeling the pressure from the caffeine, and it must be mental, but she was immediately hit with an urge to pee.

The detective glanced over at her with sympathy. "Maybe half an hour."

Thirty-five minutes later, Kelso took the exit for Vermont Avenue. "I can't believe you made me fucking do that."

"It was an emergency," she protested.

"It's an abuse of authority."

"Would you prefer I peed in your car?"

"It's LAPD property. What do I care?"

Nadia laughed despite her full bladder. "You'd care if Gabby made you sit in it."

"I always drive," he muttered.

She had whined at Kelso, forcing him to use the police lights so they could use the shoulder about a mile from their exit. They'd been crawling on the freeway for thirty-five minutes and the caffeine plus water made it an unbearable journey. Besides, she was in this predicament because she was working overtime and she hadn't eaten. She felt justified enough that she was working for the benefit of the city.

"We're almost at the deli, but I see some nice shrubs over there," Kelso said when they passed a gas station with landscaping separating it from the road.

"Don't be a smartass to a woman who's barely holding on to her bladder."

Kelso mumbled something.

"What?"

The vehicle went over a speed bump.

Her bladder didn't like that.

"Eh, I think I just peed a little."

Kelso glanced at her in horror. "Say it isn't so, Powell."

Nadia burst out laughing. She wasn't sure if that was a good idea either. "You should see your face. Don't worry, I didn't."

Her friend chuckled and patted her on the shoulder. "You've been hanging around us guys for too long. Our toilet humor is rubbing off on you. You're double-dosing between our team and the three old farts at your apartment with your dad."

She grinned. "I'm glad you didn't include my dad in the three old farts."

"Is it my imagination or is Dugal not fond of me?" Kelso swerved the SUV into the Mediterranean restaurant's parking lot.

Nadia didn't answer and hopped out. Before slamming the door, she said, "Hold that thought. Get me a lamb gyro with extra tzatziki."

After her much-needed stop at the ladies' room, Nadia grabbed a basket and started grocery shopping while Kelso waited for their orders. With her unpredictable hours, it was best to run her errands with whatever sliver of time she could scramble. Among some of the diverse cuisine in Los Angeles, Persian food was something she and her dad were fond of. Her dad's former girlfriend, Sara, was an Iranian widow. They were together for two years and Nadia was treated to the most delicious home-cooked meals. When they broke up because Sara had to return to Iran to take care of her ailing mother, Nadia cried. She wasn't sure if it was partly because she was going to miss Sara's cooking or her nurturing soul. However, the woman, bless her kind heart to the sixteen-year-old Nadia, made sure she and her dad were equipped to cook the food they loved from her.

She wondered if Stephen would have married again. He hadn't been serious with another woman since then. He told Nadia that her mother was the greatest love of his life. She also wondered if her father wanted her to have a sort of mother figure growing up, especially during her adolescent years.

Putting a pack of dried limes, dried fenugreek, and a bottle of pomegranate paste in her basket, she headed over to the nuts section to weigh some walnuts for Stephen—and her —Fesenjan, a stew made with pomegranate molasses, and crushed walnuts. Saliva pooled under her tongue. She'd been craving the sourness of pomegranate recently.

Kelso signaled that he was done and stood aside so his big frame wouldn't be in the way. Nadia walked toward one of the counters to pay. As she was adding a container of pastries, the store's bell tinkled and for some reason her senses made her look in that direction.

Two men walked in. Caucasian. One was blond and the other had brown hair. The blond man was almost albino-like. Swedish maybe? The man's neck was covered in ink. His gaze strayed to her briefly before looking up at the menu above the food counter.

Nadia's eyes flew to Kelso who was already making his way toward her. The amiable detective was nowhere in sight, his face closed off, his jaw hardening. When he got to her side, he easily blocked her from the newcomer's view.

"That'll be forty-eight dollars and twenty cents."

Her attention momentarily diverted back to the cashier, and she quickly settled her purchases. Normally, Kelso would offer to carry the bags, but not this time. He was making sure he could draw his gun quickly in case the suspicious strangers proved hostile. They exited the store, on alert for any lurkers.

It was a relief when they got into the vehicle and merged onto Beverly Boulevard.

"That was weird," Nadia said. "You felt that creepy vibe too?"

"Yeah." Kelso checked the rearview mirror. "I've been interviewing guys who fit their profile. Both men were wearing jackets, but I could see their tattoos peeking out on the back of their hands. And you saw their necks?"

"Yes. You think Russian Bratva?"

"Another guy I interviewed in relation to Brandt's case revealed that the Kremlin, through the Russian Bratva, is working with the Argonayts on a special mission."

Nadia's blood chilled. They were elite hackers who targeted countries opposed to Russian policy. The Argonayts went after electrical grids, banking systems, and other services that were computerized for blackmail or ransom.

"That's our worst nightmare. The rolling blackout last summer—"

Oncoming vehicle lights blinded her. A scream lodged in her throat as Kelso cursed and yanked their vehicle into a swerve. Their tires rolled over rumble strips and it veered one way and then another.

"Hang on!" Kelso yelled. All Nadia could do was hang on, her fingernails digging into the handle and the dashboard.

Nadia glanced behind them. "They're following us."

"I know," Kelso gritted. "Those men in the store—fuck!"

Something rammed the front of their vehicle. The seatbelt

bit across her body, sending excruciating pain in its wake. Screeching tires and metal scraping over metal shrieked in her ears.

Her head hurt.

Her spine hurt.

Nadia struggled to shake the cobwebs from her head and tried to reach for her backpack. Her gun.

"Get out of here," he told her. "Move!"

Her hand closed on the handle, but her door was yanked open, and she was hauled bodily from the vehicle.

"Nadia!" Kelso roared.

Gunshots exploded around her as her assailant dragged her to a waiting car. She scratched and kicked.

"Do you have her backpack?" A voice shouted.

"*Tak.*" Another answered.

Ukrainian?

She stomped on her assailant's foot and rammed her elbow into him. The masked man let go of her, and she tried to scramble away. "Kelso!"

Fingers dug into her scalp, almost ripping her hair out while the force of it shoved her against the side of a black SUV. That jolt of agony stole the breath from her lungs, the strength from her legs. Giving in to gravity, she crashed to the ground.

The spray of lead escalated around her. Oh my God, Kelso was alone!

"Get up!"

A boot hit her thigh. Nadia tried to lever up, bracing for a second kick but it never came.

A body dropped in front of her.

It was her assailant's.

"Kelso!" she croaked, trying to push up.

But it wasn't Kelso who gathered her into his arms.

It definitely wasn't Kelso who gave her a searing kiss that ended quickly.

It was a kiss Nadia would've recognized anywhere.

Sounds buzzed around her.

The face was shadowed but there was no mistaking that imposing profile.

Garrison.

9

"ARE YOU ALL RIGHT?" John demanded.

A gentle shake snapped her out of her stupor. She couldn't believe he was standing right in front of her. Her gaze jerked to Bristow and Levi. They were checking the downed hostiles, but her eyes were searching for someone else.

"I'm fine," she wheezed. Her body shuddered from the adrenaline withdrawal. "Kelso?"

"Here," a voice said from the side and she was yanked from John's arms and engulfed in a Kelso-sized bear hug. "I'm so sorry, Powell. That was my fault."

Nadia leaned away. "How was it your fault?"

"We'll do a post-mortem later," Garrison interjected, grabbing Nadia back from Kelso.

She was too outraged to react. The man probably saved their lives, but she could still be annoyed with him, right?

"Bristow, how long before the cops get here?" John asked.

"Six minutes."

Garrison glanced at Kelso. "You got this?"

"What the fuck?" The detective scowled. "How am I supposed to cover up this shit? I don't know who was after us."

Yes, John, what the fuck?

Levi approached their group and crouched beside the man who had dragged Nadia out of the car. He lifted the mask over his face and took a picture. "We have confirmation on Maxim Vovk."

"Vovk?" Nadia cocked her head at John in disbelief. They had killed a member of the Odessa Order, the ruling committee of the Ukrainian Brotherhood.

"We're trying to flush out his brother, Dmitry," John answered. "Killing Maxim wasn't the plan, but it seems we've just moved up our schedule."

"What do you mean?" Kelso asked.

"We'll discuss later." Garrison clasped her arm to lead her away, but Nadia refused to budge.

"Hold on. Hold on. What the hell, John?" She wrenched her arm from his grip. "I have a scene to process."

"Bristow needs to look you over." Garrison crossed his arms over his chest. "There's something more important to discuss."

And here she was trying to act mature and not think about his broken promise, but she ended up sneering. "If you're talking about your no-show that Monday, don't sweat it. And an EMT can look me over." She straightened her spine with self-righteous anger and walked away from him. "I feel fine." In reality, it felt like she'd gone ten rounds with a gorilla, but any second longer in his company and the carefully constructed fortress around her emotions was going to crumble. John was a sledgehammer when it came to her resolve.

"Dammit, Nadia—"

"Four minutes, Garrison." Bristow reminded, while John's crew headed for their Escalade.

Kelso glanced from Nadia to him and smirked. "Just so you know, there'll be no kidnapping on my watch."

"Fuck it," John clipped and captured her arm, ushering her behind their assailant's SUV and out of earshot from the rest of the men.

Nadia had had it with this overbearing man. "If you don't want to be singing in falsetto, let go of my arm."

John positioned her against the side of the vehicle, his fingers clasping her shoulders. Something in the way he was assessing her made her nervous.

"Are these men after my dad?" she asked.

His eyes seemed surprised by her question, after which they softened to a degree and lessened Nadia's anxiety.

"No."

"Then what's so important it couldn't wait?" Her irritation returned.

His fingers tightened on her shoulders as if he was expecting her to bolt.

"You could be pregnant."

Those words were so absurd she thought she misheard him. She exhaled the breath that went stale in her lungs. "Ha. ha. You almost got me." She shoved him aside to move past him, but he was persistent and caught her arm again.

"Broken condom."

Those two words sent Nadia's mind cartwheeling back to how consistent she was with her birth control pill. One that needed to be taken as much as possible at the same time of the day. Her ears started buzzing.

Shit!

"G, three minutes," Bristow hollered.

"A minute!" the man before her yelled back.

All Nadia could say was "Shit."

John's face was impassive. "Let's go." His voice was firm and in her spiraling panicked state, she followed his lead without question. Her brain processing. Her body processing. She was due for her period any day now. Her mind calculated. Two days from now. She wasn't pregnant. She couldn't be pregnant.

Before she knew it, she was bundled into the back of the SUV with John getting in beside her.

A choking feeling gripped her throat.

Fear.

JOHN SHOULDN'T HAVE BROKEN the news that way to her, but he couldn't keep it from her a second longer. She deserved to know. Nadia looked like she was going to throw up. Nothing wrong with her reaction given his own response to condom-gate. He had two weeks to process the possibility of becoming a father, especially since he spent majority of those days locked in a dank dungeon. Now he had to help Nadia get through her shock, so they could prepare for either outcome.

"Do we need to take you to a hospital?" he asked. "Did you hit your head?"

"No. I'm fine. Just got tossed a bit."

"I can give you a once-over when we get to Garrison's house," Bristow interjected from the passenger seat. Levi was driving. "I have my med-kit in the back."

"I said I was fine," she snapped.

"Whoa. Chill there, Powell," Levi said.

She was anxious, John assessed. He reached out and took her hand in his. Nadia resisted, but he held fast, giving her hand a squeeze, letting her know she wasn't facing this alone. She cocked her head at his gesture. Yeah, he wasn't sure where that came from either.

She asked, "What in the world did Maxim Vovk want with me? Does this have something to do with one of our cases?"

"Kenneth Huxley."

"Shit," Nadia said, looking out the window. "So that's what it was."

"Were you guys able to secure the Crown-Key?" John asked.

"What? You don't know?" she retorted.

"We've been out of the loop, but we're back now," he answered mildly, ignoring her sarcasm.

"I need to talk to Gabby and Kelso before I release any info."

"Of course."

"If they'd planned to grab me and failed, would Dad be in danger?"

"I've messaged Declan," Bristow said. "He communicated with Gabby to send a patrol over to your apartment. She's heading there right now to tell your dad that you're okay, before she joins Kelso to clean up the mess we left them."

John tried not to let this close-knit circle give him claustrophobia. Staying in that dungeon was more familiar than this weird family vibe he seemed to have formed in LA. A muscle twitched beneath his right eye, and he let go of Nadia's hand. He could feel her studying him. This situation between them was begging for a discussion, and he couldn't wait to get her alone.

The second they arrived at his house, he asked Bristow to give her a look-over. Nadia didn't balk this time and let the former SEAL make sure she was okay. John paced behind the two while the other man gave Nadia a checkup.

Levi joined them, tucking his phone in his pocket. "That was Kelso. He said we need to get on the same page, same line, and same fucking word before this blows up in their faces."

"I agree," Nadia said.

"So much for saving your asses." Bristow shined a light on Nadia's eyes before he strapped on the blood pressure cuff and oxygen meter.

"Don't get me wrong. I'm thankful, and I'm pretty sure Kelso is too," she said. "But if there was any way you all could have given us a heads up that this was going to happen, then we wouldn't have been in that situation."

Bristow glanced at John, and he gave the SEAL the go-ahead nod to disclose their information. "We've recovered intel in Kiev. Maxim had been in the U.S. for a week, so someone else took the hit on Huxley."

"Our gut tells us it's Morris," Nadia said, cutting her glance to John. "You had a run-in with him at the party."

"Why it took them this long to make a move ..." He stopped his pacing and gave her a penetrating stare. "I think you have the answer."

"Where were you all this time?"

"Unavailable," John said. "I'd like to repeat the story only once, so let's wait until the detectives want that debrief."

"Depends who's debriefing whom," Levi muttered.

"Good point." With Maxim dead, big brother was unpredictable. CTTF was going to be in its crosshairs, so John was making sure they had what they needed to bring Dmitry Vovk down. Also known as the Gray Wolf of Odessa because of the color of his hair and eyes, it was common knowledge he doted on his brother. John would be a hypocrite if he said he didn't want him to feel the pain he had when Vovk wiped out an entire special forces team under John's command. Thirteen years was a long time to plan Vovk's demise.

Nadia was a complication to his focus on the capture of the elusive crime boss.

Either she was pregnant or not. But by the way her already pale face turned bloodless when he mentioned the broken condom, she wasn't confident about her birth control either. John had used his resources to check her medical records on the flight back from Kiev. She was on the progesterone pill which was pickier than the combination one and had to be taken more consistently. He'd done his research. He'd obsessed every bit with the possibility that she could be pregnant and ... he wasn't as horrified as he initially reacted.

The only thing he hated about this whole scenario was how it preempted his plans in figuring out this 'thing' between them. John was always one step ahead, but fate had its sassy ways of messing with the best-laid plans. It had a way of making him wonder if he'd run out of his nine-lives when he didn't give a fuck before. But the other side of the scale was luck. And Lady Luck certainly pulled through when Kade and the rest of the team rescued their asses from certain execution, not to mention that cache of information recovered from the house where Bristow and Garrison were held was instrumental in stopping Maxim from taking Nadia.

"What time is the debrief?" John asked.

"Eight a.m. We left a lot of paperwork for them with four dead hostiles, and they're one tech down." Levi looked pointedly at Nadia. "But, since Nadia appears to be the target, Kelso appreciates us keeping her safe and said they'd deal."

"You're good to go," Bristow told her. "Take it easy for the rest of the night. Maybe a Tylenol or two if you're in pain."

She shrugged. "I've been more sore after workouts with Kelso."

"You're a trooper," John said.

Bristow cast him an amused glance.

Nadia arched a brow. "Is that ... is that ... a compliment?"

"Don't be a smartass," John shot back and walked over and took her hand, drawing her in. He searched her face. "You really okay?"

"Yes, I am." Nadia's face was starting to get back some color, and she tipped her head to their audience. "I think we're embarrassing the guys."

Judging by her heightened color, he figured she was the one getting embarrassed.

He faced the men. Bristow had a shit-eating grin, while Levi was staring at his boots, a smile playing on his lips.

"That's why he was so distracted." The ginger-haired SEAL directed his statement at Nadia.

She raised a skeptical brow. "He was?"

"Enough. Go home. Get some rest," John ordered. "Be here at oh-seven-thirty."

"Kelso said eight," Levi protested.

"I might have to go over things with you guys before the briefing."

"Fine," Bristow replied and the two started whispering between themselves about being glad they were contractors so they could abandon his ass at any time.

John followed them to the door. In reality, he was having cold feet about confronting the woman in the dining room. "Bitch all you want. You guys love working for me."

"Yeah, yeah." Grumbling voices faded up the driveway.

He still had his back to Nadia as he slowly shut the door, but what had been left unsaid since he packed her into the SUV hammered at the back of his skull.

Exhaling a deep breath because it could be his last, he turned to the woman in the room whose hands had flown to her hips, her eyes shooting sparks of fury at him.

"What the fuck, John?" Nadia yelled. "Why did you wait to tell me about the broken condom?"

"If you would have just answered your phone—"

"Your paranoid ass couldn't have made that exception?"

He shot her an incredulous stare.

She started pacing. "I can't believe it. I could've taken a morning-after pill if you just told me, and we wouldn't be having this conversation."

"Just imagine how I felt."

She spun around, invaded his space, and poked him in the chest. "You could have sent word." Her lips twisted in a sneer. "Oh, wait, your job is too important, so you didn't give a rat's ass that our carelessness could change my life."

"And you think it won't change mine?" he shot back. "You think I'm going to let you do this alone?" He scrubbed a hand over his face and raised his arm in her direction. "We're jumping the gun, don't you think? Can we just calm down?" He huffed a breath. "You're on birth control, right?"

Nadia glanced away briefly before returning to meet his stare, mouth twisting. "I haven't been consistent since that time after Mexico. Since I found out you were threatening to expose Dad to the people after him."

John regretted using that as leverage against Nadia, but he needed her to help him run the Mexican op to rescue Ariana and retrieve the bioweapon. "You should've called my bluff and kicked me in the gonads."

"I'm still debating the latter suggestion."

"You did threaten to make me sing in falsetto earlier," he reminded her.

Nadia smiled weakly, lowering her arms to her sides, and sinking into the chair behind her.

John approached and took the seat at the head of the table which was directly adjacent to hers. "How soon can we use those pee sticks?"

"I don't know … I think after a missed period. And no, I haven't gotten it. It's due any day." She blew out a breath. "Tomorrow, I think."

He tried to keep a straight face. This whole thing was … foreign … but it was turning out he didn't mind it very much. It was a novelty, talking about a woman's monthly cycle instead of laying out the groundwork to a covert operation. This was why he welcomed his phone chats with Fiona Mason, it was his link to a life when he was normal, when he could be a son who cared deeply for his mother. What he'd not had since he became a Delta Force operator was have a woman he could plan a future with. Not that he was thinking it was a sure thing with Nadia. But this was as close to a normal relationship as he'd had in decades.

"You're right." She rubbed a finger across her brow. "I'm probably overreacting. We really might be fine."

"I'm clean, in case you're wondering," he shared.

"I am too." She stopped worrying her brow and started tracing the lines on the wooden table.

John scrambled for something to say and ended up with, "Are you hungry?"

"Now that you've mentioned it, I'm starving. And thirsty." Nadia got up when he did, but it wasn't to follow him to the kitchen but rather head into the living room, hooking the backpack on her shoulder.

Maxim's men wanted her and the backpack. If John were to guess, since the Argonayts couldn't fully hack into Huxley's code repository, they planted malware that would notify them if someone had been successful. If Morris was involved, why wasn't he with Maxim in the assault?

He checked his freezer for frozen dinners. If he were by himself, he'd probably grab an MRE from the pantry and nuke it. When living the life of the spy, one had to be flexible. He could tough it out in a rainforest and hope the water or the wildlife wouldn't kill him, or don a tux and dine on caviar and fine wine. When they were rescued, the first thing he and Bristow requested were big juicy burgers and fries. Surprisingly, they didn't lose too much weight since their diet of oatmeal and beef jerky sustained whatever muscle mass they had. Plus, they were mostly sedentary. At the moment, his craving was for home-cooked meals. The agency had a house-keeper who maintained a couple of the homes on Assassin's Hill, and she regularly stocked up their freezers with food.

"Chicken pot pie okay for you?" He hollered from the kitchen.

Nadia had already booted up her laptop and simply gave him a thumbs-up without looking at him. He set the food in the toaster oven. It would take forty-five minutes. He strode over to the pantry to find some snacks to feed her. Christ, was he this way with Nadia before? Was he treating her as if she were already pregnant?

Fuck. He shoved that thought aside, but it kept nagging at

him because he'd turned the idea over and over in his head in the past two weeks. It would be better if she wasn't pregnant. Then he could resume his original plan of treading carefully into a possible relationship. Weigh the pros and cons. Consider how it would affect his job. Could he stand being away from her for months on end and stay focused? If she wasn't pregnant, John would feel both disappointment and relief.

He wondered if he was losing his mind.

He rarely felt conflicted.

Nadia. She was the source of these damning feelings.

His eyes perused the chips and jars of different salsas. Then he glanced over at the woman in the living room, shaking his head as the surrealness of the situation. John walked over to the center island and did something as mundane as putting chips on a plate and the salsa in a bowl. He retrieved their drinks and set them on the tray with the snacks and headed to the living room.

Nadia and John might be heading into unknown territories, but he'd be damned if awkwardness was going to be part of the problem.

10

"Hope this will hold you over until dinner is ready."

Nadia glanced up from the screen, not quite sure what she was seeing. John was serving her chips and salsa. As far as she remembered, the guys were nothing this civilized. They always ate out of Styrofoam containers. Mostly it was Bristow who liked eating chips, and he usually had one of those single-serve packs you see out of a vending machine.

Chips and salsa? Her mind repeated. That was something she would expect at Gabby and Declan's house. Although, from what she had heard, Gabby had joined Kelso in his shredding phase. So, no carbs.

She cleared her throat. "Thank you." Her eyes returned to the screen but doubted if she could get any work done because John perched on the slope of the armchair she was sitting in.

"What are you looking for?" he asked.

"I'm trying to see if there was an attack launched on our servers," she said. "So far all looks good." Right now, her brain wasn't fully processing the case. She was still annoyed at John for not finding a way to leave her a message. She closed her laptop and set it on the table. Then she picked a tortilla chip, dipped it in salsa, and popped it into her mouth, chewing very slowly. John got off his perch by her side and sat on the coffee table.

"You're pissed at me."

"Geez, John, I wonder why that is."

"You shouldn't have wrecked the agency phone I gave you."

"So sue me for not wanting to be at your beck and call … and stop looking at me like that." He studied her as if she was a delicate puzzle he was trying to solve.

His brows shot to his hairline. "Like what?"

"Like you don't want to hurt my feelings." Her eyes slitted. "Wait. Are you assuming I'm already pregnant and I'm acting hormonal?"

He shrugged. "Just covering my bases."

Hmm … she could milk this situation to get answers.

"Uh-oh," he said. "I don't trust that look in your eyes."

"Like what?" And John saying 'uh-oh'? Nadia was wondering if she was living in an alternate universe. Or could this be John in domesticated mode? Or was he using one of his practiced covers? Paranoid much, Powell?

"Like you discovered a way to flay me alive," he continued, his expression wary.

"Just covering my bases." She crunched away on more chips. "Why don't you answer this? I'm curious why you don't leave voice messages."

His face shuttered. "It's discouraged in our tradecraft."

"But under extenuating circumstances, it's not against any rulebook."

"It's bad practice and a habit I haven't broken in thirteen —" John caught himself and cursed.

"Thirteen what? Months? Years?"

"Years," he clipped.

"Did something happen?"

"Classified. Let's just say a recording of my voice exposed my cover and nearly got my entire team killed."

"I'm sorry, John."

"In this job, you learn fast."

"Okay. But I don't see how leaving a message saying 'the condom broke' would constitute a national security threat."

The mask cracked. Frustration mingled with humor in his eyes. "I would disagree," he said.

"Oh? Explain."

"Say someone is trying to break me, but me being me, that's close to impossible."

Nadia emitted a *pfft* sound. "Everyone has a breaking point."

"You know what I noticed," John said. "You don't roll your eyes."

"Uh … and that's relevant, how?"

John shook his head and chuckled. "This getting to know you stage."

"We were talking about a breaking point." But Nadia was already seeing where John was going with this.

"If someone got a hold of my message to you. They would know that I deemed it important enough to leave such a message. If they held me prisoner, unable to torture any information out of me, they could say that they'd also captured you and that you're pregnant with my child."

"Leverage."

"Exactly. What we think is inconsequential, the enemy has a way of twisting it to have big enough consequences that could be used against me. I may not care about myself, but I'd definitely care about the mother of my child and my unborn baby. You just don't see it from my point of view …" His mouth hitched in one corner. "And now you're staring at me like I've grown two heads."

Nadia realized she was indeed squinting. "Wow, that's some paranoia."

"Life in the fast lane, babe."

"Maybe you need to slow down."

"Maybe I should get off the train," John returned mildly.

She regarded him doubtfully. "You'll never quit."

He gave her a brief smile. "I'm going to check on dinner."

Ha! Deflection again. She had his number now. If she didn't know what he was capable of, she would think they'd entered a twilight zone. She didn't know how to handle this John. She was used to bluntness from him. Not this treading-on-eggshells guy. But … she glanced behind her. He wasn't in the kitchen. She exhaled an irritated breath. He said he was going to check on dinner. Where the hell did he go? Okay, this was more of the Garrison she knew. There was relief in knowing that. Nadia would hate it if a torn condom was the downfall of this badass CIA operative.

He came down the stairs with something in his hand.

Shit.

He approached her and held out a phone. "Since you insist I leave you voice messages, I thought you'd want another one."

Nadia grabbed the device from him. "This doesn't mean anything."

"Huh, if someone has commitment issues, it certainly isn't me."

Speechless, she wondered who was this John that returned from two weeks away. Squinting, she realized he look more weary than she'd ever seen him. Thinner? His cheekbones sharper? It was hard to tell with his beard.

John chuckled. "If you could see your face."

She stepped into his space, reached up, pinched his cheek, and then pulled at the flesh. Had the CIA perfected the full facial disguises common in Hollywood espionage films?

"Hey," he protested.

"Who are you and what have you done to John Garrison?"

"Come here." He reeled her into his arms. "It's still me."

An emotion flashed through his eyes. "Just did a bit of reprior-itizing, that's all."

"While you were on the trail of the Argonayts?"

John released her and headed toward the kitchen. "That pot pie smells good."

Nadia didn't press, assuming that his mission was classified.

"It's been barely in there for ten minutes."

He peeked into the oven.

"Stop opening that. You're going to let the heat out," Nadia grumbled. She was hungry and she didn't want chips; she wanted that pot pie. She yanked him away from the oven and their bodies collided. He gripped her elbows, steadying her.

Their eyes locked. His grew heated. Okay, Nadia was feeling warm too, and she was feeling it between her legs. Damn him. Would she always want to jump him?

"I can think of a way to pass the time," he murmured, his head lowering to kiss her.

Nadia pushed away and stalked back to the living room. "No, John."

"We could be pregnant," he called behind her back.

She pointed at him with the hand holding the phone he gave her. "Why are you being so … so"—ugh, with John, she couldn't even find the right words—"so unconcerned about this?"

"You said it's an unlikely possibility, so why can't we make a joke about it?"

"It's not something to joke about." She paused. "Wait, is this your way of coping? Are you afraid to become a father?" It certainly didn't fit his lifestyle.

John chuckled. "Now you're projecting. Stop psychoan-alyzing."

"Psychoanalyze you?" she scoffed. "I'd be terrified of what I might find in that brain of yours."

John muttered something like 'compartments.'

"Compartments?"

His eyes flashed with annoyance. "You're right. You wouldn't want to see what's inside my brain."

"That scary, huh?"

"Very," he said gravely, and even when there was mirth in his eyes, Nadia wasn't sure if it was dark humor. Spies had morbid ways of seeing things.

She moved closer, and his expression grew wary. "Have you ever been to see a CIA shrink?"

"Many times."

"Oh."

"What? You think I'd deny it?"

"That's good," she said faintly. "You must see a lot of shitty things in your job."

He glanced in the direction of the kitchen. "It's going to take another half hour. Why don't you go freshen up?"

"I have no clothes."

"You can borrow mine."

CHRIST. The urge to kiss Nadia was excruciating to resist, so John had to send her elsewhere. There was no denying that he missed her. Craved her. There was something to be said about knowing what mattered most when you were faced with your own mortality. He'd long made peace that his mother might never find out the truth in case he was killed in an op. It depended on how the agency would cover it up. He left a letter with Kade just in case something did happen to him.

Was he ready to make the same provisions for Nadia? No, because he wanted to pursue a life with her. It was the biggest mission of his life right now, except there was real fear of the unknown. The unknown being these weird emotions rattling inside him.

He certainly didn't want to make excuses as to why he didn't return that Monday. He should have known better than to make that promise given what he did for a living. Although getting captured by the Ukrainian mob and thrown into their dark dungeon was certainly reason enough to miss the date.

He'd been gritting his teeth all night, trying not to wince when his bruised ribs screamed. John had been through worse and was just glad that he survived with all his limbs and appendages intact.

The mob hated to be put in the spotlight. The bioweapon plot that had been linked to the Ukrainian Brotherhood was still too fresh in people's minds, and the death of CIA operatives wasn't good for business. However, nabbing John and Bristow and stowing them away meant the agency was getting close to the truth. There was something bigger at play that the Order was planning. Or maybe the Argonayts were planning something below the Order's radar. A side job.

And it had everything to do with the Crown-Key.

As for Garrison, it served his purpose. His plans for Nadia were singular. There was something about her that had him coming back for more. And, in a few days, they might be tied together forever.

Or maybe not.

The timer dinged. The pot pie was finally done.

He reached into the oven, the aroma of buttery crust assailed his nose. An odd nostalgia pricked at his chest. A time when he'd come home from football practice and his mother would have a whole tray of this just out of the oven.

Shuffling behind him made him turn.

"That smells good," Nadia said.

He'd momentarily forgotten about dinner. She was standing in his shirt and nothing else. Her hair was piled up in a towel, her feet bare.

He cursed and strode past her and double-timed it up the staircase to the hallway closet that held emergency supplies.

Usually, he'd just point the operatives where to look, but hell, apparently with Nadia he felt compelled to do this.

John rummaged through the slipper supply. They were decent looking, made of soft and strong rubber. He remembered the guys saying they were durable enough to run in. Grabbing two of different sizes, he headed down and back to the kitchen.

"I think you're more a six than a seven."

Nadia was giving him that look again like he'd grown an extra head. He went down on his knees and tried a pair of them on her feet, brushing the dirt from her sole before slipping them on.

"John."

It was the right size. A smug grin started to form on his mouth.

"John!"

He glanced up.

"Stop treating me like I'm already pregnant."

His brows drew together. "I'm not."

She shook her head and left him kneeling on the floor. "Well, I'm hungry." Opening and closing the cabinets, she asked, "Where are the plates?"

Before he could answer her, she found them on the shelves above his collection of Scotch and out of her reach.

John got up from the floor and went to the sink to wash his hands. Toweling them dry, he approached behind Nadia, feeling her stiffen. She was skittish of his advances, but the tension rolling off her informed him she wasn't as immune as she was letting on. John grinned, leaning closer and brushing up against her back as he reached above her. "These need washing. I don't remember the last time I've used dishes."

He laid the plates beside her on the counter and put his hands on her shoulders, turning her around. She leaned back, her mouth curled into a smile. "I see where your priorities are."

"What can I say? I like Scotch."

He stared at her mouth and heard her breathing hitch. John was tempted to skim his hands down her sides. It would be so easy to slip his fingers under the shirt she was wearing ... and squashed his imagination viciously when it went into the direction of what she was *not* wearing.

Her lips pursed together and then she very firmly pushed him away and grabbed the plates. The sound of the water started. John didn't immediately turn around as he willed himself to regain control. The look on Nadia's face caused unease to knot in his gut. She was actively rebuffing him.

"Let's eat," she said.

John faced her and they stared at each other across the counter. Before he could utter a word, she held up a hand and said, "I thought about this in the shower."

He grinned faintly. "I probably shouldn't have sent you to take a shower."

"John—"

"Don't over think this right now."

"I just want to be clear about something ..."

John held his tongue. It was so instinctive for him to override any objections to his agenda. And he had quite an agenda planned for Nadia, but instinct told him she wasn't in a receptive mood. He ground his molars.

"No matter what happens, whether I'm pregnant or not, nothing changes."

"You have to be clearer about that, babe."

"You and I are done."

His jaw hardened. "You don't think I'm going to abandon my kid."

"No. No. Nothing like that. We'll co-parent," she exhaled heavily. "And that's as far as I'm discussing right now. I don't want this to be a reason for us to fall back into bed and pick up where we left off."

"I told you that I was coming back that Monday which meant there was still something to discuss between us."

"But you didn't return—"

John chuckled darkly. "Believe me, babe. There were extenuating circumstances."

"I'm sure there were, but remember what I said about not wanting your scraps?"

Goddammit. This woman. John wanted to sit her down and shake some sense into her.

"That hasn't changed—despite this new development," Nadia finished. She nodded to the table. "Now let's have dinner."

11

Nadia didn't regret drawing a line in the sand the night before, and she was glad John didn't attempt to pull that line to his favor. They ate dinner and maintained a civil conversation that had nothing to do with what was going on between them. John didn't talk about his two-week mission to Ukraine. He asked mostly about her dad and her team. He was particularly interested in Kelso, maybe because he was the lead on the Crown-Key investigation.

John put her up in a separate bedroom, but she slept terribly. It was the first time they'd spent the night together in a house. She had no doubt he expected them to pick up where they left off. She'd even hazard a guess that he was ready to explore more, but his total radio silence these past two weeks only reiterated her decision to resist him.

Any kind of relationship with John Garrison would only end in heartache. And it was neither of their faults. Nadia wanted something stable and certain, and that wasn't John. That man wasn't meant to be anchored in one place.

Noise in the hallway drew her attention, and she rolled over in her bed and snatched the phone. It was five thirty.

Minutes later she heard the coffee grinder go. The kitchen

was equipped with one of those fancy industrial ones. Her sleep-deprived brain immediately responded to the promise of caffeine, and she scrambled out of bed. Crap, she didn't have clothes. She texted Kelso last night to swing by her place to grab a few items. He had a key to her apartment like she had a key to his. It wasn't unusual that they ran errands for each other. Gabby used to be in the mix until Declan walked back into her life.

She padded to the bathroom to take another shower. Afterward, she put on another fresh shirt and went without panties again. Nadia's thoughts strayed to their encounter last night.

They'd almost kissed.

Again.

Dammit.

The sooner she escaped John's clutches, the better. Those little gestures from him … the chips and salsa, making sure she wasn't walking barefoot on cold kitchen tiles were … endearing and so not good for her resolve. It was so unlike John and, yet, seemed such a part of him. He was an enigma.

That was his spy craft, her suspicious mind whispered. The first time she'd met him, he'd been pretending to be a suit from Homeland Security. He let Declan do all the talking, but he slipped in and out from the background. He could blend into the walls if he wanted to, but if he needed to be heard, he spoke with authority. And everyone listened.

Her lady parts quivered, reminding herself again that she was going downstairs without panties. She seemed to lose her panties whenever John was around.

She stuck her head out of the bedroom door and immediately inhaled the glorious aroma of freshly brewed coffee. But when she arrived in the kitchen, he was nowhere to be found and she wondered if the coffee machine was set on a timer. Oh well, didn't mean she shouldn't partake. However, she noticed the front door was slightly ajar, and she heard the gates.

Shit, she never checked her phone when she came out of the shower. Nadia had a feeling that it was Kelso.

She headed to the door, but before she reached it, voices filtered in from outside.

John entered, holding a black gym bag with Kelso following closely. John's eyes raked her from head to toe, his mouth flattening.

"Sorry!" Nadia chirped, deliberately ignoring his displeasure at having a surprise visitor sprung on him. "I forgot to tell you Kelso was stopping by."

The detective didn't appear too happy himself. Did John say something to him?

"As you can see, Lieutenant, Nadia is fine."

"I wanted to see her with my own eyes," her teammate shot back. "After the last time I had to pick her up—"

"That was a misunderstanding," John clipped.

Her brow arched. *It was?*

But Nadia was familiar with the clash of testosterone in her line of work. And it hung around John and Kelso as thick as the LA smog at rush hour. And was equally as suffocating too.

She needed to diffuse the situation. "It really was."

"You sure?" Kelso asked, doubt tinging his tone.

"Yes."

"You two are not—" Kelso started.

"None of your business," John growled at the same time Nadia said, "No."

Silence.

She exhaled in exasperation. "John is watching out for me because you and Gabby have enough on your plate. Besides I'm sure after our meeting later, it'll be back to normal."

John shot her a look that stated, *don't count on it.*

She shot him one of her own communicating, *wanna bet?*

"Fine," Kelso said. "I need to check with our CSI tech regarding the prints they lifted off the other three assailants, but we're pretty sure if they're not related to the Brotherhood, they're hired mercenaries."

"I can find out if they can't." Nadia returned her gaze pointedly at John.

Translation: I'm sure the CIA will let me check their databases.

"Okay, then," the detective started backing out the door. "See you at eight." His mouth quirked. "I'm sure I put *every-thing* in there and your dad says hi."

Pivoting on his heel, he left the house.

"You can drop the bag there." Nadia already turned to head back into the kitchen. "I need coffee."

She heard something plop on the floor, the door shut, but nothing else. Nadia went on tiptoes to get the coffee mug— why was everything put up on a shelf that was hard to reach. She was five-seven. Before she was able to grab one though, she was spun around and pinned against the countertop.

"What the hell—" Her voice caught at the fierceness of John's expression.

He leaned in, hard face a scant inch from hers, his harder body keeping her own hostage.

And he was hard *everywhere*. And pissed.

"Don't tell me this is about Kelso showing up unan-nounced," she said.

"I'm used to that. Try again." Clipped words.

"I don't know, John," she returned with a touch of sarcasm. "Why don't you enlighten me?"

She might have regretted those words.

Or maybe not. Because the gleam in his eyes changed, and it made her nipples harden.

"If you need anything that touches your body, you tell me first."

"This is about the clothes he brought me?"

"Yes. How did he get them?" He must have pushed closer because she was leaning further away. And why was she taking this? "Get off."

"Answer me!"

"How else? He has a key to my apartment. I'm warning you, John." She was going to knee this asshole in the balls the first chance she got.

His eyes narrowed. "Get it back."

"What the hell? What's wrong with you?"

"You should've asked me first."

"Why make it complicated? I'm not your responsibility."

"Yes, you are."

"Is this about the 'I might be pregnant' again?"

"No, it's about me staking a claim."

How could his bossiness make her hot and indignant at the same time? "Stop being such a caveman, and let me—"

John crashed his mouth on hers, and she squirmed against him. She opened her mouth to protest, but he slipped his tongue inside. Big hands cupped her bare buttocks, and she felt him groan. He squeezed her ass, and she felt warmth pool between her legs.

He boosted her up, spun around and walked over to the center island, all the while still kissing her. Then he tore his mouth away as she landed on her ass on the cool granite surface. He hauled her to the edge, and the shirt rode up, her pussy bared to his eyes.

Indignantly, she braced herself on her elbows but seeing John staring solemnly at her core stifled the words she wanted to say. His gaze flicked to hers momentarily. "You're wet."

A finger stroked her slit.

"Yes, so what?"

"You want me, Nadia, even while you try so hard to push me away."

"You're bad for me."

His mouth tightened. "I'll change your mind."

Without saying another word, he bent forward, tossed her legs over his shoulders, arching her back and then his head disappeared from view.

The first lashing of his tongue on her pussy had her biting back a moan. She slapped the back of her hand on her mouth to keep from crying out as he licked and assaulted her with broad strokes, fastening on her clit, sucking the bud between his lips.

Nadia exploded and bucked against his mouth. Exquisite pleasure drummed at the tip of her mound, and he knew what she needed to extend that feeling, pressing down on the top of her pelvis and prolonging those pulsating sensations.

Then he hauled her up and started kissing her again. Letting her inhale her own scent on his skin, he devoured her mouth with a consuming possession that couldn't be denied.

Finally, he pulled away, and Nadia sucked in an instinctive breath. "What the hell?" she mumbled against his mouth.

They were face to face, his hips between her legs. She was in a very precarious position to be fucked. All he had to do was lower the waistband of his track pants. His erection wasn't trying to be shy either. He was long and rock-solid underneath that thin fabric. He read her mind.

His eyes crinkled at the corners. "I can fuck you right here, right now."

"And if I say no?" She arched a brow.

"Then I won't."

"I don't get it. You're willing to suffer through that." She didn't dare brush his shaft and tempt fate. If he was experiencing blue balls, he brought that on himself.

He stared at her intently. "Oh, it's not suffering."

"It's not?"

"No. You're going to remember how easily I made you scream while tongue-fucking you on this counter. The guys will be here any moment. They'll be sitting around that table, but you won't be thinking about anything but this …" His large hand wrapped around her skull to bring her face forward. His indigo eyes studied her reaction, and then he grinned, but it wasn't exactly in humor. "My head between your pretty thighs, your hips squirming to feed that pussy into my mouth. That's the image you're going to see in your head today, babe."

"You sound possessive."

John shrugged.

"You don't get possessive, John."

The fingers around her scalp tightened. "I'm possessive of you."

"You didn't listen to what I said last night."

"I listened. And I gave you a chance to stew over that foolish assumption."

"I was very clear that I don't want anything to happen between us anymore."

Very deliberately, he raked his teeth over his bottom lip in an attempt not to smirk.

"You manhandled me!" And it got her all lusty and hot. "I didn't have a chance to say no." Even as she sluttily opened her legs the moment he wedged his hips between them.

"I dare you to say I forced you." His stare continued to hold hers captive.

Nope. He didn't.

"I dare you to say that you didn't lay awake in your bed last night, hoping I'd come to you and end your stubbornness."

"Self-preservation is not being stubborn," she said.

John stared at her for a scant second longer before turning away from her. He searched the cabinets and hooked two coffee mugs in his fingers.

"I get where you're coming from," he said finally.

Was he admitting defeat? A desolation swept through her. Wasn't that what she wanted, though? Argh! *The conflict is real!*

He grabbed the carafe of coffee and started pouring it into a mug before handing her one. "Black?"

She nodded.

Filling his own with brew, he took a measured sip. "There's a lot I want to say. Part of it you'll hear when the guys get here. But know that I've always intended to explore whatever this was between us, even before I left for Ukraine."

She started to protest, but he cut her off. "Nadia, I'm not proposing marriage, but something incendiary is happening between us. I'd be stupid to let my job get in the way of what could make me the most human since I've lost the ability to empathize … well, empathize like a normal human."

Nadia snorted. "Glad you made that clear. You're not a sociopath, John. I've seen you care. Does it come naturally to you? No. But that's not even the issue here. It's the nature of your job."

"Don't worry about it."

"Don't worry about it?"

"We'll cross the bridge when we get to it."

"See that's the whole problem!" Nadia's voice rose. "You're not seeing my problem."

"I'm seeing quite clearly. You think I don't have what it takes for a long-term relationship."

"Are you denying it?"

"No. Your fears are legitimate, but, like I said, I want to change your mind."

"By giving me orgasms?"

At this, his grin widened. "Among other things, but—"

"See! You think because we've got this chemistry—"

"But—" he cut in firmly with that authoritative voice that made her obey. "But, we're going to take the emotional shit slow."

"Oh, as long as we continue with the physical shit."

"Have I ever given you shitty sex?"

Nadia crossed her arms and clasped her biceps, looking

away. "I mean you want to continue having sex and wait until you feel something? That's what you mean, right?"

"No," John said, making her eyes snap back to his. "I'm not fucking you until you ask me to."

"That's not what happened just now."

"Call that a preview of what I can give you. You're going to allow me to touch you, but no sex. And what I mean by no sex is the actual act. Penetration. Filling you with my cock, you feeling me move inside you—"

"I get the picture." Nadia squeezed her legs together. "You can stop the dirty talk."

He smirked. "Is it working?"

"Damn you, Garrison," she said under her breath.

He chuckled softly before drawing her into his arms, putting a finger under her chin and tipping it up. "I've been damned many times, babe, but now I'm ready for my reward."

Nadia didn't dare ask him what he meant because it was clearly etched in his eyes.

And she was a little bit afraid.

Because John was everything that was exciting to her, and in his determination to change her mind about giving them a chance, she was afraid that he would be successful. But what if he realized it was not what he wanted and craved his nomadic existence again.

Where would that leave Nadia? She wanted stability; she didn't want uncertainty.

John cursed under his breath. "You're still hesitant."

She sighed. "Do you blame me?"

"No. This can't be solved in a morning." He glanced at his watch. "And there's only so much I can say, but we're out of time. The guys will be here soon. Go get dressed."

"You don't want them to see me in your shirt? Wouldn't that be more your caveman speed?"

"I'd rather they not see your nipples or imagine you without panties."

"They'd never—"

"They're men, Nadia. Fuck it, I don't even want to think about it."

She was surprised how strongly he felt about that. He let her go and walked over to where he dropped the gym bag. Returning to her side, he handed it to her and nodded his head toward the staircase.

John was lucky she found his bossiness hot, otherwise, his crotch would be meeting the contents of her coffee cup.

She gave one of her dramatic turns and strutted out of the kitchen. Let him drool over her swaying ass.

And when she heard his strangled groan, she smiled wickedly.

12

NADIA WAS STUBBORN AS FUCK, but John couldn't blame her for resisting his advances to pick up where they had left off. The truth was, he hadn't tried to win a woman over since his freshman year in college. He was rusty. Sure he'd done it on assignment or when he was undercover. It was so easy to lie and not care that he'd lied.

John tried to stay away, but after having her again after Huxley's party, he knew it was useless to resist the sexy walking contradiction that was Nadia Powell. She was a nerd at heart, but she had the moves of a siren. Sassy on the streets, scorching between the sheets. A lethal combination in John's book. Whatever conscience he had told him to leave her alone to find a decent man, find the California dream and raise two-point-five kids.

A roar inside him protested it wouldn't be any man but him.

Jealousy was a dormant feeling he hadn't experienced in a long time. He thought he was practical, logical, and pragmatic. Man, was he mistaken.

But what exactly could John offer her?

Nadia wasn't a risk taker, and it seemed a lot to ask her to take a chance on him. He'd read her file. He knew of the time when she was twelve and was yanked away from the security of a Virginia suburban neighborhood when there were leaked CIA files that might have exposed her father. It was eight months of safe houses until they landed in Seattle and then finally made their home in Los Angeles. John was a reminder of that life when everything was uncertain.

He refilled his coffee and headed to his bedroom to change into faded denims, a crewneck tee, and military boots. There was an image he wanted to project especially with the detectives coming over to talk about the case. If they needed to head somewhere after this, he wanted to be ready. Grabbing his tablet, he made his way to the first floor and was surprised to see Nadia already seated at the dining table, on her laptop, and tapping away at the keyboard. She had on red cat-eye glasses and her blond hair was piled up in a high ponytail. She was wearing one of her nerd-themed t-shirts. He walked over to where she sat and slid out a chair beside her.

"Watcha up to?"

"Checking to see if there's an update on those other DBs."

John woke his screen and checked communications as well. Bristow had already sent him the files on the three assailants from yesterday. "I got them."

She glanced up. "Bristow?"

"Yep."

"See, you can depend on him. I don't know why you keep yanking me into your ops."

Nadia raised her mug to take a sip while shooting an inquiring brow his way.

"You're prettier than Bristow."

She started coughing, may have spewed a bit of coffee on her screen before glaring at him. "You did that on purpose!"

"Sorry, babe, that was hard to resist."

The gates sounded on its tracks, so Garrison checked the

surveillance app on his phone. "Speak of the devil. They're here."

Not long after Bristow and Levi showed up bearing to-go paper bags that smelled of pancake and bacon, the detectives arrived. They all scattered around the dining table to review their own data before the briefing commenced. Kelso handed Nadia a large to-go cup of caramel macchiato, and it irritated John how her face lit up. How did he miss this about her? So he was competitive as fuck when it came to wooing a woman.

Trying to swallow the annoyance boiling inside him, he asked, "Shall we get started?"

The detectives glanced up from their position behind Nadia's seat while she accessed the results from their forensics lab.

"Yes." Kelso eyed him shrewdly. "It appears that you're more aware of our cases than we are. How about you tell us what you know about Maxim Vovk and why he's after the Crown-Key?"

A corner of his mouth lifted. "My trip to Ukraine with Bristow yielded interesting intel."

"That must be some intel gathering." Nadia's eyes were full of scorn. "How did five days of business end up being two weeks of silence?"

John glanced briefly at Bristow who suddenly got up to check out the untouched Styrofoam containers of food.

"For starters," he replied evenly, directing his gaze back at Nadia. "We got abducted as soon as we got off the plane and thrown into a dungeon."

Shock registered in her eyes, as the entire room went silent. "You didn't think to mention this yesterday?"

Kelso appeared equally taken aback by his announcement, while Gabby didn't show surprise.

John continued holding her eyes. "I didn't want to make an excuse that I didn't keep my promise to you."

"That's a pretty damned good excuse. Are you all right?" Her gaze flew to the SEAL. "You, Bristow? You okay?"

"John and I were roughened up, but we'll live," he quipped. "I could eat pancakes and bacon for a week."

Kelso turned to Levi. "That's why you and Roarke were suddenly called away?" And then looked at his partner. "And that's why you were distracted this past week? I thought he wasn't picking up overseas jobs any longer. That he was banned."

"Someone higher than the JAG authorized the op," Levi said.

"And Dec wouldn't have gone if it weren't Garrison and Bristow's lives on the line," Gabby said.

The SEAL grinned. "We're honored."

"Any idea why you guys were held?" Kelso asked. "Was it the Brotherhood?"

"The men who captured us were members of the Argonayts," John said. "When we were rescued, Bristow managed to retrieve several hard drives and computers. We found the plot to secure the Crown-Key and that they had a person on Huxley's security team."

"Cain Morris, right?" Nadia asked.

"Yup."

"But why did they feel the need to detain you?" Kelso asked.

"Ilya, our asset in Ukraine had this same information and was about to hand it over, but he was too high profile in Kiev society to kill, and it was too late to stop us from leaving the U.S."

"So they abducted you guys so you wouldn't interfere with their plot to steal the Crown-Key," Gabby postulated.

"That. And tried to find out what we already know … without leaving permanent marks on us," John said.

"As if we're going to admit to having our asses kicked," Bristow said.

The men chuckled. The women glared.

"How can you all be so cavalier about this?" Nadia snapped.

He shrugged. "Only way to stay sane in this job."

Kelso asked, "So what can you tell us about Maxim?"

"Maxim Vovk was the leader of the Argonayts, the Ukrainian hacking ring, which the U.S. government believes is responsible for the SillianNet hack last year."

"There were speculations that the Kremlin was behind that," Gabby said. "The government couldn't prove it, right?"

"To prove it would expose several of our assets in Russia and eastern Europe," John admitted. "Many of them are deep cover, and such documentation—if revealed—would start a witch hunt. We couldn't allow that to happen."

"Okay, so with Maxim dead, would that mean whatever they're planning is also dead because their activities are not sanctioned by the Brotherhood, right?" Nadia asked.

"The Brotherhood is a collective name for Ukrainian organized crime," John said. "They're closely related to their Russian counterparts and usually do business together. In reality, they're made of several groups. A few of them would get together for a job and then disappear after it was done."

"Yes, we see that happening here," Kelso replied. "That's why they're so hard to pin down."

"Their ability to adapt is what makes them dangerous, so there's no telling what Maxim's death will do," John said. "Someone else could take over. We need to know exactly what that Crown-Key software can do. Nadia?"

She gave a shake of her head as if attempting to refocus her attention on their meeting objective, making John momentarily doubt if he spilled the circumstances of the Ukrainian trip too early. But it was relevant to their case, and he hated keeping secrets from her that would affect how they moved forward in his plans for her.

"I'm still deciphering the extent of its capability." She exhaled a heavy breath. "But it's not looking good."

"She's already given us a brief rundown about how it could propagate and bypass a company's security," Gabby said. "We've informed Homeland security of this, but we're not getting priority."

"They're dealing with cyber threats elsewhere." John kept his face neutral when he said this. In reality, he and the admiral agreed to keep the DHS on the periphery of the investigation. "My opinion?" he continued. "You've got all the resources you need right here." He nodded at Nadia.

"Your confidence in my skills is endearing." She gave a small smile that slightly lightened the cloudiness in her eyes.

"You have no idea," John murmured. He immediately felt a blast of displeasure coming from the detectives. He returned their narrowed gazes with one of disinterest. He understood Gabby's protectiveness, but Kelso could just fuck off.

Bristow cleared his throat. "Maxim Vovk's last date of entry into the U.S. was Friday a week ago." The SEAL named the unidentified assailants from yesterday. "They're Russian mercenaries who have been in the U.S. for a while—associates of the Russian Bratva."

"Could that be our link to Moscow then?" Gabby asked. "You think the Kremlin is behind this?"

"We know they made an offer to Huxley," Bristow said.

"Really?" Nadia asked. "That's not in our files. You have supporting data?"

"Yup, sending you a drop," the SEAL replied. "Those are from the disks we retrieved from the house where we were held."

"Okay, that's an important piece of the puzzle," Gabby said. "So, back to my question earlier. With Maxim gone, should we still be concerned about a looming cyberattack?"

"We're not sure if someone has the Crown-Key device, so

I wouldn't be complacent," Nadia told her. "We're not sure if it has any part of the source code installed in it."

"Shit," Levi, who'd been quiet through all this, spoke up. "Does CTTF have anyone looking for it?"

"Huxley has several properties in the U.S. and around the world," Gabby said.

"And Cain Morris is still missing," Nadia informed them. "And he's not tripping any of our surveillance on his accounts."

Bristow looked up from his laptop. "If you study the intel I sent you, he's got experience forging identities, so, don't be surprised if he already had one waiting in the wings when they axed Huxley."

"This is what doesn't add up," Gabby said. "Why kill Huxley if they don't have everything yet?"

John had been trying to piece together what little bits of info he could remember from his time in captivity, so he floated up a theory. "The men who held us said Maxim botched the operation and would be trying to salvage it. What I could infer from that statement is that they managed to get the Crown-Key and either killed Huxley before verifying that they could get to the source code, or they killed him accidentally."

"Two shots to the chest don't seem accidental," Gabby said. "Nadia found malware that tried to sneak around to grab the program when she managed to break into Huxley's code repository."

"It could be a tracking malware alerting them that the source code was now unlocked, and that's why they attacked yesterday to grab Nadia" John said.

"And you were watching us too?" Kelso asked. "You knew they were going to make a move?

"It was a hunch," John said. It had been a struggle to let it play out the day before as he fought the urge to steal Nadia away and lock her up safely.

"Looks like we need to operate under the assumption that our enemies do have the Key and intend to use it," Gabby said. "Let's identify the potential targets."

"ENERGY INFRASTRUCTURE IS the most vulnerable right now," Nadia said. She was struggling to concentrate on the meeting and trying to ignore how John turned her resolve on its head after the bomb he dropped earlier. How could she hold that against him? He was abducted, thrown in a dungeon, and tortured. The coffee she'd drunk this morning turned sour in her stomach.

"There are water treatment plants," Kelso speculated. "Not long ago a hacker changed the ratios of chemicals in the water to unsafe levels."

"Government databases. The Office of Personnel Management had already been victimized."

The public didn't seem alarmed by the breach. If they only knew that every single background check that was done by the government was stored in those databases. Hmm … databases. Her analyst's brain went to work on the files Bristow had sent her. Working on a hunch, she let the rest of them identify potential threats.

"Defense contractors and research facilities that are developing new technology for the military are high-value targets for rogue states," John said.

"So, let's throw in the CIA and the National Security Agency," Bristow smirked.

"Financial institutions," Gabby added. "In short. If this gets into the wrong hands, there would be chaos. We have two kinds of perps. The ones whose purpose is to cause instability in the country, and the ones who are in it for the money. Both have the potential to cause chaos."

"All right, so we concentrate on the Argonayts," Kelso said.

"That's our best chance to find the Key," John agreed and split a look between the detectives. "I'm going to work with Nadia to offload the rest of the hard drives we were able to collect from the house where we were held. I have a feeling we'll get more intel from them." He turned to her. "But priority is the source code and finding the device."

It was on the tip of her tongue to say she didn't take orders from him, but, at this point, that was going to sound petty. She didn't know how to process both the emotion and information she'd gotten in the last five minutes. Besides, the hunch she had just came back with a hit.

"Guys." She glanced up from her screen. "The partial print lifted off Thomas Brandt's homicide scene matches the print of one of our assailants from yesterday. That's not a definitive win, yet. But that's something."

"Fucking A," Gabby said and fist-bumped Nadia. "Put in an order for detailed DNA cross-analysis on both Huxley and Brandt's cases and match it against our DBs from yesterday."

"Already did," she said.

"You're the best, nerd girl," Kelso added.

"Excellent work, *babe*," John cut in. "One more thing. There's a likelihood that the Order will retaliate. We were hoping to capture Maxim to flush out his brother Dmitry Vovk. It's our belief he's the real mastermind behind the Argonayts hacking ring, and his brother was simply a puppet. I'm hoping he shows his face Stateside and we can link big brother to the whole plot and arrest him."

Somehow Nadia didn't think that putting the mafia boss behind bars was exactly what John had in mind.

After the meeting broke up, Bristow left with Levi. They were taking some much-needed R and R but staying close to LA in case John needed them. The detectives were giving last-minute instructions to Nadia who was given permission to telework although she preferred to have all her gizmos around her. But she missed her own bed and was freaking tired from lack of sleep.

"I can run you home," Kelso said.

"I got her," John answered behind them.

"All right," Gabby glared at John with suspicion. "Is there something going on between you and my crime analyst?"

"This is your business, how?"

"Guys—" Nadia started, even raised her hand in a weak wave.

Kelso gave a humorless bark of laughter, but it was Gabby who answered, invading John's personal space. "Oh, it is when it's you."

"Did I interfere when you and Roarke mixed business with pleasure?" he asked.

"That's different!"

"Diff—"

"Guys!" Nadia cut in in exasperation. "Goodness." She yanked Gabby away from John and positioned her beside Kelso, so she could yell at them together. "John's right, it's none of your business if I sleep with him—"

"Technically, there was no sleeping—" John drawled.

Nadia spun on the infuriating man in the room. "You shut it, Garrison!"

A brow hiked. A corner of his mouth tipped up. "Sure, babe."

Nadia blew imaginary wisps from her forehead and faced the detectives again. "I'm thirty-two-years old. I have a job I love, and I support myself. I sure as hell can pick any man I choose to sleep with—"

"We know that," Gabby said. "And did you see us interfere with any other man you chose to date?"

She didn't say it was because there was hardly a second or third date because her mind kept imprinting the image of this annoying CIA man on their faces. "So, why now?"

"Garrison's different," Gabby said.

"Sure hope so," he commented behind her, and she cast him another quelling look.

"He's not the usual boyfriend material." Gabby glanced past Nadia to look at John. "No offense."

"None taken."

The detective continued, "With his job, he's not good relationship material either."

"Now, I take offense to that."

Nadia wanted to scream. She gave up and left them where they were standing. Let them duke it out for all she cared. She grabbed her backpack which carried all her essentials. The gym bag was upstairs, but she didn't need everything in it if she planned to make a quick getaway.

Aware of John's eyes on her even as he exchanged barbs with Gabby, Nadia marched up to Kelso and said, "Just get me out of here."

She wasn't expecting to be spun around quickly and slammed into hard muscle.

She definitely wasn't expecting John's mouth crashing down on hers, forcing his tongue between her lips, and kissing her senseless.

His fingers dug into the flesh of her ass and brought her closer and he simply consumed her, her body still tingling from the super-hot foreplay from this morning when he tongue-fucked her to mindless orgasm. Now her nipples were hard, and she was pretty sure her panties were drenched.

Her palm on his chest felt the vibration of his groan, and she came back to her senses that they had an audience. She pushed at him and he stopped kissing her. John lifted his head and stared at her with unwavering intensity.

"Oh, wow," Gabby's voice broke her 'John Garrison haze,' and they both turned their heads toward the detectives. "Now, that was hot."

Gabby fanned herself. "How did I not know that Garrison's got the moves?"

"Your husband better not hear you say that," Kelso told her.

"But this is news! Garrison is not a cyborg."

"Apparently," Kelso muttered, then asked Nadia. "Sure you're okay?"

Nadia speared John a 'zip it' look, because *clearly* he was going to answer for her again. His mouth flattened. Good.

"Yes, but I think I have a ride."

Kelso nodded while still glaring at John. John clasped her shoulder from behind and drew her against his chest.

Overprotective meets possessive.

Heaven help her.

13

GARRISON COULD DO this stare-down all day.

"I need more bacon," Nadia announced and left the three of them standing by the doorway.

Meanwhile Gabby pointed two fingers to her eyes and then turned them on him, letting John know that she was watching his every move.

"That's right," Kelso added and leaned in to him. "Watch yourself, Garrison."

"Get out of here." He gave a shake of his head, feeling more annoyance than intimidation from Nadia's team.

"Just saying ..." Gabby backed up to the outside, before shooting him a smirk and swiveling on her heel to leave. John and Kelso remained laser-locked in their gazes for a second longer before the other man followed his partner's exit.

He promptly let the door swing shut.

When he turned to face the woman who was at the center of contention, she was busy stuffing bacon into her mouth.

"They're overprotective," Nadia told him. "And it's irritating the hell out of me."

"That's fine."

"It's not fine if we're still trying to figure out what's going on between us. We don't need them sticking their noses in it."

"Agreed. However, it's another hurdle I'm prepared for. Besides, I think they're the least of our concerns."

Her head tilted in question.

"Your father and his friends."

Nadia groaned, but she gave a breathy laugh that John felt straight to his dick. Damn, her face was already gorgeous, but when she laughed like that, it transformed to a beauty that mesmerized him. He knew exactly why she wore glasses. She didn't have a vision problem. It was part of a disguise since she was twelve. She hid behind her jeweled frames and trendy shoes, using them as a form of expression. But when she lit up like that? Her genuine Nadia smile was blinding, and he absolutely adored the sound of her laughter.

"Why are you even smiling?" she asked. "If you think Kelso and Gabby are annoying, wait until you meet the MoMoS."

"MoMoS?"

"The merry old men of SkyeLark apartments."

He crossed his arms. "Oh, I know everything about them, down to their favorite takeout restaurants."

"Seriously? Stop pulling files on people around me. That's blatant invasion of privacy that has nothing to do with your job."

John uncrossed his arms and advanced on her. Nadia took a step back, but she was trapped by the counter bar. He braced a hand against either side of it, boxing her in.

"I disagree. You're right smack in the middle of a case I'm working on. But, more than anything, I intend to focus my time and attention on you."

"When did you decide that?"

"I had a lot of free time on my hands to stop and ponder my priorities."

Her eyes clouded, but John didn't want to get into his

epiphany during his time in captivity. "No, Nadia. I'm not going to give you a play-by-play of my journey into self-enlightenment." He smiled faintly. "I'd rather show you.

"Stop making light of your abduction."

He leaned in. "I'm not. But if you're going to use it as an excuse to drive a wedge between us, I'd rather not discuss this here. I still need to pack a few things."

"You're leaving again?"

"No. I'm moving in with you."

John relished seeing the shock on her face. Nadia's mouth formed an "Oh," so of course he kissed it. Actually, he could think about several other things to do with those lips, but John was a fan of working for things.

"Are you insane?"

"You need my secure Wi-Fi," he told her.

"I have one at home."

"Not as secure as my portable one."

That made her pause. "True, especially since we're dealing with hackers ...hmm..." she tapped her fingers on her lips as if weighing the pros and cons.

"We could stay here—but," he quickly added when he saw the mutiny in her eyes—"I know you wouldn't want to be separated from your dad. And I don't think Stephen would appreciate me sequestering his daughter."

"You got that right, buddy, but I'm not stupid either. Is it going to be safe for me to stay where I am after what happened with Maxim?"

"You know their MO. If these motherfuckers can't get to you, they'll go after the ones you love, and most of the time, that's worse." Which was why men like John rarely formed attachments. It was a lonely life, but he thought he was good with it. Apparently, this smart and beautiful crime analyst was his downfall. "We keep up with the whereabouts of your dad and the other guys. I doubt they'll agree to a safe house."

"Oh, God, no," Nadia snorted a laugh. "They're great

friends but I don't doubt they'd start killing each other if they lived in the same house."

John chuckled. "I figured that." He started backing away because her freshly showered scent was an unholy temptation to dirtying her up. "I'll be a minute."

"WE NEED to stop at the pharmacy to pick up Dad's meds," Nadia said. She texted her father before they left John's house and she volunteered to pick up his prescription. Stephen was healthy except for his elevated blood pressure which was manageable with medication.

She told John where to go. He grunted in acknowledgement but kept on driving.

It was a bit weird to come home with John in broad daylight. She usually expected him to sneak about in dark alleyways, behind a bank of elevators in an underground garage, or emergency stairs of a building. Not here riding side by side like a couple.

Wait. They were a couple, right?

Well, not a couple-couple, but two people trying to figure things out. She could give him that chance at least, but her confidence that anything but a rollercoaster awaited them was not encouraging. Sure, John had a reason for breaking his promise, but it was that exact reason why a stable relationship with him was not possible. And he seemed like the hornet in a nest of vipers that could bring danger to her and her dad. And, yet, he alluded that he was ready to make a change.

Was that a tiny niggle of hope in her heart? Or was that niggle a fear of heartbreak?

"Might pick up a few of those pee sticks," he said suddenly when the sign for DTS pharmacy came into view. He cast her a quick glance. "How soon can you try it?"

She shrugged. "My period is tomorrow. So, day after is the soonest? We can wait a few more days."

John wheeled the Escalade into a parking spot. "We can try one day after."

"I'll just be a sec." She unbuckled her seatbelt.

"I'm coming with." John unharnessed himself from the seat.

She frowned. "You don't have to."

"Listen, babe. I wouldn't want to miss a thing."

Nadia hopped down from the vehicle and slammed the door, meeting John at the back of the vehicle. "You're taking this to the extreme."

He grinned. "I don't want to be accused of not being hands-on."

"I guess not. Come on then." The sliding doors to the convenience store opened. This particular pharmacy was one of the few in LA that was piloting automated medication dispensers that were already in use at several hospitals around the country. The margin of accuracy of the unit was ninety-nine percent, better compared to the higher rate of errors by humans. Trained professionals still performed quality checks.

She approached the counter. "Hi, Rosa."

"Nadia." The tiny Hispanic pharmacist with a short bob and a round face smiled.

"How's Dr. Powell?" Rosa asked as she scanned the QR code on Nadia's phone.

"He's well. Blood pressure has been good, though he can't resist the salt."

The pharmacist gave a tsk sound. "Same with my husband. He said I'd be prying the salt shaker from his cold dead fingers. I'll just be a minute, honey."

Nadia glanced behind her wondering where John was. Good heavens, he better not be in the feminine care aisle picking up pregnancy tests. She craned her neck to search for him but the robotic arm of the RX auto dispenser distracted her. A light tendril of fear wrapped around her heart. This was another vulnerability that could be hacked.

In the past decade, hospitals had embraced digital information in a big way. Computerizing records made it easier for sharing patient history between hospital systems. But what if their medical records were hacked? What if a rogue state decided to change medication requirements and allergies for a demographic. That would be a disaster on so many levels.

Many people would die.

"Nadia?"

She realized that Rosa had been calling her name.

"I'm sorry," Nadia said. "You know I'm always fascinated with Mr. Roboto."

Rosa's grin faded as her eyes narrowed at the person behind Nadia. Somehow, she knew who it was.

"If you step back, sir, I'll be with you in a minute," she told him sternly. What the pharmacist lacked in height, she sure made up in attitude.

"I'm with her." Boxes of pregnancy tests were dumped on the counter followed by three crisp hundred-dollar bills.

"Jesus, John, how many women do you have on the maybe-impregnated list?" she sassed.

"Only you," he deadpanned.

There were eight boxes on the counter.

"I'm a fan of backup," he added. "Trust one, but verify with another. And you said we might have to try several times. I'd say we try one tonight."

Nadia turned to Rosa whose earlier scowl had transformed into a wide grin.

"Believe me I told him that it's better to test after my missed period which is supposed to be arriving tomorrow."

"He's anxious, honey," Rosa said.

"Hmm," she turned to John. "Are you anxious in a good way or anxious in a bad way?"

He only shot her an enigmatic smile.

· · ·

THE PHARMACY WAS a short distance from the apartment complex. There was a section for visitor parking behind the buildings and was usually empty by late morning. Unfortunately, it made it conspicuous if someone pulled into the spot. Also, unfortunately, it was a spot that Clyde's balcony was facing, and her neighbor was currently sitting in his favorite porch recliner having what he called his second breakfast.

Nadia's eyes dipped to her outfit, thankful she wasn't doing the walk of shame.

Clyde surged to his feet when she exited the vehicle. She and John hadn't even rehearsed how to introduce him.

She ducked her head back into the SUV as John was getting out. "Shit, how do I introduce you?"

"Your dad knows me as John Garrison. I'm sure Clyde has seen me around so just introduce me as your bodyguard slash tech support. Let's play the facts close to the truth." John grinned. "Relax."

Grrr... easy for him to say—he did this for a living. She shut the door and slung the backpack on one shoulder while her fingers clasped the bulging paper bags in one hand that contained the eight pregnancy tests and her father's meds.

"Morning, Clyde."

"Morning? It's almost noon."

Technically it was ten forty-five, but okay. "What's for breakfast?"

"Chocolate beignets."

"Yum. Did the Rivoli food truck come by?"

"Yup. I got you some, doll."

"You're a sweetheart. I'll come grab it on the way up." She didn't wait for Clyde to answer. She'd rather not holler and introduce John in an apartment parking lot ... because he was CIA and shit, you know.

Holy crap. He *is* the CIA and shit.

Nadia was contemplating a relationship with a spy.

Beset with a thrilling and frightening thought that threatened apoplexy, she didn't notice John coming up beside her until he was unhooking the backpack from her shoulder. "Go on." The strap of his giant duffel was fixed across his chest while the majority of it was supported by his back. Her gym bag was emptied of its contents and folded into his things. He'd slipped on a navy-blue Henley over a white crew neck, sported threadbare jeans and military boots. He appeared to be a normal guy, albeit a hot normal guy.

Still, her legs were uncoordinated because a fizz of anxiety shot down from her throat to the pit of her stomach as they negotiated the staircase.

She was processing what to tell Clyde.

The Clyde who was already waiting at his front door with a Styrofoam container holding her chocolate indulgence. "Do you have chicory coffee to go with this?" he asked.

"I'm good." She accepted the beignets with the hand not holding the paper bag. To her horror, the pharmacy bag was ripping at the edge where the staples were holding the fold. "Thanks again, we'll see you—"

Nadia knew better than to think she could escape the busy body of the apartment complex, but she wasn't expecting John to make the first move.

"Name's John Garrison," he said smoothly, extending a hand. "I'm sure you've seen me around the top floor."

"Yes." The old man acknowledged the handshake. "I see you either very early in the morning or late at night."

"I like the Late Show," John said. The Late Show was the midnight shift for the LAPD.

Clyde being Clyde, understood this of course. "I see. So what brings you here?"

"Okay, stop interrogating my co-worker," Nadia cut in.

"And bodyguard," her fake co-worker added.

"I thought I heard you, *sonyashnyk.*"

Nadia groaned. Of all the times for Stephen to show up.

"Did I hear you say bodyguard?" her father asked. "So what happened last night isn't resolved? Under control?"

"What happened last night?" Clyde asked.

She turned around to see Stephen glaring at John. Arthur stood behind her father and was giving John a dubious look as well.

Nadia glanced at Clyde. "We can't talk about an ongoing investigation."

"Well, at least tell me if my daughter is safe," Stephen said, still directing his ire at John.

"Dad," she butted in. "I'm right here. Let's just take this upstairs."

"But I wanna know," Clyde protested.

"Is that my prescription?" Stephen nodded to the paper bag in her hand and her grip instinctively tightened on it.

"Yes, but I have other things in there." A sense of foreboding paralyzed her limbs. "I'll give it to you—"

"Here. Let me help you," Stephen offered. "It's about to rip."

"No, Dad!" she panicked as he reached for the paper bag that she instinctively jerked away.

The horrific sound of tearing and the clattering boxes on the concrete flooring played out like one of her worst nightmares.

14

THE SILENCE WAS DEAFENING, and Nadia was frozen.

All eyes were on the pregnancy tests scattered on the floor.

"What's that?" Clyde asked, bending at the waist and squinting at the items.

"Well, Clyde, my friend," Arthur started. "That's how women of the past ... hmm ... thirty or so years have found out if they're pregnant."

"I see that." Clyde straightened and glanced at her. But why eight?

Her face was on fire, and she wished she was hot enough to melt and disappear into concrete. Her father's gaze burned with a question even without her having to look at him. And she couldn't look at John because that would be akin to screaming ... *it's his fault.*

"Well, gentlemen," John drawled, crouching in front of the test kits, and collecting them into a compartment of his giant duffel. "The show and tell is over. Nadia and I have work to do."

"Now, wait a moment." Stephen yanked John by his sleeve.

"Dad!"

"Your daughter is an adult." John stared at him steadily. "When she's ready to share, she will."

He shook off her father's hand and stepped protectively beside her, shielding her not only from her dad, but from the curious stares of Arthur, Clyde, and the rest of her neighbors who had come out of their apartments and seemed to have a radar for gossip.

John ushered her to the third floor, and Nadia didn't care that she meekly let him.

Mortified didn't even begin to describe how she was feeling.

The CIA man who was branded as her potential baby daddy fished out the keys from the side pocket of her backpack, opened the door, and turned off her alarm without asking her for the code.

Nadia wasn't surprised.

When he shut the world outside behind them, she zombie-walked to the couch in the living room, collapsing into it, and buried her face in her hands. "Thanks for rescuing me from what could be the most embarrassing moment of my life."

"There's nothing embarrassing about it."

John stood in front of her in his usual arms-crossed stance. She was beginning to see this was his stance of patience, where he didn't see any problems, but he was willing to listen to other people's concerns.

His calm demeanor at handling the situation started to send blood back into her brain.

"Look, I understand your father's outrage," John sighed.

Nadia gave a small smile. "He knew I was torn up over something I did for you."

"The Mexico op?"

"Yes. I just wasn't the same after that."

"I'm sorry I was such a fucking ass about it."

She raised a brow.

"Not about the sex," he huffed. "But what I said to you."

"What you said was true."

"It was explained to me that how you reacted was because you care."

At this Nadia's smile grew wide and genuine. "Oh, who explained that?"

"Roarke said it, and then later when we were in the Ukrainian cell, Bristow and I could only talk about some things. We spoke in vague terms, in case the cell was bugged. I didn't want those assholes to find out about you."

She sobered at this. "I'm sorry that happened. I was so mean to you when you came back."

"With reason."

Nadia nodded. One thing she also learned about John was that he didn't like to waste time rehashing things ad nauseam. She glanced over at the door. "You know our reprieve won't last, right? They'll come knocking on that door any minute now."

"Oh, I know. They probably called for reinforcements. Like that lumbering Scot for instance," John said dryly.

"Dugal," Nadia groaned. She stood and sized up the man before her. "I think he can do real damage to you. He's pretty scrappy. I think he took those *Braveheart* reenactments to heart." She frowned. "And you're hurt."

"Just bruised ribs. I'll survive. He's also got twenty years on me," John said in an amused tone. "I'll be fine."

"We can say … the pregnancy tests were Gabby's."

"Too late for that."

"You shouldn't have admitted it immediately," she groused.

"I didn't exactly admit it," he shot back. "And you were just standing there frozen and tongue-tied."

"Well, what do you expect? My dad just found out I had sex in the last few weeks."

"I'm sure he didn't expect you to be a virgin or celibate,"

he scoffed. "His outrage was because it was me. He doesn't trust me."

"I should have my head examined when nobody seems to be trusting me to be with you."

"It's about my job."

Nadia nodded and grinned. "I know. I'm a big girl and I —" she slapped a palm to her forehead as another thought struck her. "I wonder if Dad thinks we had unprotected sex." All her life she hadn't wanted to disappoint Stephen. It wasn't because he demanded she follow any rules, but it was because he'd done so much for her as a single dad that it was instinctive to make him proud of her. "I mean, I'm even on birth control ... I was just so stressed in the last two months. I haven't been taking it regularly. Shit—"

John gathered her into his arms and gave her a gentle shake. "Hey ... hey..." he repeated until she could focus on him. "Don't overthink it. No birth control is a hundred percent. Let's leave the reason at that."

"Okay."

"It'll be fine."

"WHOSE BALLS SHOULD I string up and feed to the crows?"

Dugal Cameron bellowed from the backdoor of Nadia's apartment.

Garrison winced at the visual and wondered if he'd been transported into medieval times. "I guess your Scot is home," he told Nadia when she rushed to his side.

To keep her mind from stressing over what transpired in front of Clyde's apartment, he encouraged Nadia to start deciphering the Crown-Key source code. It also helped that the detectives required her help, so that kept her busy all afternoon while John caught up with his own correspondence which had piled up in the past two weeks.

"Let me take care of this," she said as she moved past him, but he hooked his thumb in the waistband of her shorts and drew her back.

"Hell no," he said firmly, turning her around and putting his hands on her shoulders.

"John, now is not the time to act all macho."

"I disagree. Look, I know it feels as if I'm running roughshod over you, but, right now, out there"— he pointed at the door—"are guys who are waiting for me to man up. Letting you take care of it is not going to make them leave us alone. They need to know I can take care of you." He paused. "Come what may."

Her eyes narrowed. "Okay, but just so we're clear, we're still on a trial basis, pregnant or not."

John accepted this. Knew he had work ahead of him to convince her to take a chance on him, that he had to be patient. But the green-eyed monster inside him was growing in leaps and bounds and it was roaring for him to make her his.

"John?"

He gave a brief shake of his head to snap himself out of his compartments, their walls becoming more permeable in the last few weeks.

The Scot was still bellowing by the door but had tried a different tack. "Nadia, we would like to meet your boyfriend. The guys and I have a few questions to ask him."

"Christ." John wondered if Chinese water torture would be easier.

"Now are you going to let me do the talking?"

His brows drew together. "Fuck no." He crossed the kitchen and threw open the door.

He was taller than the Scot by a few inches and, although the other man was wider and appeared beefier, John was more muscular and toned. Dugal's eyes widened when he laid eyes on him. He doubted the Scot had seen him before. Did the man expect hipster geek or maybe someone like Kelso? He squashed the thought of the detective from his head. Jealousy not only extended to romantic love, but it also applied to anyone who was taking care of Nadia, apparently. And it appeared he had to share her with these grumpy old folks of SkyeLark apartment. Well, at least they were grumpy to him.

"You must be Dugal." Like he did when he met Clyde, John extended his hand. "John Garrison." The other man had mastered the unwavering stare, but he returned it with interest.

The handshake lasted more than it should have, and John smiled briefly when Dugal squeezed his hand for good measure. The Scot's blue gaze slitted. "You're Nadia's boyfriend?" he asked, releasing his hand.

"No," he answered, deliberately baiting the other man who scowled at him. "I am the man Nadia is seeing." And fucking … or will be fucking soon enough.

The Scot crossed his arms over his chest, punching up his massive biceps and forearms probably from years of butchering or maybe bludgeoning imaginary foes in reenactments. "Aye, you may be. But know that lass is precious, and we won't let just any man have her."

"All right, guys." Nadia bumped her hip against John to make room beside him, but he slung an arm around her and kept her plastered to his side, all the while holding the Scot's stare.

"If my honor is at stake," Nadia said. "I intend to be part of the conversation."

"You don't have to marry him, you know," Dugal said.

"Oh my God, you stop it right now, Dugal Cameron." She wiggled out from John's embrace and invaded the scary-looking Scotsman's space. John wouldn't mind having him around for her added protection. According to his file, he was skilled with the battle ax and sword.

"Just saying," Dugal grumbled.

"Shoo." It was cute to see Nadia manhandle her burly

neighbor, spinning him around and giving him a shove. Maybe she could handle them better.

Cute. John grinned.

He hadn't associated that description to a woman in a long time. Cute had no place in his world. It was linked to a lightness of feeling and a smile on his face.

"I brought dinner from the butcher shop," Dugal said as he lumbered off. "A stew Colin made. We're setting up at Stephen's place."

"I'm not sure—"

"We'll be there in five minutes," Garrison answered.

"John, we have work to do." Nadia cocked her head at him and frowned.

"And you need to eat," he countered, and then tipped his chin to where the older guy disappeared. "They just need to be assured that you're fine."

"When did you suddenly become this considerate?"

He smiled faintly. "No idea." But he did. His parents. His mother in particular. Fiona Mason taught her son how to treat a girl right. And that you needed to respect the feelings of the people who cared about her. Over the past few weeks, as Nadia seemed to occupy more of his mind space, it felt like a stranger had taken over the control of his thoughts and his actions. But since returning from Ukraine, John was realizing it wasn't a stranger at all, but the shadow of the man he used to be.

It was a curious and terrifying thought.

***

"So, how long have you known Nadia?" Arthur asked.

"Over a year," John answered.

Nadia felt like she was in an awkward scene of "Meet the Parents." When she and John arrived at her father's apartment, four pairs of eyes glared in his direction. She had no doubt that John could handle the scrutiny, but she was still amazed at how he deflected their displeasure as though they weren't using him as target practice. Even Kelso, on occasion, couldn't hide his irritation when Dugal wouldn't stop harping about the fake protein shit.

"And what exactly do you do?" Dugal stuffed a piece of buttered roll into his mouth. Nadia took that time to serve herself with Scottish beef stew to avoid witnessing the interrogation.

"I'm with Cybercrime at Homeland Security," John replied affably while taking a swig of the stout that Arthur suggested would go with the main dish.

Her dad cleared his throat but didn't say anything. The corners of his mouth were pinched, and she tried to catch his eyes, wanting to let him know she was fine, but Stephen mostly kept his eyes averted.

"I call bullshit on that," Dugal scoffed. "You don't look like you work on that cyber stuff."

John raised a brow. "What makes you say that?"

"You don't look as smart as our girl," Clyde piped in. "I agree, Cameron. I think he's making it up to look good to us."

"Nobody is as smart as Nadia." John smiled. "Which is why our department needs her expertise and assigned me to her. And to protect her as well."

Well played, Mr. Garrison.

"Oh-ho-ho," Dugal chuckled. "Good answer, my man. So, are you firearms-trained?"

"All of us are," Nadia said. "You know that."

"Yes, but can he shoot while under pressure?" Clyde wanted to know.

"What does that have to do with him being our girl's boyfriend?" Arthur asked.

"He said he's not her boyfriend," Dugal said.

The three men at the table gave a start, swinging their condemning gazes to the man on the hot seat.

John sighed.

Dugal grinned. "He says he's her man."

"Oh, that does sound better," Arthur murmured. "One shouldn't use the word boyfriend when the man is past twenty-five."

Nadia always wondered about that, but Clyde answered the question in her mind. "It's because men were usually husbands by that age in my time."

Huh, that made sense. She finally relaxed enough to taste the stew. The sauce was velvet on her tongue, and the beef was fall-apart tender. "This tastes incredible. Give my compliments to Colin."

A devilish gleam entered Dugal's eyes. "See, lass, I told you Colin is the man for ye." He glanced at John. "Strapping lad, my Colin." He smirked. "Closer to Nadia's age too. How old are ye?"

For the first time since Dugal had been needling John, his affable expression disappeared and his eyes hardened. "Forty-two."

Nadia had never been sure about John's age. His beard and hair were threaded with gray, and lines scored the edges of his eyes, but Nadia thought it was due to the challenges of his job because she could attest that his body and stamina belonged to a man in his prime. Of course, *prime* being relative. A piece of beef lodged in her throat, and she started choking as all things sexual starring John Garrison flashed through her mind. Her face warmed and it had nothing to do with the stew.

"You okay, Nadia?" her dad asked when she finally stopped coughing. There was a somberness in his face, a worry. Oh, God, she needed to talk to Stephen. Assure him she was fine. She'd planned to drop by his apartment earlier to personally talk to him, but John had been a tyrant about keeping her mind off the pregnancy tests incident, and the detectives had also been on her ass.

"My Colin is thirty-four."

John seemed to recover from his earlier annoyance, and he grinned one of Bristow's shit-eating grins and raised his beer to the Scot. "But the experience of a mature man is like fine vintage." He tilted his head back and drained his beer.

"True that," Clyde murmured and raised his beer too. "Maybe we should be drinking wine."

Dugal grunted in agreement.

Arthur, eager to ply the table with more alcohol, got up from his chair and went to the kitchen.

Nadia stifled a laugh. Somehow John managed to turn the conversation back to his advantage, while at the same time compliment the men at the table. She stole a glance at Stephen. Even he had a ghost of a smile on his face.

The opening of the Napa Valley cabernet shut the interrogation down when the men started to compete regarding their knowledge of California wines. She was impressed with John's wine IQ, and he seemed to hit it off with Arthur when it came to the tasting notes and the nose of that particular vintage he uncorked. Clyde kept nodding his head while Dugal kept interjecting that Scotland had wine too—the fruity variety.

As for Nadia, she chose a non-alcoholic beverage at the start of dinner because she wanted to get more work done tonight, and partly because she didn't want to get into an argument with any of the guys. No one seemed to want to touch on the subject of her potential pregnancy. She had a feeling her dad had put a gag order on the MoMoS.

Gah, how she wished this uncertainty would all be over.

"Help me with the dishes?" Stephen asked her.

John made to get up, but her father gestured for him to sit. "No, John. Sit. Enjoy the wine. My daughter and I haven't had a chance to catch up after all this excitement started."

"Sure." His tone was uncertain as he cast Nadia a questioning look.

She gave one shake of her head, and started clearing the table, and followed her father to the kitchen.

After donning vinyl gloves, Nadia started rinsing the dirty plates, handing them to her dad who put them in the dishwasher. It was their routine, something familiar they did as they discussed events of the day.

"Are you really okay, *sonyashnik*?" her father asked.

"Absolutely." She glanced at him briefly and smiled before returning her attention to the dishes. "It was just embarrassing you know, having your father know about your sex life." Might as well mention the elephant in the room.

Her dad chuckled. "Yes. I keep on forgetting that you're not sixteen anymore."

"Yes, *Dad*, you didn't have to intimidate my boyfriends."

"They were kids, and it was easy." He stared at the dinner table. "But John is a man who lives dangerously. I worry for you."

"He's not going to hurt me."

"He already did."

"That was a confusing time. Garrison was being *Garrison*."

"And now?" her dad asked incredulously.

"Let me clarify. John was being the no-bullshit CIA officer. That John sitting at that table?" She gave her dad her befuddled look. "You wouldn't actually believe this, but I think there's a human underneath that skin."

"Like the Locke Demon?" her dad asked.

Nadia snorted a laugh and then caught herself. Was that why she was so enamored by the breakout creature of the *Hodgetown* series? "Yes, exactly like our Locke friend."

Her dad studied John again as if seeing him in a different light. "Now that you put it that way. It's possible."

15

"What did you tell Stephen?" John asked when they returned to her apartment. "He seemed to be more ... accepting that I'm sleeping with you."

Nadia laughed. "Honestly? I still think he doesn't like the idea of a guy sleeping with his daughter. But I was able to explain to him that there's more to you than a cold CIA operative."

John closed the back door and slid on the bolt. "I hope you didn't trash my credibility as a super spy."

"Don't worry. Your credibility is intact."

"Thank God." He drew her into his arms, his eyes full of speculation. Her chin was tipped up to him, and a smile tugged at her lips.

They were in the kitchen. And she was reminded of their hot encounter this morning.

His blue eyes narrowed. "There's more."

"It's funny. I couldn't explain that you were more than a hard-nosed CIA officer until I mentioned the Locke Demon to him.

John drew back. "The what?"

An exasperated sigh escaped her. "The Locke Demon,

John. It's the breakout character from the last season of *Hodgetown*. You do know what *Hodgetown* is?"

"Of course."

She raised a brow.

He looked away in exasperation before returning his attention to her. "Theo's show. I've watched a few episodes when I was putting together a file on Gabby's division."

"Of course," she replied with candor. Trust John to be thorough when he was researching a job. "Anyway, the Locke Demon is a creature who used to be a man. Cursed with no emotions and meant to guard the thin line separating the dimension of monsters and humans."

John's eyes grew progressively slitted. "You compared me to this creature."

"Not exactly."

"This unfeeling demon."

Nadia laughed briefly. "The point is, my dad finally understood that there may be hope for you yet."

"What exactly is the problem here?"

"You heard Gabby. She compared you to a cyborg."

"Christ. How callous do people think I am?"

"Hmmm… I remember Gabby saying that Declan said you'd throw your own mother under a bus."

He let out an intelligible string of expletives. "Declan said that?"

The expression on his face begged for closer scrutiny. "You seem weirdly offended."

"And I shouldn't be?" he barked. John let go of her and marched to his duffel bag to unearth a bottle of Scotch. She wondered what else he kept in there, because he seemed like a magician pulling rabbits from its depths these days. He searched the cabinets for a glass, grabbed one, and poured whisky into it.

He seemed really, really … hurt. Hmmn. "I thought you'd be wearing it like a badge of honor."

"I can't believe Declan would say that." He sipped on the whisky.

"It might not be his own words," she hedged.

"And that's supposed to make me feel better?"

"They're exaggerating. And if it makes you feel better, Gabby also added that Declan said you'd risk your life first before others."

"Whatever." He took another measured nip at his whisky and stalked away from her to scoop up his duffel. The impassive expression she hadn't seen on John's face since he returned from Kiev was back. "Which room should I take?"

Wow, he didn't even ask to share a room.

Why was she feeling hurt?

"There are only two rooms and mine is the one beside the kitchen."

He stalked, or rather, stomped away from her.

"Wait. Are you mad?"

He stopped and glared at her over his shoulder. "Maybe. I don't know what I'm feeling anymore."

"Is this about the 'mother under the bus' remark? You know the guys are just speaking metaphorically."

He shot her a derisive smile. "Yeah, but I happen to have a mother I love very much."

With that statement he disappeared into the hallway between the rooms and then she heard the door slam.

But what was reverberating in her head was the weird fact that John Garrison, who many had joked had sprouted from the ground fully formed, actually had a mother.

SINCE WHEN DID he become a fucking snowflake? John thought savagely.

No, it had nothing to do with the 'mother under the bus' remark although that had grated on his nerves more than any insult thrown his way. And there had been many. He was usually a Teflon shield about these things. Nothing fazed him. It was nothing personal, just the job.

He realized he was circling the room like a caged animal, so he sunk into the edge of the bed, resting his elbows on his knees, and linked his hands, flicking his thumbs together to give his fingers something to do.

This was personal.

That was the difference.

Fuck.

He needed to get a grip. The deeper he got involved with Nadia, barbs that didn't affect him before would take on a new meaning. He'd just been compared to a demon for fuck's sakes. An unfeeling demon at that. He was realizing more and more that he had a lot of work ahead of him, but John didn't want to pretend to be someone else.

At least not with Nadia and the people she cared about.

They were going to see the real him.

Except John wasn't sure which one was the real him. Over his long career as a CIA operative, he'd assumed several identities. Each time he would absorb a nuance of that identity after a mission, adding a layer of that person to the core of him and each time that happened, it hardened the shell around his heart, strengthened the compartments in his head. In recent weeks, the shell had started to crack as shades of the man he used to be seeped through those spaces and started manifesting itself in his actions.

Shit, he just left her out there. There was some relief in knowing he could still be an asshole. Shaking his head, he got up from the bed, went to the closet, and slid a pocket door open to stuff his bag inside, but it was a tight fit. Columns of clothes in clear garment protectors took up majority of the space. No. Not clothes exactly. He peered closer. Costumes.

Nadia talked about cosplaying before she joined the LAPD. Is that why he was drawn to her? In some ways, they were the same. They formed a kinship in the way they slid into a second skin. John did it for a job, and he had an inkling of why she did it. It went back again to the time she was twelve.

The puzzle pieces that made up Nadia Powell began to fall into place.

A light rap on the door followed by its opening called his attention.

Nadia ducked her head into the room. "Is it safe to come in?"

An unbidden smile touched his lips. "Smartass. Come in."

She entered the room and padded to his side as he returned his attention to the things in the closet.

"Careful, you might find some of my skeletons in there," she teased.

John chuckled because there was indeed a skeleton body-suit among them. "Was this for cosplay or Halloween?"

"Both," Nadia said. "Speaking of which, Halloween is in two weeks."

There was an open-ended question in her statement, so he cocked his head her way. "No."

"Oh, come on. It's going to be fun. Our division used to have a contest. Now that we've broken off into a task force, it's going to be more intimate."

John didn't answer, but carefully shut the closet, contemplating the wood panel before he leaned against it and faced her. "Convince me."

She grinned. "I'll think of something. Maybe you can go as one of the *Hodgetown* monsters."

"The demon thing."

"Yes, but it's too recent. I don't think they'd have any good replicas."

"You do realize Levi's wife is a makeup and special effects guru on the series," John said.

"Oh my God, you think you can ask him?"

"I was saving my requests to her for emergency purposes." He was opportunistic. John admitted this to a certain degree and knew Levi's wife was a great resource if he ever needed to build a cover—physically.

But seeing Nadia's face light up at the prospect of having access to a Hollywood special effects expert sent a jolt through him. An overwhelming desire to make it his mission to put that expression on her face every fucking time settled inside him. That genuine Nadia smile.

"Okay, okay… wait," she continued. "We might not want to waste it for a simple Halloween costume contest at the office." But then again, the way he could see the gears turning in her head made him wary of whatever scheme she was cooking up in that brain of hers. It was a conundrum. What attracted him to her also terrified him. "StreamCon is happening the week before Thanksgiving and it's in LA."

"StreamCon? Sounds familiar."

"Yes! It's similar to ComicCon but dedicated to streaming networks." She glanced up at him expectantly.

He grew warier. "What?"

"We can go."

"When you say *we*, you mean *you*, right?" John said dryly. "I'll go with you but only one of us is going in costume and it ain't going to be me."

"What do you have against costuming up anyway? You do it all the time," Nadia grumbled.

"Don't want to lose my street cred lumbering around in a one-ton body suit."

Nadia laughed. "Now that'd be hard to imagine you doing. You slip in and out of places with ease." Her brows furrowed. "Which reminds me of the reason I came into this room before I found you snooping through my closet—"

"I wasn't snooping. I was trying to be considerate and not leave my shit lying around. You might kick me out."

"Somehow I think you don't like leaving 'shit'"—she air

quoted the word—"around. Anyway, if we're going to work closely, you need to let me know how to deal with this new John Garrison."

What the hell is she talking about? "I'm still me."

"Hmm … maybe. Why is this the first time I've heard of your mother. Who else knows?"

John shrugged. "Only Bristow and Kade Spear." And the admiral of course.

"Not Declan and Levi?"

"I haven't known them as long as I've known Spear and Bristow." In a way, he and Kade had come full circle. He rescued the former green beret from an Al Qaeda prison when the DoD didn't launch any plan to rescue him. And now Kade had extracted them from the Ukrainian dungeon. "It's not really a secret, but it's not something I'd advertise."

She stared at him for a second longer. "Is your real name even John Garrison?"

"I've been John Garrison for a long time." He kept his focus on her eyes and tried not to stray to the exposed skin of her legs. Legs that were wrapped around his head earlier this morning while he consumed her. Christ, he could still remember her taste on his tongue. He erased the distance between them, still not letting his gaze leave her face. He gently drew her in and lowered his head, loving the way her breath caught, and how her eyes darkened. She wanted him.

He captured her lips in a slow lingering kiss, and then he raised his head, drinking in the features he found so compelling. "Jacob," he said.

"What?"

"Jacob Mason is my real name."

Nadia's slow smile sent a ripple through him. "Well, hello, Jacob Mason."

16

"I'll do it when we get home." Nadia glared at the man holding her coffee hostage. Didn't he know he just put his life in peril? "Now give me that."

"Why can't you take the test now?" John insisted.

"Because I may still get my period later, and it's too early." She extended her hand. "Hand it over, Garrison, if you value your life."

He deposited the travel mug in her hand, and she stalked out the door. "We're running late as it is," she threw over her shoulder, leaving John to lock up since he liked reminding her so much about upgrading the security of her apartment.

Surveillance-wise, she had everyone's apartment wired. And that was Dad, Clyde, Dugal, and Arthur's in addition to her own. What she needed was extra hardware for the doors and to hook those up to what she already had.

John caught up with her just as she reached the staircase. "Relax," he said. "We're driving straight to the scene, and we'll probably get there before Gabby and Kelso. The ATMs aren't going anywhere."

"True, and it could be another false lead," she grumbled. Promising leads in the past week turned out to be dead ends.

A computer glitch here and there, denial of service attacks, and a few incidents similar to the call out this morning had turned out to be ATM skimmers. Her pulse quickened, but what if it was the real deal this time. There were seven reports in a three-mile radius.

"You won't be able to do anything without permission from the bank's IT, right?" John asked.

"Correct. But they usually have their ATM techs already there before they call us. And since it's not a singular bank, that means different IT departments. We're also there to give advice and take their statements. I should have set my wake-up alarm," she groaned. Instead of the smooth crescendo of her morning alarm, the blare of her call-out notification jolted her awake from her position on the couch where she'd been sleeping horizontal with her feet propped on Garrison's lap.

"Someone suggested starting the *Hodgetown* series last night," John said.

"It's good, right?"

"You fell asleep," he reminded her.

Nadia laughed. "I did, didn't I? I've already rewatched season one a couple of times. I swear every time I do, I find an easter egg I missed the first time."

"I hope you're not suggesting I watch it a couple of times. I'd rather you fill me in on what I missed."

"You're such a spoilsport. Did you sleep at all?" she asked. "You should've just left my ass on the couch and gone to the bedroom."

"It wasn't so bad, and I can sleep anywhere," he told her. "Besides, I'd carry you to bed first before I'd leave you on the couch."

When they made it to the ground floor, she said, "Hah! We managed to escape the apartment without Clyde cornering us."

John chuckled. "Think again."

She glanced up from looking for her keys and sighed. Clyde and Arthur were returning from their morning walk.

"A bit late for you guys, isn't it?" she called. John held out his hand for her keys. She hesitated for a moment, but the quicker they made their getaway, the better. He beeped the locks.

"What's the verdict?" Clyde asked.

"Verdict on what?" Nadia knew exactly what they were asking. She yanked the door open.

"Are we pregnant or not?" the older man asked in exasperation.

"Well, Clyde, I don't know yet." She climbed into the Subaru without waiting for his answer. John already had the vehicle backing up.

"Well, when will you find out?" he yelled as they passed the two men.

Nadia just grinned and waved.

John muttered. "The great escape."

That it was.

"You can't dodge them forever. You know that, right?" John told her after they emerged from the drive-thru for breakfast burritos. Nadia was craving them hard this morning.

"I know." She took a giant bite out of one and chased it with coffee.

"You should have done it this morning."

She ignored him and took another chunk out of the wrap, chewed very slowly before she put it down, and turned in her seat to face him. "One more word out of you and I'm going to wait until this weekend—which is three more days—to pee on that damned stick."

The Subaru made a turn on South Highland Avenue.

He glanced briefly at her. "You couldn't wait until Saturday."

"Wanna bet?"

"Jesus, didn't expect this part to be stressful."

"Why are you stressed?" she asked.

"Finding out whether I'm going to be a father or not—that's not stressful? Aren't you even a little anxious?"

Nadia didn't answer. She was trying very hard not to think of the eight pregnancy boxes in her apartment.

"I don't want to be distracted at work."

"Wouldn't you be—"

"Stop it!" she hissed. "You're the one stressing me out. Geez, John."

He exhaled heavily. "I'm not doing this shit right."

They fell into silence. Traffic was starting to back up as they approached Wilshire Boulevard.

"You're always pragmatic," she finally said when their vehicle crossed the intersection. "The voice of reason. Can you be that for me right now? Before I eat myself sick." Her stomach started protesting everything she just put in it.

He reached over and took her hand in his. "I'm sorry, babe. I'm such an ass about this."

"I realize we're handling this situation differently," she said. "It's just that when I missed my period this morning, I kinda panicked." She was still hoping that all the stress since Mexico was the cause of all this. "I just, I just want to reiterate, that if it turns out I'm having your baby, I won't stand in the way of you wanting a relationship with him ... or her. But I don't want you to feel obligated to have a relationship with me too."

John released her hand and clutched the steering wheel with both hands. The temperature in the cabin dropped significantly, and when she chanced a peek at him, every angle of his jaw was stark. What she just said must have pissed him off, but Nadia wanted to get that off her chest. She didn't want him to feel trapped to be with her. Hysterical laughter threatened to burst from her lips at how ridiculous they were jumping the gun on things. She swallowed. She did miss her period this morning.

Oh God.

After another ten minutes of chilly silence, and as they sat in traffic on Santa Monica Boulevard, John said in a measured tone, "I understand where you're coming from, but I'm shutting down that shit right now—

"John—"

"Quiet and listen," he snapped. "Because there's something we should be clear about. Me wanting to be with you has nothing to do with the possibility of you being pregnant. It may have accelerated my timetable but can't say I'm regretting it. I'm actually looking forward to it."

"You are?"

"I am. So no matter what that test says, I'm not leaving your side. Clear?"

Their SUV took the exit for South Figueroa street. Without taking his eyes off the road, he repeated, "Are we clear?"

Nadia exhaled a resigned breath. "Yes." The situation between them was confusing because there were two relationships to consider here. Their relationship with each other if there was a child and, their relationship with each other when and if they decided to make a go of it. At this point, she didn't even have the chance to be clearheaded enough to think.

"Son of a bitch," John growled. Their vehicle swerved and spun a sharp ninety-degree angle just as a black blur blew past the intersection narrowly missing her side. And like in freeze frame, she turned her head toward John, his mouth was moving but his voice receded in a vacuum as her scream filled her ears.

"John!"

A red pickup was barreling right toward his side. Their SUV zipped further, and the pickup rammed them in the rear causing them to fishtail and face oncoming traffic. Nadia held her breath as another Toyota sedan tried to avoid them, braking and sweeping sideways before screeching to a halt a car length from them. A Corvette braked and shoved the Toyota closer to the nose of her Subaru. It was surreal. Like they were in the front seat of a Hollywood action movie watching the unfolding chaos of cars smashing into each other.

But as the pile up in front of them died down, the sound of crunching metal behind them escalated to epic levels.

They whipped around to see what was happening. John was still cursing, already whipping his phone to an ear and using the heel of his hand to steer the Subaru within a metal cushion of stalled cars that were already lodged tight with nowhere to go.

John tossed the phone on the dashboard and turned to her, releasing her seatbelt, and touched her all over. "Are you hurt?"

"No, just shaken." She didn't even hit her head, but her shoulder and neck were starting to feel the burn of the seatbelt.

"Are you sure?" His gaze scanned their surroundings.

"I'm fine." She forced air in and out of her lungs to avert the signs of an oncoming panic attack. "Oh my God, did the …"

"Traffic lights," he clipped.

"This is the real thing," she whispered. Her eyes searched the sea of disabled vehicles, her thoughts turning to the injured, the fatalities. "This is a mass casualty event." Goosebumps raised on her arms. "What if the Crown-Key—"

"You don't know that," he said tersely.

People started to get out of their vehicles, stumbling around in a daze. She was debating the prudence of staying in or getting out of the Subaru.

But John was already on it. "I need to get you to safety.

Don't get out until I come get you." He grabbed his phone on the dashboard and left the SUV.

Screaming and crying replaced the noise of steel scraping on steel. Nadia spotted a woman in the Toyota, trying to get out of the vehicle. She was pounding on her windows. "Help me!"

"John …" Nadia said.

"I'm on it." He yanked open her door and helped her out and rushed her between the remains of pancaked vehicles amidst people wandering around like zombies. She realized why John wanted them to leave the scene.

The smell of gas was strong.

"Get inside the building." He shoved her toward the structure that was beside the roadway. "Get into Cal Traffic Control. Check if they've been hacked." He started running back toward the mangled mess of vehicles, gesturing for people to get off the street. "Go! Go! Go! Get off the road!"

"Hurry, please! My baby!"

The red-haired woman in the Toyota was still screaming. A good Samaritan tried to work the handle, but John could see both sides of the vehicle had sustained damage. They needed to break the glass. The fumes were stronger as he approached the car with the trapped woman.

John unscrewed the antenna from the Toyota. "Stay back! Cover yourself if you can!" he yelled as he pulled his shirt over his head and wrapped it around his hand holding the antenna. Going in at an angle, he positioned it against the base of the window so the tip would strike the center. Pulling it back like a bow he turned his head away and let it fly.

The glass cracked and spiderwebbed on the pane.

"Hit it from inside!" John ordered.

The redhead didn't hesitate and used her jacket to knock

the broken glass into the pavement. She twisted around to grab her little girl and handed her to John.

The toddler started crying.

"Hold her." He shoved the kid to a young man—a good Samaritan. John leaned through the window to adjust his leverage on the woman and hefted her out. The redhead was sobbing in relief and gave him a tight hug. "Thank you! Thank you!"

She collected her toddler from the other man.

"Come on!" John urged, scanning the wreckage of twisted steel for anyone else who was trapped. He shook his shirt out of the broken glass and put it back on.

Sirens echoed in the distance. A blast shook the ground, sending flame and smoke shooting up a few intersections ahead.

The flashing lights of first responders appeared. John blended back into the crowd that congregated in the parking lot of the building where he left Nadia. It was a mayhem of casualties, of people scrambling to help them, and spectators who had their phones filming the scene.

Filming him.

Shit.

"John!"

Nadia rushed toward him and hit him with such force, he took a step back and grunted. "Oh my God, that blast … I was so scared."

He cupped her face and tipped it up to him. "You worry about me too much."

Her eyes flashed, and she punched him on the shoulder. "If you don't want people caring about you, then what the hell are we doing?"

She tried to wrench away from his arms but he held fast. "Nadia."

"Let me go, asshole!"

"Nadia!" He gave her a light shake.

She didn't answer but continued to murder him with her eyes.

"I like it."

A puzzled look came over her face. "What?"

He kissed her lightly. "I like it that you worry about me."

Her puzzlement turned into incredulous amazement. "What?"

Turning her in his arms, John marched her back to the building. "Come on, Miss Powell, there's some sleuthing to do."

"CAL TRAFFIC CONTROL confirmed anomalies in the feedback data of the magnetic sensors in the road strips," Nadia said.

Gabby and Kelso arrived with the full force of the CTTF team. CSI techs and detectives were dispatched to the original call-out locations of the ATMs that had been emptied of cash. Their team had moved to a nearby police station a few blocks from the building where Nadia and John first took refuge.

First responders established a command post in front of the police station. Over sixty cars were involved in the pileup —two deaths reported along with numerous injuries. But because of the vehicle height and weight restrictions on South Figueroa, catastrophic crashes were minimized.

In the station's war room, Kelso was on the whiteboard, mapping out the intersections and the traffic lights that were affected. "So it was localized to these?"

"Yes."

"Explain to me how all those lights turned green?" Kelso asked.

"The computer managing the traffic lights has the ability to send minuscule adjustments to the timings depending on data it receives," Nadia said. "But historical data has been built into its database so it doesn't make knee-jerk reactions to a momentary crush of cars. The data analysts are taking a snapshot of the information that was fed into the system at the time of the anomaly and comparing it to their historical information. We'll get a report soon."

"Where are we on the IT departments of the banks?" Gabby, who was sitting at the end of the table, asked.

"Two banks already sent their initial findings. It's not a skimmer, but a hack that controlled the ATM software and bypassed the withdrawal limit that saw a high balance in a bogus account. The perpetrators also managed to wipe out the surveillance camera footage of every single camera within a half a mile radius of the ATM."

Muttered curses went around the room.

"The Crown-Key did all this?" Henderson asked.

"There seems to be a misunderstanding of what the Key does," Nadia said. "It's a penetration tool. It just finds a way to enter the network and deliver its payload."

"You're saying any malicious software can use the Key to figure its way into the system," Gabby said.

"That, and from what I can see from its source code, it also has the ability to learn the best way to deliver a particular program."

The door to the room opened as John and Bristow walked in. John signaled to Kelso who nodded in return. Kelso addressed the rest of the CTTF squad. "We'll pick this back up at HQ. I imagine top brass will want an update on this ASAP."

Nadia, Kelso, and Gabby stayed behind while the rest of the team exited the room. Henderson, though, was casting suspicious glances at Garrison and Bristow.

"Please don't tell me you have more bad news," Kelso groaned when the door closed.

"Dmitry Vovk left Kiev on a plane bound for LA," John said.

17

IT FELT LIKE A LONG DAY—AND John was used to long days, used to waiting for more information, biding his time to make a move. Fourteen hours since the crash this morning, and they were still at CTTF HQ. But he was also impatient. He could compartmentalize, but at that moment, everything in his brain was focused on the woman he was watching through the transparent glass of the CTTF lab that was Nadia's domain.

She'd been assisting Cal Traffic run some tests to protect their infrastructure from the recent hack. Nadia was halfway through deciphering the source code. These latest attacks on the traffic network as well as financial institutions had been picked up by major news channels. That brought increased scrutiny from the mayor and from federal agencies. Nadia had transferred her data on the bank fraud to the Secret Service.

Bristow, meanwhile, was doing his best taking down videos on the internet of John. So far, only two had shown a clear capture of his face. It was still two too many. Exposure of this kind sounded the death knell for an operative's career, and he wondered what made him throw all caution aside and rush headlong into the fray to help people.

That was something Jacob Mason would do.

His gaze focused on Nadia again, and he checked his watch.

Kelso exited the lab, spotted him, and headed his way. "I told Nadia to go home. She should be done in a few."

John nodded.

"Thanks for your help today and with the DHS," the detective continued. "Nadia would be heartbroken if they'd taken this case away from her. No matter what an asshole Huxley turned out to be, he was still her friend."

"I just cut through the bureaucracy, ego, and bullshit," John replied. It also helped that he reported directly to Admiral Porter. "To send this to DHS would only have us starting from square one. Nadia's prior friendship with Huxley is an advantage."

"Yeah," Kelso agreed. "She put out feelers on the dark web for information. There are several white hats eager to help she said."

His phone buzzed. Levi had been monitoring travel into LA. "I have to get this."

The detective gestured for him to go ahead and walked back into Nadia's lab.

John swiped the screen. "What do you have for me?"

"He's a no show," Levi said.

His muscles locked. "What?"

"The plane's manifest just updated and put him as a no-show. I've accessed the surveillance at the gate the aircraft deplaned and he wasn't on it."

"The fucker knows we're watching him," John said. "How about our contact in Kiev?"

"He assured me he saw Dmitry clear the security gates."

"Follow up with him and see if he's somehow evaded surveillance and returned to any of his residences."

"Already did."

"Also crosscheck his aliases on any flights, from any destination in the U.S. If you don't get a hit, expand your search to Canada and south of the border."

"My search is running now. It's going to take a while."

"Damn. You're beginning to think like me," John said. "Want my job?"

"Not a chance." Levi chuckled then hung up.

He tucked away his phone just in time to see Nadia exiting her lab in brisk strides. She was practically bouncing. He sighed. Kelso had been plying her with caffeine much to John's annoyance. Still, he wasn't about to stand in the way of how she interacted with her colleagues … yet. He understood what was needed.

"Ready when you are," she chirped as she took a sip from the latest caramel macchiato Kelso had served her.

John gave her a quick kiss on the lips. "You look wired."

She raised the sixteen-ounce cup and grinned. That was her third one of the day from what he'd counted and that didn't include the coffee he handed her this morning.

"Obviously." His gaze past her shoulder and spied Kelso locking up Nadia's lab and leaving with a guy from their tactical team named Henderson.

He asked Kelso, "Where's Woodward?"

"You didn't see her sneak out?" the detective asked. "You're losing your touch, Garrison. Declan ordered his wife home."

John raised a brow. "Ordered. Now that I find hard to believe."

"Don't ask," Kelso grumbled. "I don't want to understand or attempt to understand the dynamics of their marriage."

"Good point." He turned back to Nadia and looped her backpack off her shoulder and slung it on his.

"You're that guy from Homeland, aren't you?" Henderson asked, his gaze scrutinizing.

"Yep," John acknowledged the man briefly before

addressing Kelso. "Well, I guess I better take our prized analyst home."

"Take care of her."

John wrapped an arm securely around Nadia. "Count on it."

"I feel so special." She grinned up at him.

Definitely wired.

WHEN THEY ARRIVED at the garage where he parked the Escalade, Nadia said, "Henderson's been asking questions about you."

John had asked Bristow to take him back to Nadia's apartment to pick up his vehicle. Thank fuck it wasn't his SUV that was involved in the pileup. He had a lot of upgrades in his including bulletproof tires and windows which would be useless in a wreck.

"And?" he prodded.

"I told him to mind his own business."

"Sassy, are you?" He kissed the top of her head before letting her into the vehicle.

When he got in beside her and started the engine, she continued, "He's a good tac lead ... well, second to Kelso when he's not leading. He's also very observant. You show up every time we face a real terrorist threat in LA. First with Raul Ortega, second with the Ebola bioweapon mutations, and now this. He said if you were truly Homeland Security, you'd be throwing your weight around, but you always stay in the background." She paused for effect. "He said that's what spooks do. That you're a spook. There's no other explanation."

He drove the SUV out of the LAPD parking lot, getting on Third to head to the 101.

Fuck, he knew this. If he hung around Nadia while she was working this big case, too many people would start to notice. The first time, he let Roarke take the lead. And the second? He remained in the background until the FBI tried to take the case from Gabby, and John had to step in. And now? It was personal as well, very personal, but he was all in.

After his actions earlier today, his CIA career hung in the balance. But what struck him after his weeks of conflict was he suddenly attained clarity.

He cared for Nadia. A lot.

He did want to build something meaningful with her, but he refused to put a label on it yet.

"Let him stew over it," he said.

"Ha! That's what I'm doing. And he knows better than to piss me off because … " She wiggled her fingers. "I hold the Key."

"You're too straight-laced to do anything illegal."

"Ha! Is that why you've been hell-bent on getting me to do illegal stuff?"

"When did I make you do something illegal?"

"No. You call it something fancier like 'rogue operations'."

"Nadia," John said, biting back a smile. "What exactly is in your coffee?"

She laughed before slurping to the end of her fancy-ass concoction. "Probably too much sugar and caffeine. I can't metabolize alcohol well, which is why caffeine is my drug of choice."

They were both skirting the elephant in the room, or rather, in the SUV. Not one word was mentioned about "the situation" since the pileup this morning.

"You'll have trouble sleeping tonight."

"Oh, I'll crash. Don't worry. If anything, I'll keep you company with season two of *Hodgetown*."

John debated on what to say, but he seemed content to let her chatter on about the several leads she acquired on the dark web. He was fascinated by her passion. Usually, he got irritated with techs trying to show off their expertise, but not Nadia. There was something about her. He probably didn't understand half of what she explained, but John hadn't felt this passion in a long time.

He learned a skill because it was what was needed for the job. His initial passion was to serve his country. But as the years rolled by and he had to deal with the scum of the earth, sometimes having to make deals with them just to preserve the greater good, he grew more detached because that was the only way he could stomach what needed to be done.

To preserve the greater good.

His stomach soured at the thought.

"John? Are you even listening?" Nadia jolted him out of his thoughts.

He glanced at her. "You said you had a lead on the dark web."

She huffed a breath. "I've said a lot since then. You just zoned out ninety percent of what I said."

Shit. John guessed it was important for her that he understood her too, but he had a knack for storing information in compartments to access later. *Claims of notoriety.* That's what she said. "There are people who are claiming responsibility."

That seemed to satisfy her. "Can you believe that? We've had at least twenty come in. I need to narrow it down. Maybe tonight. But we have a more urgent matter."

"What?"

"I need to pee."

NADIA RACED INTO THE APARTMENT. John was right behind her and shut the door, muffling the protests from Clyde and Dugal who followed them.

"I can't believe they were waiting to ambush us on the second floor," she groused. "It's almost midnight."

"Where are the pregnancy tests?"

"Can we do it tomorrow?" she cried when he grabbed her arm to stop her from entering the bathroom. "John!"

"We're doing it now," he dictated with a determination and fierceness she felt all the way between her legs. Oh God, she really needed to pee. That last macchiato seriously did her in.

"It's on my vanity. In the bedroom."

"Stay here," he clipped. "Do not move. If you move——"

"John! Will you just freaking get it?"

She danced in place, her bladder about to explode. He came back with two boxes, already extracting the stick from one and giving it to her.

"Take two. If one fails, we have a back-up." He unboxed the other and handed it to her.

"Whatever." With sticks clutched, she ran into the bathroom, slamming the door.

The moment she sat on the toilet, immense relief flowed out from her.

Pounding came from the door. "Don't forget!"

"Not sure I want you for a baby daddy with that bossiness!" she yelled, picking up one stick and doing as he ordered.

"Don't jinx it."

"You … what?" Her voice caught on that statement. Did he mean he wanted her to be positive?

"Don't forget the second one."

"Do you have X-ray vision?" she grumbled, her ire returning. She laid the first stick carefully on a few squares of toilet paper and picked up the second to do the same. When she was done, she got up and washed her hands, and then opened the door.

John was standing in front of the bathroom, leaning against the wall, arms crossed.

"Five minutes." His gaze went past her and zeroed in on

the two sticks that could determine their future. Whatever that meant.

"Oh my God," she mumbled, hands covering her face.

"Yeah," he grinned, drawing her into his arms, one hand behind her head, resting her face on his chest.

She glanced up, and puffed a short laugh. "I can't believe we're doing this."

His grin widened. "Believe it."

"But…"

"No buts, babe, if you're not pregnant, it doesn't change what we're trying to build here."

"What are we trying to build here, John?"

"You and me," he said seriously. "I like the kind of man I am with you."

Her heart somersaulted upon hearing those words, and as much as she thrilled to hearing them, there was still a part of her that threw out all alarms.

A part of her that rationalized how John was all kinds of wrong for her because he was too complicated.

The girl in high school who was never popular and never attracted the attention of the jock.

The woman who overcame all that, who thought she was finally happy in her own skin, until this man barreled into her life and showed her she could have more.

She was teetering on the precipice of heady feelings, not to mention sex with this man was a mind-and-body-altering experience.

And Nadia was just greedy enough to take the leap. Or was she?

John's eyes searched hers. "I know I'm not getting through to you yet."

"I still need to understand what has changed from Mexico until now. You've been you for a long time. How can you suddenly change your nomadic and clandestine lifestyle?"

"Ask yourself that question."

"I love being in one place."

"Yes, it's safe, isn't it?"

Her mouth flattened.

"For years, I was comfortable with who I was," he said. "The jackass who didn't care much about anyone's feelings, with the singular goal to get a job done. People I continue to work with understood that, and, to some extent, we shared the same values which made the detachment easy. Understood that men like me are needed so others won't have to get their hands dirty." He let out an extensive sigh. "But I wasn't always this way. I cared, Nadia, but caring too much got people killed. But … today was eye opening."

"Bristow sent me a video of you being badass while shirtless," Nadia grinned.

John chuckled. "Yeah … today I realized I missed the man I used to be."

"Is that man going to stay?" she asked.

"I hope so."

Not a straight answer, but she didn't expect him to promise anything. Everything was still new between them, even though they'd known each other for over a year.

"So," she said as she turned to look at those sticks sitting on the bathroom counter.

His brows furrowed as he glanced at his watch. "They should be good. Come on."

He tugged her along and together they entered the bathroom, stopping over the sticks that would define how they moved forward.

She stared at them and blinked.

John came around her, hugged her from behind, and rested his chin on her shoulder.

"Hello, mama," his voice rumbled.

Her breath swooshed out.

Two pink lines on one, and the other one said: "pregnant."

18

HE WAS GOING to be a father.

Fuck.

John was excited, and a little bit terrified, but he'd been prepared for this possibility for weeks. He could even say he had hoped for it.

Nadia turned in his arms, chin tilted up, eyes huge. "I'm really pregnant."

"Hey, now," he said in amusement. "Are you claiming all the hard work?"

Her expression grew pensive. "Are you sure you're okay with this?"

John cupped her face so she couldn't look away. "Listen up. I'll admit to the same panic you had when I found the torn condom. But clinging to the hope that you might be pregnant gave me a semblance of self-preservation in that dungeon."

"What do you mean?"

"My objective was surviving and getting back to you," he said. "You heard about the time I nearly got beheaded by Al-Qaeda?"

"Gabby told me about it." Nadia shuddered. "That really happened that way?"

John nodded. "I was reckless at times in wanting to push my enemy's buttons. Call it an instinct, that drive to fulfill a mission at all costs." And no consequence to his own life. "But fear sometimes is good." He stared at her intensely. "My biggest fear is leaving you alone and pregnant."

"That's just it. Will being with me and our baby make you less effective in your job?"

John thought back to all his friends that had recently married. Kade, Roarke, and Walker. His thoughts also strayed to Antonio Andrade—the billionaire who fell for Charly—the CDC's spunky virologist. Complete opposites, but somehow they fell in love. "I think the solution is not putting myself in a situation that makes me ineffective." John had a feeling a different kind of ruthlessness would surface.

"And you're okay with that?"

He grinned briefly. "I think it's time I slowed down. Put down roots."

Nadia still looked doubtful.

"I know you still need convincing, but I'd rather show you than tell you."

The corners of her lips tilted up. "A man of action."

He grinned roguishly. "That's right."

"Let's see what kind of man-of-action you'll turn out to be."

"Hit me with what you've got."

"You'll be at every doctor's appointment and birthing class."

He stilled, and with difficulty, swallowed the knot in his throat. "Okay."

"And if I have any middle-of-the-night cravings, you're going to satisfy them."

"I heard pregnancy makes women horny."

Nadia rolled her eyes.

John chuckled. "Did you realize …"

"That I rolled my eyes … that seems to be the urge with you recently. I finally gave in."

There was a knock on the kitchen door followed by, "Nadia…"

She exhaled a resigned breath. "That's Dad."

"What do you want to tell him?"

"I sort of want to keep this to ourselves for tonight."

"I agree. Although I think Dugal and Clyde were more concerned about the pileup this morning."

"Yes. So, let's just show our faces?"

John agreed and ushered her to the kitchen. Nadia leaned against him, and he figured she was still dealing with the shock of finding out she was going to be a mother.

He yanked open the door and they both stared at their nighttime visitors.

Stephen and Clyde in front.

Dugal and Arthur behind them.

"Are you both okay from this morning's pileup?" Stephen asked. "I know you sent me that text, but that's what's all over the evening news and the images are horrible."

"We're fine," Nadia said.

"I thought I saw your Subaru," Dugal said.

"Yep, that was mine," she answered. "I was just glad John was with me. Otherwise, I would have been t-boned from the side."

"You would have seen it," John said grimly.

"Well, we just wanted to make sure you were both okay," Stephen said, turning to walk away. Clyde was still staring at Nadia expectantly.

John cleared his throat in an obvious way and awarded Nadia's nosy neighbor a look.

"Oh, yeah," the short man said. "We'll leave you both to rest."

"Thanks," John said firmly and without waiting for all of them to turn away, he shut the door.

"Wow," Nadia said as they headed into the kitchen. "You're quite the warden."

"You bet your ass I am. Anyone giving you a hard time, you send them to me." John leaned a hip against the counter as she opened the fridge and ducked in to rummage through its contents. Guess he'd have to get used to his woman always being hungry.

His woman.

He liked the sound of that.

"I hope that doesn't include my bosses at work." Nadia straightened from the fridge with a bowl in her hand.

"You know me better than that," he said, even when he knew it could become a lie. This overwhelming urge to protect her, to be the buffer against anything that could upset her or harm her, surprised him. John was including himself in that assessment.

He erased the distance between them and took the bowl from her hand, setting it on the counter.

"Hey, rule one," Nadia warned. "Don't get between a pregnant woman and her food."

"So you're playing the pregnancy card now?"

"Every opportunity I get."

"Fair enough," he said. "But this is new territory for both of us. There's going to be a learning curve. I may irritate the fuck out of you. In return, you'll give me more gray hair, but what we won't do is blame this pregnancy when the going gets tough between us." At the question in her eyes, he continued, "I'm finding myself protective as hell over you. If anybody complains to you about it, that's not your problem, it's mine. Send them to me."

She looked at him doubtfully. "Not sure about that. You might get me fired."

"Luckily, you report to Kelso and Gabby. They're used to me."

"Still, I don't need you to fight my battles," she argued.

"Don't get me wrong, I feel all warm and dainty when you say these things, but the woman who worked so hard to get the LAPD to give her one of the most advanced forensic labs in the county is itching to kick you in the balls."

He choked on a laugh. "Noted. You wouldn't be the woman I—" he caught himself at what he nearly said. "I'm obsessing about."

Her mouth quirked. She caught that. Nadia picked up the bowl John had snatched away from her and popped it in the microwave.

"What are you eating?"

"I have a craving for day-old, greasy, shrimp fried rice."

"You're very specific."

"I'm pregnant, so be warned," she sassed, then she announced that she needed to take a shower and flounced off. Doors opened and closed. There were two rooms but only that one bathroom in the hallway. The water turned on, and he tried very hard to ignore the stirring in his jeans. How long had it been since he'd been inside her?

Over two weeks, but he had a taste of her this morning, and he was dying for more. She was as fucking sweet as he remembered. He was all kinds of stupid for promising not to fuck her until she made the first move, yet there was still a part of him that wanted to give her that choice. Because as John was finding out, he didn't want to give Nadia many choices when it came to him. In fact, they were sleeping together tonight in one bed, with him wrapped around her.

Dammit. He was some fucking possessive son of a bitch.

Did he care? No.

The microwave dinged with Nadia's food and he walked over to check on it. It was warm enough so he left it in the appliance.

He grabbed a bottle of water for himself and sat at the counter, thinking he needed a shower as well. There was the one and only bathroom in the hallway. He knew Nadia was attached to her dad and the people in this apartment complex, but soon, they may need more room. John needed to plan ahead because that was the man he was. He fished out his phone which was always in secure browsing mode and started to search.

He'd been down the rabbit hole of Westwood real estate when Nadia emerged. She was in sleep shorts and was wearing a shirt, but all John could see was the shadow of her nipples. Her shampoo and soap mingled and he had the oddest desire to dirty her up. Wipe out her clean smell with the scent of sweat, musk, and sex.

Fuck.

"You want to relax in the living room while eating this?"

She declined. "I'll end up watching television and I really want to sleep in my bed this time." Opening the microwave, she picked up her bowl and started chowing down. John returned his attention to his phone, but this time went to a site he bookmarked.

"You should head to bed," she said. "You've had less sleep than I have."

He glanced up. "I'll wait. Because we're sleeping together."

She swallowed the bite in her mouth and sighed. "A part of me wants to say no and not rush into this, but then another part of me says I'm being ridiculous because, hey, I'm already knocked up. It's not like you can get me pregnant again."

John shrugged. "Or you could say it's a matter of principle, and that you haven't had your pound of flesh yet for the times I've been such an asshole to you."

Nadia put her spoon down, rested her elbows on the counter, and leaned forward, her gorgeous eyes narrowed at him. "Is this one of your techniques of getting someone to agree with you?"

He chuckled. "It's hardly a technique."

"No. It's called reverse psychology."

"Is it working?"

"I never thought I'd use these words to describe you, but you can be a charming scoundrel when you want to be."

"Only with you, babe."

NADIA WAS IN BIG TROUBLE.

Every layer she peeled away from John, she was falling deeper and deeper under his spell. His bossiness was catnip. Add in his protectiveness and that roguish charm of his ... who the hell was he hiding beneath that badass CIA persona he'd been showing everyone?

She took a sip of water before spooning more fried rice into her mouth. John had returned his attention to his phone, so she took that opportunity to reflect on the past forty-eight hours.

"I like the kind of man I am with you."

A simple, heartfelt statement that she felt right in her soul. Like John, Nadia had worn many identities not only in her foray into cosplay, but also the many different times she dyed her hair. But with John, she'd uncovered a passionate woman hiding inside her. All her life she loved living in the land of make believe, but in real life? She liked to play it safe. She liked numbers, science, and computer code because it was something that had order and logic. They were quantifiable. She understood now why she was pissed at John when he threw her headlong into the Mexican op. He was pushing her outside her comfort zone. She had a feeling he did that on purpose. He was perceptive. That asshole. But he was her asshole. She thought possessively.

He glanced up from whatever he was scrolling. "We need to make an appointment for your prenatal."

Nadia stopped chewing. "Ah ... I think that's best when

I'm four weeks?" She wasn't sure. Nadia hadn't even opened one website about pregnancy.

"Yes, but the first ultrasound can be done at six weeks," he told her. "We also need to start you on prenatal vitamins, ASAP."

"Okay, I guess you're on top of it," she laughed.

His eyes crinkled at the corners. "So, in about two weeks then." He put down his phone. "I'll try not to make decisions for you, but I know an agency physician I trust."

"John?" She watched him carefully. "Are you paranoid because you have enemies who could get to me?"

He blew out a breath. "I'm trying not to think that way, but Bristow and I have been *made*, and we're not sure how Dmitry Vovk will react to his brother's murder."

"That's on the CTTF. I've read Kelso's report. Kelso dropped Maxim, and the ballistics that belonged to your team were attributed to a Latino gang that had a beef with the Ukrainians. Followed them, and ambushed them when Maxim attacked Kelso."

"I still want to take precautions," John said. "DNI is concerned with what happened with the Automatic Traffic Control System. If that happened to air traffic control, it could be catastrophic."

Nadia had been helping Cal Traffic safeguard their systems all day that she didn't have the luxury of thinking of any other threats. But John once told her the difference between the CIA and the FBI. The FBI was reactive, while the CIA identified future threats, especially those coming from outside the homeland.

She finished her fried rice, and the carbs didn't take long to make her sleepy. The caffeine in her system lost its effect as her brain wanted to shut down. Nadia hadn't slept well in the past few days.

"You ready for bed?" he glanced up from his phone again, alert to her every movement.

"You need to stop doing that," she groused.

His blue eyes widened in surprise or pretend-surprise. "I don't know what you mean."

"Declan said you have the ability to think one step ahead, and it's great when it comes to ensuring the safety of the country. But doing it with me? It's freaky."

His grin turned apologetic. Not really. Nadia was beginning to discern his tells. He was fiddling on his phone because he couldn't wait to carry her off to bed. She could blame it on her hormones, too, because after satisfying the hunger in her stomach, another type of hunger took over.

"I'll try not to act too freaky. I just want to anticipate ... your needs." His gaze turned meaningful.

Oh, boy. He was determined to turn up the heat. Could she at least hold him off for another day? Show some self-control around this man. *Geez, Powell.* Nadia hopped off the bar stool, anxious to get away before she ended up jumping him. "The bathroom is all yours. Sorry if I got all my feminine crap all over it. You're probably not used to sharing."

He caught her arm before she could flee to her room, and she glanced at him questioningly.

"One more thing, babe," he said. "You be you. I'll adapt. Got it?"

She melted a little.

NADIA WOKE up to a wall of warmth at her back and a rod of hardness tucked between her ass cheeks. She dared not move. She didn't remember falling asleep last night. She thought she'd be too nervous about sharing a bed with John for the first time, but she was more exhausted than she realized. After all, yesterday was a lot to pack in.

John had his arm flung over her torso.

They were spooning.

And she was hot ... and not in a good way.

And as much as the idea of spooning with him tickled her heart, the idea of perspiration trickling down her back did not, so she attempted to extricate herself, lifting his arm ever so slowly. But when she tried to scoot away, he tightened his hold and pulled her back to him. He burrowed his nose even deeper into her hair and she felt his chest contract as if inhaling her.

She huffed. He was awake. He was a spy, and probably slept with one eye open.

"I'm hot," she said.

"Yes, you are," he rumbled behind her, but there was laughter in his tone.

"Did you sleep at all?"

"Some. Sleeping with a hard-on is proving quite difficult."

"Are you hoping I'll put you out of your misery?"

"Not at all. No pressure. Go back to sleep. You have another two hours before your alarm goes off."

Was that another attempt at reverse psychology? He let her go and the mattress shifted beneath his weight. Coolness touched her back and she was suddenly missing his warmth. She also switched her position, turning to face him where she could see the outline of his profile.

"I can feel you staring at me." His voice was rough. "Go to sleep, Nadia. You need it."

She closed her eyes and must have drifted off to sleep soon afterwards, because next she blinked, it was morning, and John was gone from her side.

19

"DMITRY SHOWED up in LA early this morning."

With the phone between his ear and shoulder, John tightened the lacings on his boots as he listened to Bristow. He transferred the phone to his hand and stood. Though he spent the night in Nadia's room, he kept his things in the spare bedroom. "Where?" He walked over to the window and peeked out the blinds, spying Clyde and Arthur returning from their morning walk.

"Club Sochi."

"Russian?" John asked.

"Yep. Any idea who he met?"

"No. Levi didn't go in because it was closing time," he told the SEAL.

"Do we know how he got into the country yet?"

"We suspect private charter."

"I need special clearance to tap into NSA Level One," Bristow said.

"I'll get on that," John clipped and ended the call, searched his contact list for Grandpa Earp and swiped the number.

Admiral Porter answered on the third ring. "Any updates on the breach of Cal Traffic?"

"Powell said there were several claims of responsibility. She's sorting through those today," he said. "Dmitry showed up early this morning at a Russian club."

"How did he get into the country?"

"No clue."

Silence, and then. "You need Level One access and it's not for a single subject."

"I need a broader scope of access for my men to figure this shit out," he told the Admiral.

The last Level One access John demanded from Porter was the file on Yehven Skoryk aka Stephen Powell. At the time he met Nadia, he didn't know she was the daughter of a Russian defector, only that the trail of the bioweapon led to Los Angeles. John had instincts for people hiding in plain sight, and when he did do his own background check on Nadia, the previous DNI slammed down his efforts, but had the opposite effect, raising red flags in his head.

So, when Porter took over the acting director position, John demanded the file on Nadia Powell and used that information to blackmail her into helping him on that Mexican op to rescue Ariana.

"You think he came in through one of our Level One assets?" Porter asked.

"He could've. Or we could find an answer if we look for it there."

Level One involved highly classified agency assets. Foreign assets like Stephen who were given new identities, and there were also companies that the agency used to shore up cover identities and move operatives. Most of the corporations were in it to facilitate doing business in foreign countries, which meant they were susceptible to a better offer.

A noise in the apartment told him Nadia was awake. The

only thing John had gotten ready was coffee. They'd have to go drive-thru again for breakfast.

"Okay," Porter said. "You trust your men, and I trust you. I'll clear the access."

"Appreciate that, sir."

After ending the call, he texted Bristow to let him know that the request was granted. John slipped his phone in his pocket and left the room. He'd meet the team after he dropped off Nadia, and probably pull Roarke into the loop. So much for R and R, but clear and present dangers took precedence.

He found Nadia in the kitchen, dressed and ready for the day, pouring the brew in her travel mug. Was coffee okay for pregnant women? He'd need to research that.

"Just one for the day," Nadia said. "Stop glaring at my coffee. I'm sure it's better than having a grouchy analyst."

"That mug is more than eight ounces."

"Oh, shut up," she mumbled.

"Already short-tempered I see."

There was a knock on the back door. John sighed.

"That's dad. He texted to come over, so be nice to him." He headed to the door to let Stephen in.

"Morning, John."

"Stephen." He stepped aside for the man to enter.

"I packed you both breakfast." The older man strode directly to his daughter. "I saw you rushing out yesterday. You couldn't have eaten."

"We woke up late and got drive-thru." Her eyes went to the items in her father's hands.

Her father glanced at John with displeasure.

"Dad, stop it," Nadia snapped. "It wasn't John's fault that we woke up late. I made him watch *Hodgetown*."

"Oh," Stephen replied, still wearing a frown. "How did he like it?"

"*I*," John emphasized, "think it's interesting, but verdict's still out. I just finished season one." He was willing to make a lot of leeway for Nadia's protective father, but John wasn't one to let other people answer for him. And he wasn't about to start now.

"Good," Stephen said. "These are breakfast sandwiches from free-range eggs. I hope you eat eggs, *John.*"

"I eat anything. Nadia, we need to go." His gaze locked with Stephen's. The other man's mouth tightened, but he nodded, backing away.

"I'll catch up with you later, *sonyashnik*. John."

Stephen left the apartment and closed the door quietly behind them.

"Why are we rushing?" Nadia asked. "I didn't see any urgent call out."

"I need to investigate a lead on Dmitry and drop you off at CTTF."

"Oh, all right. I heard you talking in the other bedroom— I wasn't eavesdropping."

John looked at his watch, a little impatient.

Nadia raised a brow. He controlled his urge to curse.

"You know the task force can lend me a car, seeing that my own was sidelined in the line of duty."

"We'll talk about that later," he said shortly. "Come on."

"I hate being rushed," she said. "And I hate keeping you from doing your covert stuff."

"Nadia," he said, transferring his impatience to the act of opening the door. "Let's go."

She gave him a shake of her head and walked out. He followed close behind, making a mental note to get new locks for her. Hell, maybe for her dad's apartment as well. John thought back to the real estate listings he was looking at a few hours ago when his head was in a domesticated cloud until Bristow's message yanked him back to earth and reality.

He was determined to give a life with Nadia a go. He was all in. But having Dmitry show up Stateside was huge and might mean the end to thirteen years of trying to pin the bastard down. For the first fucking time in his life, he was envisioning a future with a woman, and he didn't want his fixation on Dmitry hanging over it.

When they bypassed Clyde's apartment and the man was predictably standing outside, John preempted the questions by muttering, "Rushing…" and firmly grasped Nadia by her bicep, making sure that their path was straight to the Escalade.

"Glad to see you're still an asshole," Nadia commented. "I keep wondering when he'll show up."

Jaw clenched, he let her into the passenger side of the Escalade without answering. It wasn't until they were on the road— after exhaling a long-suffering breath—that he said, "I'm still getting used to your nosy neighbors."

"You said we can't dodge them forever, right? They're a part of my life, John. Granted they can be annoying sometimes, but I like them in my life. Is that going to be a problem?"

"No," he gritted. "Look, I'm not making excuses. I've always been single-minded in pursuit of a case. It'll sort out, all right?"

"Fair enough. But don't be surprised if they're forming bad impressions of you."

"I'm used to bad impressions." He thought back to Stephen's expression this morning.

"And you're doing nothing to dispel that, and you don't have to. But I'm just caught in the middle, okay? Change can't be forced. And I'm not asking you to change, because I know what that feels like, but we're having a baby together, and I just want to bring him or her into a stable environment as much as possible."

That pissed off John. "And I told you not to bring your pregnancy into our disagreements."

Nadia went silent and looked out the window.

When they were about to get on the freeway, he glanced at her. "I don't want you stressing about how I handle your dad and the other guys. I get that they care about you. I may not live up to their standards yet, but I intend to exceed them, but not on their terms, but mine. Got it?"

"They have their quirks, and I'm sure you've done a background check on them. Clyde——"

"I know about his daughter," he cut in. Clyde's daughter died from a traffic accident which could explain the ambush from the merry men last night when they got home. "But don't feel like you're a replacement."

"I'm not a replacement. People care, John. You seem to have a problem grasping that."

"I'll cop to my inability to empathize at times, but it's because it helps me not let emotions rule my decisions. But see my side of it. I'm trying to avoid resentment in the future. I've seen this happen many times when someone tries to be everything to everyone and has nothing left for themselves. They start to resent it."

She didn't say anything.

"I'm just saying we need boundaries, all right?"

Nadia glanced at him then, and he was surprised at the relief he felt when he saw a dawning understanding in her eyes. Then she fucking smiled.

Christ, that was all he needed to start his morning on the right beat.

A genuine Nadia smile.

I'M SORRY ABOUT YESTERDAY. *I just wanted to help my mom, but older brother tainted the program and inserted the worm.*

Help me,

Harriet V.

Nadia stared at the unusual message from the CTTF chatroom. The userid was Anonymous_754, but interestingly enough it was signed. After John dropped her off at her lab, her priority was going through the three hundred messages that had come over their secure boards that served as their tip line.

Nadia marked the message to double-check later.

She was in the middle of wrapping up this task when an aha moment about John's behavior came to her.

Boundaries.

With that one word, Nadia understood where he was coming from. It still didn't mean he was right. It was his CIA training, the instinct to look at future threats. He was preempting the nosiness of the four merry men at her apartment by setting boundaries early with a precision strike—nip it in the bud, so to speak. She shook her head, knowing John needed some help decompressing from what was second nature to him.

Clyde, Arthur, Dugal, and her dad had a median age of sixty-five—far from terrorists conspiring to do evil in the world.

A smile touched her lips.

"Now, who could have brought that smile to your face?"

She glanced up to see Gabby striding through the doors.

Nadia felt like she'd been caught daydreaming, but she just shrugged.

"I knew Garrison was up to no good when he kept on pulling you into his crap." Gabby made a funny face. "Although some of it was to my benefit."

"The first time our team went rogue was for your benefit," Nadia reminded her.

"Yeah." The detective smiled slyly. "So, how is he?"

Nadia's mouth gaped open. "I hope you're not asking me to spill about how he is in … you know. I mean, do you hear me asking personal stuff about Declan of the sexual nature?"

Gabby laughed. "You have a point there. It's just that

Garrison is this anomaly. I couldn't imagine any woman putting up with his steamroller personality."

She hunched behind her computer screen to hide her smile, but she remarked primly, "Some women may dig that."

Her swivel chair went spinning as Gabby whipped it around, the detective's shocked comical face almost sent Nadia into a fit of laughter.

"Tell me," Gabby lowered her voice conspiratorially. "Is he like ... one of those Doms?."

"What? No! He's just ... a lot..." Nadia faltered, feeling her cheeks flame.

"Aw, come on. I was hoping you could give the kinky scoop on Garrison."

Her brows knitted together, suddenly feeling protective of him. "Why?

"You know, so we can hold something over his head. He conveniently has dirt on all of us while he remains controlled and detached."

"He's not as controlled as you may think, and that's all I'm going to say about it."

"Who's not as controlled?" Kelso asked, walking in and joining the two of them.

"Garrison," Gabby said.

"Yeah, that man doesn't know what hit him." Her partner winked at Nadia.

"What am I missing?" Gabby demanded.

"If you didn't keep disappearing every time your husband crooked his finger, then maybe you'd know what's going down between Powell and our favorite spook. John hung around all evening to take Nadia home," Kelso continued. "And, from what I've gathered, he dropped her off this morning."

"Don't you have something better to do?" Nadia snipped.

"Just looking out for you." Kelso's sincere expression warmed her heart.

"So, this is getting serious?" Gabby asked.

Is getting pregnant serious enough? Nadia didn't say. "We're taking it slow." She almost choked on those words.

And she knew better than to fool these two detectives because they were staring at her dubiously. So she tried to distract them. "Aren't you all going to ask if I have any lead on our cyber actors from yesterday?"

Gabby snapped out of her I-know-you're-lying stare. It was funny how she always played the bad-cop when she and Kelso were doing their good-cop-bad-cop routine. "What do you have for us?" she asked, switching to all business.

"A couple of white hats said a new malware emerged from their pen test on universities and government agencies with weaker security. They sent me a sample of the code and parts of it look like a copycat of the Crown-Key source code."

"Are you saying …" Kelso started.

"That someone might have the device. But, like I said before, it can only contain certain modules of the source code at a time."

"Because Huxley was paranoid?"

"Depends what you mean by paranoid. But if it's having a device with all the power then yes. He was wise to keep it separate."

"Anything else?" Gabby asked.

Nadia turned in her chair to show them the message from 'Harriet V'. "I don't know why there's something about this message that grabbed my attention."

"Because Harriet is apologizing, not bragging," Kelso said, staring at the message again. "She wanted to help her mom. Is this about money? The ATM thefts?" He paused and tapped the back of Nadia's chair. "We haven't looked in-depth at the backgrounds of the employee roster of Hux Technologies." He glanced over at Gabby. "Wanna go over them now?"

Though they were able to get a warrant for the employee roster, it was tougher to get the personnel files on them, so CTTF decided to do their own data collection via their driver's licenses or social security numbers. Any further background check would require the employee's consent, especially medical records. But Nadia was confident the detectives would be able to infer information with what was readily available to them until a further warrant was needed.

Besides, suspect number one was Cain Morris. John had provided his link to Maxim. The man had been low profile. No hits on a credit card or any online transactions. Morris probably had a separate identity ready and had vanished.

"Yes, but my bet is it's still Morris," Gabby said.

"But he's not a hacker. He must have had help," Kelso said.

"Sisters? Brothers? Cousins?" Gabby said. "Harriet could be anyone to him."

"He's got a sister," Nadia said. She'd looked quite a bit into his background. "Estranged. Husband with three kids. An event planner."

"And his parents are both deceased, so it couldn't be the mother Harriet is referring to."

"We're looking at this wrong," Gabby said. "Send all the files you have on personnel. Maybe we didn't ask the right questions when we interviewed Morris's colleagues."

Hux Technologies was in limbo. For a company that made millions, it had a very lean staff. A total of thirty people. Fifteen of them were his software engineers, but Ken was still the brains.

"Many of them were told not to leave town while the investigation was ongoing. A few of them are already applying for jobs elsewhere," Kelso said.

Henderson took that moment to sprint into the lab. "You won't believe who walked through our door."

Gabby and Kelso turned to their tac team leader.

"Dmitry Vovk."

20

"John, you can't just walk in there."

Levi James grabbed his arm as he was about to barge into the building that housed the CTTF. When he received the call informing him that the head of the Odessa Order strode into the last place he expected the man to be, John dropped everything he was doing. He had Bristow pack up their shit, and they raced to get to Nadia's place of work. It was a wonder that the highway patrol hadn't pulled them over.

He shook off Levi's hand and began to prowl in front of their vehicle.

"Just think. Whatever's going on in there you *do not* want to show your face. You think he doesn't have your picture and Bristow's in his files."

John recalled the phones held to their faces when they'd been captured. It had been the most exposed he'd ever been. Bristow was conspicuously quiet, as if he understood his turmoil.

It wasn't that Dmitry Vovk was in CTTF.

It was that Nadia was breathing the same air as that bastard, and he wanted her nowhere near him. "I'm good."

He threw up his arms to warn Levi off and scrubbed his face with his hand. "Text Gabby and Kelso that I'm outside."

He whipped out his phone to see if Nadia responded to his text about not going anywhere near the Ukrainian mob boss.

Thank God, she responded. "Okay."

When he glanced up, Levi and Bristow were both staring at him. "What?"

"What's up with you?" Levi growled. "I know you've had a hard-on for Vovk for a while, so I can't believe you'd blow our cover by rushing in there."

"Cover's already blown. He knows who I am."

"Not as John Garrison. You and Bristow were traveling under assumed identities that your Ukrainian contact gave up."

John was rarely wrong. He was also rarely in a place ruled by emotions, by fear, and by his attachments. He never expected to be so sorely tested today. And yet he owed it to his team to know where his head was.

"Nadia and I have a serious thing going."

Levi crossed his arms and glanced at Bristow, whose face was relatively neutral. "You knew?"

The ginger-haired SEAL shrugged. "Garrison gets chatty when stuck in a dungeon about to be packed off to Siberia."

"Somehow I can't believe that," Levi said.

"Ahhh, there were extenuating circumstances," Bristow smirked. "But, it's the first time I've heard him say it's serious."

John debated telling them the exact situation, but Nadia wanted to keep it to themselves and she hadn't told her father yet. He was going to respect that.

"I'm new to this … thing." Hell, he even couldn't say *relationship*. "So, thanks for stopping me."

But both men had such irritating grins on their faces, John wanted to smash their heads together.

Levi's attention dropped to his phone. "They have Vovk in an interview room. Nadia's already behind the one with a two-way mirror, observing and crosschecking Vovk's statements. Figured you want in?"

"Hell, yeah."

After a beat, Levi said, "One of their guys will escort you in."

"Be on the lookout," John said as he started for the CTTF HQ. "And raise Roarke. It's time to pull him into this."

"Shit, are you sure you want husband and wife on the case?" Bristow said.

"It's bound to happen sooner or later," John threw over his shoulder.

"He's right about that," Levi said to no one in particular.

THE GRAY WOLF of Odessa sat on the opposite side of the two-way mirror. Chills went through Nadia as she stared at the man. His eyes were almost silver like he was blind. His hair was also threaded with more gray than black. His face was hewn in so many harsh angles it couldn't be called handsome, but one couldn't help but be fascinated by the feral edges that sculpted it.

And he was huge.

He should be called a bear more than a wolf, but Nadia could see how he earned his nickname. Vovk was a common surname in Ukraine, which meant wolf. His brother Maxim was tall, lean, and was the handsome one with a head of blond hair. Nadia had been sure they were half-brothers or not even related, but tracing their familial lines proved they shared the same parents.

"Is it inconceivable that I would want my brother's body back? Give him a proper burial?"

"Understandable," Gabby said. "But how exactly did you come into the country? There's no record of your entry."

"I have friends in high places."

"And would these friends in high places know about the illegal activities of your brother?" Kelso asked.

The Wolf smiled but didn't answer.

There were four Vovk brothers. Maxim was the youngest and the black sheep. The other two were entrenched in Ukrainian politics.

Dmitry, on the other hand, was very private. Little was known about the forty-eight-year-old mobster since he withdrew from the public eye following the failed assassination attempt of Ukrainian presidential frontrunner thirteen years ago. The Order, a secret society, was implicated. What was known was that they defined the rules of the Ukrainian Brotherhood—a hybrid organization of criminal and legitimate business activities.

The door to the observation room opened, and she felt John before she saw him. He took his place by her side. She glanced at him, but he was transfixed on the person in the interrogation room. Another chill passed through her. In profile, the iciness of John's features was evident. As much as she'd seen him with a poker face, she knew this was not it.

Cold fury radiated from him.

"Has he said anything of consequence yet?" he asked.

She returned her attention to the interview room. "No."

Kelso pressed, "Mr. Vovk?"

"Am I under arrest here?" Dmitry asked.

"Maybe. We have no record of you arriving in the U.S." Gabby said. "Can we assume you came in through illegal channels?"

"I did not." Vovk's smile was all teeth, reminding Nadia of the big bad wolf. "And it's better if you keep your nose out of what you don't know."

"Shit," Garrison muttered. "They need to stop that line of questioning now."

"Why?" she asked.

"Just text them."

Kelso received her message but continued to stare at Vovk for a few seconds longer. "Fair enough."

Gabby backed off as well, receiving the same message.

For the first time, Vovk stared directly at the two-way mirror, gaze piercing. "Who do you have back there?"

"Someone who can double-check if you're lying," Kelso said. "Why don't you answer why Maxim ambushed my vehicle? Was the traffic incident yesterday payback for his death?"

Vovk's attention swung back to the detectives. "This is what I intend to investigate after I bury my brother."

"We're doing the investigation, Mr. Vovk. It would help if you cooperate," Gabby said.

He leaned forward and sneered. "Then who murdered the rest of my brother's men? The news said the Colombian gang. My brother had no problems with them."

"Yes, but the Ukrainian Brotherhood does."

"There are many factions—" he started.

"And your Order oversees them," Gabby cut in. "So don't tell me you don't know shit about what's going on."

The Gray Wolf leaned back in his chair, flicked his eyes to the two-way mirror again and then said, "Is that what your analyst tells you?"

Nadia froze.

John moved closer to her side. Their arms almost touching.

"Face it, Mr. Vovk, after what happened with the bioweapon fiasco a couple of weeks ago where several of the Brotherhood were arrested, your secretive society isn't a secret anymore. Is your brother an assassin? Sent to terminate everyone who was involved in exposing the Order? Is that why Maxim went after Kelso?"

"You know nothing about the Order," Vovk spat and surged to his feet. "We are done here. Either charge me with something or let me go." He looked directly at the two-way mirror again. "And tell your analyst to be careful where she treads."

Shit! Nadia's hand flew to her throat.

"Son of a bitch," John bit out.

"That seems like a threat," Kelso said, then added. "And we never said our analyst was a woman."

The Gray Wolf grinned and walked around their table and approached the double mirror. "Nadia Powell. I am a man who likes knowing what he is walking into." He turned to face Kelso and Gabby and chuckled derisively. "So paranoid. Your names are on the LAPD's organizational chart."

Nadia exhaled a brief laugh. "Oooh, that man is good." She glanced at John. "I don't want to be locked in a room with him."

"That'll be over my dead body." His eyes never left Dmitry until the crime boss left the room.

"John?" He looked at her and she was frowning. "Did I miss something?"

He gave a shake of his head. "No. It's good. He just wanted to get a rise from the detectives."

"Okay."

"Bristow and I will continue our work here. Fill me in on what you've found."

———

HER NERD LAB had a full house. After Dmitry left, Bristow and John set up shop in one corner. Kelso was behind Nadia as she typed away on her keyboard, scrolling through her messages in the chatroom.

"Sally Davis is on Huxley's software development team. I

have a note here that you interviewed her right after Ken was murdered," Nadia told Kelso.

The detective stared at the photo on screen. Brunette. Big-framed square glasses. Bangs and straight shoulder-length hair. "I remember her. I visited her house. She was distraught actually."

"Did you ask her about Cain Morris? It's not in your report."

"She didn't say anything relevant. I did remember her saying that she was worried about losing her job with her mother in the hospital."

Nadia scored the report and saw his footnote about it that Sally hardly had any interaction with Morris.

"She's quite shy," Kelso continued. "Not a people person. One who liked to fly under the radar. Typical nerd."

"Hey, are you bashing my people?" Nadia interjected. "I'm not anti-social." Saying that, her attention flew back to the screen. "Wait a minute. I know her."

"From where?"

"Huxley's party. John?"

Garrison came up behind her while Bristow took to her side with his laptop on his arm.

"Do you recognize her?"

"She looks familiar. She was in that crowd surrounding Huxley."

"Yes, the one who asked about StreamCon." She glanced at Kelso. "Definitely my people."

The detective rolled his eyes.

"Why are we looking into …" John squinted closer at her screen. "Sally Davis."

"We're looking into possible perps who may be in a financial hole," Nadia told him. "I flagged a possible legitimate claim of responsibility from a Harriet V. Kelso pointed out that Sally Davis's mother is in a coma at the hospital and is on dialysis. Calls to Sally go to a disconnected phone."

"Which hospital?" Bristow asked.

"Downtown Medical," Nadia answered. If there was going to be unlawful hacking into medical records, she'd leave it to John's team.

"Hold on a sec," Bristow said.

Nadia sat back and waited. "It's handy having spooky friends." Kelso snorted behind her.

After a few minutes and lots of patience, Bristow finally said, "Seems like a bill payment came in this morning. They were overdue for a while."

"The evidence is circumstantial," John said.

"Then I'll pay Miss Davis a visit and maybe some of her neighbors." Kelso was already walking toward the exit. "Yo, Woodward!" he called to his partner as the door to the Nerd Lab slid closed and muffled his words.

"Okay, what else have we got?" John said.

"Nadia, have you started tracing the IP where that 'Harriet V' message came from?" Bristow asked.

She shook her head. "It's almost impossible to trace since it came in through the Onion router. I've attached an IP tracer for the next time 'Harriet V.' logs into the relay chat," Nadia said. "But if she's on Huxley's design team, she'd be prepared for that."

"No need." Bristow grinned and moved closer, as though conspiratorially. "I thought John had given you the keys to the kingdom."

"What?" Her brows furrowed.

"I was going to, but then you spoiled the surprise, knucklehead," John said dryly.

She swiveled around and glared at him. "What surprise?"

"NSA Level One! I can't believe you were holding out on me!"

John swallowed a smile as Nadia grumbled at him. They left the CTTF headquarters after his revelation. Bristow followed behind them in the Expedition. While Kelso and Gabby pursued the Sally Davis lead, Levi continued to trail Dmitry. His last message to John was that the Order boss left the county coroner's office and went back to his hotel.

Nadia checked the database. Maxim's body was scheduled for release tomorrow morning.

"You didn't require that kind of access before," he told her.

"So the rumors are true! Intelligence agencies are slyly funding some of the servers on the ToR network."

"I'm not confirming or denying."

"John!"

"All I'm saying is you have a backdoor to trace that IP, but we need to use my network access to get to those servers."

"Does Bristow have access?"

"He's an agency contractor. Of course he does."

"And I'm what exactly? Your side piece?"

He cast her a brief glance of amusement. "You're so sassy today, and you can't blame the caffeine."

"Maybe it's the lack of caffeine, so be warned."

John barked a laugh and caught himself. His unrestrained laughter sounded so foreign to him that it left him bemused. He gave her the side-eye again, his mouth still threatening to break into a grin. And then he let out a breath.

Driving down Sunset Blvd and then making a turn into Westwood, he was hit with an epiphany. He adored this woman. Every single quirk, every bit of her personality—even if she appeared to have several. But who didn't? John certainly did. That was why he connected to her immediately. Add to that her intelligence. He derived immense satisfaction in feeding her appetite in shiny things of the technological kind. Which was why he wanted to punch Bristow earlier for spoiling his surprise.

As they approached her apartment, a tiny pinch of guilt nagged at him. The look on Clyde's face imprinted in his mind. The man's face lit up when he saw Nadia this morning and started to dim when John brushed him off.

Fuck. What was wrong with him? These things hadn't bothered him before, but then again, they were usually people who were used to it or humans of the unsavory kind. But those four men in the apartment mattered to Nadia. John cared about her and by extension, he should include them. But was it a hardship? No matter how grudgingly he hated to admit it, he was growing fond of those meddling old farts, even the big Scotsman who would rather see John hanged, or drawn and quartered given a chance.

"We should tell them tonight," he said.

"I'm not going to pretend to misunderstand what you mean, but you meant my pregnancy."

"Yes. I didn't think you'd want to wait to tell your dad."

"Normally, people wait four weeks to tell family and twelve to tell the rest of the world."

"And it would be cruel to tell Stephen and make him keep it from his buddies."

Nadia laughed. "Especially after the pregnancy test fiasco, I'm sure they're all impatiently waiting."

He reached across the console and took her hand and gave it a squeeze. "Then we tell them."

When they arrived at the SkyeLark apartment complex, Clyde's unit appeared to be dimly lit. The raucous noise on the rooftops told them where they were.

"There's a chill in the night. Big Dugal takes every opportunity to tell Scottish folk stories around the fire pit."

"Sure hope there's food," Bristow said behind them.

"You can be sure there's whisky," Nadia said.

"You can't drink alcohol," John told her.

Bristow's mumbled "holy fuck" made John shut his eyes at his blunder.

They stopped in their ascent, and he turned to face the SEAL. Flabbergasted was an apt description for Bristow's face.

"Holy fuck." The SEAL repeated and then glanced at Nadia. "You're pregnant."

"Uhmm…" Nadia mumbled.

Bristow burst out laughing and smacked his thigh. "Fucking hell, G. This is priceless. Wait until the guys—"

"You will say nothing."

"But"

"Zilch." John did a slicing motion across his throat. "Got it?"

The SEAL's eyes danced with humor. "But … you should be proud. Oh man." That could be tears of mirth at the corners of his eyes.

Son of a bitch.

"We're telling Stephen." They resumed their ascent.

Nadia looked over her shoulder at Bristow. "You would have found out anyway."

"I'm honored," came his smartass reply.

He unloaded to Bristow in that Ukrainian dungeon. Guess the man deserved to be the first to receive the news.

"For a spy, you sure have a big mouth," Nadia informed John cheekily.

He grunted. That was a terrible lapse, and it made him uncomfortable that he had let his guard down when he got too comfortable.

When they arrived at the rooftop to what appeared to be a huddle around the fire pit, he tamped down the urge to retreat with Nadia to her apartment and start working.

All sets of eyes went to the woman beside him, and then to John, and then, finally, with curiosity, to Bristow.

The regular four men were present. There were also the additional two who John knew were Dugal's sons Colin and Alec. John's resolve to be nicer was put to an immediate test. He couldn't help thinking that the big ole Scot was trying to matchmake his sons to Nadia. Tear her away from the hands of the interloper—him.

It didn't help that Nadia emitted an excited cry as she wiggled out of his hold and rushed to greet them.

"Alec!" she gushed at the dark-haired one that was a carbon copy of his dad. "Did you just get back from Scotland?"

"Aye, lass, and you're as bonny as ever." The younger Cameron engulfed Nadia in a bear hug.

He rolled his eyes at the affected brogue, at the same time wanting to yank his woman back into his arms.

Nadia oohed and giggled. "I like that accent. You need to try out for that new Highlander series."

"Aye, that's the plan. That's why I did some immersion to prepare."

"Hand her over, you knave." Colin pulled Nadia from her brother's embrace and gave her a squeeze and a kiss.

Bristow moved up to John's flank. "Easy, killer."

He grunted even as the edges of his vision started to haze in red. Or maybe it was green.

"Have we entered into a Robert the Bruce alternate reality?" his friend chuckled.

"Tell me about it."

"Now, lads, you don't want Nadia's man to be breaking your noses for hugging her too long," Dugal stepped forward and held out a tumbler to John. "You haven't tasted whisky this good. My boy brought it back from Scotland."

John accepted the glass. He'd definitely be needing a drink.

Dugal turned to Bristow. "You're flame-haired like my Colin."

"Irish," the SEAL replied.

Thankfully the Scots and Irish usually got along. John had enough of having Nadia being sandwiched between Dugal's two sons who seemed to ignore their father's warning.

"Babe," John cut in. "Shouldn't you say hey to Stephen." He flicked his attention to the two men who eyed him with a mixture of amusement and hostility. "Name's John. Nadia's man."

"Take note. That's not boyfriend," Clyde called out as he and Stephen approached.

"Boyfriend is for boys," Dugal piped in. "John's got that right."

John's grin was smug. So that was all it took to swing Dugal to his side. He exchanged handshakes with the younger Scots. There may had been a test of strength in their grips, but he was used to it. Alpha posturing was so common in his line of work.

"Dad," Nadia greeted Stephen and then moved on to kiss Arthur and Clyde on the cheek.

"Have you all eaten?" her dad asked. "We had an early dinner and didn't know that you guys would come home early."

"We've come home to work actually," Nadia said, glancing at John. "But we can hang a bit, right?"

John shrugged. "No rush. You've put in a lot of work today already."

"Have a drink at least," Alec said. "Got one that's been aged seventeen years."

John took a nip of his whisky. "This is good stuff." The smoke and body was definitely top-notch. "However, Nadia can't have alcohol."

The four older men perked up, their mouth parting in expectation.

The younger ones glared at John.

"You controlling arse." Colin advanced menacingly toward John.

Alec cracked his knuckles. "Aye, looks that way, bro."

What was it with these Scotsmen always on the ready to brawl?

"You two stop it." Nadia insinuated herself between him and Dugal's boys.

It turned out to be the wrong move because John's protective instinct roared to the forefront. Everything happened so fast.

A fist went flying straight for his face, and John automatically yanked Nadia away, shoving her into Bristow.

He threw up the other arm to block the blow, the glass in that hand shattering on concrete. That left his torso wide open for Alec to throw a punch into his solar plexus, stealing his breath. John folded over, gritting his teeth, because his bruised ribs from two weeks ago still stung. He exploded with an uppercut, catching Colin under his chin. Spinning, he threw a back kick that nailed Alec at the hip, sending him careening onto his ass.

"Jesus Christ!" Dugal bellowed as he waded into the melee and dragged Alec up by the scruff of his shirt.

Nadia was immediately at John's side. "Are you all right?"

He would be damned before he admitted he was hurting, so he exhaled slowly and smirked. "Yeah."

She wheeled around and yelled at Dugal's sons. "What the hell is wrong with you two?"

"They're being protective, lass, and are already a wee bit into their cups." Dugal scowled at his boys. "Still no excuse. Shame on ye all. Yer mother would be turning in her grave."

In the midst of this, the other three older men edged closer, waiting patiently for the mini-brawl to come under control. Stephen broke away from the trio and approached Nadia. "Is there something you both want to tell us?"

She grinned at her dad and took her place at John's side. Linking their hands together, she smiled. "Yes. The tests are positive."

John put an arm around her and grinned crookedly at the guys. "We're pregnant."

Nadia glanced up at him, her eyes seemed to gleam in the firelight. He lowered his head and kissed her.

"Should we kick his arse for that?" Alec wondered.

"Shut yer mouth," Dugal growled.

When they faced their audience again, John's eyes zeroed in on Stephen. "I'll take care of her."

"Is he going to make an honest woman out of her now?" Clyde wondered.

Dugal crossed his arms and puffed his chest. "But, of course."

Stephen and Arthur exchanged a look before awarding John their expectant gazes.

He may be sweating a little, and he definitely needed another drink.

Thankfully, Nadia rescued him from answering. "Guys, I'm only a little over two weeks pregnant. We wouldn't have mentioned anything if it hadn't been for that pregnancy test fiasco."

"What pregnancy test fiasco?" Colin wanted to know.

"Apparently, John bought eight pregnancy tests," Dugal said. "I wasn't around, but the paper bag tore and spilled them out in front of Clyde's apartment."

"Man, I'd hate to be in your shoes right now," Bristow said behind him. "But this is so entertaining."

John glanced over his shoulder. "Fuck off."

"I don't want to make a big deal out of it yet," Nadia wailed. "We're not supposed to tell anyone until twelve weeks."

"Och, lass, you think you could keep it from us? We'd never stop pestering ye," Dugal said. "Don't worry, I'll make sure we feed ye right so your bairn will be strong and feisty."

"Why don't we drink to a healthy baby?" Arthur announced and then looked at Nadia. "I can make you a non-alcoholic one."

"John, may I hug my daughter?" Stephen asked.

He chuckled. "As long as I can have her back."

Nadia's dad smiled and opened his arms. His daughter dove into them, and they hugged each other tight.

A knot backed up in John's throat and he thought about his own mother. He was going to break the news to her soon. But he knew once he told Fiona Mason she would be a grandma, John better have his shit together.

Alec came up to him and handed him another dram of whisky. "Congrats, man."

"Thanks."

"Let me get this straight," Bristow said. "The man steals and hides the Selkie's …"

"Seal skin," Dugal offered.

"Right, so he can force the Selkie to remain on land and become his wife."

"Aye, but she eventually falls in love with him."

Nadia hid a smile behind the glass of hot apple cider. The Selkie Wife was one of Dugal's favorite tales of these mythical creatures from Scottish folklore. A seal that can shape-shift into a person—usually a beautiful woman who captures the heart of a human male.

Bristow scratched his trim beard. "Yeah, and they have kids, but after a few years she eventually finds the seal skin in a trunk and returns to the ocean."

"Aye, it's her true nature."

"And she leaves her family behind."

"Aye." Dugal finished his dram of whisky. "In some versions, the mother still shows herself to her kids when they are playing on the beach."

"And the husband sits by the fire grieving the loss of his love." Bristow shook his head and grinned wryly. "Man, that's some tragic tale."

Dugal guffawed. "Most Scottish folklore involving romance between shapeshifters and humans rarely ends well."

Everyone laughed.

The menfolk were getting along, gathered around the fire pit and passing around the bottles of whisky that Alec brought home from the Isle of Skye and Talisker. John never left her side, though. Nadia suspected he was keeping Dugal's sons away, which was funny because she was already pregnant with his baby. There was no reason to be possessive.

"I believe there's a metaphor there," Stephen said.

"Let's hear it," Dugal invited.

"I've heard you tell this story so many times, but I wonder why I never get tired of hearing it."

"I never get tired in the telling of it either." Dugal smiled a bit drunkenly.

"The seal skin is the wife's true self." Her father fixed his spectacles. The fire reflected in them, but Nadia could feel his gaze on her. "Many times we put on different skins and invent personalities in our search for happiness, but somehow in the end we're not truly happy unless we embrace our true nature."

Nadia raised her glass to her father. "Way to go, Dad. Is that your sideways method of reprimanding me for all the money I spent on cosplay costumes as a teenager?"

"You were finding yourself," Stephen said. "And you were a good kid. You made the grades; that was your reward."

"From Knightress to Black Widow," she said. "I do have lofty goals."

Alec waggled his brows. "I remember you in that bodysuit."

John's laugh was a bit maniacal. "And I'd stop right there ... lad."

"Halloween is coming up," Colin piped in. "Do you have a costume yet?"

"I have yet to look." She threw the man by her side a mischievous look. "John is dressing up as the Locke Demon—"

"Not a word," Bristow cut in. "I haven't watched this season yet." The SEAL smirked at the man beside her. "But John as our demon ... now this I wanna see."

John shot to his feet. "Wow, look at the time." She cringed at how fake he sounded, and Bristow, who had a finger over his mouth, was trying not to react.

"This was fun," he continued. "But Nadia said she's got work to finish up, so we're turning in."

"Make sure she doesn't sleep too late," Clyde said.

John didn't answer the older man but gave a nod. Nadia noticed he'd been more tolerant toward the menfolk in general, so maybe he was able to resolve his boundary issues on his own. It must be his skill in adapting to any situation.

She was also surprised the others hadn't asked questions when Bristow went inside her apartment with them, but maybe they were suitably imbibed that they didn't think it was strange. She already thought to say that Bristow worked at Homeland, too.

Although Nadia wondered how long she could keep her stories straight. They needed a cover for John, Bristow, and everyone who worked around them that would hold up to scrutiny.

They settled around her kitchen counter.

"Okay," she demanded, rubbing her palms together in anticipation. "Gimme."

"Depends," John drawled, cocking his hip beside the counter and facing her so Bristow couldn't see his expression. The smolder in his eyes sent a pulse of heat between her thighs. "What are you willing to do to get that Level One?"

"Christ," the SEAL grumbled. "Do I have to ask for tips from Kelso on how he handles the flirting between Roarke and Gabby?"

Ignoring Bristow's quip, and without taking his eyes off her, John pulled his laptop from his duffel of magic tricks. "Here. Use mine for now. Your access hasn't cleared yet and since your laptop—"

"Isn't agency vetted." Nadia extended her arms. "I know the drill. So, gimme."

"Just so you know, Garrison's never let anyone touch his personal devices," Bristow said.

"I'm very protective of my personal devices," John deadpanned and turned over his laptop.

Nadia gave a shake of her head at the double meaning and booted up his machine. A shiver went down her spine when he came up behind her, not even bothering to hide that he was crowding her deliberately.

"I'll pass if it means losing my personal space," the SEAL laughed. "Seriously, do I need to be here?"

A login screen popped open with a skull and crossbones and a warning that misuse of that property was subject to prosecution on charges of treason.

"Uhm…" Nadia said.

"Here." With both arms around her now, he typed in his

access credentials and then authenticated using his phone. When the screen dissolved into the desktop one, Nadia inspected the icons that were available. None of the programs were familiar. It wasn't a stretch that it was created solely for the CIA. The shiver in her spine became a thrill of anticipation.

High technology and a sexy spy … Nadia was extremely turned on. Maybe that was why John had Bristow stay. So *real* work could actually be done.

Her eyes zeroed in on a program, and she instinctively knew it was the one she needed.

The OnionShaver.

To negotiate the Dark Web with anonymity, many of its clients used The Onion Router software called Tor. She clicked on the icon and the screen transformed into a hologram map of the world, but quickly adjusted and zeroed in on the west coast.

"This might take a while," Nadia said. "I've identified several exit nodes for Anonymous_754."

"You're talking about the final server that reassembles the message?"

"Yes." Network traffic analysis was time consuming because of the millions of packets going over the wire which was why Nadia wrote a program that could parse the data specific to what she was looking for. Still, the volume took time.

"So what do we do next?" Bristow said.

"Identify the hops that Anonymous_754 use," she replied. "Judging from how long it takes the packets to travel, I'm thinking four, but …" Nadia grinned with glee as she poked around the OnionShaver program. "I have a feeling the app simplifies this." The data could hop from Los Angeles to another node in Canada, and then bounce off to Russia before heading to its target destination.

"Bingo," Nadia whispered as the path of the first IP was revealed on the screen—a location in New York.

"Holy fuck," Bristow muttered.

"I'm assuming you're getting somewhere," John said with amusement.

"Yup," she said. "This is still going to take a while."

"How long?" John asked.

She glanced up at him. "I guess you never used this app."

A brow arched. "Does it look like I know that shit?"

"I don't know, John, it looks pretty basic," she teased. "But in answer to your question and with the rate it's going, two hours?"

"All right," John replied. "Maybe we should get more comfortable in the living room."

Seventy-five minutes later, while John was watching the second season of *Hodgetown*, Nadia's tracing returned with a familiar address.

"Stop the episode," Nadia said, sitting up straight on the couch beside John.

Bristow got up from the armchair adjacent to hers and went behind her. "You got something?"

"Not an exact street address, but the coordinates put it around the vicinity of Club Sochi."

"Damn, the club Dmitry went into yesterday?" John asked.

"Yes."

"Interesting." He thumbed through his phone. "Levi said Vovk checked into his hotel and hasn't left."

"I have a line on him." Bristow tapped around his keyboard. "He ordered room service. Do you want to know what he had for dinner?"

Nadia could only shake her head again at the illegal surveillance activities these guys were doing. Well, illegal if you weren't the CIA. They operated under the as-long-as-you-don't-get-caught code, which sounded thrilling to her.

Maybe that was why she was attracted to John. She wanted to live vicariously through his experiences. And that was why she was so pissed at him—because he was pushing her before she was ready to shed the skin she'd donned over the years since finding out Stephen was a Russian defector. Was she, indeed, like the Selkie who was ignoring her true self? Did she really want to live on the edge? Maybe a little?

"Has he made arrangements for a flight back to Kiev?"

"Ooh, I can tell you that," Nadia jumped in. "He's booked tomorrow on Oceana flight 314." She glanced up from her screen. "Have you guys found out how he got in?"

"Yes," Bristow said. "Evan Wagner's private plane."

"Why does that name sound familiar?"

"Primeflix," John said.

Her eyes widened. "Wait, we're talking about Evan Wagner the former action star?"

"Yup."

John glanced over his shoulder at Bristow. "See if Sochi is a hangout for Wagner."

"Already did. And it is."

"Was he there last night?"

"Checking."

While the two men hashed out Wagner's whereabouts, Nadia was staring at another message that came into the CTTF chatroom.

It said: "Lisbeth freed the reporter from the basement."

This time it wasn't signed.

22

"ARE you sure you're up for this?" John asked by her ear.

Embracing her from behind, he was a wall of muscle engulfing her in security for this undercover op. They were standing in line to enter Club Sochi. It was Saturday evening, two nights after they discovered where Anonymous_754's IP had pinged. Her arms wrapped over his own, and she squeezed them, assuring him she was raring to go. John had his misgivings about her participating in this mission because of her pregnancy, but she managed to convince him that there was no other officer who would be perfect going in as his partner.

Gabby was too recognizable for the Club Sochi crowd and decided to stay in the comms van with Bristow. Declan and Levi were not entering the club but were keeping an eye on the perimeter.

For this op, going as a couple attracted less suspicion. She leaned slightly and gave him a quick kiss. "Of course."

"If you're uncomfortable, just tell me. We've got backup."

Ahead of them in the line was Kelso with Henderson playing his wingman.

"Yes, but I'm the only one who can deploy the Wasp."

Nadia was excited to test her new toy; yet another reason why she was hellbent to be on this operation.

The second message from Anonymous_754 finally made sense of the first. Sally Davis verified her identity with her knowledge of Huxley's fondness for Lisbeth Salander. Her first "Harriet V." signature was in reference to a character in "The Girl with The Dragon Tattoo" who was being abused by her brother. The only purpose of that message was to verify her knowledge of Huxley and then inform them about her mother, making sure she was receiving care.

Speculation was that Cain Morris kidnapped Sally to operate the Crown-Key. Club Sochi had an exclusive dance floor in its basement level. It was quite possible she was being kept in one of those rooms with the device. It wasn't unheard of for mobsters to use clubs like this to hide their business dealings. It would hardly raise a brow for organized crime personalities to make an appearance. It was the perfect business to move drugs, launder money, and hide illegal transactions.

The line to the club moved, and Kelso and Henderson were allowed through. It was an exclusive club that was very selective with who they allowed to enter so Nadia dressed with care.

Her black dress had a plunging neckline and long sleeves to cover her tattoos. Its asymmetrical skirt crisscrossed mid thigh in front while it skated longer to a point in the back. Classic satin black pumps with four-inch heels completed the look that was sophisticated yet edgy. A red wig styled in a classic vintage wave covered a part of her face. Her skill through years of cosplay came in handy as she spackled on foundation and contouring product to rework the angles of her face.

John, on the other hand, wore a dapper black suit with a crisp white dress shirt, no tie. His hair was tousled to contrast with his previous look of a seventies mob boss. Taking advantage of the shadow and light of nightclub lighting, he changed the contours of his face with makeup as well. John finished his look with a pair of glasses, leaving Nadia in awe of this master of disguise. Not even a scholarly look diminished his sex appeal, but she could be biased.

The whole purpose was to thwart facial recognition software that technologically advanced criminal groups like the Argonayts were using. There was a possibility that Cain Morris was in there and watching.

In the past three days that they'd shared a bed, they hadn't had sex. Well, the second night, Bristow stayed over late, and there wasn't time for any sexy shenanigans. The night before when they had a mission briefing, she was too exhausted to feel sexy. John actually ordered her to bed since tonight was going to be a long one.

So here they were, standing close together, bodies touching, teasing. There was something to be said for being fully rested and having the whole day to relax and primp for the evening. How her life had changed in the past few days. Homicide, cybercrime, finding out she was pregnant. John moving in with her and declaring he was making her his woman. All of that was a lot to take in.

"Have I told you how beautiful you are tonight?" John's husky voice sent delicious chills snaking up her spine.

"Might I remind you guys that you are on comms," Gabby interrupted.

"Thank you, Woodward," Kelso said dryly.

"Payback's a bitch," John remarked. "Twenty on any of our targets?"

"Negative," Kelso replied. "But we're only at the entrance. It's slow moving."

A part of their briefing before the op was getting familiar with the different possible disguises of Cain Morris, Sally Davis, and Evan Wagner.

The bouncer at the door spied Nadia and John who were

about ten people away. He pointed at them and signaled them over. Ten pairs of eyes glared at them for skipping the line.

The low-cut dress was meant to show off the cluster diamond necklace that hung below her cleavage. She was almost afraid to wear it because it was the real deal. Her discerning analyst eye, that had inspected evidence involving jewelry in other cases, placed the price of the rope on her neck north of six figures—probably even seven if it was designer. Apparently, the bouncer at the door had a trained eye as well. Hopefully, that meant they had a chance of getting into the basement level.

As they entered the club, the bombastic bass of techno-music vibrated around them. They weaved through the crowd to get to the expansive circular bar surrounded by high-top tables. Off to one side were regular tables and exclusive booths, while on the opposite side, people writhed and swayed to the music on the dance floor. They arrived at the bar that was three people deep, but John managed to find the tiniest opening and positioned her against the bar with him actively shielding her.

He ordered a Scotch neat, while she ordered a virgin piña colada. They spotted Kelso and Henderson at the opposite side of the bar in conversation with two women while surreptitiously observing the crowd as they were. It was too loud to speak through comms, but she knew she had to deploy the Wasp soon, so Bristow and Gabby would have eyes in the club.

But not yet.

They needed to play club-goers first.

"Can't wait to dance!" Nadia yelled into John's ear. She probably deafened the people in the comm van. She raised her arms and shimmied her ass against John's crotch.

"Finish your drink, sweetheart, and we can have fun."

In front of them and past the high-tops, people bounced to the music and more than a few were out-of-sync with the beat, but no one cared. Glasses clinked, laughter and chatter swirled around them, and with the backdrop of pulsating music, everything coalesced into one rip-roaring club scene. No wonder this place was so popular.

After about ten minutes of dancing in place and feeling John's erection growing harder against the softness of her butt, she turned around and pressed her breasts against his chest. "How about it, old man?" she teased.

That got his brows cinching.

Laughter erupted in their comms.

"You have what it takes to keep up with me on the dance floor?" she sassed.

The gleam in his eyes was enough to make her wet. Nadia was in trouble, and she was excited.

"Ready when you are, baby," he drawled with a smirk, embellishing his own endearment for her as they slipped into their roles.

He took her hand and led her to the dance floor.

"Don't forget to deploy the drone," Gabby yelled.

Oh shit. She laughed and made a u-turn, leading John toward the ladies' room.

"Whose bright idea was it to get these two lovebirds on an op?" Declan cut in. "Are we going to get anything done?"

"Speak for yourself," John shot back.

They passed Kelso and Henderson who were already dancing with their choice of partners for the night.

Once they slipped into a dimly lit hallway, John pushed Nadia against the wall and started kissing her. It was part of their act, but when his tongue pushed through her mouth, her body ignited, and the acting went up in flames. John tore his mouth away only to scrape his teeth over her jaw, his fingers gripped her thigh and pulled it over his own and let her pussy ride his leg.

"Are we still acting?" she breathed.

John groaned, "Is it on this leg?"

"You guys better not be fucking," Gabby warned.

"Yes, under the garter," Nadia moaned. But his fingers bypassed the lacy band, and slipped between her thighs, using his knuckles to rub against her panties over her clit. She moaned again. He didn't say anything, but his chuckle let her know that he loved finding her wet.

"This is like listening to a live sex-show," Bristow said.

"John's got the moves," Gabby commented.

"How do you know that?" Declan asked.

"She didn't tell you, man?" Kelso asked.

A muffled "What?" came over their comms, probably from Kelso's dance partner.

Gabby told her partner to mute his mic.

John's fingers slipped through her garter and extracted the tiny drone and then, after giving her mouth one last kiss, handed her the device and lowered her leg.

"Whew, that was hot," Nadia said, more for the benefit of teasing the people on comms.

"Powell, I'll have you know that that was very unprofessional," Gabby deadpanned.

"It was John's fault." She twisted the drone and let it fly. "Okay, it's up."

"Getting a read … and …. have control," Bristow said.

"Take care of my baby," Nadia warned.

John slung an arm around her shoulder and pulled her close. "And I'm taking care of you, sweetheart."

Everyone grumbled.

———

JOHN COULDN'T REMEMBER the last time he was in his element and loved what he did. He was used to playing roles, but it was always a job to him. This time? Everything he did with Nadia, he felt it. As he suspected, she had it in her to be daring, she just needed to break free of the old constraints she'd developed over the years. It turned out Nadia had to come to it in her own time.

And now, to the drumming beat of a sexy Caribbean tune, they were rocking their hips together in the thrust and roll rhythm of sex. With her leg wrapped around his hip, her pussy was wet heat riding his thigh. Gazes locked, searing each other with a promise of what was to come while they continued to grind against each other.

Nadia broke eye contact and buried her face against his chest, and he held her tight as she shuddered against him. Shit, he was aching to drive into her and feel her clench around his cock, but there was work to be done.

The blatant display of sexuality was a ruse to get them into the basement level which was whispered to be more than a dance club. It was rumored to be a swinger's heaven. People looking to swap partners for the night. Over his dead body. No one was going to get their hands on Nadia except him. But for the first time since he'd begun clandestine missions, an unsettling ambivalence gripped him.

So far, the drone hadn't picked up shit from anyone on the main club level. Bristow was reluctant to send it to the basement because underground spaces didn't offer good signals. They didn't want to send Nadia's new Wasp into its depths without a manual retrieval.

His watch buzzed with a notification from the club app. They'd been selected.

The music and the lights in the basement were more subdued. Large and small booths surrounded the dance floor that was cornered with scantily clad women dancing in metal cages. The clientele was distinctly foreigners—European, Asian, and Middle Eastern. Most of the men were in suits, the women in skin-tight clothes with short skirts and heavy makeup. He was glad Nadia didn't exactly stand out and both of them blended right in. At that moment, his Nadia was channeling a Russian trophy girlfriend to a lucky bastard like him. He dimmed his presence, hanging back, letting his shoulders slump. They'd practiced his cover. He was a successful tax accountant with questionable clientele, and she was an aspiring actress.

As the hostess led them to a small booth, John could feel eyes on them. Probably some asshole already marking Nadia as a target. The dance floor in front of them was unlike the one upstairs where it was crowded with writhing bodies. Down here it was couples in a slow dance. Two women were dancing in front of a booth as the men chatted and did business.

"Are you here to meet someone?" the hostess asked as she slid the menu and a card to them.

"Just observing," John said.

The hostess frowned. "I don't understand." She glanced pointedly at Nadia.

"Shit," Bristow said through comms. "They're expecting your accountant persona to be a mail-order bride broker and are bringing Nadia to one of the customers."

Adapting to changing situations on an op wasn't new, but acting as Nadia's pimp started an itch at the back of his neck.

"I have a few offers," he said smoothly. "After a drink, I'll display the merchandise." He winced as Nadia's nails dug into his thigh.

The hostess smiled widely. "Very good, sir."

"What would you like, *moya dorogaya.*" He turned to see Nadia smiling sweetly at him.

Her fake smile. Fuck. "Just a Shirley Temple."

"Your best Macallan for me."

When the hostess left them, laughter erupted through comms.

"Nice save, G," Bristow chuckled.

"What the hell did you get us into, John?" Nadia groused.

"Minor setback," he said. "Get moving, Bristow. The

drink will buy us time, then I'll lead Nadia to the dance floor to buy us more."

"On it. Moving the Wasp down the hallway to the private rooms. There's a whole network of corridors down there... and more rooms."

"A sex club?" Gabby wondered. "I'm checking the blue-print of the building, and it's not matching what the drone is picking up. It's supposed to be one hallway with rooms that end. But the Wasp seems to have gone through where a wall was supposed to be."

"What?" Bristow interjected. The two conferred between themselves. "Yes, I'm checking our GPS against our drone. It's in the next building."

"They're connected underground?" John asked.

"We can't investigate without drawing attention," Nadia said.

The hostess returned with their drinks and left again.

"There's a restroom in the corridor that will lead to the next building," Bristow said. "Think you guys can check that one out?"

Nadia took a sip of her drink. "Yes."

"I'll follow you after a few seconds," John said. "Make it look like we're getting our freak on and indulging in some kinky shit."

"Before you hand me over to some pervert buying a mail-order bride?" Nadia asked dryly.

He shot her a hard look. "Never."

NADIA WALKED through the hallway with trepidation. It was oddly empty and dimly lit.

Initially she was pissed at what John said to the hostess about displaying the merchandise. But as she was learning from John and in his line of work, you adapt to the situation.

So here she was—adapting. When she walked away from their booth, she did it with sass and might have overdone it a bit. She took the long route to the corridor, strutting past the booths, and feeling strangely empowered. It was because she knew John had her back.

"Looking good, Powell," Gabby said with pride.

"I wish I could see," Kelso said after almost half an hour of radio silence. "I guess we weren't kinky looking enough."

"Powell looked like a wet dream," Henderson added.

Someone growled over comms.

"I'm bringing the drone back, so we can watch you," Bristow said.

"What did you see back there?"

"A bunch of offices and definitely some living quarters," the SEAL replied.

Nadia reached the ladies' room and glanced over her shoulder. "Where's John?"

"Fucking hell," John muttered.

"Checking it out," Bristow said. Nadia saw the Wasp fly past her. It was barely visible since it camouflaged its appearance with the mirrors making up its body.

"Okay, I'm going to—" Nadia broke off when her eyes caught movement and she came face to face with a young woman.

"Holy shit." It was Sally Davis.

"Didn't mean to scare you," the woman said, then nodded at the bathroom door. "Are you heading in?"

"Oh, sorry." Nadia recovered and opened the door letting Sally go ahead.

"Where did you come from?" she asked the newcomer.

"I work in the back offices," Sally said, before disappearing into one of the cubicles. Nadia's disguise must be holding up because there was no trace of recognition in the other woman's eyes. Nadia decided to take care of business as well.

"Powell's talking to someone. Cough if it's one of our targets." Bristow said.

She cleared her throat.

"Is that an affirmative?"

She wanted to snap but realized that wasn't what Bristow told her to do. She coughed.

"Nadia has Sally. And fuck, the man talking to John is Evan Wagner. Things are happening, people."

"Who has eyes on Nadia?" Kelso demanded. "John can take care of himself."

"Roger that. Swinging Wasp back," Bristow said.

There was a flush from the other cubicle, so Nadia finished up as well.

Stepping out, they both washed their hands. Sally had her eyes downcast, not looking at her.

"So, what do you do, exactly?" Nadia asked.

Frowning, Sally glanced up. "Why are you interested? You're the first ever to ask me."

"Just making conversation. You look …" Nadia grasped for words. "Like you need to talk to someone."

Everyone groaned on comms.

"What? Like I'm pathetic?" the other girl's chocolate eyes flashed.

"No… I didn't mean …"

But, at that point, Sally tore out of the ladies' room. Nadia hurried after her.

"I didn't mean—" Nadia repeated, but she was suddenly caught in a steel trap.

Rancid breath exploded under her nose as a man in a dark suit jacket and a cream turtleneck pinned her against the wall.

"Where are you going, *moya dorogaya*,?" The Russian endearment that sounded sexy coming from John's lips was downright creepy coming from this man sporting Elvis sideburns and glazed eyes.

A jumble of voices erupted in comms.

Nadia jerked her head to the side, spying Sally who backed away, a torn look on her face. Another man came into view behind her, and she registered a possible build for Cain Morris, but the sloppy kiss that landed on her neck and the fingers sliding under her skirt had her on the defensive.

"Powell's in trouble," Bristow alerted everyone.

"How much?" the man slurred.

"Not for sale, asshole." Nadia managed to slip her arm between them and used the heel of her hand to keep the man's face away, trying to get into a position to knee him in the groin.

"Let me—"

The man's weight disappeared in a blur of motion.

John was there, and he had the man up against the wall by his neck. "You dare touch what's mine, *mudak*?"

Nadia's assailant wasn't a big man, maybe five-ten, and John had fifty pounds of muscle over him.

"I'll pay!" the man choked.

"What's going on here?" a voice said beside them.

Nadia barely hid her gasp. It was Evan Wagner in the flesh. The image on file didn't do him justice. He used to be a popular action hero back in the day. Interesting because he wasn't very tall but obviously kept in shape. He was in his fifties but appeared to be in his late thirties with his boyish looks.

"My girl and I are leaving." John was speaking with a Russian accent.

"Come on, man, let's have some drinks and talk about this," the Primeflix executive said. "My associate just got a bit too eager."

John let the man go, grabbed Nadia's hand, tugging her along, and invaded Wagner's space. Two burly black-clad men flanked the executive.

"There's a misunderstanding of what I'm offering. It's

certainly not prostitution. Miss Petrova is here to find a suitable husband."

"Ahh, yes… and many clientele here are willing to offer marriage, but they want to be certain of … the merchandise."

Nadia glanced at John. He'd used the same term when describing her, but someone else using it had him looking ready to explode.

"I do not want him." She edged closer to John and his arm wrapped around her.

"*Konechno, malyshka,*" John murmured and gave a kiss on her forehead.

Wagner eyed them with interest. "It seems you're attached to this one." He glanced over his shoulder and signaled to someone. A woman with straight, glossy, blond hair stepped up beside Wagner. The girl couldn't be more than twenty despite the heavy makeup on her face.

"I have young Belina here. She's Romanian." Wagner swiped his tongue on his lower lip. "Maybe you would consider an exchange for the night? We have private rooms in the next building." His eyes raked Nadia from head to toe.

"Holy shit," Henderson groaned. "I wanna see."

"Get your ass out of there, Garrison," Gabby ordered. "This op is over."

John gripped her fingers convulsively, causing her to whimper in distress, and although he loosened his hold, his rapidly fraying temper crushed against her.

"Not tonight. Maybe we'll return." John tucked her to his side and brushed past Wagner.

"It's a one-time offer, Mr. Stratford. This level is very selective."

"You can stick that offer up your ass," he muttered for only Nadia to hear. "We're outta here and never coming back."

23

"I'm reviewing video footage from all exits. Several vehicles exited the garage of both buildings when you were talking to Wagner," Bristow said.

They all congregated in the comm van. Nadia was still wired from going undercover with John and she was still bouncing with excitement. This was so different from when they went to Huxley's shindig. He was undercover, she was playing herself, and they had no surveillance at all.

"Can you confirm that who you saw with Sally was Cain Morris?" the ginger-haired SEAL asked her.

"I can't. He had the same build but sported a buzz cut and a beard. The Morris we know had a crew cut and was clean shaven. If that was him, he's changed his appearance."

"We can assume it was him. Should we get a warrant to search the premises?" Kelso asked.

"On what grounds?" This from Gabby. "Whatever evidence we have so far has been obtained illegally. And we can never use the IP address as a reason because that would alert them that we have a way of tracking them. That would open a whole can of worms I don't think the CIA wants exposed."

"You bet your ass," John seethed. "I want to nail those fuckers to the ground as much as anyone else, but that would jeopardize not only this op, but many others that use this back door to the Onion Router."

Nadia frowned. He was still strangely seething. She understood his fury when he rescued her from Wagner's handsy associate, but they escaped unscathed. It was all part of going undercover, right?

"Mail-order brides are not illegal, and neither is the kinky shit they're doing down there," Kelso said. "The prostitution argument can be a gray area. We need more evidence."

"It may be possible Morris saw through Nadia's disguise," John said. "It's one thing to blend into the crowd, another when isolated in a hallway like that. The light was dim, but men like Morris work on hunches and take precautions. My gut says he's in one of those vehicles that exited the building. Can you isolate the license plate?"

"Working on rendering," Bristow said.

"My take? He'd be prepared for that as well," Kelso said. "He'd probably ditch the vehicle or switch license plates."

"Okay, let's back up a little," Nadia spoke up. "We're concentrating on Morris too much but Wagner is right there. No way does he not know what Morris and Sally are doing."

"Excellent idea," Gabby said. "But I might have to recuse myself from investigating him simply because he was one of the executives who refused to expand the budget of *Hodgetown* in the recent Revenant Films deal."

"Really? But *Hodgetown* is so big right now," Nadia said.

"Right? It doesn't make sense," Bristow added.

Gabby sighed. "Something about the direction of the company. He said production costs are too high because of the special effects and those expenses are being passed to Primeflix. Wagner said he wanted more human-interest drama-type series, but no one is giving it to him."

"He's such a hypocrite. He made his name in action movies," Nadia grumbled.

The team agreed to wrap up, take Sunday to regroup, and would pursue the Evan Wagner angle on Monday.

It was around three in the morning when they arrived at the apartment. John was still strangely quiet on the way home, which was unusual for him. He was the only one who hadn't told her she did a great job. All kinds of thoughts raced through her head. Did she fail his standard of undercover work? They were nowhere near closing in on the Key, but they did uncover a different angle.

After he let them into the apartment, he went straight into the kitchen and grabbed two glasses, filled one with water and handed it to her. "You need to hydrate."

His jaw was still hard, and a muscle jumped in his cheek.

She took the glass, noting she was indeed, thirsty. "I'm sorry we didn't get to investigate the other room."

"It's fine." A terse response.

"I'll look more into Wagner tomorrow."

His eyes flashed with something like anger. "I'm with Woodward. Take tomorrow off."

Nadia, meanwhile, had had it. She took another sip of water because this might be a long tirade. She lowered the glass on the counter. "Look, I'm new at this undercover crap, okay? I'm not expecting to get it right the first time and get a pat on the head—"

John's face morphed into unmoored rage, and she took a step back. His glass slammed on the counter, and it was a wonder it didn't shatter. He grabbed her by the shoulders and yanked her forward. "You think that's what I'm pissed about?"

"Well … yes—"

"I'm pissed because I failed you!"

"What?"

"That stupid fucker touched you."

"John, you can't control everything." He was withdrawn

because of that? "And I have self-defense training. I would have kicked him in the nuts if you hadn't intervened. It's part of the job, right?"

"When it comes to you, it's not," he spat. "You're pregnant with my child." He let her go and turned around, raking his fingers through his hair. "What the hell were we thinking?"

That pissed her off and she gave his back a shove. He turned to face her.

They glared at each other.

"Oh, because I'm pregnant? I can't do this kind of work anymore? Fuck you, John!"

He lowered his head and snarled, "You can't do *this* kind of work."

She reared back. It was like he'd slapped her.

John let her go and gave her space, his hands resting on his hips, looking down and everywhere except at her.

"What are you saying?" she pushed through gritted teeth. "Now that I've tried to give it my best shot, it's not good enough?"

"Haven't you been listening? I was the one who fucked up." He stalked away from her so fast, he was already yanking her apartment door open before she registered that he was leaving.

"What the hell, John?" she snapped, hurrying toward him. "You take one step out that door and you negate every promise you've made regarding making this work."

He paused and glowered at her. "Our professional work shouldn't interfere with our personal lives."

"Why? When I'm right smack in the center of both. Given our line of work, scenarios like these are bound to come up again, so why not hash it out now?"

"Nadia ..." He shut the door, scrubbed a hand over his face, and said, "This can't happen again."

Confused, all she could say was "What?"

His face darkened. "Tell me, Nadia, would you have gone with Wagner to his special rooms?"

"No."

"Because if you were truly an agency operative, you would have gone all the way."

Nadia swallowed as bile settled in her gut. "If I wasn't with you, would you have gone with that woman?"

"It burns, doesn't it?" he taunted, backing her against the console table and caging her in. "The few seconds I imagined Wagner's hands on you, I wanted to tear him apart right then and there."

"Well, would you?"

A dangerous gleam entered his eyes. "What do you think?"

She tried to shove away from him, but he kept her in place. "Fuck you! I don't have time for these games."

"And you're pissing me off," he said under his breath. "If you believe after what I said about making our relationship work that I'd turn around and sleep with another woman—"

"But your job—"

"I'll adapt," he told her. "For one thing, I haven't used sex as a weapon in years. And second? Remember I said I wouldn't put myself in situations that would make me less effective?"

"Yes." Her eyes dropped, and she stared at the base of his throat.

John tipped her chin up with his finger. "I didn't consider a scenario where you were in the thick of it. Tonight was my fuck up, but you were a pro."

Okay, that made her feel better, but why was John still looking at her as if she'd committed a federal crime. "So … I did well?"

"You did better than well." His mouth came close to hers, a scant hair's breadth away, but it was as if he was still taunting her, teasing her. "You played your role so well in making me crave you, made me want to fuck you in front of them to show them who you truly belong to."

Her heart pounded, and the area between her thighs pulsed with wet heat. Her high from the op turned into a baser need, and John's hand slipped under her skirt, his fingers making their way to her damp panties, stroking the slit between her legs. With their faces close together, their gazes still locked, his knuckle rubbed against her sensitive core.

Nadia closed her eyes. She was on the verge of coming. "That ...oh my God, John."

"Tell me yes, babe," he murmured.

Her eyes shot open in confusion, then she remembered his promise not to fuck her unless she asked him.

"Fuck me," she breathed.

His eyes flared, and before she knew it, she was boosted up the console. John worked his fingers between them, and she heard the clinking of his belt, the lowering of his zipper. Nadia looked down at the swollen head of his cock that seemed as angry as he was. She glanced up and the unbridled lust in his eyes stole her words. His next move stole her breath.

Not even bothering to remove her thong, his finger nudged it aside and he dropped her on his cock. Nadia gasped, the fullness impaling her. With his hands under her ass, he lifted her and then let her weight take care of the downward motion.

He did this quick-like. She was bouncing on his cock.

"Look at me," he ordered.

She did.

His lips curled back in a feral snarl. "This is it, Nadia." A sheen of sweat appeared on his brow as he continued moving her up and down his cock. "Mine. You're completely mine. This body," he panted. "This body was meant to climb only mine. This pussy," he growled. "Will only know my cock from now on."

Her teeth clattered. It wasn't easy to form words when she

was riding his dick at the pace he set. Just the thought of how he was owning her body sent her into a mindless orgasm.

"Got me?" he snarled.

"Yes!" she screamed. "Yes!"

Nadia's inner muscles clenched as another pulse shook her whole body, and she could hardly feel her lower limbs. "Don't stop!"

John moved them against the wall as he continued to drive into her. She was coming down from her high when his head reared back, and then he buried his face in the crook of her shoulder and muffled his roar.

His hot seed poured inside her.

He branded her, marked her as his.

And yet somehow in that moment, Nadia felt that John had surrendered to her too.

They ended up on the floor, and she was cradled on his lap. Her head resting securely on his chest.

Both of them were breathing heavily.

He kissed the top of her head. "Sorry, I didn't even make sure you were ready."

Nadia glanced up. "Can I be honest?"

The corner of his mouth turned up, giving her the go-ahead.

"I've been ready since we did that sexy dance at the club."

He closed his eyes as a rumbling sound made its way up his throat. "That was torture. Your pussy riding my thigh like that?" His eyes flashed open "You were so wet, I bet you left a mark on my pants."

Nadia laughed. "I probably did."

"Fuck, you know what I wanted to do right then and there?"

She squeezed her legs together. Goodness, couldn't she get enough from this sexy man. "What?"

"Bury my face between your pretty thighs and eat your pussy."

JOHN COULDN'T SEEM to get enough of being inside Nadia, and he couldn't get enough of her taste either. After working themselves up into a frenzy exchanging dirty talk, he hauled her into the bathroom. He gave them both a quick shower to wash off the makeup and the filth of the night club. Afterward, he toweled her dry.

With their flesh still damp, he laid her on the bed.

She barely had time to prop herself up on her elbows when he followed her down. Shoving her thighs apart, he buried his face between them the way he'd been hungering to do all night.

Her moan was music to his ears. She was sopping wet, but the slickness wasn't from water. He lashed, ate, and sucked down every bit of her sweetness. But her pussy was a gift that kept on giving, and he continued to feast on each drop that fell on his tongue.

"John, I want more ..." she moaned. "I need your cock."

Jesus, she was as dirty-mouthed as he was, and he loved it.

He gave her pussy one final lick, before he crawled up her body, relishing the way her legs cradled his hips. "You want more of this, babe?"

She grinned up at him. Her blond hair spread like a cloud on the pillows, the moon casting its beams through the blinds, bathing her in a heavenly light.

John's breath caught, as the inkling of the word love played on his tongue.

"You're gorgeous like this." He slowly pushed into her, the squeeze of her inner muscles making him groan in pleasure. "Damn, I could stay buried like this in you forever."

Nadia's laugh was cut short when he thrust. "You feel so good," she moaned. "Why did I fight this for three days again?"

"Not complaining." He kissed the tip of her nose as he

continued to rock into her. "The wait was worth it. I wanted you to be sure this is what you wanted."

A delicate brow arched. "I do like your bossiness. I find it sexy."

He grinned wickedly. "In that case—"

"Still," she paused and arched her back which sent him deeper. Jesus, this woman was his perfect fit. There was no place else he wanted to be. Staying deep in Nadia like this, he could die a happy man, except he wanted more.

For-fucking-ever.

"Still, I appreciate you dialing back your *bulldozerness*," she said and then chuckled. "And no that's not a word, but I think John Garrison is a synonym."

"Smartass." He captured her lips as he continued to take her at a leisurely pace.

When he came, it was not as explosive as the first, but it sent him spiraling into a web of contentment. He slowly pulled out of her and tucked her to his side, feeling her fingers splay on his chest, tracing random circles. His eyes drooped.

"John?"

"Hmm …"

"You didn't fuck up."

He exhaled heavily. "Nadia—"

"You didn't fuck up," she repeated. "If you did, Kelso and Gabby would have reamed your ass. What we have between us is too new, but we'll figure things out."

He kissed the top of her head. "No more field ops for you."

She pinched his torso. "We'll see about that."

He chuckled. "Looks like I've created a monster. What happened to not pulling you into my shit anymore?"

"I think this is more mine than yours."

"All right, but I don't want you near any perverts again."

"I really could have taken that man down."

His arms tightened around her. "Still hated it, babe."

She fell quiet after that. If John were honest, he loved working that op with Nadia except that hairy part where she nearly got mauled by that bastard. He doubted this would be the last time they would be working together given he was thinking of putting down roots here.

But she was right. They were a work in progress.

He welcomed the sands of sleep sucking him in, and he welcomed it more because he was wrapped around the woman who'd become the most important part of his life.

24

IN THE TWO weeks that followed, Nadia and John fell into a routine. Adjusting to each other wasn't as impossible as she first thought. John seemed to adjust well to her family of nosy neighbors although they continued to have some sort of competition in her care and feeding. It was amusing to watch until she had to jump in to referee.

John and Dugal would always tell her, though, that they were men just being men.

John surprisingly found the time to sneak in episodes of *Hodgetown* and declared he had finished season three. Perfect, too, because that day was Halloween and Nadia couldn't wait to see him in the costume she ordered for him and that arrived a few days prior. She was hosting a Halloween party that night at her apartment and she invited the CTTF crew. The food and drinks were going to be prepared at her apartment and the guests could spill out onto the rooftop.

Halloween was one of her favorite days of the year. Was it because she could get to be someone else without guilt? She thought back to what her father said about being happy in her own skin. She was beginning to appreciate what he meant. She'd stopped wearing the spectacles she didn't need and was thinking of letting her hair grow back into its reddish blond roots from the platinum she'd been favoring.

As for the investigation, she usually worked from her apartment with Bristow, staying clear of the Nerd Lab since anyone could just walk in when they were accessing a site that was for CIA eyes only. Nadia was feeling very special.

But she was getting frustrated at the lack of progress of the investigation in finding the Crown-Key.

There hadn't been any big cyberattacks like the traffic light incident, but no one was breathing a sigh of relief yet with the device still missing.

Kelso's theory was the device had already been sold to an arms dealer or a rogue state. The traffic light incident was a display of what it could do. Whether Evan Wagner's involvement was simply to provide Club Sochi as a venue to conceal the transaction remained to be investigated.

However, digging into Primeflix business yielded interesting information regarding their financials or, rather, that of one particular board member. Evan Wagner owned an investment company, and they'd scrutinized all his business dealings. They all seemed legit, but further investigation led to an incongruent line of business. Why would a gas station chain in Ukraine invest millions of dollars in the media giant? In recent years, speculations abounded that Primeflix was partly mob-owned and was used to launder money, not only in its operations, but also through production companies it did business with. And maybe that was why Wagner had a hard-on for *Hodgetown* because its production company, Revenant Films, refused to play.

As for Dmitry Vovk, several of the CIA's European assets had confirmed his very public appearances from Kiev all the way to Paris while chatter with the Argonayts all but died. No more messages came from Anonymous_754. Nadia continued to send her messages in their secure chat room, telling Sally that CTTF could help her if she was under duress. She even gave Sally her own task force cell number to call. But there was only complete silence.

The clanging of a pan brought her attention back to the present. Dugal and John were arguing in the kitchen over oatmeal.

Over oatmeal.

This was a roll-your-eyes moment and it was amusing to witness.

"You do realize there's the microwave kind." John was being a smartass again.

"Bite your tongue, man," Dugal boomed. "There's nothing like Scottish porridge to make sure you have a healthy bairn."

"Right now he—or she—is the size of a vanilla bean," Nadia called from the living room. "That's a speck."

"You want big, healthy boys or girls, then you want to feed them porridge. The right kind."

"There's a wrong kind?"

Oh, John, shut up.

Dugal told him, "Scottish porridge is made from stone-ground oats. It makes creamy oatmeal, not the gummy kind you Americans like to eat."

And so their argument went, but finally, after half an hour, Dugal finished giving his porridge lesson to John and they were finally sitting down to eat except for the big Scot who headed to the backdoor to leave. Had John pissed him off that much?

"Are you not joining us, Dugal?" Nadia stared at the big pot in front of them.

"Nay, I have to go to the butcher shop early, so I can come home and get your roast started."

"Aww, thanks for doing this!" she beamed. Dugal and her dad were helping out with the party.

"No problem, lass." And he waved off. Dugal, even at his

age, was a big Hallowed Eve fan. Halloween, after all, had its roots in Samhain, a popular Gaelic festival.

"Hmm," John said beside her. He had a serious look on his face as he tasted the creamy gruel topped with blueberries and walnut pieces. He chewed slowly and appeared to roll it on his tongue and then, "Damn, this is really good."

"See? You might learn a thing or two about good food," she said.

"Yeah, not a bad idea to learn this homemade shit." His eyes warmed as he looked at her. "I want our kid to be healthy." He glanced at his watch. "Speaking of which, we have an hour before we make our appointment." He gave a shake of his head. "Only you would think it's a good idea to schedule our first-prenatal visit on Halloween."

Nadia grinned. Proof that the holiday was her favorite day.

WHEN YOUR BABY daddy was a spook, there was no waiting room. They arrived at a nondescript, three-story, gray building. From the outside it looked like an abandoned building. He drove the Escalade around to an underground parking structure that was sealed off by folding gates. He tapped his watch to a scanner and it raised on its tracks.

When they went underground, Nadia was surprised to see an almost-packed parking lot.

"What's this place?"

"It's a division of the agency. Medical research. But some operatives have their surgeries and medical procedures here."

"I guess it's understandable with your line of work and wanting to keep anonymity."

"Yeah. Most of the medical staff work at regular hospitals."

"Like Hank?"

"Yeah. Bristow was a plant in the hospital system, but after the Ebola bioweapon, I needed him more in the field."

"Gotcha."

John parked their vehicle and went straight into an elevator, taking them up to the third floor. When the doors slid open, she was relieved to see the modern interior and not a hole-in-the wall clinic. She knew with John's protectiveness, giving her the best care was a priority. She found comfort in that.

A woman in scrubs at the reception area smiled when she saw John.

"You're here for Dr. Fern Ryan."

"Yes."

"I'm Taylor." The woman held out a tablet. "Just register here."

John signed the electronic log, and they were immediately accompanied down a brightly lit hallway. Unmarked rooms dotted both sides.

Taylor opened the door to the last room on the right. "I'll let Dr. Ryan know you're here."

Nadia sat in a chair, while John remained standing.

"Where's everyone?" she asked.

"First and second floor mostly. I was surprised we were directed to the third." His grin was lopsided.

"Must be a special occasion when John Garrison requests a prenatal."

He chuckled. "Fern was shocked for sure when I asked her. This is only for the first visit. She's going to recommend someone she trusts in the area at the end of this appointment."

"Wait. She's not from here?"

"She's based at Langley."

"You had her fly across the country for this?"

"She owes me one."

"How high-maintenance an operative are you?"

The door opened and a woman in her sixties with silver hair rolled in a severe bun stepped in. "Very." She quipped and extended her hand. "Hi, Nadia, I'm Dr. Ryan." Her gray eyes flicked to the man beside her. "John."

"Fern." He gave her a kiss on the cheek. It was weird seeing him this familiar with someone, but it also added a point to the humanity column. The life of a CIA officer must be lonely, but she was glad it seemed there were people that John felt close enough to request this cross-country favor. Nadia wanted her people to be his too.

"I told John that I can't continue to be your obstetrician for obvious reasons, but don't worry. I've been the first line of consultation many times with nervous super spies becoming parents for the first time."

Nadia gave a snort of laughter. John grunted.

"It's a hard transition, from trusting only a few people inside the CIA, to having to deal with institutions outside the agency. But as I told a few of John's colleagues, the CIA medical facilities specialize in emergency response. We leave the prenatal and children's wellbeing to the experts."

"Sounds good to me."

"We're not going to do an ultrasound. It's too early and it will only do more harm than good, psychologically. I presumed you'd done an over-the-counter pregnancy test?"

"Yes, I took two over two weeks ago and then another one, hmm, last Saturday and …" Nadia grinned. "I'm still pregnant."

John frowned at her. "You didn't tell me you did that."

"I didn't want to sound paranoid. And I didn't want to waste an appointment just in case I'm not pregnant, especially since I insisted on Halloween."

"Please don't hide anything from me in the future," his voice was so gentle, it warmed all over.

"Oh my," Dr. Ryan said, grinning. "I'll tell you one thing, whatever you're doing to this man, continue it."

John scowled, "Fern—"

"Do you know how many times I had to treat him, or one of his crew, and his abrupt, get-it-over-with attitude?"

"Believe me, I know." She beat back a smile. "That was one of the problems I had with him."

"And I'm standing right here," John said dryly.

Nadia and the doctor shared another laugh, and then Fern put her serious face on and started asking questions about her medical history.

The blood test she ordered confirmed that she was, indeed, pregnant, and, even if they were clear when conception may have happened, they officially dated her pregnancy to the last date of her menstrual cycle which would put her roughly around six weeks.

"Is it strange that I'm not feeling any symptoms?"

"You're one of the lucky ones."

"And, ah, Fern," John put a finger over his mouth as if he wasn't sure of what to say, and his face was unusually ruddy. "I… have a question."

"Is this about sexual intercourse?" The doctor's eyes twinkled. Obviously, she was used to this question.

"Yeah."

"John!" Nadia exclaimed and her own face was suddenly flushed with embarrassment. They'd had this chat. Nadia already knew from her friends that sex wasn't a problem, which was why she wasn't worried when they had that vigorous sex after the nightclub op. Apparently John did his research on that, too, so why was he asking this now?

"We've been having lots of it and … I read somewhere that it was fine."

The doctor grinned. "It is perfectly fine." She winked at Nadia. "I don't see anything in her medical history to preclude sex."

"Thanks, doc." John winked at Nadia.

That time she did roll her eyes.

Dr. Ryan gave an amused shake of her head. "I've sent your info to Dr. Stephanie Stahl, and, yes, it's because John requested a female doctor."

"For obvious reasons," he said.

Oh, her caveman.

AFTER THEIR DOCTOR'S APPOINTMENT, John dropped her off at the Nerd Lab and went off to do what super spies did when they were not attending prenatal checkups. It still felt surreal when she thought of their relationship. He'd always been the man of mystery in their little group ever since Gabby and Declan got back together. When their division spun off into CTTF to address terrorist threats in LA that could have nationwide consequences, John became a fixture ... well, a fixture in the background.

The sliding doors to her lab swooshed open. "Hey."

It was Levi.

Her brows furrowed. "Where's John?"

"He got held up a bit."

"Oh, no, no, he wouldn't dare." Nadia grabbed her phone and called him. It went directly to voice mail. He sent her to voicemail! The nerve! "John Garrison," she fumed. "You're not getting out of wearing the Locke Demon costume."

She ended the call and chucked the phone into her backpack and gathered the rest of her things. Levi was trying so hard not to laugh, but she shot him a glare just the same. On the ride home, she typed and erased messages to John, trying not to come off as a needy, pregnant woman.

Argh.

"He had something significant come up. It appears Dmitry Vovk boarded a plane for the U.S. again."

"He could have answered his phone or sent me a text."

She blew on imaginary bangs. "He knew how important this was to me."

"Maybe he's a coward," Levi said, glancing at her briefly. "He didn't want to hear the disappointment in your voice."

Nadia sighed. "It's better than ignoring me, leaving me in limbo."

The other man chuckled. "He's got a long way to go to be trained."

"Is that so?" she grinned. "Is that what Kelly did to you?"

"Believe me, John is smarter than I am navigating this shit. My only excuse? I'm younger."

Nadia grinned and stared out the window. They were at the neighborhood road now. Some kids and teenagers were already strolling on the sidewalks. The kids were about to be let loose. The police vehicle patrolling their apartment complex was parked in front of the main entrance.

"You can drop me right ahead."

"Nope. I'm coming up with you."

She frowned. This was the first time she'd come home without John since Maxim's ambush. She looked up ahead and saw another two cops stationed at the entrance to the complex, and then another patrol up ahead in addition to the one assigned to watch the SkyeLark apartments.

"Look, your girls are waiting for you, right?"

A muscle ticked at his jaw. "They understand daddy has a job to do."

"And you weren't supposed to be doing this. John was. Your girls are going to be disappointed," Nadia added. She was getting pissed at John for putting Levi up to this. "And Kelly, too, because I'm sure she's going to make your daughters rock."

A wistful smile touched his lips. "She always does."

Nadia went in for the kill. "So, screw John. I'm protected like Fort Knox. If you want, I can bring one of the officers up with me."

Levi's jaw hardened. "No. I'll walk you up and make sure there's an officer stationed at your door."

Nadia sighed, whatever would let Levi go home to his girls and wife faster. She was going to have a word with John about this.

"ARE you sure you don't want to try this, officer?"

"I'm on duty, ma'am," the fresh-faced cop said.

"It's your loss." Nadia turned away from the entrance and closed the door, still holding a sample of the appetizer Dugal had made. Poor Levi. He wasn't comfortable leaving her with a cop who looked like he was fresh out of the academy. It wasn't until John texted that he was five minutes away that the SEAL left.

It was six o' clock. The festivities had started. John was going to be in the doghouse if Levi completely missed trick-or-treating with his girls.

She headed back to the kitchen where Dugal was checking on the roast. He shut the oven and stared at the sausage roll in her hands.

"Nay?" He frowned.

"Nay," she replied.

"It's Halloween. Even cops are allowed to have fun."

The walkie-talkie on the counter sounded. "We're starving."

It was Clyde.

The Halloween festivities were set up in the parking lot. The stairs were blocked so kids couldn't come up. Clyde and Arthur were handing out candy along with the other residents.

"I can bring them something," she said.

"I'll do it," Dugal said. "You stay here and watch the roast."

"You just want to show off your pirate outfit," Nadia told Dugal as he fixed a patch across one eye. A bandana covered his bald head. He fastened the wide belt around his waist. His Claymore sword was sheathed in a scabbard that hung off the belt.

"Be careful with that thing," Nadia warned.

"Aye."

"Don't let the children touch it."

"They'd love to see it. A real Scottish sword."

"Scottish pirate?"

"Aye." His grin was all teeth. "Ye don't look bad yourself."

"Yes, but it's getting hot." Since the Locke Demon didn't have a romantic interest in *Hodgetown*, Nadia decided to go with the vampire-warrior of her favorite vampire-werewolf franchise. It was a bodysuit; a corset-like top and chunky boots completed the look. She also slathered white foundation on her face and finished with red lipstick. She skipped the fangs though. Nadia didn't want to deal with them tonight.

As Dugal stalked out the backdoor, her dad came in. He was the only one of his friends who didn't don a costume. He said Nadia did enough dressing up for both of them. Spoilsport. He was carrying a tray of pies. "I hope these turned out okay."

"Dad, I told you we could have just gotten those from the supermarket."

He stared at her from under his spectacles. "And I've said many times those are bad for you."

"The sugar in these is probably as bad as all the preservatives."

Her dad proceeded to lecture her about high-fructose corn syrup and polyphosphates. She'd heard this before and let him chatter as she surreptitiously checked her phone. The adults were coming at eight after the kids were done trick-or-treating.

There was a message from Kelso that he was ready to chow down. Gabby said she was having a problem fitting into her costume and might be late. John said he was having trouble finding "fuckin' parking." She did tell him the parking lot was occupied. Served him right.

But her eyes zeroed in on a text message from Anony-mous_574. She'd finally used the number Nadia left her in the chatroom.

The message was: "Get out now!"

Was this a joke?

"Excuse me, Dad, I need to call someone." She went to her bedroom and called the number on the text message.

"Hello?" It sounded like Sally's voice.

"Sally? How—"

"I escaped," she was whispering. "I thought I'd come to you, but I realized they're tracking me."

"How?"

"Just get out, please! I think I led them to you. I cut out the tracker…" Her voice went shaky as if she started running.

"Who's tracking you?"

The line went dead.

She tried to call back, but it kept on ringing.

Leaving the bedroom, she called John.

"I'm parked up the street," he growled. "I'll be there in—"

"Shut up and listen. Sally called …" her voice died, and blood drained from her face.

Two black-clad men, their features covered by balaclavas, stood in her kitchen. One of them had a gun pointed at Stephen.

"Hand me that phone." One of them spoke tersely. "Now." He pressed the gun against the back of her father's head.

She did so without hesitation even when John was cursing at the other end.

"Your boyfriend can't help you now." The man looked at the phone, swiped to end the call, and handed it over to his comrade. "Check the messages."

Nadia and her father kept their gazes locked. She hated

the fear in his eyes. It wasn't for him, but for her. Did her own gaze reflect the same?

Get out now!

She should have checked her phone sooner. But how could she have known? There'd been no contact with Sally since that Lisbeth message and later when she saw her at the club. And now …

She led those men here.

"Where is she?" the man pointing the gun to Stephen's head asked.

"I don't know. You saw the messages." She glanced at her father. "Please let Dad go. You have me."

"*Sonyashnik*, no," her father pleaded.

Dammit.

The second man swiped the number and walked over to Nadia. "Tell her to come here."

"She knows you're looking for her. She won't come."

"Then maybe we can use you and your father as incentive, hmmm…?"

"Nadia?" Sally's voice whispered.

Nadia swallowed. "Where are you?"

"I'm still … Are you still at the apartment? I told you to leave."

Too late.

"Why don't you come over? It'll be okay. I can help you."

"They're there, aren't they …You're going to … I thought I could trust you. You said in your messages to me—never mind."

"Don't. Don't hang up!" The line went dead and Nadia wanted to scream.

At least John would be here soon.

"There's a cop outside the door," she said, trying to steady her voice "You—"

A bloodcurdling cry roared in the apartment. A battle cry that chilled the air.

Nadia watched in horror as the glint of a medieval sword hacked through the arm that was holding the gun to Stephen's head.

Screams filled the apartment.

Something crashed.

Someone cursed.

As the man holding her father hostage dropped, Dugal's brutish form appeared. The man beside Nadia tried to grab her, but she ducked and twisted that man's arm.

"Everyone freeze!"

Muffled pops and gunfire exploded.

A force sent Nadia flying to the floor. She hit the tiles hard, her arms taking the brunt of the fall. When she looked up, it was all over.

Her assailant was pinned to the wall by Dugal's sword.

No one else was left standing.

25

TWO SUCCESSIVE GUNSHOTS exploded from the top floors just as John cleared the first step of the staircase.

Two patrol officers were following him, but he was way ahead as he climbed the steps two at a time.

"Nadia's in trouble." John had Levi on the phone. "Need you back here."

"I shouldn't have left her," Levi groaned in remorse.

"Stop dwelling," John said. "Get Bristow and Roarke. All hands-on deck. Now."

He rounded the stairwell to Nadia's apartment door. It was wide open. A young officer was sitting against the wall, radioing for help.

But what he saw defied all reason.

A man in black was slowly slipping to the floor, the sword that affixed him to the wall through his chest succumbing to gravity.

His fucking heart lodged in his throat.

"Nadia!" John roared.

He skidded into the kitchen.

Blood.

So much blood.

But Nadia was alive, her hands drenched in bright red as she tried to stop the bleeding from Dugal's chest. Off to the side, Stephen sat against the center island, pale as death, holding a kitchen towel to his shoulder. At his feet, another man in black had his arm partly shorn off, swimming in a pool of blood.

"I can't stop the bleeding," Nadia choked, summoning John's attention now that he'd assessed the situation. Tears streamed down her cheeks, smudging black makeup into the white paint on her face.

"I've got it," John spoke calmly, taking over the towel she'd been using to hold pressure to the wound. "Ambulance is on the way." He nodded to her father. "Stay with Stephen."

Dugal's lids were fluttering. His mouth moved.

"You foolish old Scot," John said. "What did you do? Charge at a man who was holding a gun?"

"The lass ..."

"She's fine."

A smile tugged at the corners of Dugal's mouth. "Nailed ... that bas...tard...to the wall."

"You did." Where was the fucking ambulance?

Dugal coughed and blood came out of his mouth. He was bleeding internally.

"Where else were you shot?" his voice grew rough. Bristow. They needed Bristow.

"So cold," the Scot mumbled. "Need ... whisky."

"You'll have all the whisky you want, man," John said. "Just stay with me."

Dugal's eyes closed, and he went still.

couldn't be who Nadia needed and stay in the shadows. He was going to be that man beside her every step of the way. Walking through the sliding glass doors of the emergency room, he tried not to flinch as several pairs of eyes flew to him. He felt every single disguise he ever wore peel away, and he tried to act rationally when he saw Colin embracing a sobbing Nadia in his arms.

Colin's eyes were red, mouth set in a firm line, but he whispered in Nadia's ear at his approach.

"Babe," John said.

Nadia raised her head, and he flinched as he took in the despair reflected in her eyes.

Make yourself vulnerable. Bristow's words repeated in his head.

He opened his arms, waited in bated breath for her rejection, his guilt weighing him down. Because despite what Bristow said, what happened was all John's fault.

He promised to protect her and the people she cared about.

He failed.

"John," Nadia's broken voice whispered before she extricated herself from Colin's arms and went to his.

His lungs labored to exhale as his arms wrapped around her.

Nadia tilted up her chin, tears running down her cheeks. "I'm scared." He could barely hear her words.

"Hang in there, babe," he told her. John never gave false promises, and he wasn't starting now. Then he realized why she voiced her fears so quietly—she didn't want to add to Colin's anxiety. He raised his gaze to the Scot. "Your father is one of the fiercest men I've ever met." And he was being honest. Pinning a man to a wall with a sword wasn't for the faint of heart. "He's not going to let those bastards win."

Colin nodded grimly.

The sliding doors to the emergency room swished open

again and Dugal's son, Alec, arrived with Arthur and Clyde. The three newcomers approached and asked for an update. After giving them one, they moved to a row of couches and chairs.

There weren't enough seats in that section for all of them and John had a feeling Nadia wanted to stay with the people who knew Dugal and Stephen the best, even though he wanted her right where she belonged.

In his arms.

Nadia drew him away, out of earshot of the rest of the group.

"I feel it's my fault," she admitted. "What if—"

"Don't say that," he cut her off. "It's mine. All mine."

She was shaking her head and starting to push away. "I can't process this right now." She glanced at the huddle. "I want to be there for Colin and Alec."

"Of course." What else could he say? This wasn't about him, and he was still drowning in his own guilt.

Raising her hand and cupping his jaw, she gave it a squeeze, but said no more before she walked over to Dugal's sons.

Three hours later, John was by himself, standing against the wall beside the vending machine. Bristow came in, took one look at John and then at the huddle with Nadia. The ginger-haired SEAL walked over to him.

"No go. Huh?"

"It's fine. Nadia doesn't blame me, but she needs them." John nodded over to the group. It was the collective strength of the people who were closest to Dugal and Stephen that was necessary for all of them to get through this. A relatable shared love for the men whose lives were currently hanging in the balance. Where one would fall under despair, the other could prop him or her up with hope. "Any news?"

"Stephen is out of surgery."

"How—?"

Bristow raised a brow.

"Never mind. You did work here before."

"Still not my place to tell Nadia but that'll be one thing off your mind too."

"Any news on Dugal?"

"Shot once in the chest, twice in the back."

John replayed the gruesome scene he came upon. "Morris got off two shots despite almost losing an arm?"

"I got the quick assessment from Kelso. Dugal hacked through Morris and went after Nadia's assailant who tried to use her as shield. The patrol officer guarding the entrance heard the commotion and barged in and was initially stunned by what he was seeing. This allowed assailant number two to get off a shot at him and Dugal. Meanwhile Morris recovered, and was apparently ambidextrous and picked up his gun and shot off two rounds into Dugal's back."

"Stephen tried to stop Morris and got shot," John concluded.

"Yes. And the patrol officer managed to kill Morris."

"Damn, did the patrol officer say if he witnessed Dugal impale our second attacker to the wall?"

Bristow grinned. "Kelso said the poor cop might be in therapy for a while."

An aching fondness expanded in his chest. "That old bastard better make it."

HE HAS TO MAKE IT.

Nadia thought miserably. The guilt weighing her heart was unbearable. If she hadn't sent Levi away, would this have happened? She stared at her fingers. She wasn't able to scrub all the blood from her fingernails. Her cuticles still bore the evidence of the carnage in her kitchen. The horror of not knowing who to save first.

"I'm fine," her father gasped. "Hand me that towel and see to Dugal."

She crawled over trails of blood, grabbed two kitchen towels, and pressed one on her dad's shoulder, before scrambling over to Dugal who was groaning on the floor.

"You're crazy," she muttered, staunching the flow of blood right below his heart. "And what are you smirking about?"

"That was quite the charge," he boasted.

But she couldn't respond because a map of red began to pool from under him. "Oh my God."

"He was shot in the back," her father said.

"Here, take this."

She glanced up to see John holding out a protein bar and a bottle of water. Three hours earlier, she received word that her father was okay. John checked on her periodically, asking her to be looked over by a doctor. She refused. It was hour six now. Nadia realized how thirsty she was.

She accepted the water but shook her head at the bar.

"You need to eat something." His tone was firm.

"Not hungry."

John sank to his haunches and held her gaze steadily. "Babe. You're scared. I get that. But Dugal's not going to be happy if he finds out you've been waiting in this ER without sustenance." His expression turned somber. "Please take care of yourself too."

She shook her head again.

A muscle bounced in his cheek, and she knew he was fighting with his steamroller nature, not to force the issue of eating, but her gut was twisted up with acid. His mouth compressed into a thin line and he nodded. "Please eat this. Put something in your stomach."

He left the bar on her lap and stood, walking back to where he waited with Bristow.

"He's right, lass," Alec said. "Pa, wouldn't have wanted you getting hungry, especially with the baby."

"This is all my fault. I shouldn't have been around your dad."

Colin nudged her leg. "In case you haven't learned this about Scots yet, fighting is in our blood. If you were in any sort of danger, Pa would've been the first one to protect you."

"Aye," Alec said. "There's nothing like a Scotsman loving to be in the thick of it."

The doors to the ER opened and an exhausted-looking man in scrubs walked out. "Dugal Cameron?"

Nadia surged from her chair with Colin and Alec. Arthur and Clyde rose up with them and crowded the surgeon.

"He's out of surgery and is stable …"

Nadia heard no more. Her legs gave out as darkness swallowed her.

"Are you sure she's fine?"

John's gravelly voice hovered overhead.

"She's dehydrated." An unfamiliar female voice answered him. "And the stress just got to her."

"She's pregnant."

"Yes. I checked the records sent over by Dr. Ryan. And we agreed that since she's not spotting, an ultrasound right now might be too stressful since it's early in the pregnancy."

"I know that!" John snapped.

There was a moment of charged silence before the doctor —at least Nadia presumed she was a doctor—added, "I'll check back later, but she has the best care with Bristow here."

A door opened and closed.

"I'm going to wring her neck when she wakes up," John muttered.

"No, you're not," Bristow said, amusement lacing his tone.

"You're going to be all over her and not let her out of your sight. Ever."

"Got that right."

"Are you bullying me even when I'm unconscious?" She croaked as she opened one eye, and then another. The blurry image of John slowly came into focus. He looked terrible and a bit feral.

"I fainted," she announced.

"And damned near shaved fifty years off of my life," he snarled. "I thought to give you space, that you needed other people around you more." An expression she'd never associated with John was carved into his face. Remorse. Distress. "I'm sorry I fucked up. If I'd picked you up when you told me to, this wouldn't have happened."

Was that why he was blaming himself? Nadia thought. Well, she could see that as much as she could see her own fault.

"I called the DNI and told him I'm out—"

"Whoa, hold on—" He was making her dizzy.

At this point, Bristow had backed away to the door. "I think you two need to have this conversation alone."

"Can you check when I can see my dad and Dugal?" she asked.

"I can do that." The SEAL retreated from the room, closing the door behind him.

At the soft click, John continued his tirade. He edged his seat closer, grabbing her hands in his. "I should have held off the intel gathering on Vovk. Nothing matters more than you, but you'll have your pound of flesh, Nadia. I'll be the best costumed Locke Demon at StreamCon and you're going to be my demon bride—"

"Okay, back up," Nadia interrupted.

"No. Listen to me—"

"John, I —"

"I'll be damned when you fainted and I was clear across the room and couldn't catch you—"

Nadia extricated one of her hands from his grip, leaned forward, and slapped it over his mouth. "Staaahp."

They glared at each other.

"Let me speak, dammit. You're stressing me out," she growled.

His eyes panicked. "Do I need to call the doctor?"

"If it's to make me relax by kicking you out, then by all means."

His mouth flattened, and he sat back in his chair. "Obviously, I'm missing something."

"You're missing a whole lot, buddy," she grumbled. "I never blamed you for Dugal and Dad getting hurt at all."

Garrison's jaw hardened. "You should."

"Then I should be wracked with guilt too because I insisted Levi go home. But you know what? In that waiting room? Colin and Alec didn't blame any of us because they know the man their father is. He will protect his friends like his own family." She inhaled and exhaled raggedly. "None of us could have predicted that Sally would have escaped Morris and come to me." She paused as her mind did a rewind. "I did hand over my phone to Kelso, right?" Everything from the evening was a jumble.

"They were able to piece together what happened from those messages."

"They weren't after me. They were after Sally." Nadia emphasized the words. "There were more than enough officers there to guard me, but the confusion of Halloween … " she trailed off.

John closed his eyes briefly and opened them again. "Yeah."

"Now is the time I say the words back to you."

A corner of his mouth quirked up.

"Suck it up, John Garrison."

His mouth twitched. "Yes, ma'am."

"So you're going to call the DNI back and say you're not quitting."

John sighed. "I was pretty final when I talked to him."

"What did he say?"

"He said I should sleep on it. I told him that's not going to change anything."

"You're going to give up your pursuit of Dmitry Vovk? I thought you've been after him for thirteen years?"

He sighed. "It appears I'm not getting through to you, so I'll state it plainly. You're more important than any job, got it?"

John's gaze was piercing and held her captive. He'd wrapped both her hands in his two as if to make a point.

"I don't know what to say." Her lips trembled. Nadia couldn't believe the words coming out of his mouth, but his the emotions in his eyes were too turbulent to interpret.

He leaned forward and kissed her on the lips. "Nothing. Just accept me as your man. Your protector."

"I do," she said. "But, you can't give up on the Argonayts case."

He sighed again. "I know." His mouth turned wry. "Because the LAPD needs my access."

Her lips curved. "You got that right."

"I feel so used," he deadpanned.

Her smile grew wider. "Suck it up."

27

"I'm going to wear my scars like a badge," Dugal said.

Three days after the carnage at her apartment, her Scottish neighbor was coherent enough to talk to the detectives to give his statement. The room was crowded. Besides Gabby and Kelso, John, and Bristow, as well as Arthur and Clyde, her father—who was released yesterday—gathered to give a full reconstruction of how Morris and his partner got to the rooftop.

"I just want to make it clear since all of you are here, everything was done by the book," Kelso said. "It was the responsibility of the LAPD to provide our crime analyst with security, not Homeland Security." John, Bristow, and Levi were still playing the DHS card. "There was a patrol car in front of the apartments. Because of the Halloween festivities, Officer Tarrant was stationed in front of Nadia's apartment. Officer Nero was positioned at the bottom of the stairs that led straight to the rooftop. It's my understanding, Mr. Cameron, that you noticed an officer down."

"Aye. On my way back from handing Arthur and Clyde their food, I noticed the officer disappeared. Is he going to be all right?"

Nadia learned that Officer Nero was shot in the back and then dragged behind the dumpster right beside that particular staircase.

"He's expected to make a full recovery," Kelso said.

"I knew Levi was reluctant to leave Nadia alone," Dugal said. "So I told him I could be counted on as extra security. I even showed him my sword."

"Impressive sword," Gabby said.

The Scotsman's grin was smug.

"Unfortunately," Gabby added. "We had to confiscate it as evidence."

Dugal scowled. "I'm not going to be charged with murdering that bastard, am I?"

"They better not." Nadia glared at her colleagues. "I'll stand witness."

"He saved us," Stephen added. "I'll vouch for him too."

"Don't worry. I doubt the prosecutor will even bring up charges what with Officer Tarrant's report insisting it was self-defense as well. Morris and his partner made an armed incursion into your apartment and held you at gunpoint. We just want to have the sequence of events nailed down." Kelso coughed. "Pardon the pun."

Everyone chuckled at the morbid humor in reference to the man Dugal impaled to the wall.

After another ten minutes of everyone giving their accounts of the incident, Dugal started waning, his eyes drifting close as he fought to stay awake. As if on cue, a nurse, followed by Colin, Alec, and their eldest brother, Jamie, the stuntman, walked in.

"All right, time's up, folks. Our patient needs his rest."

Kelso and Gabby thanked Dugal for his time and left.

As the rest of them filed out, Clyde grabbed Dugal's hand. "I'm so glad it was you watching Nadia. I wouldn't have known what to do."

"You will find your courage when ye need it, old man," the Scot said.

Stephen added, "Nevertheless, we're thankful you took one for the team."

"You did too, Stephen," Dugal said. "Your love for your daughter saved us all. If you hadn't stopped that bastard from shooting, I would be dead.

Arthur concurred.

"I wasn't going to let anyone take my family from me again," Stephen replied fiercely. "And my family includes crazy old Scots."

Dugal chuckled, then grimaced. "Don't make me laugh."

"All right, everybody who is not family needs to leave," the nurse repeated more firmly.

Bristow waved at Dugal and left with the MoMoS.

Nadia and John took their turns by his bedside.

"Thanks for saving my woman," John said.

"Anytime." Dugal's lids flitted to half-mast. "Just take care of her."

John wrapped his arms around Nadia. "Count on it. I doubt I'll let her out of my sight."

"You keep threatening that," she groused.

"I don't think it's a threat, lass ... and I'm trying not to laugh," Dugal groaned.

At the disapproving look from the nurse again, Nadia slipped out of John's embrace and went to hug Dugal's sons. "Your dad is such a brave man."

"He'll be a tough act to follow," Colin agreed.

"You all are talking about me like I'm dying," Dugal complained.

Giving the younger Scots another squeeze, Nadia returned to Dugal's side to give him a kiss on the forehead before leaving the room with John.

GETTING ALL the MoMoS into a safe house was proving to be an exercise in patience.

Arthur needed to bring some of his exotic plants.

"They'll die without meticulous care," the botanist said.

It was a wonder that John kept his sarcasm in check. Of course, the plants would die. They were native to the damned Amazon, not California.

And Clyde couldn't go without his leather chair.

John had told him. "I did mention the house was fully furnished, right?"

"My sciatica has special needs," Clyde sniffed. "I had that specially made from Burmese rosewood."

Which explained why the leather chair weighed a ton for something that looked like a regular armchair. The premium timber was similar to mahogany. John made sure to wrap the whole piece in moving plastic because that shit was expensive, and he'd hate to fuck it up.

Surprisingly, most of the men were not ornery. John was thankful for that, but they were set in their ways and just the change of environment might turn the merry men into grumpy ones. Nadia didn't need that shit, and John was sure they would keep it from her, but the downside of reading people so well was they couldn't hide it from him, and he didn't need that shit either.

Although mostly he was patient because he'd grown fond of the old buggers and making them happy was making him … happy.

Shit.

Stephen, thank God, was a pro when it came to living in safe houses.

John made two trips with the U-Haul truck. Granted the biggest truck wasn't available, but with the way Clyde and Arthur packed, one would think they were leaving for a year instead of a few weeks. Dugal would be joining the rest of the MoMoS once he checked out in another few days. Colin was staying to help his dad. He must have packed Dugal's entire kitchen when John informed him about the concept of take-out. Besides, they had a fully equipped kitchen.

To which the younger Scot scoffed, "If they are to heal faster, they need proper nourishment."

Proper nourishment.

Who said that?

Thank fuck, Bristow agreed to stay in the house too. There were six bedrooms and seven full bathrooms. More than enough room and facilities that they wouldn't be on top of each other. Roarke and Gabby were just a few houses down the same road.

He sent Levi home to Kelly and his daughters. John didn't want to be on his wife's shit list, seeing that he was going to be needing a favor from her soon.

When he drove through the gates, he was surprised to see an Audi RS Q8 he didn't recognize parked right at the side of the house. He couldn't recall anyone he knew driving one, and he immediately went on guard, but eased up when he spotted Nadia laughing with Arthur. They were carrying some pots to put on the bare driveway garden border probably to catch the midday sun. The pavement sloped down from the gate and wrapped around the house to the back where the entrance of the residence was located. Were their visitors Arthur or Clyde's children? John sure hoped they weren't handing out the address. The menfolk had been briefed that they were going to a safe house, not Club Med.

The driveway allowed plenty of room for two vehicles to pass side by side. John had a feeling he would derive immense pleasure if his vehicle kissed the Audi just a little bit. Still, his ego wouldn't allow him to make such an error—even delib-erate—because there *was* enough room for the U-Haul to pass through.

When he pulled the truck in front of the double-door entrance, Nadia bounded up to him. He got down from the vehicle. After giving her a quick kiss, he asked, "Who came in the Audi?"

"Antonio and Charly are here!" Nadia announced.

His brow furrowed, but a grin touched the corners of his mouth. "Aren't they supposed to be on their honeymoon? They just got married ... like what ..."

"Two weeks ago," Nadia finished. "But Charly heard about dad ..."

Charly had been infected with a mutation of the weaponized Ebola virus which didn't work with the antiviral she created. However, Stephen happened to be the scientist who synthesized the virus's backbone and was able to tweak the existing antiviral to save her.

John had to admit, their group had formed an indelible bond given the numerous dicey situations that had come their way. Add to that how some had started coupling up, they'd become close to a blended family. Not only personally but professionally as well. John always had planned to build his resources inside the LAPD, but he didn't expect it to get personal. And now?

He braced for that suffocating feeling to hit him whenever people got too close. That need to disappear when attachments were getting too personal.

Nothing.

He exhaled a breath of relief.

He was all fucking in.

"Who's the Audi?" Roarke asked. He and Bristow ambled up to Nadia and John.

"Andrade and Charly," John answered.

"Why are they here?" Roarke asked, then his brows shot up in realization. "Oh, Stephen." Then he frowned. "How did they find out?"

All eyes swung to Bristow who shrugged. "Charly and I still communicate. I thought she should know."

John smiled as an idea took shape. "Know what?" he

clapped Bristow's shoulder. "That gives us an extra body to help unload the truck."

When they entered the house, Charly was on the couch talking to Stephen, while Clyde was keeping Andrade busy—moving furniture. John had to keep from laughing. The billionaire appeared game, though. One could even say there was an indulgent look on the man's face.

John's thoughts turned somber. Maybe Andrade was missing his friend Luis. Though Antonio didn't have any military background, the man could hold his own in any fight whether it involved guns or fists. And he could be ruthless if any of his loved ones were threatened. John suspected Antonio had something to do with cartel boss Benito Carillo getting murdered in prison. It was a good thing the billionaire was on their side.

"Guys!" Charly jumped up from the couch and strode over to greet them. She gave him a hug and then pulled back to stare at him accusingly. "You disappeared from the taco party. Antonio and I haven't been able to thank you properly."

"No thanks needed. Just doing my job," he said.

She gave him a squeeze on the arm, before transferring her attention to Bristow and gave the SEAL a tight hug.

Antonio strolled over to them. "Garrison, heard you were recent guests at a Ukrainian dungeon."

"I've had better accommodations," he deadpanned. "Perfect timing. We could use your muscles to move shit."

"So it seems," Antonio answered absentmindedly. His attention was on his new bride who was still chatting animatedly with Bristow and Roarke. Andrade moved closer to Charly, clasping her shoulder, and drawing her against his chest.

A move John was familiar with. He'd seen it with Roarke, he'd seen it with Migs, and John remembered a couple of times he'd done it too.

Possessiveness.

This burning, intense desire to be the source of your woman's every joy and the recipient of that expression that depicted said joy.

Garrison angled his body toward Nadia who gave him a raised brow. He put his arm around her shoulder and squeezed her to his side, touching his lips to her brow.

"I can't believe it," Charly gasped, extricating herself from her husband's hold and walking up to them, eyes wide, gaze transfixed. "Bristow said something was brewing between you two—"

Bristow coughed. "It's past brewing—"

John shot the ginger-haired SEAL a glare. "And Bristow has a big mouth." He was the only one on the team who knew Nadia was pregnant, but John had a feeling that secret was not going to remain a secret for much longer.

"So did you grovel?" Charly asked.

"Why should he grovel?" Nadia leaned away from him and shot him a suspicious look. "Is there something I don't know that you've done?"

"*Minha Linda.*" Antonio retrieved his wife, putting an arm around her shoulder. "Are we causing trouble here?"

"Oh …" Charly laughed. "Not really." Her eyes dipped to Nadia. "We were wondering where you were when the Z-9 series was happening because Hank was having trouble—"

"Hey, I managed as best I could," Bristow protested.

"You seem to be digging your hole deeper, *gatinha,*" Antonio drawled. Yet in the way he was gazing fondly at his wife, there was no doubt the bastard was smitten.

"Soooo," Charly addressed Nadia. "We asked where you were, and Garrison said you quit. Everyone came to the conclusion that he'd been an asshole to you… which he confirmed." She paused and glanced at John. "Or was it because you didn't deny it?"

"Don't fucking remember." John shifted Nadia to the front of him, his arms around her in a full embrace, to keep her from bolting just in case the doctor let her mouth continue to run. Christ, he wasn't expecting to get roasted. His eyes lifted to Andrade. "Please rein in your wife before I end up sleeping on the couch."

Charly grinned and shook her head. "I still can't believe it."

"Hey. Any food?" Bristow interjected, and then winked at John in a move to change the subject, ushering the crowd at the entrance further into the house. "We're starving."

Not that he needed saving from the feisty doctor, but John didn't want to rehash the Mexico thing. It wasn't one of his proudest moments.

"Lasagna in the oven," Nadia said.

"You cooked?" Roarke asked.

"No," Nadia replied. "I reheated. I'm quite impressed. The freezer came fully stocked with food that can feed an army."

She was about to follow into the kitchen when John pulled her back.

"What?" she asked.

"We're okay, right?"

Her brows furrowed. "You're talking about the Mexico thing?"

"Yeah."

Arguing from the kitchen interrupted her reply. Roarke and Bristow were at odds with Clyde and Antonio on whether the lasagna was ready.

"The timer says ten minutes more," Roarke said.

"The cheese is bubbling, and it's browned on top," Antonio said. "It's done."

"What do you know? You have a housekeeper," Bristow shot back.

"Antonio has become an expert in reheating food," Charly defended her husband.

"For fuck's sake," Nadia muttered and made to go to the kitchen again.

John held her back. "Let them handle it."

She blew out a breath and relented.

"It *is* ready." Clyde put in his two cents. "I wouldn't trust the timer because Nadia set it. She can't cook, much less reheat stuff."

"Hey, I can reheat stuff," Nadia protested. "Some." She added under her breath.

John waited patiently for her attention to return to him. Somehow, he had a feeling Nadia was doing it on purpose to mess with him.

He was right. When she glanced up at him, there was a mischievous glint in her eyes and her mouth curved coyly. "Maybe Charly has a point. You were pretty mean. I need to make you grovel."

He looped an arm around her and murmured into her ear. "As long as you don't deny me access to this body. I'll do whatever you want."

John grinned when she shuddered against him.

The noise around them seemed to have died down, and when both of them looked around, all eyes were riveted on them.

Stephen had risen from the couch, but a faint smile was playing on his lips. Arthur and Clyde were looking on like indulgent uncles. Declan, Bristow, and Antonio were smirking. And Charly? Charly was staring at them with a goofy smile on her face as if she'd witnessed the most romantic scene.

Fuck.

For the first time ever, heat rose up his cheeks.

"Oh my god, I'm swooning," Charly called from the kitchen.

Declan said something about taking a video for Gabby to see.

Bristow said something about Roarke's wife already knowing that Garrison's had the moves.

"Fuck," John muttered.

"John, are you blushing?" the woman in his arms beamed at him, flashing her genuine Nadia smile.

He grinned. "I believe I am."

28

NADIA OPENED the door to Gabby and Kelso.

"You're late for the moving-in party," she told them. The guys had worked efficiently to unload the U-Haul, and they were lounging around the backyard patio, drinking beer. Her dad still got tired easily, so Nadia made sure he was comfortable in the bedroom before she continued unpacking items in the kitchen.

"We come bearing pizza," Kelso said, his biceps bulging from the weight of the boxes. Gabby was carrying two smaller ones.

"Hurry in before you drop them." Nadia waved them through. She closed the door and followed them to the dining room. "Are you done with your shredding phase?"

Kelso lowered the pizza on the dining table. "No. Just taking a cheat day."

"I'm taking one with him," Gabby winked.

Declan took that moment to stride in probably getting a heads-up text from his wife. He went directly to Gabby and reeled her in for a kiss. "How was your day?" he asked.

Awww, Nadia swooned.

"Evan Wagner has been a drag," Gabby declared, wrapping her arms around Declan's torso. "I need a hug."

Her husband dutifully obliged. "Do I need to kick someone's ass?"

"I wish. But I don't want to get you into trouble," she pouted. The dynamics between them were cute. Gabby could be a no-nonsense cop but had no problem giving up control to seek comfort from her hot and protective hubby when they were among close friends.

Kelso said, "Wagner denied knowledge specifically about any device. He said since the Vovks were close business associates he didn't see any problem with their request to use the office spaces beside the Club Sochi basement."

"How did the search of the premises go?" Nadia asked.

John, Bristow, Antonio, and Charly took that moment to walk into the house from the patio.

"Still looking for clues that may lead to Sally's whereabouts. She hasn't returned to her house for sure," Kelso said, and then he smiled. "Don't worry. Your place is with your dad. Let us worry about finding her."

She blew out a breath. "How's her mother?"

"We have a man undercover at the hospital just in case she shows up."

"So far, bills are getting paid," Nadia said. "Any hopes of her coming out of a coma?"

"I can dig deeper," Bristow offered. "I know John has given you the access, but we agreed it might be better for plausible deniability if anyone questions how you came into the medical information."

"Oh." Kelso slipped out a phone and handed it to Nadia. "You may need this. I've sent Sally several messages encouraging her to turn herself in. That we can help her."

"No response?" She asked it more as a statement than a question.

Kelso shook his head. "We put out news of the apartment home invasion. Stated that your dad and Dugal were hurt."

"Trying to guilt her?" Nadia sighed.

"Yep."

She crossed her arms. "I have complicated feelings about Sally."

"We may have an insight of what's going on," John said. "We've noticed the influx of high-ranking mob bosses coming into the country. Dmitry Vovk was spotted in LA just last night, and he wasn't hiding his movements."

"Sicilian crime families were seen in Vegas," Bristow added. "And Levi said Russian Bratva lieutenants were seen crawling the clubs on Spring Street."

"First I've heard of this," Kelso said, face turning concerned. "Any idea why?"

John and Bristow's attention cut to Antonio.

"Something big is happening in LA," the businessman said. "I've heard noise about it from my associates inside the cartel and the Sicilian mafia."

"Well, don't keep us in suspense," Gabby said.

"A mob convention," Antonio said.

Nadia's eyes widened. "A mob convention?"

John nodded. "The disks we retrieved from Ukraine yielded interesting business dealings between Wagner and the Vovks. Revenant Films refused to work with the mob, and we're thinking Maxim and Wagner originally hatched up a plan to cause an incident at StreamCon and derail the production company"—he looked at Gabby—"your production company."

"The board has discussed this," Gabby replied. "We refused to work with the Vovks."

"But with Maxim dead, Morris was left in charge of the Crown-Key," Nadia speculated. "The traffic incident was meant to be a test of its capability. StreamCon is going to be held in the convention center which is located in Sequoia

Global City … and, oh crap!" SGC was a high concept urban development where the utilities and banking were computerized and highly interlinked. "This is bad. The Key can potentially shut down that city with just one malware."

"Not to mention if we're looking for persons of interest, they'll be in costumes," Gabby pointed out.

"Fuck," Kelso muttered. "They could dress as a mobster and say they're emulating that mob film that won the Oscar last year. These sons of bitches are going to use StreamCon to hide their activities since many of the participants are associates. They're going to blend." The detective studied Nadia. "Fancy going undercover? This gig would be right up your alley."

Excitement pulsed through her veins. The idea that she would be doing what she loved in the line of duty seemed to be the perfect storm.

But when John clasped her shoulders and gently turned her toward him with an apology in his eyes, she held her breath, knowing she wasn't going to like what he was about to say.

"I think you should sit this one out."

NADIA THREW up her arms and broke his hold, putting some distance between them. John wanted to yank her back in his arms and keep her there as he wrestled between his emotions and the job that needed to get done. It was a murky path, and one that blindsided him.

"Oh hell no," she snarled. "You do not get to make that choice for me."

Gabby got in between them, more in John's face, eyes shooting warning sparks. "She's right. Not your decision. She works for me and Kelso. It's an LAPD op. Don't fucking overstep."

His mouth flattened, and two simple words forced through clenched teeth. "She's pregnant."

The air around the room stilled, and Gabby's mouth gaped. "What?" Her brows shot up, and a look of incredulity crossed her face.

"Holy fuck," Declan chuckled, clapping Bristow on the shoulder. "You knew, didn't you?"

The SEAL was just grinning his shit-eating grin.

"You're pregnant?" Charly exclaimed while Antonio had a smirk plastered on his face.

John closed his eyes briefly. Fucking fantastic.

Kelso folded his arms and stared at Nadia. "I'm kinda hurt you didn't tell me, nerd girl."

Gabby wheeled around and glared at her partner. "Lay off. It's her prerogative when to share." She glanced back over her shoulder and smirked at John. "Although the baby daddy jumped the gun."

"More like he should've holstered the gun," Kelso coughed.

Everyone started laughing.

Roarke had tears in his eyes and couldn't hide his mirth. Fucker.

"I'm sorry," Roarke wheezed, and John hoped he choked on his next breath. "I mean, you're the most hardcore, mission-oriented operative among all of us." He wiped the corners of his eyes.

"Wait a minute," Kelso interjected. "You're not with him because of this, right? Because——"

"Stop right there, fucker——"

"All right, everyone calm down," Bristow stepped in. "We have a case to discuss."

"I agree," Nadia said, but John didn't like the cloudiness that descended on her face or the way she was staring at him. "We have several issues here and it seems it's more yours than mine because I trust you to do your work. Question is, do you trust me to do mine?"

"That's not a fair question," John growled.

"Oh, is it because I'm pregnant?" Nadia challenged. "Because, as far as I know, women have been pregnant since the beginning of time, and they're quite capable of working." She flared her arms down her sides. "I'm not even showing yet."

"How far along are you?" Kelso asked.

"Almost five weeks," Nadia replied.

"There are things we need to consider," Kelso's eyes shifted to John. "But it's up to Nadia if she wants to do it. Clear?"

His jaw clenched tight, as he bit back the urge to roar at everyone. He reined in the urge to lock Nadia away in a room, but judging from the stubborn set of her jaw, it was a losing battle. He gave a tight nod.

Everyone moved to the patio area, and the fire pit was lit for another chilly evening. The pizza seemed to mellow Nadia's mood to a point that John was able to sit by her side without a glare coming his way. He'd always been high-handed, more so after hearing the plan. His outburst asking her not to go on the mission bothered him, but he was slowly accepting how Nadia had become the center of his universe. Wasn't this what he wanted—her confident in her skills? But it was her skill to run an op safe in a room far away from danger, not in the middle of one.

Turnabout was fair play, apparently.

He stared at her profile, her features basking in the firelight. She was beautiful beyond words and vulnerable. The mother of his child. He was coming to terms with each tumultuous emotion that was wrenched out of him each time he worried about her safety. Was he in love? An emotion he'd scorned, that he'd promised he'd never feel for a woman. Was this what it was?

He'd damn everyone else, every other mission objective to protect Nadia. He would always choose her. He would find a way to do his job, but fuck, he would always choose her. And that was the main directive he'd assigned to all the compartments of his brain. He glanced around the men who'd gathered around the fire—Roarke and Andrade. They would do ruthless things to protect the women they loved. He understood Walker now too.

"It's Walker's wedding today," John murmured.

"I thought the man was already married," Gabby said.

"It was a Vegas wedding the first time," Andrade smirked.

Charly slapped him across the chest with the back of her hand and told everyone, "I find this reaffirmation of their vows very romantic."

Andrade gathered her in his arms. "More romantic than the wedding I gave you?"

His new bride leaned away and smiled at him. "No one can be more romantic than you."

Bristow coughed. "Challenge thrown."

"Why weren't any of you invited to Migs and Ariana's wedding?" Nadia asked.

"They wanted to keep it in the family," Bristow said. "Man, but I do like Mexican food."

Roarke shot him a look. "You like all kinds of food."

"I concur," Antonio said dryly.

"Bristow needs a woman who can cook," Nadia teased.

"Don't need one or the headache." He winked. "There's always takeout."

"Don't let Dad hear you about takeout," Nadia warned. "Or you'll never hear the end of it. Finish the pizza. Let's hide the boxes. Though I think I'll save a few pieces for Clyde."

"Where are the MoMoS?" Kelso asked.

"MoMoS?" Charly asked.

"The merry old men of SkyeLark," everyone who knew the acronym chorused in unison.

"Stephen retired early," John said. "Arthur and Clyde

turned in after the first beer. It's been a long day for them …" He frowned when more than a few heads tilted his way in a baffled look. "What?"

"You sound … almost … fond of them," Gabby said.

"Don't be a smartass," Roarke nudged his wife. "Whatever magic the MoMoS are weaving on Garrison, he seems to be more tolerable to work for these days."

"Fuck you, man," John grumbled.

After everyone had their amusement at his expense, Kelso called attention back to their yet unresolved plan to find the Crown-Key.

"With no device, will the mob still converge at Stream-Con?" the detective asked.

"Sally's status is unknown. We don't even know if Dmitry Vovk has found her," Gabby pointed out.

"I have a feeling she won't miss StreamCon." Nadia told them of the excitement she remembered in the woman's eyes at Huxley's party.

John already had his phone out, searching the StreamCon website. "We have exactly ten days to come up with a plan." He stood and started pacing, fingers rubbing across his chin, trying to work in the other angle. "So, how does the mob come in?"

"Maxim Vovk was a performer," Andrade said. "I've had dealings with him before our association fell apart because he loved publicity. Good or bad didn't matter."

"Seems he and Wagner are made for each other," Gabby said.

The businessman smiled briefly. "Yes. I have a feeling the organized crime groups at the event are there to witness the power of the Crown-Key."

"That's some kind of sales pitch," Roarke said.

"It starts a bidding war," the billionaire explained.

Andrade sure knew the inner workings of the underworld, John thought with amusement. It was definitely to their

benefit that he was on their side. Otherwise, they wouldn't
have thought to look deeper at the appearance of other criminal organizations. That was why Dmitry was very public in
the past few weeks, to draw all the attention to him, and let his
associates slip under the radar.

"But with Maxim dead …" Kelso started.

"It's up to Dmitry to deliver," John said. "He has to
produce something his brother promised."

"But with Sally missing," Nadia said. "He must be
desperate—"

"Dmitry doesn't get desperate," John murmured. "We
have to prepare for the possibility that he already has Sally,
and that's why she hasn't responded. She may have even
reached out to him."

"Dammit, Sally," Nadia muttered.

"Don't get too attached," Kelso told her.

She glared at him. "I'm not."

The detective raised a brow. "You said yourself that you
have complicated feelings about her."

"Ugh, yeah," she admitted. "But why would she reach out
to Dmitry? There's nothing in her profile that says criminal, so
what's driving her is paying the medical bills. Maybe we can
cut a deal with her. I'll continue to message her." She glanced
around. "We can, right? Give her immunity from the traffic
incidents and the ATM scam."

"Definitely," John said. "But that doesn't solve the problem
of her mother's medical bills."

"Yes, but if Maxim was the one who stole the Crown-Key,
maybe we can offer a reward for its return," Nadia argued.
"That'll go hand-in-hand with the immunity deal."

John's eyes softened. "Babe, you're making this too
personal, but it's not too farfetched."

"We don't know what transpired when Dmitry went to
Club Sochi," Kelso said. "You've seen him in action. He can
be charismatic. If there's truth to the rumor that he's indeed

the leader of the Argonayts then he would have been more appealing to a computer nerd like Sally."

Nadia turned to John. "If the ultimate goal is to hit StreamCon, and Sally is there, I'll be the person most likely to be able to reach her. Appeal to her."

"Geeks unite, huh?" John stared at her as the indecision battled inside him.

She offered a tight-lipped smile and gave a subtle nod.

He knew she was right. He couldn't let his overprotectiveness derail the relationship they were building. He told her he was going to adapt, but he sure as fuck thought it had everything to do with his job, not hers.

He hadn't counted on Nadia being in the line of fire.

The crackling of the fire pit was the only sound that could be heard around the patio.

Finally, John exhaled with a heavy breath. "Then, we'll make sure you're protected as fuck."

29

Sometimes, Nadia wondered how John put up with her shit. She could always blame her pregnancy hormones when she responded badly to his suggestion she sit out StreamCon. Later that evening, she realized that John reacted that way because he cared about her and the baby.

He had already proven his commitment to her and the baby when he'd been ready to resign his job so it wouldn't conflict with his responsibilities toward her.

Relationships were about compromise. And knowing the kind of man John was, he appeared to be compromising a lot when it came to her. So, when he insisted she get a thorough checkup from Dr. Stahl to make sure she was physically able to run after or escape from a perp and strengthen her self-defense skills, she didn't argue.

And now, after receiving a thumbs-up from the doctor, John had something else up his sleeve.

She stared at the text on her phone.

John: Go to our bedroom. Put on the dress in the box and be ready at six thirty.

She glanced up from her phone and stared suspiciously around the living room where Bristow and the MoMoS minus Dugal—who was still in the hospital but due to check out the next day—were assembled. Arthur and Stephen were watching television. Clyde was reading a book, and the SEAL, as usual, was on his laptop. Nadia had been with them all morning after John left to do whatever a spook did when he wasn't catering to the whims of a pregnant girlfriend or merry old men.

The menfolk appeared to be actively ignoring her.

Hmm…

She went upstairs and headed to their bedroom. Opening the door, she looked inside. It was hard to miss.

A long fancy box on top of the bed with a shoebox beside it.

Grinning, she moved further into the room and resisted the urge to fling the box open to see its contents. She took a picture of the box and sent it to John.

Me: How did you manage to sneak this in?
John: You know what I do for a living, right?

Nadia rolled her eyes.

John: You're rolling your eyes right now, aren't you?

She burst out laughing and looked around for cameras.

John: No cameras in our bedroom.
Me: OMG, stop. You're freaking me out.
Me: Seriously, how did you sneak this in?
John: Trade secret.

She shot off a tongue-out emoji and returned her attention to the boxes. She lifted the lid of the dress box, and her breath caught.

JOHN PULLED the Audi RS 5 in front of the house and got out of the sports car. In lieu of the Escalade he usually drove, he wanted to give his date with Nadia a different feel. He wanted to leave this craziness behind them for just one night. John texted Bristow, telling him to make sure Nadia didn't meet him outside.

He was going to do this right, dammit. This wasn't a role he was playing or a cover he was maintaining. This was real.

But he wasn't going to ring the doorbell.

He smirked and walked right in.

The MoMoS were in the living room and looked up when he came in. Clyde and Arthur rose, a pleased look on their faces. Bristow, who had his back to the door, turned and shot him a grin. "She's going to knock you off your feet, but you don't look so bad yourself."

"Thanks for the pep talk." John was wearing a black designer suit, blue dress shirt, and a thin tie. "Where is she?"

"Upstairs getting ready," Stephen said. "Arthur, can you go get her?"

Nadia's dad got up from the couch and approached John. He still had on a sling on from where he was shot in the shoulder.

"Thank you for doing this for her," Stephen said. "She needs a break from us."

"Though I agree with your sentiment, my reasons are selfish," John said. "I want her all to myself tonight."

"Ha! Good answer, man," Clyde said.

Stephen smiled. "You both certainly need alone time."

He was saved from answering when movement from the stairs caught his eye.

Nadia.

Holy fuck.

As her heeled feet cleared the bottom step, she glided toward him in the black cocktail dress that caught his eye on the mannequin when he was shopping for her dress. The saleswoman called it a sweetheart neckline. It showed off her shoulders and shapely arms with her dragon tattoo on full display. The skirt was edgy yet elegant. Short in front and skating longer toward the back, it was reminiscent of the dress she wore at the club. But John realized why he liked Nadia in short skirts. It was a sin to hide her mile-long, shapely legs.

"You can pick up your jaw now," Bristow murmured beside him.

He couldn't even muster a comeback, because as Nadia inched closer, her radiant face simply captivated him. Her hair was twisted up in a stylish knot, with tendrils framing her oval face in just the right places, exposing her swan-like neck and reminding him of what he had in his suit.

"Hey, handsome," she grinned up at him. John lowered his head and kissed her with just the right amount of tongue so as not to give the MoMoS a heart attack.

"Feels like a prom date," he murmured after he broke the kiss.

"Not with a kiss like that," Clyde interjected.

Nadia gave a breathy laugh while the other men chuckled.

"Turn around," he said.

With a bemused smile on her lips, she did as she was told.

Slipping out the necklace he had in his pocket, he placed it around her neck and clasped its ends together.

A few oohs and ahhs escaped their avid audience.

With his hands on her shoulders, he guided Nadia to the hallway mirror so she could see.

"Oh my God, John, this is too much!" Her hand flew to the necklace.

"It's a lariat necklace," he said. "At least that's what the jeweler told me."

"It is." She fingered the diamonds that paved the chain. "Are these …"

"I'd like to think they're sunflowers."

"It's exquisite," she continued, leaning in closer to the mirror and inspecting it with an analyst's eye. "It's very intricate. I see round, pear, and marquis-cut …"

"All right, babe," John chuckled as he turned her back around to face him. "Let's go before I start getting jealous about a piece of jewelry."

"He said he wanted to command all your attention," Stephen informed his daughter. "Maybe he should have held off on the necklace until later."

"I should've," he muttered.

"Hey, I'm not that bad," Nadia protested, but he was already ushering her toward the door. As much as he had grown fond of the MoMoS, he was anxious to be alone with his girl.

"We'll be back tomorrow," he told them.

"Wait, I don't have stuff with me," Nadia said.

He continued to move her out the door. "I took care of it."

Bristow had the sense to stop the menfolk from following them out the door. Great, because John had something to say to Nadia before they left.

Her eyes were riveted on their ride. "Wow."

He grinned. "Like it?"

"You're pulling out all the stops," she commented.

John leaned against the passenger side of the Audi and faced her. "One rule tonight."

She cocked her head in his direction.

"No talk about the case or the MoMoS. We can talk about StreamCon or *Hodgetown*, but nothing about how it pertains to the case."

"How about your job?"

"If it's about how it affects our relationship," he said. "Ask away."

"Wow."

"Tonight is about us." He opened the passenger door, letting her get into the vehicle, before ducking his head in so their faces were almost touching. "You and me. Our baby."

She flashed him the smile he loved, and John knew they were on the right track for tonight.

———

NADIA STILL COULDN'T BELIEVE how much her life had changed in the past few weeks. Couldn't believe how John was turning out to be the man of her dreams, or rather, the man she didn't know she needed. She always wanted safe and predictable. John was in no way safe or predictable. But when he made something or someone his mission, he was dependable.

Steadfast.

And in the pursuit of their relationship?

Swoony.

He took her to a highbrow French restaurant on Melrose Avenue. What made their outing special was their reservation at the chef's table—that pricey section at high-end restaurants where foodie patrons received a unique service from the chef. Nadia wasn't one for fancy dinners, but she was excited about this one.

They ordered their drinks. Wine for him and a raspberry-infused seltzer for her.

"Where's the menu?" she whispered.

"Why are you whispering?" John said beside her, amusement in his tone.

"I don't want to offend the chef in case he had something planned for us," she worried. "What if he prepares something

I can't eat? And because we're at this table, he'll see. He'll get offended."

The deep timbre of John's chuckle made her toes curl, momentarily chasing away her anxiety about restaurant etiquette. Everything about this man was sexy. Sweet Lord, she was getting James Bond fantasies with how impressively he filled out his suit. And the kicker? He wasn't a fantasy. Because John *was* a spy, and at that moment, he was sexier than any 007 in memory. If she wasn't already pregnant, her ovaries would be screaming to have his babies.

"First of all, the executive chef *is* a *she*," John said. "And second? You're going to love the food. I promise."

She smacked her lips together, still dubious about his assurance. Nadia wasn't particularly fond of French food because of its rich taste. However, she trusted the man beside her to do his research.

Trying to recall where she'd ordered food in the past few weeks, there were no places that were exciting. She had that failed gyro expedition with Kelso. She wondered if John had Bristow compile her favorite takeout places and restaurants. Didn't John say he knew what the MoMoS' favorites were? There were also those food trucks in front of their HQ. Her tastes were wide and varied, but French cuisine wasn't at the top of her list save for its desserts like the beignets Clyde had gotten for her.

A woman in a chef jacket approached their table. A toque cap sat on her head instead of the tall ones most chefs wore. "You must be Nadia," she said. "I'm Parisa, and I have a special evening planned for you." The chef glanced at John. "Mr. Garrison was very specific with his requests when we planned the menu."

"He's very demanding," Nadia shared, tongue-in-cheek.

"Only the best for her, right, chef?" John drawled.

Nadia wasn't sure whether the chef was Italian or Middle

Eastern, but her name gave her a clue. "Your name ... I think—"

"Persian." Parisa smiled back. "I'm a classically trained chef, but I learned my love for cooking from my mother. Sometimes I infuse our French menu with a touch of my Persian heritage. So when your boyfriend approached me about doing this for you, I was all over it."

They chatted for a bit about Iranian culture and its culinary delights, about how it was so underrated in comparison to Italian and Mediterranean cooking. After a while, Parisa said, "Well, I better get back to the kitchen. Evening rush is about to start. I'll get those appetizers out to you."

When the chef walked away, Nadia turned to John excitedly. "I can't wait to see what she prepared for us. I mean, I do have an idea." She was babbling, but she didn't care. "I trust you to be thorough in your investigation." She leaned in and gave him a kiss on the cheek.

His hand on her thigh gave a squeeze. His mouth twitched, and the gleam in his eyes was nothing but indulgent and it made her heart skip. "If tempting you with your favorite dish gets me this exuberance every time, then you can be sure it's duly noted."

She tucked her arm into his, thankful they were in an alcove facing the theatre of the kitchen. But despite the hectic rush, blurs of white, and yells of "yes, Chef," Nadia hadn't felt this relaxed since Halloween, before her world had flipped on its axis. Her dad was on the mend, and Dugal was coming home. The days were looking up.

"Hey, where did you go?" John asked.

"I was just thinking of Dugal," she replied. "I know you said tonight is about us, but—"

He put a finger on her lips. "Say no more. Dugal is family. Of course you can't simply push him out of your thoughts."

"But they weren't bad thoughts," Nadia reassured him. "I was thinking about how resilient people are."

Their server took that moment to present them with an appetizer tray. She eagerly sampled the offerings. Nadia couldn't believe the texture of the hummus and its balanced flavor of garlic, lemon, and tahini. Parisa's Persian cucumber yogurt that always reminded her of tzatziki was the creamiest she'd ever tasted. She also savored the creative little bites she hadn't known existed, and they all combined to tickle her palate for the main event.

She was pregnant after all. It was the perfect excuse to eat.

The pomegranate-walnut stew that her father's girlfriend, Sara, used to make was the star of the evening menu. In looks, Fesenjan wasn't a very appetizing dish. Typically, its color ranged from maroon to dark brown. The one presented to them was a shade in between, and the suspicious looking pieces poking from its thick, grainy sauce hardly invited a diner to dig in. When she caught John scowling at the dish, laughter bubbled up her throat.

"Aren't you going to try it?" she asked.

"Ladies first," he muttered.

"It tastes a whole lot better than it looks."

"I'll take your word for it."

That time, she did burst out laughing. "Here, have the rice first." She prepared a plate for him, relishing the act of introducing him to her favorite cuisine.

"Smells good," he murmured.

A shiver ran up her spine. Somehow, she knew it wasn't the food he was referring to, but she feigned innocence anyway. "The aroma of saffron basmati rice is my favorite. Dad and I usually burned the crust, though." When she looked at him, his eyes were riveted on her as she suspected. "Give it a taste."

John continued holding her gaze captive as he raised his wine to his mouth, taking a sip. Heat flashed between them, and the area below her pelvis pulsed. Then he oh, so deliberately lowered his wine glass before finally giving attention to his food. Nadia grabbed her own seltzer water to quench her throat which had suddenly gone dry.

His brows shot up after his first tentative taste of Fesenjan. "Interesting flavors. Tangy. Sweet. Earthy." His mouth quirked. "Not as bad as the blood stew I had when I was in the Philippines."

Nadia proceeded to fill her plate. "I guess you're trained to eat whatever."

He grimaced. "Yes. Doesn't mean I don't struggle."

"What were you doing in the Philippines?" She paused. "Or is that classified?"

"The mission specifics are, but we were tracking terrorists in the southern islands."

John regaled her with stories of his life in the CIA, skimming over the details, but they were no less fascinating. "You've led an exciting life."

Refilling his goblet with more wine, he took another sip and leaned against the padded booth. "I'm ready to settle down."

Her grin faltered and she dropped her gaze to her plate. She pushed a piece of chicken around. "You mean quit the agency?"

"Look at me, babe."

Reluctantly, she did. The determination and intensity in those indigo eyes made her squirm in a good way. "What work I will do for the agency will depend on how it will affect you and the baby. They can take it or leave it."

She averted her eyes again. "I don't know what I can give in return."

"Hey," he said, lifting her chin with the tip of his finger. There was a firmness in that gesture that prevented her from looking away. "Our relationship is not quid pro quo. You being you? It's enough. And ... I've come to care for you so deeply, babe. It pissed me off when Kelso suggested that I was with you because of the baby. Let me squash that statement now." His face inched closer. "I would have pursued this relationship whether there was a baby or not. Your pregnancy accelerated my timeline, but we were going to happen. Baby or not. Are we clear on that?"

"Yes." Giddiness suffused her system.

"You remind me of the man I used to be. The kind of man I hope you can be proud of."

"John." She cupped his jaw. "I'm proud of whoever you choose to be. This world needs men like you, but I'm happy to volunteer and keep you grounded."

"Oh, babe," Their lips were almost touching. "You have no idea ..."

A crash in the kitchen broke the spell between them. Two servers had collided and were standing in a mess of shattered porcelain and food. A ruckus of yelling ensued. John chuckled while she gave a quick, if not embarrassed laugh. Sometimes they forgot they had an audience. She hoped their amorous display had in no way distracted the servers.

They resumed eating the feast before them. She cast surreptitious glances at the man who was the reason behind the secretive smile currently lurking on her mouth.

And when the dessert of the evening turned out to be a chocolate beignet topped with crème fraîche ice cream, she could unequivocally say she loved the way her man planned their date.

John took her favorite things and elevated them to perfection.

30

"THERE'S ONLY one way you could have found out about the Fesenjan," Nadia told him.

After dessert, they lingered over a digestif. Nadia favored the decaffeinated ginger tea, while John went for Armagnac. By the time they finished their three-hour dining experience, it was past ten.

Instead of answering her, he secured the wrap around her shoulders before taking her hand to walk the short trek across the street to their hotel.

"My dad," she continued. "I had all these theories about how you and Bristow combed through my credit history to find out which ones were my favorite restaurants, but it was my dad, wasn't it?"

"Intel from trusted human assets are the most valuable," he deadpanned. They entered the hotel lobby where John gave a muted nod to the concierge. He was certain they'd been spotted from across the street. All subtle interactions inherent to embedded agency operatives were in play. This hotel was one of the few hotels in the city the agency used for clandestine work, and the top two floors were reserved specifically for men like John and were routinely swept for bugs and surveillance.

"Hmm," Nadia said. Her heels made clacking noises on the Italian marble flooring, underscoring the ensuing silence that made him glance over. Her head was angled away from him. She was studying her surroundings.

Lowering his head, he said, "You should watch where you're going."

She shot him a look. "I trust you not to let me run into a post or stumble on steps."

"You're scoping around this place like it's a museum."

She bit her lower lip, the edges of her mouth tipping up as though she was controlling a big smile. Mirth filled her eyes. "Is this place like …" she lowered her voice. "Assassin's Hill?"

John sighed in resignation. "You make it very hard to date you."

"That's what you get for setting your cap on a crime analyst."

Arriving at the bank of elevators, he stabbed the call button, impatient to get her to their suite so he could show her the consequences of her flirtatious taunts.

"You're such a challenge," he muttered. He'd been living a jaded existence for long, he finally understood why Nadia just did it for him. There was no question they burned the sheets in the bedroom, and there was no question her beautiful face took his breath away with those expressive hazel eyes and a smile that dazzled him. But a man like him needed more than beauty and lust to twist him up in knots. He needed a woman who kept him on his toes in a way that cracked the walls of his hardened heart, letting dormant feelings soar. Feelings he didn't know existed.

Nadia Powell did that to him. He would never, ever let her go.

"What?" she asked innocently. "You don't like challenges?" She looked very pleased with herself. The minx. The wrap had come loose and exposed the soft swell of her breasts. He couldn't wait to peel the rest of her clothes off.

The elevator was taking too long. He stabbed the button again.

Nadia edged closer, molding her softness to his side. She nipped his ear. "Someone is impatient."

A groan vibrated in his throat, and he gritted his teeth. She definitely had his number, but goddammit, it was messing with his plan to fuck her slow and gentle.

The elevator doors finally slid open, and he resisted the urge to drag her in.

He flashed a keycard against the panel that would turn off the carriage cameras and take them to their floor. It also increased the temptation to push her against its mirrored walls, sink to his knees, toss up her skirt, and lick her between her thighs.

Instead, they stood side by side, still holding hands. But both of them were so still, as though frozen. No words passed between them. They stared at each other in the reflective steel of the elevator doors.

When they reached the twelfth floor, they both released a deep breath. Nadia burst out in nervous laughter, letting go of his hand, and skipped ahead of him. John followed more leisurely, shoving his hands in his pockets, chuckling in self-deprecation at how his woman so easily put him on edge.

"Which one is our room?" she asked, her breathless voice raised goosebumps of need from the top of his shoulders to the base of his spine.

"End of the hall," he clipped. He flexed his fingers to let out the tension.

Alone with Nadia.

There was no one else on this floor, and the walls were soundproof. No one to hear her scream as he brought her to orgasm over and over.

When she got to the door of their room, she spun around and shot him a seductive smile.

He narrowed his gaze. "You keep doing that and we'll never make it to the bed."

"I love wall sex."

Jesus, that mouth. Just slay him now.

But he was supposed to be this cool-as-shit CIA officer. He had a rep to protect, and he had a feeling Nadia liked him to boss her around, daring him to do filthy things to her. With their gazes unwavering from each other, he tapped his wallet to the electronic reader and opened the door.

Nadia tugged him in by his tie, leading him into the room.

"Hold on," he said, engaging the safety.

Her mouth curled in a smile, "You're so hot when you're protective."

"Are you making fun of me, Miss Powell?"

"Of course not, Agent Garrison."

John winced. CIA operatives weren't called agents no matter what the public thought. He spun her around and pinned her against the wall, making her feel his erection at the base of her spine.

"We're not called agents," he whispered in her ear, lowering his hand around her and under her skirt, slowly sliding it up her thigh. "Every time you call me that, it makes me want to torture you right here." His finger touched the core of her, touching wetness through the scrap of fabric hiding her pussy. She was wearing a thong again. Her arousal immediately coated his fingers. Her breathing fractured. His grew ragged as he pressed two fingers inside her, feeling the tight fit of her inner muscles clenching around him.

Fuck.

He rocked his body against her as he continued pumping with his fingers.

"Agent Garrison, please fuck me," she breathed out.

"You're so wet and ready for me," he snarled softly. He

withdrew his fingers and scooped her into his arms and carried her to the bedroom. "But you're going to know slow and torturous from me."

She might have whimpered at this statement. Good.

Because this evening was about showing her there was more than lust between them, and he intended to show her just how much he cared by worshipping her body in the way she deserved.

He lowered her gently to the bed. "Don't move. I'm undressing you."

He doffed his jacket and undid his tie. When he started unbuttoning his dress shirt, Nadia propped on her elbows and watched him remove his clothes with hooded eyes. He was in no way doing a strip tease, but these slow deliberate movements certainly ratcheted up his anticipation. He didn't know whether this was a good or a bad thing.

"Don't take off your pants all the way," she whispered.

"Why?"

"I love the way the clothes rub against my inner thighs … makes it feel so deliciously dirty."

Damn, she was perfect.

He slid off his shoes, unbuckled his belt and lowered his zipper. Then he put a knee on the bed, reaching for her leg to pull her to him. Settling between her thighs, he raised himself up on his arms and framed her face. "I'm on the brink of falling really hard."

Her brow arched. "Is that so?" Her voice sounded nonchalant, but there was no hiding the hitch in her breathing.

"Yes. You've ruined my perfectly ordered existence."

"Oh, you mean I made you more likable?"

"Smartass."

"Bossy."

He kissed the tip of her nose. "You like my bossiness."

"And you love my smartass mouth."

"What am I going to do about you?"

She smiled slowly. "Make love to me?"

He didn't answer her with words. He answered her with a kiss. Slow and deliberate, he kissed her. Tongues tangled, plunged, and swirled, searching each other deeper. They searched for their truths and yearnings, exposing their aspirations and that tiny niggle of uncertainty in defining their feelings for each other. Passion threatened to take over, but John was determined to take it slow and managed his pace, making her lips swollen with his kisses.

He nipped at her jaw and worked his mouth against the sensitive pulse at her neck, before he angled her body to undo the zipper at the back of her dress, pulling it painstakingly down her curves to reveal her tits. The image he'd been trying to push out of his mind all night was finally here—Nadia naked with only that diamond necklace around her neck, still wearing heels.

After removing the dress, he slipped off her thong. Rising to his knees between her thighs, he stared down at her for a moment, taking in the sensuality of how the light from outside cast a pearlescent glow to her skin. He committed her in that moment to memory.

"So fucking beautiful," he whispered.

A sensual smile curved her lips.

Grinning, he adjusted himself on the bed in the perfect position to go down on her. "I love this view," he murmured against her pussy. "I love the smell of you right here." He ran a finger through her folds. "And you're wet. So fucking wet."

From his position, he could see her chest rising and falling rapidly. "You're being so good and patient. You need me so badly here. Want me to fuck you hard, but that's not what you're getting tonight. I'm going to love your body, Nadia. The way it deserves."

He lowered his head and tasted fucking ambrosia. His tongue darted out and swiped broadly from her opening to her clit. It was always this way with her. The madness between plunging inside her with his cock and making her come over and over on his tongue. He added two fingers to his assault, crooking them up where her sweet spot was and she shot off like a rocket. She screamed and it became his mission to make her scream some more, until the yanking of his hair told him to back off. He withdrew his fingers but continued to suck on her swollen clit.

Then he trailed kisses up her body until they were face to face once more.

Her makeup was smeared, yet she looked glorious. A satisfied smile touched his mouth because he was the one who mussed her up. He was the one who wrecked her.

He linked their hands together and he rocked into her, reveling at the slick heat clenching his cock in a vise. He saw her eyes close and watched every expressive nuance fleet across her face. He was mastering Nadia Powell in a way that would ensure she would crave only his touch. He tried his best to keep it slow and make it last. But taking Nadia skin to skin always worked up the beast inside him.

Gritting his teeth, he reined in his feral lust, making his heart take control of the demands of the flesh. He ground his hips in a circle, knowing the contact with the top of her pussy triggered her pleasure.

"Oh! Harder. There."

He was right.

She was coming again. Her moans of pleasure almost causing him to come undone. When she rounded him with her limbs, he knew it was time to let go.

He sped up his thrusts, his cock growing impossibly hard. The clenching of her pussy demanded his surrender. After a few more shallow thrusts, he planted himself deep.

Emptying himself inside her, pleasure jolts rippled endlessly all over him as he continued pumping into her.

"Fuck," he groaned, rolling off to her side to avoid

crushing her, yet not wanting to lose the connection, he dragged her into his embrace.

His heart throbbed in his ears, and he wondered if he would ever recover his breath. So much for slow, the anticipation and holding back nearly stroked him. Nadia snuggled into his side, and slid a bare leg across his thighs.

"Thank you for tonight. This is some date."

"Nothing too good for you," he said. "Night's not over yet."

"I wondered," she said huskily. "Can we do it doggy style?"

His dick jumped in response to that. "You'll be the death of me, woman."

31

"WE'VE BEEN through this a gazillion times."

Nadia puffed a breath, feeling sweaty, and more than a little bit annoyed at John, but she couldn't help admiring how his shirt hugged his shoulders, how his tattooed arms bulged out from his sleeves. After the spectacular date two nights ago, she tried to be more tolerant of his pushiness that sometimes got the better of her.

"One more round."

"What's the use anyway, when we go in slow motion," she griped. "That's not the reality of it."

His face hardened. "You want to go on this op. I want you to be prepared."

"Can I just kick my attackers in the balls?"

His eyes crinkled at the corners. "That's what we're working up to. Nose, face, throat, and groin. Weakest parts."

Then without warning, John grabbed her shoulders. Nadia instinctively lifted her right arm, pivoted sideways to the left and brought her arm down, breaking his hold and followed it by ramming her elbow to the side of his face.

"Fuck!" John grunted.

"Oh my God!" Horrified, Nadia instantly checked on him, but he spun around her and captured her from behind.

"Never let your guard down," he rasped in her ear as she squirmed against him. It was hard to concentrate when John was with her in this way. Images of him fucking her from behind last night flashed through her mind.

"Well, I wouldn't have if it wasn't you," she snapped.

"How do you get out of this?"

I don't want to. Take me to the floor and fuck me.

But Nadia grabbed his forearms, pulling herself in and shifting her hips to one side. She faked to strike his groin, but John released her.

Straightening up, and swiping the hair that had escaped from her ponytail, she glared at him. "Satisfied?"

His mouth quirked at the corners. "You're hot when you're badass like that."

Her brow arched. "I am feeling hot." And just as she said that, heat pulsed between her legs. It must be the pregnancy hormones, or it was simply Mr. Garrison. She was eternally horny when he was around, and most especially, when it was just the two of them.

He pulled her into his arms, eyes smoldering. "Oh, yeah, what else?"

"Is this still part of defense training?"

He shoved his crotch against her and she could feel a semi forming at her lower pelvis. "What do you think?"

"We shouldn't."

His face came closer …

"Ahem."

John's eyes lifted past her shoulder and narrowed.

"Sorry for the interruption." It was her dad. "Levi is here with his wife …and …"

Nadia frowned, turning around, wondering what had gotten Stephen sounding breathless. "Are you okay, Dad?"

"Theo Cole is here."

Her eyes bugged out. "Oh my God."

"Yes!" Her father's eyes were equally huge.

She wheeled around and faced John. "You know anything about this?"

"Roarke mentioned something last night. Gabby wasn't too keen about it." He hitched his shoulders. "Theo made his own decision."

"This plan is going to rock!" Nadia clapped her hands together.

John nudged her forward. "Yeah, let's hope we don't get Theo hurt, or worse, because Gabby *will* have Roarke's balls … and mine."

Nadia didn't know who to fangirl over first. Theo Cole, Gabby and Declan's son who played Billy Mayhem on *Hodgetown*, or Kelly James, Levi's wife, who was an award-winning makeup and special effects (SFX) artist of Nadia's favorite fantasy and sci-fi shows of recent years. It wasn't the first time she'd met them, and she was used to hanging around Theo. But his character on the show had developed over the years, and as he had gotten more popular, she'd seen him less and less. And she was obsessing over the Locke Demon. Gabby and Declan were always complaining that they hardly ever see Theo anymore as the *Hodgetown* production cast promoted the show on the road.

Dugal and Clyde were entertaining Theo and Kelly. Roarke was standing beside them, eyes keen on his son who was his spitting image. Arthur was his usual self, observing in the background.

Levi was standing on the other side of Kelly. They were not back together yet but were doing their best to co-parent their girls. A complicated backstory led to their separation. Gabby indicated it was because of Levi's former job as a private military contractor, but the former SEAL was getting his shit together to try and win back his wife.

Theo grinned when he spotted Nadia and John.

"Couldn't believe what I was hearing when I heard you two hooked up." The teen star met them halfway across the room, gave Nadia a kiss on the cheek while he and John exchanged a one arm hug. "Heard you guys need our help." Theo gave them a charming wink.

Kelly approached and exchanged hugs with Nadia. Leaning away, she smiled broadly. "Any woman who manages to get John to StreamCon can call me any time."

"Ha! You don't know what you've signed up for." Nadia warned her.

"I wish I wasn't laid up," Dugal spoke glumly from the couch. "I'd make a good character."

Kelly glanced over her shoulder and grinned at the grumbling Scot. "That you would, and you've got an interesting face to work with."

"Did you just insult me, lass?" the Scot asked.

Nadia was used to his feigned outrage.

"She's blunt," Levi said. "Get used to it, because you're going to see her for the next few days."

"Dugal is a drama king. Don't mind him," Nadia said. She was so relieved that he was making big strides in his recovery. There were moments when he got easily tired like her dad, but John said he believed Dugal's resistance to being laid out for long was helping his recuperation.

Colin walked in from the kitchen and handed his dad a glass of water. "And you should be lying in bed."

"I'm bored," he told his son. "It's more entertaining here." Colin rolled his eyes and sunk into the armchair.

John cleared his throat. "Let's take this to the work room I've prepared for us."

Translation … there are too many ears in this room, and it makes me uncomfortable.

This was an LAPD op working closely with the CIA. The fewer people in the know, the better.

The garage of the safe house was huge, it could be

described as a garage bay that could fit five SUVs. Right then, it was empty of vehicles. There were four garage doors, and two of them were open. Levi was backing up a white, heavy-duty, commercial truck. When the rear was just inside the mouth of the garage, he cut the engine and jumped down from the vehicle, going around to lift the gates in the back.

"Chairs and the table," Kelly said. "I need to get a mold of their faces."

"I get to keep my beard, right?" John asked.

The brunette assessed him. "I'll trim it down to make a smoother mold. I've worked with many actors who were attached to their beards, I've become a pro."

"You are a pro," Theo said, walking to where Nadia and John stood. "So I heard back from Nick," the teenager continued. "Mom talked to him this morning, and he was fine with John walking around as the Locke Demon with the other Locke Demons during the *Hodgetown* panel. "

Declan grunted. "Was there any concern he was going to say no to Gabby?"

His son shot him an exasperated look. Though Theo and Gabby owned the majority of Revenant Films, Nick Carter was the CEO. He was also Gabby's ex-husband. Apparently, Declan still hated the guy.

Theo shot his father an exasperated look. "It's been over a year, dude. Aren't you two ever going to be in a room and not be at each other's throats."

"Don't count on it."

Rolling his eyes, Theo addressed John. "You'll be joining at least one dress rehearsal."

"Christ. Can't you just coach me?"

"It's a team effort," the teen said. "And we need to give you a rundown of what's tolerated behavior from the fans and where to draw the line. We'll have simulations there." Theo grinned. "The Locke Demon is the most popular character from the show right now aside from me. You may be mobbed."

"Do not antagonize the *Hodgetown* fans," John scoffed. "Got it. Easy-peasy."

Declan said, "Hmm … that could be a problem."

"No," Theo contradicted. "It might work in our favor. The Locke Demon is supposed to be a gray-area character. Garrison is the perfect person for this role. He can be himself. Some ornery behavior is expected."

Nadia didn't know whether to laugh or be more worried.

"Hey. Some help here," Levi hollered from inside the truck.

Declan didn't make any move to help. "Don't know, bro. Kelly looks scary seeing how she orders you around."

The woman in question turned toward them and gave Declan the finger.

Nadia burst out laughing. "A woman after my own heart."

John looped an arm around her neck and drew her close. "It seems we all have a type."

"It takes a special kind of woman to be with men like us," Declan winked at her.

"One with a lot of patience," Nadia said under her breath.

———

JOHN WAS BEGINNING to hate the sound of the compressor powering the airbrush system. He was getting fidgety, especially after sitting for almost two hours in a chair. How do people do this shit? This was nothing like the times he'd had to sit with an agency cover specialist.

Kelly flitted between him, Nadia, and Levi who was a last-minute addition to their monster squad.

In the days leading up to StreamCon, Nadia and Sally Davis were in contact via messaging. Nadia had tried to get the computer hacker to turn herself in to no avail. However, the other day, Sally sent a message that she would, indeed, be at StreamCon and might decide to surrender the Crown-Key in exchange for immunity.

There'd been several theories.

First, Sally was telling the truth and needed those few days to decide to turn herself in. According to her, she still didn't trust the LAPD to drop the charges in return for the Key.

Second, Dmitry Vovk had her, and she was being coerced into lying to get to Nadia who still had access to the source code. As a precaution, Nadia entered a duress code within the program in case the op went sideways, and she was captured. John gritted his teeth at that thought, which was why he added Levi as extra eyes.

The third speculation was that Sally was leading them on and continued to use the Crown-Key for monetary purposes and had no intention of giving it up.

The buzzing of the compressor turned off, and Kelly appeared in his line of vision. "Don't move. I'm going to let this dry, but I think you look perfect."

"Fucking finally."

"I'm going to check on Nadia," Kelly told him as she disappeared from view.

"How are you holding up, Demon Boy?" Nadia called from over the divider. The corners of his mouth quirked up, but judging from his reflection in the mirror, his smile looked more evil than amused.

"I look fuckin' scary." John stared at the mirror. The Locke Demon had a squarish face. His eyes were sunken, and his large forehead loomed over them. Two horns, one broken in half, rose from his bald head. He was thankful he didn't need a padded bodysuit. The costume was a combination of black flexible armor, topped with cascading shoulder plates, edged with badass rivets. Mobility wasn't a problem, and he could hide a gun in his thigh holster masked by the handle of a knife.

"I can't wait to see!"

"Keep still," Kelly admonished.

"I'll probably scare the kids," John said.

Nadia didn't respond, but Levi, who was on the other side of her, answered, "You'll probably be under siege by the *Hodgetown* fandom. Even my girls love the Locke Demon."

"Hmm … has daddy been letting Ashley and Whitney watch too much TV?" Kelly said in that 'you're so busted' tone.

The compressor of the air brush machine started again, so instead of admiring his ugly mug, John ran through several scenarios in his head. None of them were to his liking because he was nowhere near Nadia at given times, but the CTTF team would be on hand, scattered throughout the convention center as regular attendees.

He, Nadia, and Levi would be walking around the Revenant Films booth. There would be others wearing the same costumes, but Kelly gave theirs a unique finish so they could be identified from the rest. They also had their assignments during the *Hodgetown* panel.

Kelly came around the divider to give him one last look. John held his breath as the woman scrutinized her work, praying like hell she was satisfied because trying to yank his hair off when he had no hair to pull was the worst torture.

"Are you ready to see her?" Kelly asked.

"Hell yeah, where's my demon bride?"

———

"HELL YEAH, where's my demon bride?"

Suddenly anxious like a bride about to meet her groom, words snagged at her throat.

"Nadia?" John prodded.

"I'm ready." She glanced at Levi, whose grin through his own MarshMan mask was quite freaky. She exhaled a stale breath and stood, thankful that the soft rubber bodysuit was flexible. Kelly's costume designer pal did a version of a corset that shaped her torso and pushed up her boobs. Her arms were on full display and she was proud of their muscle tone. Kelly even improved its definition with strategically airbrushed makeup but had to hide her dragon tattoo.

Unlike the Locke Demon, the demoness had hair and she was wearing a bright red wig.

"Let me see you, babe," John said gently.

Nadia realized she was frozen. She swallowed the knot in her throat and stood. Why was she so nervous? She stepped around the divider, with her eyes pinned to the ground.

Her gaze picked up scuffed boots, and then slowly lifted, taking in muscular legs she knew belonged to John that were in no way special effects. Flexible armor flared onto a bulky chest which might have been padded and molded, but John was no lightweight in any way. The shoulder armor was badass, and finally, finally, she got to his face.

Her eyes warmed as she erased the distance between them, her hand going up to touch John's demon face. Her beloved Locke Demon was looking at her with such tenderness and her love for the character and the man …

Oh my God, she loved John!

"You're perfect," she whispered in wonder.

John smiled, his gaze unwavering. "And you're sexy-as-fuck gorgeous." His eyes roamed down her heaving chest and then back up her face. "Damn." He lowered his voice. "The things I wanna do to you."

"Oh, wow, talk about smoking up the screen," Kelly laughed lightly. "Pardon the pun."

John stared at Nadia a second longer before glancing at their SFX artist. "This paint is smudge proof right?"

Kelly squinted at him in warning. "What are you up to?"

"Can I kiss her?" His focus returned to her. "Because I've

got a strong damned urge to do so, and I don't think I can fucking stop myself."

Without waiting for Kelly's response, John lowered his head—and their foreheads collided.

"I was gonna say," Kelly said in an amused tone. "It's high-quality makeup but you might have issues."

"Nothing a little adjustment can't fix." John tilted his head to the side at the same time lifting Nadia's chin, and he kissed the fuck out of her. The mouth portion of their masks blended into their real ones which technically allowed kissing.

"Hey!" Someone called from the entrance of the garage. "The convention is rated PG. Just in case you all forgot."

They broke apart and turned to the newcomers. Declan and Bristow were their escorts to the convention. Gabby was taking Theo and his girlfriend.

"Are you guys ready?" Declan asked. "Or do you guys need a moment? It seems Levi wants to take a page from John's book."

"Behave, MarshMan," Kelly warned her husband. "You guys better head over to the convention center before the doors open.

"Show time, folks," Levi announced.

32

THE *HODGETOWN* FANS fell in love with John's Locke Demon.

It was a hit for Revenant Films publicity machine, but a disaster for the joint CIA-CTTF effort. Nadia could only watch in horror and disbelief as John got mobbed by the crowd inside the convention hall hosting the *Hodgetown* panel. The actor playing the Locke Demon was actually up on the stage with the rest of the cast, but apparently the fandom was more interested in the costumed version. And Kelly James's demon creation for John was no comparison to the other Locke decoys.

"Agent down, agent down," Levi chuckled through comms. As the MarshMan, he had to sidestep a bit of the fandom's ire because he was the one who sent Billy Mayhem and the Locke Demon into the monster dimension.

"Someone rescue me from … what the fuck? No, I can't be your Bae," John growled. "I'm taken."

"John understands Gen-Z lingo?" Kelso laughed.

"It's required training," Bristow deadpanned, or at least it was said in a deadpan tone.

Nadia received a message from Sally Davis informing her to wait for further instructions during the *Hodgetown* panel. She kept her phone conveniently in a slit pocket along the thigh section of her bodysuit.

There was a distinct increase of murmur coming from the crowd as the panel took their seats after chatting with select fans along the sidelines. Nick Carter, Revenant Films CEO, took the podium as the evening's emcee.

"Ladies and gentlemen." Carter touched the mic and looked over to where John was being mobbed. "And monsters."

Clapping and laughing ensued.

"Let's take our seats, please. I promise, you won't want to wait a second longer for the much-anticipated teaser for season five."

Cheering erupted across the entire *Hodgetown* fandom and even in comms where Bristow said, "Hell yeah." A thrill went through Nadia. She couldn't wait to tell her dad and find the official video online.

The room shrunk as the lights dimmed.

She tensed, even when she knew it was part of the program.

As the chatter died away, Carter continued, "We've filmed half of the new season's episodes, and the footage is fantastic. There are critics who said we should have ended the show at season one"—loud booing erupted from the audience—"but we don't care about the critics. We care about the fans. We care about you."

Whistles and chants of—"Mayhem, Mayhem"—rose in the room.

"Hell, I know you don't like the guy, Roarke," Levi said through comms. "But he sure knows how to rally the crowd."

Nadia grinned as everyone gave Declan a hard time. Surprisingly, his wife was quiet, but Nadia might have heard a snicker from Gabby.

Thankfully, Carter kept his speech short. "Without further ado, I present, *Hodgetown* season five."

"Levi, John, keep your eyes peeled," Kelso said. "Nadia and Bristow are momentarily occupied."

She laughed. He'd be right. Her eyes were glued to the stage. The *Hodgetown* title flashed on the screen, and a new version of the theme song came on. The crowd quickly hushed when the beginning of the video showed a hand, palm up on a wet ground. The fingers twitched and then the camera panned out to reveal it was Billy Mayhem amidst the foggy forest-like floor of the monster realm. When the Locke Demon appeared and grabbed Billy and looked like he was about to chomp off his head, the crowd gasped.

"Hmm, Kelly's version is better," Levi commented.

"Yeah, John is more handsome," Nadia laughed, but her laughter faded when confusion at what she was seeing set in. It started creepily enough, a hallway in an old house, a door creaking open, but she was confused to see what Cain Morris was doing on the screen. He was arranging Ken Huxley's body on the bed.

A wave of confused murmuring swept across the room, and Nick Carter yelled at someone on his phone.

"What the fuck?" John bit out.

Shouting and curses erupted in her ears as the screen went blank, and the lights came on.

Nadia's phone vibrated. Quickly fishing it out, she checked what came in.

Anonymous_754: I was part of the cover up.

"She's made contact," Nadia said through comms, heading rapidly for the exit. She typed back.

Me: It's okay. We can talk about this.
Anonymous_754: Stairwell beside the Sparbro booth. Come alone.
Me: Got it.

"Wait for Levi," John ordered. "This could still be a demo for the mob."

Or Sally was making one last ditch effort to come clean. "She wants me to come alone. Stairwell beside Sparbro booth."

"We talked about this …" John cursed at someone again. Revenant Films might regret allowing the LAPD to use their company for cover.

"I'll watch her," Kelso said. "I'm right beside the booth. Crowd is thin. Woodward, anything from your end?" She was in the CCTV room of the convention center, monitoring security feeds.

"This is a nightmare," Gabby replied. "I can't tell the real gangsters from the fake ones."

Or the real monsters from the make-believe.

The phone in her hand vibrated with another message.

Anonymous_754: Are you in costume?

Nadia hesitated.
Bubbles for a long time … and then…

Anonymous_754: Well? Don't play me again.
Me: I'm in a demoness costume. You?
Anonymous_754: No costume. I'm me.

Nadia cleared the door. She was stopped a few times by fans who wanted to pose with her and after the third photo op, she turned down the rest. "Boy, Revenant is going to get bad publicity for its ornery creatures."

"We're just staying in character," Levi said as she heard a roar in her earpiece followed by delighted screams from the crowd behind her.

Nadia glanced briefly over her shoulder. "I think you missed your calling, Levi."

Facing forward, she weaved through the crowd and spotted Kelso who shook his head. "Haven't seen signs of her yet."

"No heat signature in the stairwell," Bristow said. "But the walls might be too thick for our drone to penetrate."

"Do not go in that stairwell by yourself," John said. "I'm heading your way."

"You're going to bring a mob with you," Kelso said. "Stay where you are. Powell, I'll follow you."

"Fuck that," John seethed. "Everybody's talking about the hijacked trailer."

"G, you better not punch anyone," Declan joined into the jumble of communication. He was acting security for the *Hodgetown* panel. "It's gone loco over here. Should I explain?"

"Negative," Kelso said. "Just tell them we're aware of the perp."

"Shit, they're still crowding me. Fucking lights. Use Theo as a distraction," John demanded. "Just get these bloodsuckers off me."

As she listened to John bitch about his fans, Nadia slowly approached the door to the stairwell. The employees around the Sparbro booth gave her a curious look, but largely ignored her in favor of making a sale of the toys and action figures representative of the many participants in StreamCon. She pretended to browse the merchandise while waiting for Kelso to get into position close to her without attracting attention.

Kelso's voice exploded, "Coming your way, Powell. Man in Witcher costume." His voice shook as if he was jogging. "Intercept—"

A stream of profanity blasted from behind her, and she wheeled around and smacked straight into a big man with long pale hair in a warlock costume.

Dmitry Vovk.

His silver eyes slitted. "You're not Sally."

"No, I'm not."

"Someone's got Powell," Kelso growled.

More shouting and cursing erupted in comms.

Nadia couldn't see beyond the mountain of man in front of her who crowded her toward the stairwell. Reaching past her, he shoved the door open and pushed her inside.

He swung her around and, with a hand to her throat, Dmitry pinned her to the wall. "Who are you?"

Her knees knocked together, but she glared at her captor. "I'm a demoness."

The hand on her throat tightened. "Do not test me. What have your people done to Sally?"

"I should be asking you that, Dmitry Vovk," she choked out.

The door to the stairwell slammed open and a roar exploded before the hand on her throat disappeared.

John had taken off his headpiece and was grappling with Dmitry. The two men exchanged grunts and punches. Levi also showed up, and his mask had a rip.

"Get her out of here," John shouted.

The SEAL held the door wide open for her to get through, and when she glanced outside, it was chaos. Kelso was bleeding from the nose, but it looked like he was directing his undercover officers to secure the groaning men on the floor who Nadia figured worked for Vovk.

"I'll stay with Kelso," Nadia said. "Make sure John doesn't kill Dmitry."

"I'll try my best," the big man muttered.

The detective was maybe ten feet away, but on her way toward him, a small figure in a hoodie turned around and grabbed her arm, yanking her inside the Sparbro booth as though they were convention goers looking at products.

"Keep walking." It was Sally.

"You were here this whole time?" Nadia snapped, wrestling her arm away.

Sally looked around her nervously and nudged her so they were in between booths. "Dmitry was hot on my tail."

"So you played him. Told him you looked like a demoness?"

"Powell, where the fuck are you?" Kelso demanded through comms.

"She's talking to someone." Levi was coming their way, so Nadia waved her arm to acknowledge.

"I'm fine," she answered. "I've got Sally."

"What?" Kelso said. "You have her?"

Was that alarm in his voice?

Nadia turned back to the woman before her, but the gleam in Sally's eyes chilled her blood to sludge. As if a curtain had been raised, and she could see the deception etched in them. Kelso's urgent words faded as she came to an alarming conclusion. They were trying to find the monsters hiding behind the masks, but sometimes monsters were comfortable using their own skin.

"Don't go anywhere," Kelso instructed. "We just got a call from Henderson. Sally's mother is awake. Or should I say, Evelyn Brown is awake—and she's not Sally's mother at all."

Nadia jumped back from the woman in front of her as though she'd been bitten by a rattlesnake. She frantically searched for Levi and saw two men intercept him in the Sparbro booth. When her gaze spun back to Sally, a stun gun was in her hands.

The lights went out.

A roar went up in the convention center just as a jolt hit her.

And then there was nothing.

33

IN THE PITCH-BLACK DARKNESS, fear took hold of John's heart.

Pure terror that Nadia was not in his sights.

"I tried to stop this," Dmitry hissed. "You shouldn't have interfered."

"You were hurting one of our own." John hauled the Gray Wolf to his feet. The emergency lights came on just as they rushed out from the stairwell, the buzz of conversation was deafening, the pandemonium adding to the chaos in his head.

"Garrison," Kelso shouted, fighting his way through a panicked crowd. "Nadia's not answering."

"Where's Levi?" John barked.

"Here." The SEAL appeared by their side. He had a body over his shoulder that he dumped at their feet. "Two men attacked me. The other got away. Nadia's gone."

"What do you mean she's gone?" John shouted.

"She's not responding to comms," Bristow came over their earpieces. "Guys. The entire city's gone dark."

34

WITH THE HELP of DHS's Cybersecurity division, partial power was restored to SGC, but its central command was down, and blackouts continued to roll. There was a provision to borrow from the LA power grid, but the immediate supply wasn't enough. Only essential facilities had power, and they kept on blinking. Patrols were brought in from other parts of the county because all the traffic lights were down.

StreamCon was shut down.

No one was sure what Sally's endgame was, but John was going to get to the bottom of it. He sat across from the Gray Wolf of Odessa in the LAPD trailer. The crime boss had already admitted that Sally Davis was, in fact, Yelena Ivanova. She was thirty-three, not twenty-four. She was planted as a student at Caltech a year before she was hired by Huxley.

"I found that information in Maxim's files," Dmitry said. "What you found in the house where you were held was simply misdirection. I'm sure you already know."

"What does she want from Nadia?" John asked through gritted teeth. Bristow was hitting a dead end locating her because her phone stopped pinging.

"The source code."

"Nadia doesn't have the source code," John said.

Dmitry raised a brow. "Don't bullshit me, Mr. Garrison. She may not have direct access to it, but she can get it through you."

"Is Sally doing the sale herself?"

"Maxim stated in his emails that Sally was becoming hard to control. She helped Huxley figure out the problem in the device, but Huxley took all the credit. Maxim told her not to argue or call attention to herself."

"That's some shitty treatment," Garrison derided.

"My brother told her to wait for the bigger payout."

"This event."

"Yes, but she hasn't reached out to any of the crime bosses yet."

John mocked, "So she made you all dress up for nothing."

"I do not find this amusing. And you're one to talk."

He leaned forward, his lips curling into a snarl. "Oh, I assure you, I am far from amused."

There was a knock on the back of the trailer. The door cracked open, and Bristow slid in. His face grim. John's gut tightened. "Nadia?"

"Negative. Levi was able to get something out of the man he knocked out." Bristow glared at the Gray Wolf.

"If he said he's one of mine, he's lying."

"He didn't, but he has a record in our agency database. He's a North Korean agent."

"What the fuck?" John muttered, and his gaze sliced to Dmitry who didn't seem surprised.

"You knew?" He spat. His chair scraped back, lunging over the table to grab Dmitry by the collar and hauling him up. "What are you not telling me?"

John slammed him up against the wall. "You better start talking."

"The Crown-Key was just a means to an end."

"The end of what?"

"CalTech has been developing a guidance system for the U.S. military's newest HellRaiser missiles."

John turned to Bristow. "Did the power outage hit CalTech?" The research university was on the outskirts of SGC.

"Yes."

"Dammit. Check if there's been a breach." As Bristow hurried out, John turned back to Dmitry. "This power outage was just a distraction."

"Maxim didn't plan the attack on infrastructure to be this elaborate. He only meant to embarrass Revenant Films for refusing to cooperate and to use it to demo the power of the Crown-Key."

"And sell it to the highest bidder."

"Correct."

"Except he didn't realize Sally Davis had loftier goals."

Dmitry's grim expression told him the Ukrainian crime boss was not pleased with how his own people had turned on him.

John released Dmitry and stepped back, raking fingers through his hair, feeling like the bald cap he wore earlier was still compressing his skull. Nadia had been gone for forty-five minutes. That was forty-five minutes too long.

"You care for this Nadia Powell."

"Don't you dare fucking say her name."

The man's lips flattened, but there was something in his silvery-gray eyes that seemed to penetrate into John's soul. An understanding. A reflected pain.

Bristow burst through the door. "I think we have something. We have several drones in the air. I directed one to CalTech and I'm getting an SOS from a building across from the university."

"The Crown-Key needs to be close to its target," John said.

"And the distress call is in Nadia's signature encryption."

"You found her." A glimmer of hope sparked through the bleakness hanging around him. Ever since his woman was taken, John fought with the panic and fury he'd contained in his ragged compartments. To find the woman he loved, he needed to be in control.

He loved Nadia.

"Kelso and Gabby are already on their way."

The door to the trailer opened again, and Roarke poked his head in. "What's the hold up? Let's go."

NADIA'S HEAD THROBBED, and she was still groggy from being stunned. She sat back against the wall, the iciness of the cold, tiled floor seeping through her bodysuit. They were in an abandoned building, or maybe it was just unoccupied office space. The outline of CalTech University loomed outside Palladian windows. The lights of the university blinked as electricity fluctuated.

With the unreliability of the power grid at the moment, only her feeling for Sally was certain.

Contempt.

She hated that two-faced, triple-faced bitch with a passion. No amount of silicone masks could hide the ugliness lurking behind that innocent, seemingly helpless face she tried to project. Who the hell was she that she duped everyone?

Sally was talking to Asian commandos dressed in black fatigues. Was she selling secrets to the Chinese? To the North Koreans?

When Nadia woke up, they'd immediately put her to work, threatening her with a cocktail of drugs unless she complied with their demands. Sally had already managed to break into Homeland Security and download the source code. That was why she'd been laying low between the time of Morris' death and the days leading up to StreamCon. However, Sally failed to break into a block of program that Nadia had inserted as an extra safeguard against events like this. Sally needed that part of the code to complete whatever nefarious goal she intended.

Making a judgement call, Nadia did as she was told because that also activated a constant stream of SOS that her drones could pick up. She only hoped her other defensive measures worked.

"We've initiated the cryptocurrency transfer," one of the commandos said.

"I'll release the missile program once I've confirmed payment."

"Sally," Nadia groaned. "What the hell did you do?"

The other woman turned to her. "That's not my name."

"Who's that poor woman in the hospital?"

"Someone Maxim and I picked up off the streets to build my cover."

"Did you betray him?"

Sally snorted. "No. I didn't. It didn't come to that, but I was getting tired of being dictated to." Her eyes flashed. "Especially by men. I elevated the Crown-Key to what it could do, not Huxley." She puffed an irritated breath. "I saved his reputation." She thumbed at her chest. "Me."

Nadia wasn't sure if she understood her right. "You were part of the design?"

"The device"—her mouth sneered— "has my code. My circuitry. Huxley was a visionary. He was also a genius, but a fraud when it came to this. And don't get me started on those morons Morris and Wagner. Maxim was tolerable, but he got himself killed and left me with those two. And then Dmitry came along."

"He wants the Key?"

Sally shrugged. "Who knows. But I'm done being used by stupid men, including the rest of the Argonayts. I told Maxim we should go big. Rogue nations like China and North Korea instead of these greedy arms dealers." She scowled. "All my life, I've been used by the mob." Her mouth twisted. "But look at them now, all costumed up for StreamCon." Sally giggled. "I showed them, didn't I?"

Nadia could understand the frustration of people taking credit for another's hard work but would never understand the extent of Sally's retaliation. But maybe she could still reach her. "Sally," she said quietly. "How are you sure these men won't kill you and steal the Crown-Key?"

The other woman rolled her eyes. "I'm not an idiot. They double-cross me, and I'll have every one of them exposed … they could never leave the country. Besides, they know I'm more useful to them working as an information broker." Sally gave her one last look before shifting her attention back to the screen.

The woman was a megalomaniac. Nausea roiled in Nadia's stomach. She hoped her baby was okay. Tears pricked her eyes. Bristow would know to use the drones, and they would find her. John would come for her.

"Funds received. Initiating program transfer …what the hell?" Sally whispered. "No. No. No."

Nadia smiled grimly.

After a few minutes of hammering at her computer, one of the commandos approached the other woman. "What's taking so long?"

Sally's face mottled red, the expression on her face evil, poisonous. Again, Nadia asked herself how she could have been so deceived. The other woman stabbed a finger in Nadia's direction. "She ruined it."

"What?" the man asked.

Sally lunged at Nadia, fingers digging into her scalp and pulling her hair, making Nadia wish that she still had her wig and mask on.

"What did you do?" the traitorous bitch screamed.

The back of Nadia's head cracked against the wall. Her eyes caught a glimpse of Sally rearing back with her right leg.

Instinctively, she curled into a ball, protecting her head with her arms and drawing her knees in to protect her belly, her baby. Sally continued her assault. Kicking her, clawing at her hair.

"Fix it!" she screamed.

"Can't you just download it again?" the commando demanded. He spoke with a perfect California accent leading Nadia to believe that he was a sleeper agent who'd lived in the U.S. for a while or he'd been trained to speak like he had.

"The window of opportunity was very slim," Sally snapped. "We had to tunnel into their network as the systems were restarting from their backup power."

"What's wrong with the program?"

"She scrambled it with ransomware."

Boots stopped in front of Nadia. Strong fingers grabbed her chin forcing her face up. "Can you fix it?"

"Fuck you," Nadia spat.

The man smirked, releasing her jaw.

Pain exploded at the side of her head.

"You can take her with you," Sally suggested. "Force her to unscramble it."

The man barked orders at the rest of the commandos and said, "We're leaving. Both of you are coming with us."

"We had an agreement," Sally yelled.

"But you delivered a faulty product." The man drew his weapon and pointed it at them. "We move back to home base. Both of you will work on it from there."

"And if we can't?" The treacherous woman continued to rant. "You're going to kill me?"

The man stepped toward her. "Yes. Because if we don't complete our mission, we're also dead."

"How much longer on those charges?" John snarled through comms. He was struggling to keep his shit together while watching what was playing out on the thermal scans.

They were hurting Nadia.

She was on the floor.

His Nadia.

The woman he loved.

The mother of his child.

The vise around his heart cranked tighter. His eyes burned with emotion that his woman was being beaten. Feeling pain. He would give anything to take that from her.

A synchronized assault was underway because any firefight lasting more than a few seconds would put Nadia at risk. That was one risk John wasn't willing to take.

Kelso and the CTTF were behind the wall right across from the hostiles. John and his men were near the one Nadia was leaning against. A drone Bristow had flown into the room confirmed it was her. She didn't look good and her mask was gone.

She was being very brave.

"Ready," Levi announced.

"Same here," Kelso replied. "On three."

"Three."

"Two."

Boom!

The walls exploded inwards, and they moved in, knowing exactly where the targets were. Going in full-kill mode.

John had the man who struck Nadia in his scope.

Trigger squeezed.

The man went down.

"Clear!" John yelled.

"Clear!" Kelso responded.

Heart in his throat, John rushed to where Nadia was still curled on the tiles.

Fuck. Fuck. Fuck. He slid to the floor on his knees and

scooped her into his arms, crushing her tight. John had a feeling it would be a while before he could let her out of his sight or even out of his arms.

"Babe, fucking Christ," he said raggedly into her ear. "I was so fucking scared."

"John." Sobs wracked her frame. "You came. I knew you would."

He pulled back, warmth stinging the back of his eyes. "I love you so much, Nadia. I hate that it had to take something like this to get my head out of my ass and say the words. But I think I've loved you since I got back from Ukraine."

"I love you too," she whispered.

He captured her lips and kissed the hell out of her, his tongue tangling deeply with hers, needing that connection to reassure himself she was alive. He ignored the jumbled voices over comms. They probably heard his declaration, but he didn't give a fuck. At that moment, it was him and Nadia. The world could go fuck itself. She pried herself away from his embrace.

His own breathing returned to normal as did his heart rate. They stared at each other, exchanging small smiles, before he helped her to her feet.

Sally was on the floor, her wrists cuffed behind her back, being read her rights by a CTTF Tac member.

Bristow hurried over with a laptop. "Homeland Security could use some help."

"Utilities still out in SGC?"

Kelso walked over. "It's limping along." He raised a boxy device. "Is this the Key? Found it in her backpack."

Nadia accepted the innocuous looking gadget into her hands, inspecting it, twirling it around as one would study a Rubik's cube. "How can such a device wreak so much havoc? I vote to destroy it."

"I agree, but maybe you'd want to restore power to the city first," Kelso said with amusement.

The smile on Nadia's face faded, morphing into an expression of anxiety, one of pain that sent her hand flying to her belly and set John on high alert.

"What's wrong?" he demanded. "Is it the baby?"

"I don't know." Tears filled her eyes. "John …"

His jaw hardened. "The rest can wait. I'm taking her to the hospital."

35

"WATER SERVICE IS FULLY RESTORED," Henderson told John outside the examination room where Nadia was waiting for the test results of her bloodwork and further diagnostics. "Powell's suggestions helped."

"Good. They've got sufficient power and water," he said. "We warned all the cities in the metro area of a possible cyberattack after the traffic light incident. SGC management should learn from this. They'll need to figure out the rest or wait until I say Nadia is ready. Clear?"

The tac team lead sighed. "I agree."

He gave the man a nod and went back into the room.

John had Nadia barricaded from her team. All communication went through him. His woman was scared and in the wrong headspace right now to be messing around with a freaking city's advanced urban living infrastructure. It should be their wakeup-call that everything could go to shit. Technology failure could send everyone careening back into the Dark Ages.

"Is everything okay?" Nadia asked. She was in a hospital gown. The body makeup on one arm was cleaned for them to draw blood. On the way to the hospital, John called Dr. Stahl who was already there to meet them when they arrived and had called ahead to have a room ready. John wasn't egotistical enough to think that the special treatment had anything to do with his relationship to the agency or the DNI. This was all about Nadia. The doctor had been briefed that her patient stopped a rogue state from stealing highly classified research that could derail the U.S. military's advanced weapons program.

"It's fine. They have that handled," John told her, settling into the stool beside her and taking hold of her hands, giving them a squeeze. "How are you feeling?"

"I'm scared, but the pain in my stomach has subsided. I wondered if I overreacted and—"

"Stopping you right there, babe," he growled. "No such thing as overreacting when it comes to our baby. You feel something, every little twitch or pain, you tell me. You *do not* hide anything from me. Got it?"

"Got it." Then she gave him another pained smile that almost sent him into another round of panic until she said, "Right now, I really have to pee." They made her drink copious amounts of water for the ultrasound.

John's exhale of relief ended on a brief chuckle. "I'll get the Doc."

As if on cue, Dr. Stahl walked in. She smiled at both of them. "Your HCG levels are on the high end of normal, so that's good. When we do this ultrasound, at six weeks, we may not hear the fetal heartbeat, so don't be alarmed. You've been through a lot today, Nadia. Anything could have caused the pelvic pain. Stress being one of them and all the other chemical reactions that come from it. You didn't even have any spotting, which I'm sure is a relief."

"It sure as hell was," John said, giving Nadia's hands another squeeze. His woman had gone through hell today, and he was certain after all the makeup came off there would be some bruising that would make John want to bend a crowbar.

He abhorred killing women in his line of work. He'd only do it when backed into a corner and only if they tried to kill him first. But at that moment, he wanted very much to bury Sally Davis aka Yelena Ivanova alive. A quick death was too good for her.

Dr. Stahl positioned Nadia's legs in the stirrups and picked-up the ultrasound wand.

"Ready?" the doctor asked.

Nadia glanced at John and he gave her an encouraging nod.

"Ready," she breathed.

Nadia emitted a tiny gasp, before she tensed up and gripped his hand tighter.

Their eyes went to the monitor, and a lump began to fill the back of his throat.

"There it is."

John leaned forward. Where? And then his gaze was drawn to the tiny arrow pointing at a spot on the screen. The lump in his throat grew into a boulder.

Nadia exhaled a laugh. "It's the size of a pea."

"That's the yolk sac," Dr. Stahl smiled. "Do you want to see if we can hear your baby's heartbeat?"

"Oh my God, yes!" Nadia said in a scratchy voice, glancing at John. "There's a heartbeat."

"Thank fuck."

The doctor changed the screen and adjusted the volume. She adjusted the grids. John's breathing grew ragged when the volume increased, and the rapid patter of their baby's heart filled the room.

"One-hundred-fifteen beats per minute," Dr. Stahl said. "You've got a fighter in there." She smiled at them both. "Your baby is fine."

Receiving the official word that their baby was okay was like escaping a firing squad. Instinctively, they turned to each other. John stood and hugged Nadia as she sobbed, repeating over and over that their baby was fine. He stroked her back and soothed her, even when his legs threatened to buckle from under him.

Sometime during their emotional episode, Dr. Stahl said she was giving them a moment and left the room.

Finally, John leaned away only to capture Nadia's face to kiss her deeply, tasting her tears. Knowing they were happy ones filled his heart with so much emotion he could hardly contain them in his chest.

"I love you," he said quietly.

"John?" Nadia said in wonder. Her fingers touched his cheeks. "You're crying."

Hell, so he was.

There was no other reason. He was a damned happy man with a woman he loved desperately and a baby on the way. He'd never felt more complete.

"I fucking love you," he repeated with more emphasis.

She grinned her genuine Nadia smile. "I love you too."

JOHN GARRISON WAS A STALKER. If watching Nadia sleep qualified as one, he'd gladly wear the title as a badge of honor. The past twenty-eight hours had been a rollercoaster, and he wanted to snarl at everyone to leave her alone. But since she was the only one who could get SGC back online and neutralize the malware that paralyzed the city's infrastructure, Nadia did what her genius always did best.

She used her skills to get a system back online after a cyberattack.

So, John did what his cutthroat personality did best.

He used everything in his arsenal to clear the bureaucracy that stood in the way of getting things done. He had no problem using his influence with the DNI to make sure every federal agency left Nadia alone to do her job. At the end of the day, the Crown-Key device was secured by the DHS with close scrutiny under the NSA.

Her job was done. His job was done.

Because it was turning out that the endgame of his crazy life was having the woman he loved sleeping peacefully in his arms. John didn't know how much this meant to him until this moment. Her forehead was smooth, her eyebrows weren't cinched, and her chest was rising and falling in the rhythm of a restful sleep. He would even say there was a slight tilt in her lips that hinted of a smile. She felt safe. She felt free to be who she was, and he damned well was making sure it stayed that way.

The possessive man in him wanted her in *his* bed as well, but they were still in the safe house, so that claim wouldn't be true. He was thinking of remodeling his home-base in Assassin's Hill, but maybe finding a house closer to the MoMoS was better. Between him and Nadia, they'd have it wired for security in no time. A house with a yard where their kids could play safely.

Something in his chest turned over. It could be the organ called his heart.

His phone on the nightstand flashed. "Grandpa Earp."

Two in the morning wasn't unusual. Porter knew John wanted some time off to spend with Nadia and wouldn't be calling him if it weren't important. He kissed her on the brow, snatched the phone, and slipped out of the bed. She didn't rouse one bit, so he exited the room and answered the phone.

"Yeah."

"I'm outside," Porter answered. "Black SUV. I've already informed Bristow to keep an eye on the house."

"Thought I made it clear. My men report to me."

"In the interest of efficiency and assurance that the people you care about are being watched over, I knew you wouldn't mind. But your point is noted."

"Thanks."

When John made it to the first floor, the SEAL was already in the kitchen.

"Sorry about that," John mumbled.

"No problem," Bristow shot him a wry smile. "Curious to see what Porter wants."

"As long as it's not my first born, I'm curious too," he said under his breath.

Sure enough, the SUV was idling in front of the safe house. It was one of those stretched SUVs that had face-to-face seating, though not quite a limo. When he yanked open the door, a growl rose up his throat.

Dmitry Vovk was sitting across from Porter.

"For fuck's sake," the admiral said. "Get in. Close the door. I'll explain."

John wasn't prepared to deal with the Gray Wolf of Odessa. He'd hoped the LAPD would hold him until the agency could spirit him away to a black ops site to interrogate him and probably lock him away forever for what happened to the special ops team that was wiped out because of him. He wasn't expecting to face this man now, just when John thought he could let that go because he was blissfully content with what he had with Nadia.

"This is a buzz kill." John got in beside the admiral.

"You'll have to face it sooner or later," Porter told him.

The vehicle started moving. There was nothing new in these rolling car meetings with the admiral.

"What? The fact that the man responsible for the Operation Bullhorn massacre is sitting in front of me?"

"As if you didn't have a hand in the death of several Russian agents who were just doing their job," Vovk said. "We were at war. The public just doesn't know about it and doesn't care as long as they keep their false sense of security."

That was why John had slowly been stripped of his idealism, but he had found himself again thanks to Nadia. He wouldn't get sucked down that hole again, especially with these two men who had started him on that path. His skin crawled to get out of the SUV.

"Things are not what they seem," Porter started.

"Are you sure you want to tell him this?" Dmitry said. "I don't care if he hates me forever."

"I don't hate you," John spat. "I just want you in a brig in the middle of the Pacific Ocean and to never see the light of day."

"Enough," Porter sighed. "Dmitry wasn't responsible for the Bullhorn massacre. He killed the general who was, then took ownership of his actions so he could be in the position to poison the Ukrainian president when Russia and Ukraine tried to have their peace talks."

"Which failed," John derided, but his brain stuttered at the switcheroo and started processing this information.

"And that was deliberate on my part," Dmitry said. "I had to prove my loyalty to the Kremlin, and the only way to do that was go ahead with the assassination." He continued to tell them about how his brother was running for President of Ukraine and was favored to win. That would mean a change of alliances.

"What could this guy possibly offer that we don't already have?" John scoffed.

"Inside information about organized crime and rogue states. You want a man they still trust and that man is me. The war has gone cyber. You know this. Timely intel is more crucial than ever."

"And the Argonayts?"

Dmitry's nose flared. "I'm going to keep a tight leash on them. As for Yelena Ivanova, I'll leave it to your government to prosecute her."

John gave a derisive snort. "So you're the one getting immunity."

"You have no proof I had anything to do with the Crown-Key plot. Having me as an asset outweighs the trouble of trying to find evidence in my involvement in this."

John's phone buzzed and he glanced at the message. He tried to keep his expression neutral, but he couldn't help the smile that pulled at his mouth.

"I think we've kept Mr. Garrison away from his woman long enough," Dmitry drawled.

He stared at the Gray Wolf. "Whatever the DNI decides, I'll go along with it. I can't say my enmity for you will disappear overnight but knowing you didn't cause the Bullhorn massacre frees me to concentrate on what's important in my life right now."

"Not sure I like this version of you, John," Porter grumbled.

"Get used to it," he shot back. "In fact, I need your driver to make a stop."

Twenty minutes later, John walked through the door carrying a paper bag of burger and fries and a drink carrier of milkshakes.

Bristow and Nadia were in the kitchen.

Her text read: Since you're out doing spooky stuff, and if it isn't too much trouble, can you pick up a strawberry milkshake and fries from In-N-Out? Bristow wants a burger.

Her face split into a genuine Nadia smile, and John opened his arms so she could step into him and hug him. Bristow reliably rescued the food.

"You got me a milkshake!" Nadia stared up at him, eyes dancing with glee.

"And fries," he said, finally able to hug her. "Heaven forbid I disappoint a pregnant woman's cravings."

"Good man." She gave him a quick kiss.

"I'll also have you know that you carry the distinction of putting the acting director of National Intelligence and a known crime boss through the In-N-Out drive-thru to get your snacks."

"Oh my God." Nadia's eyes widened, and Bristow started chuckling.

John grinned. "And since I didn't have my wallet …"

Her mouth fell open. "You didn't—"

"Of course, I did. Porter called me away from my woman, he could damn well pay for your milkshake."

Nadia shook her head, her expression one of horror and awe.

"Man, this burger is going to taste extra good," Bristow declared.

Hell yes, it would.

EPILOGUE

"Ma?"

"Is that you, Jacob?"

"Yeah." John glanced briefly at Nadia, who was sitting nervously beside him. To say he wasn't anxious was a lie, but he was more than excited to tell his mother the news.

"You changed your number again," his mother sighed. "How was Romania?"

His mind did a double-take. Oh, right. That was where he told her he was going when he'd gone to Ukraine. That seemed so long ago. So much had happened since then.

"Jacob?"

"There was a bit of trouble but nothing I couldn't handle."

"Are you calling because you're coming home for Thanksgiving? Because I wished you would have called sooner. Your Uncle Patrick is hosting. I know you don't like his turkey, because he makes his too dry. If I knew you were coming home, I would have prepared a whole feast ..."

"Ma—"

"But come home anyway. You need to meet my Zumba instructor—"

"Ma!" he interrupted more firmly. "No matchmaking, all right?" Nadia squeezed his hand, and he looked at her again. She was covering her mouth with her other hand, hiding her laughter.

John wasn't finding this funny.

She huffed. "Well, I'm just trying—"

"Because I've already met someone."

Silence.

"Ma, are you there?"

"Praise Jesus, Jacob, you better bring her home. I'll call Patrick to make room for two more."

"Do not call Patrick," he barked. "We're not coming to Montana. Nadia and I have plans with her family here in LA. It's low key, but we're hoping you can make the trip."

"Oh, I'm afraid I can't find a flight! It's so late. Thanksgiving is next week, and you know I hate last minute. Maybe we can plan for Christmas?"

"What? You're not excited to see your son?" John chuckled.

"Do not put this on me, Jacob Mason," Fiona said in her sternest voice that used to make his balls shrivel. "I haven't seen you in two years. You've rejected each invitation for Easter, Thanksgiving, and Christmas. I'm trying to be understanding, and I'm trying to stay healthy, so I'll still have a chance to see you get married and meet my grandbabies."

His chest constricted. "You're going to be a grandma soon."

"What? I'm not sure I heard you right. I heard I'm going to be a grandma soon. Maybe it's my wishful thinking—"

"Nadia *is* pregnant."

Silence.

John gave his mother a chance to recover from the news and find her words. But as the seconds ticked by with no answer, he got worried. Shit. He was sure his mother didn't have a heart condition because he got notifications on her medical history. Still, he got anxious there for a second.

"Ma, are you okay? Sorry for—"

A strangled sob broke over the line. "Please tell me you're not joking," his mother cried.

"I'm not," he said gently.

A howl broke over the line followed by more sobbing. "Fuck," John mumbled and glanced at Nadia, whose face had transformed from nervous into an "oh shit" expression that was probably reflective of his own.

He covered the mouthpiece and told her, "She's crying. I don't know what to do."

"Wait for her to digest the news," she said. "Is it a happy sobbing?"

John wasn't sure, so he asked his mother, "You okay?"

"Give me a minute," Fiona's garbled voice responded.

John looked at Nadia again and shrugged. His woman's exasperated huff told him she was not impressed with the way he was handling the situation.

"Jacob?" His mother appeared to be walking and shuffling things around.

"I'm here."

"I'm just so happy ... and congratulations. I want to jump on a plane right now ..." she broke off crying again but seemed to have it more under control. He heard the clattering of a keyboard. "I can't find any flights. LA, you said?"

"Don't worry about it. I can get you here. Just tell me when."

"Oh, Jacob," his mother whispered. "Is she there? Can I talk to her?"

"Just a sec." John covered the mic and turned to Nadia. "She wants to talk to you. That okay?"

Nadia's face brightened. "Of course!"

He grinned, handing her the phone.

"Mrs. Mason? ...thank you." Nadia faced him with a

radiant smile. His mother must have congratulated her on the news, too. Fiona Mason was a gracious woman, and John was confident she would be thrilled knowing her son was finally ready to settle down.

"Mid-June. Yes, J—Jacob is taking good care of me."

A slew of emotions swirled inside him, making him rub the center of his chest. He'd been doing that more lately. And this moment was surreal. Two women he loved with all his heart were discussing a future he was looking forward to.

"Yes. We're looking for a house. We haven't decided where yet."

The MoMoS would be moving back to their apartments after the holidays, but Nadia would be staying with John at Assassin's Hill while they looked for a house. Dugal insisted on switching units with her should she want to return to SkyeLark.

"It's great talking to you, Mrs. Mason. Of course! I'm sure I'll get used to calling you Ma soon."

After several more moments, Nadia handed the phone back to him.

"I had a chance to think about it," Fiona said. "I think I'll fly out for Christmas."

His brows drew together. "Why?"

His mother spoke quietly as if afraid Nadia would hear, "I don't want to intrude. It seems you two need some time together and not have your meddling mother to worry about."

"You're not a bother."

"Have you asked her to marry you yet?"

Fuck, no he hasn't. "I'm waiting for the right time. We haven't been together that long." And they sort of did things out of order. The marriage and baby part that was. He stood, suddenly feeling put in the hot seat worse than any interrogation he'd ever experienced. He walked to the window, but he could feel Nadia's anxious regard drilling into his back. He shot her a grin to reassure her all was good.

"Nadia said you took an indefinite leave from your job."

"Yeah, I wanted to slow down." Enjoy this experience with her and the pregnancy. Hell, his mother was right. "Spend time with her."

"Now you understand what I mean. This time is special between the two of you."

He exhaled heavily. "I want to see you too. We've been dying to tell you."

"And I'm glad you finally did! But I'm not going anywhere. I've had you for eighteen years, and I miss you, but do everything you can to make Nadia feel special."

"I'm in love with her." The words sounded strange coming from his mouth, and he realized it was the first time he'd told someone else he loved Nadia. Hollering the words through comms for everyone to hear didn't count. "I found *the one* who can put up with my ass," he chuckled. He turned to face Nadia and caught her eyes. "I didn't know what hit me."

"Mason men. They fall hard."

She was right. Words of wisdom from Fiona Mason. "A week before Christmas. I'll expect you, Ma."

"Try and stop me."

FIONA MASON WAS STUNNING, and she was hard to miss. A shapely woman wearing an elegant floral dress that hugged her figure emerged from the security gates. Large-framed sunglasses were propped on top of thick silvery blonde hair. But it was the blood-red lipstick against creamy skin that drew the eye first. John said his mother enjoyed traveling around the world. It certainly appeared that she was a pro and trés chic while doing it.

The pictures didn't do justice to John's mother at all. She had hips Nadia would kill for and an hourglass figure reminiscent of the Hollywood sirens of the fifties. Maybe those

Zumba classes at the gym were worth looking into if this kind of aging gracefully was the result, although she suspected good genes had something to do with it.

Fiona broke into a wide grin when she spotted them. "Jacob!"

"We need to do something about that." Nadia kept her smile on her face, as she muttered the words out of the corner of her mouth. It was jarring having her baby daddy being called another name.

"Working on it," John muttered back as they approached his mother.

Nadia had expected this emotional reunion. She braced herself for the tears, but she had a hard time breathing when a massive lump formed in her throat when John enveloped his mother in a powerful embrace after two long years.

"Jacob," Fiona's voice sounded garbled. Pulling away, she wiped away the lipstick on John's cheeks before turning her tear-streaked face to Nadia. "He looks happy," she said, then her face crumpled as she dragged Nadia into a tight hug. Fiona whispered into her ear, "I've never seen him this happy. Thank you. Thank you for bringing my son back to me."

Nadia didn't realize she was bawling until John engulfed them both in his arms.

It was a reunion she would never forget.

"SHOULD I set out the appetizers, Mrs. Mason?" Nadia hurried back to the kitchen after letting Kelso in. The rest of the guests were on the patio enjoying the cool December weather around the fire pit.

It was two days before Christmas. Thanksgiving had been a subdued affair because most of the guys were wrapping up the investigation on the Crown-Key plot. John thought they needed the gathering before they broke off for their own family celebrations.

"How many times have I told you to call me Ma?" Fiona tutted at her.

Nadia blushed. "I'm working on it."

For a few days, it had been difficult for John's mother when he'd revealed the truth about his job. Fiona had a hard time not calling him Jacob. That morning, something seemed to have transformed in his mother. Her face appeared lighter. Maybe after hearing all the bits and pieces about the sacrifices John had made in the service of his country, she finally had the context to his double-life.

Fiona smiled. "The deviled eggs and the brie dip are ready. I know Dugal was hovering around the kitchen waiting for it."

Nadia fought a smile. Little did John's mother know that it was her that the big Scot was hovering around—not the dip. To say that Mrs. Mason made an impression on the MoMoS when they first saw her was an understatement, and Dugal's infatuation since that first meeting seemed to have only intensified—much to John's annoyance.

"Is this the famous Fiona Mason?" Kelso was leaning against the counter at the entrance to the kitchen.

Nadia made the introductions and then promptly glared at the detective, jerking her head toward the patio.

Kelso's mouth stretched into a sly grin.

"I wouldn't say famous." Fiona laughed, unaware of their silent exchange. "From what I gathered, people thought Ja—oh, I mean John—sprouted from the ground fully formed. I can't believe my son was so awful that people think he couldn't actually have a mother."

Kelso seemed to relish adding to that statement. "Yes, Gabby said—ouch."

Nadia *accidentally* stepped on his foot with the heel of her shoe while walking across the kitchen. That mother-under-the-bus comment better not see the light of day in Fiona's presence.

"Our Nadia certainly softened him up," Kelso muttered instead.

Fiona's eyes fell on her. "She certainly did. It's so romantic. A man—"

"Gabby's out on the patio with Roarke," a new voice interrupted the conversation. John stood at the other end of the open kitchen that led to the patio. He fixed Kelso with a stare that could pierce armor. "Why don't you join the rest of the gang? I'll help Nadia bring out the appetizers."

The two men held mutual respect for each other, but sometimes when it came to Nadia, they had these testosterone-laden stare-offs. Nadia figured it was because John didn't want anyone to be the boss of her except him, but he also knew that she loved her job.

"You two okay in here?" John moved to her side and gave her a kiss on the temple. "Dugal said Colin and Alec are on their way with the prime rib."

"I'm fine in here," his mother said. "Just make sure everyone is set with their drinks."

"Arthur has that handled." John left her side and gave his mother a hug. "Thanks for doing this, Ma."

"Anything for you, Jacob."

And Nadia's heart swooned.

***

"I STILL CAN'T BELIEVE John has a mother," Roarke whispered to Gabby loud enough for John to hear him. After dinner, the group had transferred to the living room where Bristow was setting up the widescreen television for a video conference with people who couldn't make the celebration.

Migs and Ariana were in San Diego with the Alcantara Walker family.

Kade and Yara were in New York with Yara's famous rock star father and supermodel mom.

Antonio and Charly were in Rio celebrating with Ida, Nico, Renata, and Oscar. John also heard that Andrade's best friend Martinez was back in the fold. He was glad. Their story resonated with him because John had not only lost brothers to death, but also to ideological differences.

"And I'll shut that down right there, Roarke," John said. The guys were lucky he was in the Christmas spirit. All because of Nadia. His woman certainly loosened him up in more ways than he could imagine. And then there was peace in knowing that his mother knew the truth. All of John's compartments were gone. As of that moment, there was only Nadia and the baby who were going to be the center of his universe. The rest of the world could wait.

His eyes sought her in the midst of this crowd. She was on the couch, chatting with Stephen and Clyde. Arthur was around somewhere in drink-mixing heaven given the size of the party. John's gaze began to wander, and then it narrowed. His mother was laughing at something Dugal said.

"Easy there, tiger," Roarke chuckled.

"What's going on?" Levi asked, walking up to them. He arrived late, saying he had to drop off the girls with Kelly who was taking them to Northern California the next day.

Hmm … maybe Garrison could play Cupid with them too. He was feeling that magnanimous.

"G's feeling protective of Mrs. Mason. It looks like our Scotsman is smitten," Roarke shared.

Someone else clapped a hand on his shoulder. Kelso. "This should be interesting. Maybe we could plan some payback, huh? Dugal never liked me."

John grinned cockily. "Well, he liked me, boy."

The detective rolled his eyes. "You're maybe seven years older than me. What makes you think you can go around calling me 'boy'?"

"Nothing accounts for experience. You've got a lot to learn. Maybe go freelance."

Kelso cut a glance to Roarke. "Has he always been this cocky?"

Gabby intervened. "Would you two stop picking on Garrison?"

"Me? He started it," her partner said.

"But it's so much fun," her husband replied.

"We haven't talked about your next assignment," John told Roarke.

"You're on a leave of absence," Gabby's husband shot back, although a wariness stole across his face. "And I'm a contractor. I can choose to pick up a job or not."

"Hmm… contractor work sounds fun," Kelso said.

Gabby scowled at her partner. "Don't you dare." She turned on her husband and Levi. "And you two stop enticing my partner into your stuff."

"I didn't say anything," Levi protested.

John grinned and left them to it and walked over to where Bristow was in front of the television. In some ways he was still a manipulative bastard.

The ginger-haired SEAL gave him a thumbs up. "I got them on the line. Sending it to TV."

The widescreen on the wall split into three sections, Migs and Ariana, Kade and Yara, Antonio and Charly.

John held his arm out to Nadia in a gesture that indicated he wanted her to be by his side. She'd been integral to the team, working comms in their multiple ops. And, recently, she was the one who enabled him to break free of his compartments and communicate with empathy.

"I'm honored for you all to join us." John raised his beer toward the screen, hugging Nadia to his side. "Merry Christmas."

There was a chorus of Merry Christmas, Feliz Navidad, and Feliz Natal.

"We wouldn't miss this. Where's Mrs. Mason?" Migs asked.

"I know," Charly piped in. "I was surprised when Bristow told me John's mom was visiting."

Maybe this was a bad idea.

"Oh my goodness," Fiona expressed. "I wasn't expecting this much attention."

His mother seemed to preen anyway. She stood up and did a small wave like the Queen of England.

Everyone clapped, and some of them whistled. Nadia held his hand and gave it a squeeze. He exhaled, realizing he wasn't annoyed at this distraction to his agenda. He was damned happy he could finally bring his mother back into his life.

"Oh my, she's gorgeous, John," Ariana gushed. "Have her come by the Vitamin and Wellness clinic."

Oh, good God.

"What vitamin clinic?" His mother, ever the health enthusiast, perked up at Ariana's statement.

"Ari will send Garrison the info," Migs chuckled. "I think we need to get on with the program."

A roar of laughter went around the room. John wasn't oblivious that the joke was on him, and, again, he didn't mind. These past weeks with Nadia worked magic on getting that stick out of his ass.

When the room quieted down, he cleared his throat. "As I was trying to say earlier, I'm glad everyone could join us. Andrade, you and Charly are honorary members of our team as are the MoMoS." He turned to the men in question.

Clyde spoke up, "I knew Stephen was hiding something. I can't believe I'm friends with an agency asset." The MoMoS had proven they would die for each other and Nadia. That went a long way in John's book. Dugal assured John his sons would keep the secret as well. They deserved to know after their father nearly died protecting Nadia.

He gave his woman a squeeze while his gaze shot across the room to Gabby and Kelso. "The CTTF had done an outstanding job addressing the terrorist threats to LA. I technically couldn't help directly—"

"But you did anyway," Kelso interjected, winking.

"Yes, we go rogue when we need to," Migs said from the screen.

"Hear, hear!" Roarke raised his beer.

"And, I'm happy to assist with smoothing the red tape," John said. "We have common goals, and that's to keep our country and our loved ones safe from all kinds of terror threats."

"But what are we going to do now that you're on leave?" Gabby asked.

"That's a terrible idea," Andrade agreed.

"John will never be hands-off whether he's on leave or not," Kade spoke up for the first time. His long-time friend knew him so well, and John communicated his thanks with his eyes. If it weren't for Kade and the team, he and Bristow would probably be spending Christmas in Siberia.

Second chances.

A new life.

He was looking forward to it.

Nadia tilted her chin up and grinned. "I don't know, Kade. I'm sure the baby and I will give him plenty to do."

The room's conversations evolved into discussions about babies because apparently Ariana was also pregnant.

His agenda was forgotten.

A ghost of a smile touched his mouth. He was damned pleased to see his family grow.

———

"I'M CLOSE, BABE."

John's back was against the headboard, and Nadia was on her knees between his legs taking his cock in her mouth.

This was after he'd woken her up with him tongue-fucking her pussy, so Nadia was more than happy to return the favor. She relished the mornings she had her man at her mercy. He would grab her hair, coaxing her mouth up and down his erection, but Nadia still dictated the motion.

"Jesus, Nadia, bring it home, babe."

Not yet, she hummed as she swirled her tongue around his cock in sync with her hand twisting up and down his thick shaft, savoring the fact that every inch of this man belonged to her. Sometimes, she'd get away with teasing him mercilessly with a blow job. But other times, she could tell when he'd had enough and would take matters into his own hands.

She was right.

John hauled her up and gave her a hard kiss, before flipping them over and powering inside her.

Nadia was taking his cock again.

"Knew you had that wicked look on you this morning," he growled. "You're merciless you know that?" he continued pounding, hiking one of her legs over his elbow so he could thrust deeper.

And it felt glorious.

"Coming again," she whimpered.

John grunted, and she wanted to laugh because she'd had multiple orgasms and he hadn't had one yet. Not that she was count—

Oh shit. His cock or his grinding hips had a knack for zeroing in on that magic button on her pussy. Exquisite throbbing spread like wildfire across her tender flesh, and she could only moan, "Harder." And then she melted into a puddle of boneless limbs, surrendering herself to John's domination.

"Fuck, you're so sexy when you come," he gritted. She was lost to his pounding and she distantly heard his muffled roar.

His heavy breath was warm by her ear, and his rapid heart rate galloped against her chest.

When John raised his head, his gaze was soft and warm. "Merry Christmas, babe."

"Merry Christmas to you, too, handsome," Nadia smiled. He levered up and got off the bed. "Be right back."

Nadia followed his sexy ass until he disappeared into the bathroom before she did a lazy satisfied stretch and rolled away to check her messages. Several unread texts greeted her. Everyone seemed to be up early this morning. It was barely seven. Holiday greetings from Gabby, another one from Kelso, and more from her squad at the CTTF. After the big-gathering two nights ago, they were having a smaller affair with the MoMoS for Christmas day lunch. Colin was making ham and turkey while Fiona was whipping up several side dishes. Bristow and Levi were stopping by since they didn't have families to celebrate with in town.

The bed dipped behind her. She grinned and flipped back for more cuddle time with her man before the craziness of the Christmas day began.

Her smile froze.

Right in front of her was a ring.

Not just any ring or jewelry, but *the* ring.

A pear-shaped diamond that almost blinded her with its fiery brilliance.

"Marry me."

"I'm feeling vulnerably naked here," she laughed, but excitement thrummed through her veins.

John smirked. "That was the idea. No excuses, babe. We love each other. You know I'd damn the whole world for you, and you're probably the only woman in existence who can put up with my shit."

"Hmm, that's true. What else?"

"The sex is fucking fantastic."

"That's also true." She tried to keep the giddiness from her voice, but she couldn't help it. She also couldn't help teasing him.

His gaze narrowed, and she was suddenly pinned under a very predatory male. "And I'm the only man for you. You're already having my baby. You're both mine. There's no choice here."

"Even with your proposal, you're bossy." The intense possessiveness in his eyes took her breath away.

An arrogant brow arched. "You like that about me, remember?"

She smiled impishly. "I do."

"So, marry me, babe."

"Yes." Nadia's face hurt from the happiness stretching across her face.

John grinned and slipped the ring on her finger. "I love you."

"Love you, too."

Those words were coming more easily to him nowadays, but, recently, he'd been giving her more reasons to smile.

He shifted on the mattress, lowered his head, and kissed her belly.

"Love you, too, little one," he whispered. "Daddy can't wait to meet you.'"

This man made her heart so full when he did this.

Every. Single. Time.

NINE MONTHS later

"YOU AND I need to have a chat, missy." John stared at his beautiful little girl cradled in his arms. Her eyes were round with curiosity, and they promised to turn into the hazel color of her mother's. "You need to stop waking up every hour of the night. Your mom's exhausted. I'm exhausted."

The baby cooed and then smiled at him.

His heart lurched. "And every time you look at me like that, you make it worth the trouble," he grumbled. She grabbed his thumb and tried to suck on it.

Ciara Elizabeth Garrison had her father wrapped around her fingers, and she knew it.

Three months ago, Nadia gave birth to the most adorable baby girl, and John lost his heart. Thank God, her features were shaping more into her mother's delicate ones instead of John's hard angles. His mother said it was too soon to tell, but Ciara's head of thick, black hair was all John.

He got up from the rocking chair and looked around for her pacifier. The little bundle in his arms must have chucked it somewhere she knew her father wouldn't be able to find. Very challenging, this one— so much like her mother. Between Nadia and his daughter, he didn't need a job to keep him on his toes.

And he wouldn't change a fucking thing.

He loved being a father. Well, except the part about waking up two or three times in the middle of the night. He loved watching Ciara sleep in Nadia's arms, and he definitely loved the quiet times when the baby gurgled happy sounds when in his.

There was such a thing as loving frustration, too, when his little girl refused to sleep, and both he and Nadia didn't know why, but then they'd stare at her perfect button nose, and they'd sigh and surrender to the rollercoaster of parenthood. Jesus, they were only three months into it.

But most of all? He loved being the husband Nadia deserved. They married in February barely two months after his proposal. He was determined to put that ring on her finger and have that piece of paper that stated she was his. They signed both documents with the double-identities as a Mason and Garrison and did the same for Ciara.

For now, Mason was in the past, and Garrison was their future.

Ciara gurgled and made a distressed little cry.

John sighed again. "Are you hungry now?" He walked over to the baby's dresser where he'd been warming a bottle. He tested the temperature and then gave it to her. Ciara promptly latched onto it. Nadia couldn't produce enough breastmilk, and they had to supplement because Ciara was a voracious feeder, growing so fast before their very eyes.

As was his habit when he fed her, he talked to her about the people around them. "Tomorrow, we're going to see your Gramps. Remember, he can be absentminded, but he's very thoughtful. Your Uncle Dugal? I know you love him because he tells great stories." Although John wondered if they were too grim to be children's fairytales. "Maybe you can keep him busy so he'll stop making eyes at your Nana, huh?" His mother had moved into the SkyeLark apartments since Ciara's birth. It was supposed to be temporary, but she seemed to be considering making the move permanent. And that was as far as John was willing to speculate. He loved how his mother could give him and Nadia a break every now and then, so he was far from complaining. "Your Uncle Arthur on the other hand, I think he's afraid to pick up a baby, so don't take it personally. As for your Uncle Clyde? He butts into everyone's business and says sh-stuff that annoys your dad, but know his nosiness comes from a good place."

He adjusted Ciara in the crook of his arm and sat in the rocking chair again. "Bristow is going to be there too. Good job with the projectile vomiting on him the last time he called you 'Michelin Man'." John chuckled. His daughter had chubby arms and thighs that his friend couldn't help teasing her. "That's how you handle boys. Don't take their sh-crap. Give it back ten-fold."

"Are you giving life lessons to our daughter again?" A sleepy voice came from the open door.

John turned his head and grinned at Nadia. "Yeah." Her hair was messy, and there were circles under her eyes, but she'd never looked more gorgeous to him.

The mother of his baby girl.

He held out his arm. "Come sit with us."

She trudged forward. "That girl is growing too fast. Pretty soon we won't be able to do this."

"Then we'll enjoy it while it lasts."

John handed their daughter to his wife.

"She's almost done with this bottle." Nadia let their daughter finish feeding and then proceeded to burp her.

"Yeah, I think she's gained a pound since yesterday."

After Ciara was done and fell right to sleep in her mother's arms, Nadia backed up and plopped onto his lap. John rearranged her so he was cradling his wife while she was holding their daughter securely in her arms.

He rocked them slowly.

His family.

He was a fucking happy man.

"Jesus, I love my girls," John whispered to them.

"And we love you, Dad."

*** THE END***

Thank you for reading! If you enjoyed this book, please consider leaving a review. It is much appreciated, and it helps authors a lot.

Levi and Kelly's book is up next. Release date to be determined. Don't worry, Bristow is going to get his HEA, too. Join my newsletter or reader's group for up-to-date news.

AFTERWORD

Every time I finish a first draft, I'm afraid to look at the headlines. I had to tweak the overarching plot of the first three books of the **Rogue Protectors** series to reduce the impact of the virus storyline because of the pandemic. I also delayed publishing the first book.

The plot for **Her Covert Protector** came to me when a cyberattack the previous year hit several private companies and government institutions. Digging into the details, I saw the vulnerabilities to the energy infrastructure. When the Texas power grid issue occurred last winter, I was in the midst of plotting, and again, I decided to focus the cyberattack to a fictional city—Sequoia Global City (SGC) in L.A—rather than take down its entire power grid. The manuscript was with my editor when another cyberattack hit the headlines, and this time, the public became more aware of its consequences. There was only so much I can tweak in my story, but I'm glad I limited it to a fictional city and changed the stakes so that it wouldn't be too ripped-from-the-headlines.

In case you're also curious, my fictional city is the area around Pasadena where Caltech is located. Also in this area, is

NASA's Jet Propulsion Laboratory. And yes, I toyed with ideas with it too, but given my track record lately with my books, I ditched that plot thread.

John and Nadia's book was supposed to be an easy one to write because there was no overarching suspense storyline to work in from the past books. Two things challenged me here. The first one was unpacking John's character slowly and making his metamorphosis riveting to read. I was not expecting the humor that was sprinkled throughout this book. Putting him in uncomfortable situations for him to work through his conflicts was enjoyable to write. As for Nadia, I loved how her character arc jived with John's and how the theme of **identity** held the book together. **StreamCon** worked perfectly for this and blended the suspense plot into the theme.

My second challenge was my big cast of characters. It took several passes with my development editor, my editor, and beta readers to make the scenes involving many characters cohesive and readable, especially since the external and emotional stakes intertwined in several of them.

So much for an easier book to write. LoL!

This book wouldn't be possible without my excellent team.

Big thanks to my developmental editor Geri for continuing to read my messy first draft. You've been a great sounding board, devil's advocate—lol, and you continue to challenge me to write these character-driven, emotional, and suspenseful storylines. It thrilled me when you agreed that the eventual villain was a good plot twist. Our brainstorming sessions are always fun and immensely helpful.

Special thanks to my beta reader, Sue. I loved your analysis of John and Nadia's journey throughout this book. I handled John's character arc differently from my other heroes because a part of him falling in love with Nadia was to open himself up to people around her and his team. Showing this through his interactions with everyone was important and I'm happy my intent came across clearly to you. I also appreciate all the notes you put on my manuscript.

A big thanks to my editor Kristan Roetker. As usual, you polish my work without editing out my voice. I appreciate your patience as I experiment with my writing and your honesty when you feel it doesn't work. You've been my friend and editor through several books and together we make a great team!

Much appreciation to Lynn for jumping in at a short notice and making sure my suspense plot was clear, and it didn't overwhelm the romance.

Thank you to Dana Dunphy of A Book Nerd Edits for proofreading and for the quick turnaround on this manuscript. It certainly helped me catch up with my release schedule when I was falling behind.

To Debra and Drue of Buoni Amici Press. You are rock stars in taking care of the ins and outs of being an indie author, leaving me to my creativity and TikTok. ;)

Special thanks to Jose Luis Barreiro for being my perfect Garrison! I couldn't have picked a better model. I appreciate all your help promoting the book.

Thanks to Wander Aguiar and his team for providing the perfect image as usual. I'm always eager to see who you're photographing next.

I absolutely love my Very Important Paige readers. A lot of you couldn't wait for Garrison and Nadia's book. I hope the wait was worth it and more!

Thank you to the book community—Bookstagrammers, BookTokkers, and Book Bloggers everywhere who continue to read, review, and share my book.

Finally, I wouldn't be able to write this book without my darling hubby who continues to take care of mundane house-work while I'm ensconced in my writing cave. Best of all, you make sure I have something to eat when I emerge. And to Loki, you are the best emotional support dog for an author whose characters give her hives. You sit still and let me hug you, and hugging you is all that I need to make me feel better.

CONNECT WITH THE AUTHOR

Find me at:

Facebook: Victoria Paige Books
Website: victoriapaigebooks.com
Email: victoriapaigebooks@gmail.com
FB Reader Group: Very Important Paige readers

* Sign up for my newsletter and receive **Beneath the Fire** for free.

facebook.com/victoriapaigebooks

twitter.com/vpaigebooks

instagram.com/victoriapaigebooks

ALSO BY VICTORIA PAIGE

Rogue Protectors

The Ex Assignment

Protector of Convenience

The Boss Assignment

Her Covert Protector

Guardians

Fire and Ice

Beneath the Fire (novella)

Silver Fire

Smoke and Shadows

Susan Stoker Special Forces World

Reclaiming Izabel (novella)

Guarding Cindy (novella)

Protecting Stella (novella)

Always

It's Always Been You

Always Been Mine

A Love For Always

Misty Grove

Fighting Chance

Saving Grace

Unexpected Vows

Standalone

Deadly Obsession

Captive Lies

The Princess and the Mercenary

* All series books can be read as standalone

Made in the USA
Las Vegas, NV
27 July 2023

75299916R00225